FIRST ED

Stardust

STARDUST
A NOVEL

SHELLY GROSS

ST. MARTIN'S PRESS
NEW YORK

Stardust is a novel. The characters involved in this story, and their experiences, are purely fictional. In portions of this story there are references in a peripheral manner to real persons and events. But the characters in this novel, except by coincidence, bear no relationship to actual people, living or dead.

STARDUST. Copyright © 1985 by Shelly Gross. All rights reserved. Printed in the United States of America. No part of this book may be used or reproduced in any manner whatsoever without written permission except in the case of brief quotations embodied in critical articles or reviews. For information, address St. Martin's Press, 175 Fifth Avenue, New York, N.Y. 10010.

Design by Kingsley Parker

Library of Congress Cataloging in Publication Data

Gross, Shelley.
  Stardust.

  I. Title.
PS3557.R62S7 1985   813'.54   85-2668
ISBN 0-312-75588-0

First Edition

10 9 8 7 6 5 4 3 2 1

To Henry M. for his patient guidance
and
To Joan for her belief in this story

Stardust

CHAPTER 1

1983

Her Own Woman was opening on Broadway and all of New York's entertainment world was agog. This was the night when America's goddess of glamour, Trudy Coles, would make her first official appearance in a five-million-dollar musical extravaganza. Even the jaded New York theatrical community was holding its liquored breath. Ticket brokers, loving every minute of it, were having a field day. This was the night of Trudy Coles, and everyone with the power and resources to participate wanted his full share.

Forty-fourth Street was choked with limousines stretching from Broadway to Eighth Avenue. It seemed as if the entire force of New York's finest was jammed into that one congested block. High above the pushing crowd, officers on horseback waved their nightsticks. As each limousine paused to disembark its mink-clad, white-tied cargo, there was a dramatic hush while those behind the velvet ropes strained to identify the newest arrivals.

Larry Hocker, the show's producer, had resisted the temptation to drape the sidewalk with Oriental rugs. Even the thought —and the expense—of five giant searchlights piercing the black sky had seemed dispensable. Money was short. Five thousand here, ten thousand there, new costumes, new orchestrations, new set pieces to replace those that weren't working. At each new expense, Larry Hocker resisted. But only momentarily. Sure, there were frightful cash-flow problems. But after tonight, the long hard winter of failure for Larry Hocker would end. Assuming that the critics were not too vehemently destructive, Broadway for Larry Hocker would become a land flowing with milk and honey.

In Trudy Coles' star dressing suite the tension was mounting. She had a shrimp platter and a pot of tea sent in at about five o'clock, but she could only pick at them listlessly. True, she was a veteran by Hollywood standards. But Broadway was quite another matter. Even Jolson had thrown up every night before the curtain rose. Fighting traditional opening-night jitters, Trudy could feel her blood pressure climbing.

Now, as Charles, her dresser, applied her makeup, she looked intently into the mirror that so cruelly illuminated every imperfection, and worried that her Broadway challenge might be too late in coming. Actually, for a fifty-three-year-old war-horse she looked splendid, but stage nerves were clouding her vision. An honest appraisal would have confirmed that no one in the business had eyes like Trudy Coles. They were green, deep emerald green. Go signals, as one columnist called them. And that is how eager males read them. The wonderful thing about eyes was that they never really aged. The iris always maintained its deep hue. Someone had once told Trudy that Iris was the goddess of the rainbow.

"All I need is green," she answered. "It's the color of money."

Her nose, perhaps, was an infinitesimal fraction too long by classical standards. Yet it seemed to bring further attention to her eyes, complementing their incredible depth. The mouth, all critics agreed, was perfect. Full, luscious, sensual, with just enough curve to make the face pleasant but not fatuous. And if the eyes were incredible, the nose near-perfect, the lips unchallenged, it was her unbelievable ivory skin, bearing no blemish even after all these years, that served as a tapestry for her cameolike features. One artist who had spent an evening with her commented that ivory normally looked cold and forbidding. Trudy Coles' ivory was soft and pliable. And the rich, chocolate brown hair (with a minor assist now to hide the first hints of gray) was the perfect framework for her astounding beauty. Hollywood scribes, even those annoyed by her constant love crises, agreed that there never had been, and probably never would be, a beauty to equal hers.

Even seated, one could sense her majestic carriage. Tall for her generation, she stood five foot eight in her stockings. "Just good blood lines," she always said. "I had an uncle who was six foot six. And my old man was well above six foot one." But this was only told to close friends. To the world she was a sex goddess who had stepped out of a Botticelli canvas. Who the hell remembered that Polish kid from the Monongahela Valley of West by God Virginia?

Of course, it was her bosom that beggared description. One could forget about Lana and Gina and Brigitte. Trudy Coles had cleavage that challenged Mount Everest. She sucked in her breath and dabbed a bit of rouge in the valley between them. No harm in accentuating the positive.

There was a knock on the door. It was Joe Ranaldi.

"Ten minutes, Miss Coles."

"Fine. I'll be ready, Joe."

Then, turning to Charles, "Charlie boy, leave me alone for a few minutes. I've got some self-collecting to do. And thank you for the makeup job. You've done wonders."

"You hardly need it, Miss Coles."

"Liar. Lovely liar. I see all the lines. My sight isn't gone yet."

She was alone now. It was an old trick she'd learned in the early days from Richie Stevens. Just before shooting a big scene, he had told her, take a few minutes alone. Take deep breaths, lots of oxygen. Stand tall. Concentrate on what's ahead. Get rid of all the help around you and be yourself, alone.

There was a soft knock on the door again.

"Trudy, it's Larry. I wanted you to know we're all smug as hell. We can't miss."

Damn. There went the concentration. Producers should know better. She didn't want to see him now.

Charlie slipped quietly into the room, almost embarrassed to break into her world. And then there was that fateful knock.

"Places, Miss Coles. Break a leg."

It may take three years to ready a show for Broadway, but the first three running hours of opening night race by in the blink of an eye. One moment there were those initial hesitant steps on entering the stage; the next had the audience standing and cheering and bouquets of flowers festooning the stage. Trudy stood there acknowledging the hysteria of her adoring admirers, wondering how it had really gone. She felt good but she couldn't be certain. She'd remembered her lines. Even the dance sequence had seemed to go well and, let's face it, Trudy Coles at fifty-three was no sylphlike ballerina. Her voice had held despite the mid-week soreness. The laughs had come in the right places. Who knew? Maybe she had pulled it off after all. The role that all the savants had predicted would be her undoing might just have given her career a new impetus. Christ, she hoped so. It had been one hell of a lot of work and she had grown to like New York. It would be great if she could stay for a while; stay, that is, as the toast of the town, not as one of its many victims. Well, they would know in a few hours. In the meantime, she would stand here regally, wave and smile and throw the expected kisses.

The foots were awfully bright but she could detect a few familiar faces in the crowd. Actually, the only people she cared about couldn't attend tonight's performance, and she was facing her ordeal alone. It was lonely at the top. But this was no time for indulgence in self-pity.

The smiling and waving and kissing continued for another three minutes, or was it three hours? God, why didn't Joe bring the curtain down and let it rest? Of course, that wouldn't please Larry. He wanted to milk every last bit of applause just in case a critic or two had lingered in the theater instead of rushing up the aisles. In a way, she couldn't blame Larry. This show probably meant more to him than it did to her. If that was possible.

They were still raising and lowering that damn curtain. She wished to hell they would stop. Finally, the din began to die down. Then the curtain was in place and only a lively hum could be heard from the audience. She turned and rushed off stage. Larry tried to grab her in a bear hug but she brushed him off. "Not now, baby. See you in ten minutes." And she dashed to her dressing room, with Charlie running interference. He had been waiting faithfully in the wings to clear the way through the crowd of well-wishers who already had poured backstage despite the increased security. Carefully, with Charlie's help, she removed her wig, which was causing her to perspire profusely. Charlie went to work immediately with brush and comb to restore order. He was shocked at how drained and fatigued she looked but resisted any unflattering comment.

"Well, Charlie boy, what do you think?"

"I think you were simply marvelous. But you know I'm prejudiced. Uh . . . Miss Coles, Mr. Hocker has been pounding at the door. Do we let him in?"

"I think we'd better. But I really don't want to talk to anyone else. Not now."

In a matter of minutes, she and Larry were alone, Charlie having beaten a strategic retreat after admitting him. It was truly an emotional moment. All the mounting tension of the past two months had suddenly broken.

"You were sensational, Trudy. Better than even I could imagine. Your best performance by far."

"Champs always save their best fights for after they leave the dressing room."

"You're a champ all right. Christ, you've owned Hollywood, London, and Rome for as long as you've wanted. Now, you've got New York too."

"We'll see. We haven't heard from the critics yet."

"They don't worry me tonight. Wait till you hear them cheer at the party when the reviews start coming in."

Now she grew kittenish, little-girl voice and all. "Larry, I can't face a party tonight. I'm really exhausted in spite of the iron-woman act."

"Trudy, you've got to show. The backers would fry us in oil if their star didn't greet them. You don't have to stay long. But I've got the whole second floor of Sardi's reserved and waiting."

"It's no go, Larry. You can make my apologies."

He started to protest. "But, just for a little while . . ."

He was fighting a losing battle. The little-girl act was over.

"I said no, Larry. You go to the party. Charlie will see me back to the hotel. Tell your backers I'm exhausted."

Larry realized further struggle was futile. "I'll call you as soon as we get the good news. TV will come in first. You can watch yourself, starting about eleven."

"I won't watch. You come over yourself when the key reviews are in. I'll be up. Too tired to sleep."

"You want me to take you back to the hotel?"

"Thanks, no. You go to the party. Charlie has the limo waiting."

Back at the Regal, Trudy kicked off her shoes and asked Lilly, her loyal maid-in-waiting for more than twenty years, to bring some wine.

"Hear you was great, Miss Coles."

"Not great. But good, I think. Charlie, why don't you run along? I'm sure your friend is waiting."

"I can stay as long as you like."

"No need. Lilly will take care of me. You've done good work tonight. Thank you."

When Trudy Coles wanted to turn on the charm no one could equal her.

"Go to bed, Lilly," she ordered after a few minutes. "Leave the bottle of bubbly near by. I have plans for it."

"You sure you going to be all right, Miss Coles?"

"I'll be fine. Go to bed. I want a few minutes alone and I'm expecting Mr. Hocker in about an hour."

"You're the boss. Good night now."

It was after the second or third glass of champagne that the phone rang, shattering the silence that had settled so comfortably around her. Irritated, she reached for the receiver, certain it was the desk announcing Larry's arrival even though she hadn't expected him this quickly. But instead, it was Higgins, the head night clerk, who had been ordered to screen all of her calls.

"Miss Coles, I'm really terribly sorry to disturb you. This woman has been calling your suite every twenty minutes for the past five hours. She insists that she's your best friend."

"My best friend?" Trudy repeated incredulously. "What in the hell is her name?"

"She says she's married now but you know her as Helen. Helen Caputo, I think she said."

"Helen Caputo? I knew someone with that name nearly forty years ago. . . . Well, if she calls again, just tell her I'm asleep."

"She's on the line now. She vows she'll keep calling unless you say hello."

Trudy paused. Helen Caputo. That little greasy kid she had palled around with way back in Hubbardsville, the seat of dusty Sarno County, West Virginia. It just didn't seem possible. Nearly forty years and she had to find her on a night like this.

"What shall I tell her, Miss Coles?"

"Tell her just a minute. I'll talk to her."

Another pause while she waited for the connection to be made.

"Gertie? Is that you, Gertie Kolinski?"

So that's how it was going to be.

"This is Trudy Coles. Has been for thirty-seven years."

"I wanted to say hello, Gert. Or are you too fancy to remember your old friends?"

It was obvious that Helen had been drinking. Trudy regretted ever having picked up the phone.

"I'm not too fancy. I'm too tired. I've just opened a Broadway show and this is my time to be alone. Can't you understand that?"

"Maybe I'm not smart enough to understand you now that you're such a big star. But you had time to talk to me in the old days." Helen's words were slurred.

"You sound like you've had one too many. Why don't you go to bed and sleep it off?"

"Why don't you go to bed and fuck yourself?"

There was a loud crash as two receivers were slammed down simultaneously.

So, after nearly four decades, buried memories had come to the surface just when they were least welcome. Hubbardsville, Sarno County, West Virginia. Dirt and poverty and hunger and want and bone-chilling dampness and cold. Dismal struggles for survival. Kids with running noses; dresses mended until they wouldn't hold a stitch; bitter women and unemployed men who owed their very souls to the company store. That was the Hubbardsville she still remembered despite years of luxury and efforts to erase the past. And now, on this night of nights, that bitch had to call and rustle up those painful, buried images.

CHAPTER 2

1944

The realization that she was now mother to five young brothers and sisters, the youngest not an hour old, came to fourteen-year-old Gertrude Kolinski at four o'clock one morning when a sad-faced nurse shook her awake and informed her that her mother had just died in childbirth. Her father, in the throes of one of his frequent bouts with alcoholism, could do little but sob and mutter incoherently.

Maturity comes early in coal towns, especially to an orphan and oldest child. Gertrude took over at that moment as head of the household. Her father Cass's sole contribution was that of his meager miner's wages. Only the fact that most of West Virginia's able-bodied men were off at war accounted for his continued employment in light of his drinking and erratic attendance on the job. It was Gertrude who, despite her youth, supervised the cooking, the cleaning, the shopping, her siblings' attendance at school, and managed the family's finances.

Amazingly, it all worked for a while. Then, the strain of her incredible responsibilities, including the chore of bringing her father home drunk from the bars every weekend, started to take its toll. A near-impossible situation became even more critical because money was always short. Only the leniency of the town's truant officer gave the young, surrogate mother more time to deal with her burdensome tasks. Even so, Gertrude's nerves were frazzled, her energies tapped mercilessly. But she struggled on to keep the family together.

Her only relief was a few stolen hours with the daughter of a neighboring family named Caputo. Nick Caputo worked in the mines with Cass. His oldest of eight children, Helen, was the same age as Gertrude. They had gone to school together for a number of years and, even though Helen was far more sophisticated sexually as well as socially, the girls had remained friends. Gertrude didn't have too many hours for the usual girlish gossiping, but every once in a while she joined Helen at the town movie or shared some ice cream at the local soda fountain.

"Hey, how about joining me Saturday night? I'm gonna visit some of those neat clubs in South Hubbardsville. They're all loaded with service guys and you never have to pay for a drink. How about it, huh?"

The invitation was tempting. Gertrude virtually never had a night to herself. And she'd heard some exciting tales about those bars just across the border in Kentucky.

"I don't think I can. The kids need me. And Pop's drinking again."

"You got more ways to say no than anybody. I'll ask my pop to keep an eye on Cass. Sometimes they play poker together. And the kids can watch out for their own selves."

Though she and Helen were below the legal drinking age, both appeared mature beyond their years; and tavern owners in Kentucky knew when to turn their eyes if there were a few quick bucks to be made.

The most popular club was Sandy's. There was a long bar circling a raised platform on which a pianist banged away with the latest popular hits. Every Saturday evening Sandy's featured an amateur contest. The winner got ten dollars and free drinks for the night.

Helen and Gertrude, together with a couple of horny soldiers they had picked up to buy them drinks, were seated at the bar, suffering through the cacklings of some bleached blonde from downstate who made the rounds on Saturday nights.

"Boy, she's stinko," Helen said.

"Putrid," agreed Soldier One.

"Double stinko and triple putrid," was Soldier Two's opinion.

"She is pretty bad," Gertrude had to admit.

"Hey, Gertrude," said Helen, "you can sing better than her. Why not give it a shot? For ten bucks and free drinks, what's to lose?"

"Hell of a good idea," Soldier One said. "You can't be any worse."

"Great idea," agreed Soldier Two, belching in support.

Gertrude demurred. "I haven't sung in public in years. They don't want to hear 'Lead, kindly light.' I'm out of practice on the pop songs."

But Helen Caputo was not one to be denied.

"Hell you're not. You're singing and humming every time we come out of the movies. Go ahead. Get up there. We'll win."

At that moment, the bleached-blond canary stopped her off-key chirping and Sandy himself grabbed the microphone.

"Okay. Who's our next Helen O'Connell?" he asked.

"Here she is," Helen Caputo yelled. "And she'll beat the ass off the last broad, too."

There was an enormous roar of laughter throughout the club and, reluctantly, Gertrude found herself being half pushed, half tugged up on stage. Although it was true that she hadn't sung in public since her days with the church choir, she had always sung at home when the radio played her favorite tunes. She had a knack with lyrics. Once she heard a record played, she remembered it almost perfectly.

"What'll it be, sister?" the pianist asked.

Gertrude knew exactly how to turn on the charm. After a brief conference with the man at the piano, she signaled for quiet and said in her most ladylike fashion, "For my best friend, Helen Caputo, I'll sing 'I'll Be Seeing You.'"

It was the perfect choice. With the war apparently headed for a successful conclusion, this sentimental ballad was the number one song in the country. For the troops in France and Germany, the boys in Anzio, and the many troops spread throughout the Pacific islands, "I'll Be Seeing You" meant a poignant reminder of all that was romantic and glorious about life in times of peace. Gertrude was no great singer to be sure, but her clear soprano carried the tune perfectly and almost brought tears to everyone's eyes. She was a tremendous hit.

Sandy McNabb, quick to capitalize on an obvious business opportunity, immediately made a speech awarding her the ten-dollar prize and extending the free drinks to her friends for the evening. As she stepped down, Gertrude was flushed with pride.

She never had experienced this kind of reaction to her singing. It was positively intoxicating. Later in the evening, Sandy approached her.

"Hey, kid, that's a great set of pipes you've got. With a little experience, you could go places."

"You got to be kidding," Trudy answered modestly.

"I mean it. When Sandy talks, Sandy delivers. You sing here every night, I'll pay you good bucks."

"I'm her agent," Helen joked. "How much?"

Sandy was serious. He offered Gertrude Kolinski, the star of the evening, twenty dollars a night for any night she would sing in his club. On Saturdays, she'd get an extra twenty. That was $140 a week! More money than her father had earned for a week during his entire life in the mines. And, Sandy added, if she would sign up now for six weeks, he'd give her $150 a week. It was a dazzling offer.

"You serious?" Gertrude asked incredulously.

"Try me," Sandy replied laconically. "I'll also buy you some new duds so you look show biz."

It was fairy-godmother time. Gertrude Kolinski, aged fourteen and three-quarters, looking more like nineteen, had launched her career in show business. Within three weeks she was a local celebrity. Within four weeks she was a sensation. By the end of the fifth week, by West Virginia/Kentucky standards, she was a star. Business at Sandy's Cafe soared through the roof. Though normally busy on weekends, now it was difficult to find room for players even during weeknights. Servicemen from miles around bribed their sergeants to get time off the base so that they could visit Sandy's and view the striking brunette with the crazy figure and the pleasant voice who made them think of the girl next door. Sandy was beside himself with joy and prosperity. What had started as a $150-a-week gamble was now his most solid investment. He did all he could to protect it. He sent a car each night to bring Gertrude to the club and deliver her home after the second show. He realized that she was far below age, and he wanted no problems with the authorities.

His gross had climbed astronomically from the first night Gertrude started her professional career. By the end of the fourth week, Sandy was determined to keep the honey flowing. He cornered Gertrude one night between shows and sweet-talked her into a six-week extension. Her new salary for the second series was to start at $200 a week. Gertrude had learned quickly. She wanted a whole new wardrobe and $300 a week. She got it. It was that simple.

Meanwhile, at home, Gertrude was treated with new respect. Although she was smart enough not to reveal exactly how much she was earning, she contributed an additional fifty dollars a week to the household budget. She also bought all the kids new clothes and generous gifts. Cass was overjoyed with the unexpected bonanza. Promising to cut down on his drinking, he even offered to help her with her household chores.

"What I would like is for you to help take care of the baby at night. It's hard enough going to school, singing at night, and running this home, but when I have to get up three times at night with the baby having colic, that's too much."

From that night on, Cass saw to it that Gertrude's sleep was undisturbed. Gertrude had voluntarily increased her weekly contribution to $100. His new assignment was to keep her happy. He wanted that money to keep rolling in.

But there was a threat to the Kolinski family's serenity. It took the form of Miss Inez Toski, the social worker employed by the town's school board. She showed up unexpectedly one afternoon and demanded a meeting with the family. Cass, just off one of his notorious drinking bouts, was scarcely intelligible. Gertrude served as family spokesman.

"How are you kids managing?" Miss Toski asked. "Seems to me this family needs some adult guidance."

"We're fine, Miss Toski," Gertrude answered sweetly, trying her best to mask her dislike.

"Fine? I hear the kids are alone most of the time. Billy's been cutting class again and Steve gets into fights all of the time. I must say your father, here, hasn't set much of an example."

"Dad's been sick. But he's working most of the time. The boys get frisky, sure, but they're not that bad," Gertrude added defensively.

"That's your opinion, Gertrude. The school authorities think otherwise. They tell me that unless Debby, here, shakes a leg she's going to flunk half of her subjects."

"I'm starting to study harder now," Debby chipped in.

"I don't understand why you kids want to do everything the hard way. We could find right nice foster homes to take care of you. You could all see each other whenever you wanted to. And

Gertrude, what with that new job and all, your life would be a heck of a sight better."

Miss Toski just didn't comprehend the unity and love that held the Kolinskis together. Now, realizing the threat of separation, they circled the wagons and fought for survival. Again it was Gertrude in the lead, Cass just standing by sadly and offering no resistance.

"We've got no real problems here, Miss Toski. We can't live apart. We're not going to any foster homes." There was an authoritative finality in her tone, which amazed even Miss Toski.

"Well, you kids better behave better. I'll be back in a few weeks to check you out. And you, Mr. Kolinski, could be a better father if you drank less."

She left abruptly. Debby burst into tears. The younger children howled in fear. Gertrude was resolute.

"We're a family. We'll stay a family. No Miss Toski is going to separate us."

The younger children didn't share Gertrude's courage. Little Mary cried pitifully and clung to Gertrude's skirt. She picked the child up, kissed her tenderly, and dried her eyes with the corner of her apron.

Debby cried on and on, her tears salted with guilt. "I shoulda done my lessons. Now she's got an excuse to break us up."

Gertrude smiled and put her arm around her sister's shoulders. Only a year and a half separated them but Gertrude's love shone like a beacon to light Debby's way. "She'll do no such thing. She's only trying to scare us. I'd like to see her try to break this family up."

She kissed Debby sweetly, then turned to Cass, who was just beginning to realize that his family was being threatened. "Pop wouldn't let that happen, would you, Pop?"

"The Kolinskis stick together," said Cass in his first sober statement.

But the next few weeks would be nervous ones, and the children were determined to maintain their united front.

One night Gertrude came home from the club and found Cass drunk again, lying unconscious in a pool of vomit in the middle of the living room. It took her more than two hours to revive him, get him to bed, clean up the mess, and resettle the children, who had been awakened by the commotion. The next night she cornered him before heading for work.

"Pop, I can't stand much more of this. You promised to help. You're drinking more than ever."

Deciding that a strong offense might just be the best defense, Cass screamed, "Listen, you little bitch. Don't be telling me, your father, what I have to do. I think that job's going to your head."

"You may be my father, but I make the money around here and do most of the work, too. I'm a woman now and you'd better start treating me that way. Otherwise, I'm gone from here and you'll never see me again."

The thought had already started taking root in her mind. Once Sandy had garbed her in that bare-midriff dress just like the fashion models were wearing, once she saw herself in that pencil-slim skirt and big flora-dora hat, she knew she was something special. The adoration of the servicemen who jammed the bar confirmed what her own eyes told her. She knew she was no great shakes as a singer, but she could entertain. She was growing more professional every day. Why should she end up like her poor mother had: a childbearing animal, overworked, never appreciated, and forced to an early grave? This whole impoverished area depressed her. If she never saw another coal tipple it would be too soon. If she never heard another miner coughing his lungs away, that was fine with her. She had been reading the fan magazines. There was a whole glittering world out there, and why shouldn't she try her luck? Just fifteen years old and here she was making $300 a week with Sandy promising more if only she'd sign for another three months. She would think about it but there were new horizons dazzling her vision now.

When her big break came, it was almost as if she expected it. She received a bouquet of roses backstage one night with a note attached. It read simply, "You are a sensation. I can help you make a million. When can we talk?" Accompanying the note was a business card that read, "Skipper Dawson, Theatrical Agent." It bore a Sunset Boulevard address in Hollywood. She had read enough in the film magazines to know that was where all the big Hollywood moguls hung out. But how could she be sure this guy was on the level? She decided to ignore him and see what happened. Four nights in a row the roses kept coming and always the same question: "When can we talk?" Finally, she sent him a brief reply: "Tonight. After the first show. Come backstage."

She wasn't sure what vision of Hollywood agents she had conjured up in her teenage mind, but Skipper Dawson was, on first viewing, a keen disappointment. He was tiny, certainly not more than five feet four; emaciated at 110 pounds; and his face was pockmarked with the ravages of what must have been a terrible case of acne. His dress was rather flamboyant and he walked with a swagger meant to camouflage his disappointing stature. His complexion was dark and greasy, but he did have warm brown eyes, and he spoke convincingly, as if he knew all of the answers. The gist of his pitch was simple and direct. He didn't care how much she was making. He was so well connected on the Coast that within six months she would be the rave of Hollywood. He would see to that. All she had to do was sign a simple contract giving him the right to be her agent for ten percent of the take, and they would both roll in riches.

Despite her apparent maturity, Gertrude was a child at heart, and the prospect of Hollywood and film glamour was overwhelmingly attractive. Besides, she was determined to leave West Virginia behind her. And yet, yearning for the excitement of Hollywood and actually having the courage to leave everything and everyone she knew were two different propositions.

At home on Sunday night, her one evening of freedom, she took a long walk. She needed to be alone to think things through with clarity and precision. An escape from Hubbardsville was almost too marvelous to contemplate. Yet it filled her with fear when she considered the full implications of deserting her family and chancing life without friends, family, or connections in an unfamiliar environment. After all, what did she know of Skipper Dawson and his real motivations?

She selected a route through the more deserted areas of town. The longer she walked, the more frightening the prospects became. What if he were not a real theatrical agent? What if she ran out of money and was stranded on the West Coast without means of support or transportation home? She would not be the first person to run away and end as a virtual prisoner in an alien locale. What if she really didn't have any talent? Would she end up being the laughing stock of the movie colony and have to come home defeated and depressed? These were all very real possibilities.

And what of her love for her sisters and brothers? How she would miss them! Fate had cast her in the role of household leader. But she was still a young girl and she'd miss their kisses and hugs and even their fights. Even when it disturbed her sleep, she loved to have little Mary climb in bed with her and cuddle like a young puppy.

Most important of all, what about her family obligations? She was the basic supporting beam in the entire Kolinski domicile. It was more than the money she contributed. She had been the household leader since the night of her mother's death. Reliance on Cass's sobriety was fragile at best. She was not quite fifteen, true, but responsibility had matured her far beyond her years. The children looked to her for leadership. She made all of the important family decisions. And now, she could not deny, there was the threat of Miss Toski and the school authorities. If she left and there was any sort of trouble, certainly there would be the real possibility that the family would be broken up and the children all placed in foster homes. That was a mental and emotional burden that she would have to carry for the rest of her days. Times had been tough, certainly, but they had always had each other for solace. Love had bound them together. How could she even consider deserting them when she was the foundation that gave their household stability?

And what of Cass? Could he function without her? Equally important, would she miss him? With all of his shortcomings, he was her father and she loved him. Life had dealt him a wretched hand, and even when she was angry with him her anger was mixed with compassion.

The streets were deserted as the night's shadows wrapped the town in velvety darkness. Suddenly, a cat leaped out of a nearby alley and screeched. Gertrude's heart pounded in her chest and she jumped against a nearby wall for protection. When she realized that it was only a stray cat, she was amused at her own cowardice. She regained her composure and walked on, somehow strengthened by the unexpected disturbance.

She continued her reflections, determined to think more positive thoughts. After all, she had a right to live her own life. She had been more than a daughter to her father, more than a sister to her siblings. She had a responsibility to herself. She had a chance, maybe a small one, but a chance nevertheless to make a big success of her life. How could she not even try? God had given her beauty and a modicum of talent. It was her obligation to use them not only for herself but for everyone's benefit. If she succeeded, there would be no limit to the comfort and happiness she could bring to her family. She dreamed on. She saw herself as the toast of Hollywood, returning in great wealth and bestowing magnanimous gifts on the entire clan. California was far away, but trains moved and airplanes flew and she'd see them all whenever the spirit moved her. As for the dangers represented by Skipper Dawson's intentions—hell, she could handle him.

She was walking more rapidly now, gaining confidence with every step. No, she was certain now that she would not be buried in the coal country of West Virginia without at least giving it her best shot. There were some questions to be answered, however, and she demanded another meeting with Dawson before formally giving her consent.

"What about the fare?" she questioned. "It costs a bundle to get to Hollywood."

"No problem," Dawson answered. "I'll stake you to the tickets and you can return the money out of first earnings."

"Where will I live?"

"I'll get you a place. A room by yourself."

"No monkey business?"

"I wouldn't think of it. You're a kid." Dawson was all of twenty-three. He pretended to be a Methusalah.

"You're sure you can get me a job?"

"If you're afraid you can't cut it in the big time, stay home and raise kids."

That was enough. She signed. She had only one more week to run on her present contract. She would honor that and then, without even saying farewells, she and Skipper would take the bus to Charleston, then the train to California. It was a mind-boggling dream but Gertrude was ready. For the next week she sang one song to herself. "California, Here I Come!"

CHAPTER 3

January 1945

Three nights after her fifteenth birthday, leaving $1,000 and a simple note behind, and having satisfied herself that she had done all that she could to provide for her sisters and brothers, Gertrude slipped quietly from the house and headed for the bus terminal. There, as had been carefully arranged, she picked up her one suitcase, which had been stowed in a coin locker, found Skipper Dawson waiting for her, and together they prepared to board the night bus to Charleston. All of the excitement that Gertrude had experienced during the last few weeks of preparation for her departure left her emotionally drained. She was like an automaton, moving mechanically as if in response to orders received from some unseen source. Skipper was aware that his newfound client was upset. He feared that she might suffer a last-minute change of heart.

"What's the matter, honey? You're gonna be a star in Hollywood before you know it!"

"I hope so," Gertrude replied glumly.

"Hope so? Hell, I know so. Once they see you out there they'll be jumping out of their skins!"

Dawson's words of encouragement were falling on deaf ears. Gertrude was purely and simply frightened. All of the bravado she had mustered during her long walk through Hubbardsville was now leaving her. Her thoughts of the children, of her father, of the many pleasant experiences she had enjoyed as a child, came rushing back to her in an overpowering emotional avalanche. She was too upset to smile, too proud to cry. Yet, if there had been a face-saving path of retreat, she would have bolted home to the loving bosom of her family. She felt tears gathering in her eyes and fought desperately to resist them. Skipper tried his best to comfort her.

"Hey, little girl, everybody gets homesick in the beginning. Don't worry. Skipper will watch out for you. You're gonna be just hunky-dory."

For a few moments, Trudy considered picking up her bag and returning home. Maybe the family had not yet read her farewell note and she could tear it to shreds before they found it. It was Skipper's mistake that saved the day. He suddenly reached out and grabbed her in a big, affectionate hug, hoping that by holding her close he could rekindle her courage. Though he would never know it, his advance prevented Gertrude's retreat.

Pushing him away from her in near-revulsion, she snarled, "Don't you put your filthy hands on me. I told you there wasn't going to be any of that stuff!" He stumbled backwards, tripping over his own luggage, and ended up looking decidedly silly sprawled on the terminal floor. Reaching over to help him to his feet, she said, "I'm sorry, Skipper. I just wasn't in the mood to be mauled."

Fighting to regain his dignity, Skipper rose, dusted off his trousers, and said little. In that brief face-off, all thoughts of returning home vanished and Gertrude regained her composure, her courage, and her determination.

After a three-hour trip, they arrived in the state's capital and found a cab to take them to the railway terminal. Gertrude was so excited she never even contemplated sleep. This was the start of her great adventure and she meant to enjoy every single moment of it. Even the fact that pimply faced Skipper Dawson still clung too closely to her for comfort did not dampen her spirits. She just pushed him away with the remonstrance, "Give me room to breathe. I need air, too. I'm human, you know."

She wasn't afraid of him. Even at age fifteen, Gertrude had learned that her beauty gave her a mysterious control over most of the men she met. Perhaps she would meet her match someday in that mythical fairyland to which she was headed, but for now she felt the confidence of absolute control.

The plane from New York to Los Angeles was now crossing the

country in the amazing time of eighteen hours. It boggled the mind. By train, the trip took more than three days. Even so, for Gertrude Kolinski, who never before had traveled more than one mile west of the Kentucky border, it was to be a great adventure. The train from Charleston would travel all day, reaching Chicago in time for its passengers to board the *Santa Fe Chief* for the two-and-a-half-day trip to the Coast. At Chicago, they would be joined by those who had ridden the *Twentieth Century Limited* out of New York. The trip from Charleston to Chicago proved uneventful. But there was excitement galore on the *Santa Fe Chief*. Crowded with servicemen, many of whom had just returned from overseas, a holiday glow permeated the train from engine to caboose.

Gertrude had not thought to ask about the sleeping arrangements. She learned soon enough that there were none. A roomette or sleeper compartment was too expensive.

"No one sleeps on this train anyway," Skipper assured her, "so what's the point in wasting money on a sleeper?" The obvious fact was that he couldn't afford it. There was no crime in that, Gertrude reasoned. He had sprung for the tickets as he had promised. As Gertrude would later learn, that had taken all of his remaining cash after a week of visiting his family.

Skipper made this yearly pilgrimage to Kentucky to visit his widowed father, for whom he held little if any affection. An ex-professional featherweight, his father had hung up his gloves some twenty-five years ago and traded them for a bartender's apron and a love for the bottle. Small at five foot seven, he still towered over his son, Thomas, whose classmates quickly nicknamed him "Tom Thumb." That ended "Thomas" and brought on "Skipper." Somehow, he reasoned, a dashing moniker would preclude diminutive sobriquets in the future. The one lesson he learned from his father was, in order to compensate for his lack of stature, to fight dirty. The second was to move as far from his family as possible. Hence, his settlement in California.

In later years it would be Gertrude's privilege to travel first class to many of the world's most glamorous locales. But nothing would compare to this, her first cross-country jaunt to the tinseled land of her dreams. Skipper had been right when he said it would be foolish to waste money on a sleeping compartment. Sleep was the furthest thing from her mind. She stayed glued to the window, drinking in every bit of scenery, from the corn and wheat fields of Iowa and Nebraska to the marvels of the Rockies. Even at night, she peered into the darkness lest she miss one sight.

They got out to stretch their legs in Salt Lake City and she was impressed with the crisp, clean air and Western garb. She had seen more of the same in an earlier stop at Cheyenne. Then back on the train and more anxious sightseeing as it snaked its way through the Wasatch range and into the vast, arid, plateau-like desert that separated that rugged mountain range from the lower Sierra Nevadas. And finally, after endless hours of dreaming, the promised land: Union Station in downtown Los Angeles. Gertrude knew that she should be tired. Her pounding heart told quite another story. She literally throbbed with excitement.

Several times while riding on the train, Gertrude had asked Skipper if there were any Hollywood celebrities aboard.

"Just some working professionals," he had answered. "No stars, if that's what you mean. They always ride in private cars."

"See any of your friends?" she had pressed.

"Not on this trip," he had answered. "They're all working."

Apparently, that had satisfied her. Now that she was in the promised land, she was a gawking tourist. Before they had even carried their luggage to the street, she wanted to know when they could see where Mary Pickford and Buddy Rogers lived. She was also dying to see Clark Gable's home. What about Bacall and Bogie? Did he know them?

"Take it easy," he answered, smiling. "All in due time. All in due time."

A tall distinguished man walked by, obviously looking for a passenger who had alighted from the *Santa Fe*. Skipper smiled and shouted "Hi," but Gertrude did not see the man respond.

"That's Mike Selznick. He and Lazar are a couple of the top agents in town. I'm working with him on a big deal that maybe's got a place for you in it."

"He didn't seem too interested in talking."

"Probably has some problems with a big client. See that dame over there? The one who's just jumping into a cab? Her name's Mary Connelly. She's executive secretary to Barney Balaban, the head of Paramount. Nice gal."

"She seems awful rich for a secretary, with that mink coat and all. And that guy with her looks like a movie star himself!"

"She isn't rich. But she's pretty loaded. When you work for the big names, you get paid plenty. Like my friend Arnie Somers. He works for Zanuck at Twentieth. Used to be with Cliff Work at Universal. Just an assistant, that's all. But he's good for forty big ones a year. This is the place to make it, honey."

Skipper originally had planned to take a bus that went out Wilshire Boulevard and connected with another one at Western, which would have dropped them a block from his apartment. But after all the name-dropping and big-time talk, he realized that might create the wrong impression. Eventually, she'd have to learn the truth about his financial status, but not while she was still flying. Time enough for that when she settled down and was in a better mood to accept reality. He sneaked a look at her as they crossed the terminal floor to where the cabs were lined up. She was incredibly stunning. Virtually every passerby turned and stared at her despite her mill dolly attire.

He hailed a cab. Even the driver was impressed with Gertrude's looks. As he piled their two bags into the trunk he asked Skipper under his breath, "Contract player?"

"No, no," Skipper answered. "Featured. A three-picture deal at MGM." Then, winking in masculine, conspiratorial fashion, "My new client."

"Ho, ho!" answered the cabbie. "Some guys got all the luck. How old is she?"

"Somewhere between six and sixty." Skipper laughed and jumped into the cab before there were any more questions.

They pulled away from the curb and into heavy traffic. Gertrude was all eyes, staring first through one window, then the other. The office buildings, high-rise apartments, and shops on Wilshire were lovely but somehow not quite what she had anticipated. Off to her right she could see the famous hills of Hollywood rising into the miasma of morning smog. Was it just a bit difficult to breathe or was she imagining it? It was certainly growing warmer and nothing would have felt better than a hot bath or shower after her days on the train. At Western they turned north toward Santa Monica Boulevard, and just beyond Beverly, Skipper signaled for the driver to stop.

"This will be fine," he said, matter-of-factly. "We'll walk from here. Hard to drive right to the door."

Exactly what Gertrude had expected, she herself would have been at a loss to describe. But what she did see was a terrible letdown. A small court, surrounded by Spanish-type, two-story white dwellings roofed with red tiles and entered through a rusted, wrought-iron gate, was crowded with running, chattering children who frolicked across a muddy central area where apparently flowers had once grown. The stucco walls of the surrounding buildings were more beige than white and marked by dirty streams of rust from damaged rain gutters and downspouts. Since this was Saturday, a variety of couples were seated on camp chairs in little groups near entranceways that separated one dwelling from the other. No one seemed to look up as Skipper and Gertrude entered. They were too involved with their own conversations. One man did greet Skipper with a nod of approval as he eyed the young beauty with him.

"I only live here temporarily," Skipper explained somewhat lamely. "My place in Beverly Hills is being fixed up. You'll like it here. Nice and friendly and close to everything."

Gertrude made no comment. They walked the entire length of the court, then turned right and found an entrance off to the side at the rear of the last dwelling. Outside stairs led to Skipper's front door, the upstairs of a duplex apartment.

"Up we go." He smiled. "Plenty of privacy."

Again, no response from Gertrude. They climbed, opened the door, and entered. The only thing in its favor was a lack of clutter, for Skipper was essentially a neat man. The furnishings, which he did not own, were meager and inexpensive, the owner having obviously outfitted the premises with the intent of renting it furnished. There was a badly sagging sofa, an overstuffed armchair, and a few tottering, standing lamps, which provided the living room with its only light. A bath, an incredibly small kitchen, and a single bedroom with a dresser, a straight-backed chair, and an ancient double bed completed the household. Gertrude, certainly accustomed to impoverishment, surveyed her surroundings without complaint.

"Well, this is it," he said pleasantly.

"And just where do I sleep?" she asked.

"Well, let's see. You take the bedroom and I'll use the sofa here. Or, we can share."

"No share, Skipper. I told you right from the start, no monkey business. Besides, you promised me a room for myself."

"Okay," he said, "here's your room. I don't mind the sofa. Besides, lots of time I'm out till real late working on deals. We made a bargain and I'm gonna keep it."

He did. For one night. By Sunday he had crawled into bed with Gertrude, and, lonely despite her attempts at playing grownup, she faced her first real dilemma. Even the thought of feeling any real affection for Skipper was outlandish. Overlooking the disparity in their sizes, he just wasn't the kind of man who could make her feel alive. On the other hand, he had a pleasant personality, had done his best to make her comfortable, and had convinced her of his sincerity in bringing her fame and fortune. Behind all of these surface emotions, however, there was the real fear that if she rebuffed him, he might lose interest in her entirely. Young though she was, Gertrude intuitively understood the power of sexual drive and its intricate involvement with feelings of self-worth. Now that she was almost three thousand miles from home, dare she risk upsetting him as a bed-mate? There were plenty of beautiful girls in Hollywood. He could just as easily drop her for another client. All of these conflicting emotions surged through her as Skipper pawed at her and tried his best to arouse her. Perhaps if she had felt the slightest attraction to him she might have succumbed to his persistent advances. As it was, she finally decided to resist at all costs.

"Skipper!" she shouted. "I told you there wouldn't be any messing around. Now cut it out!"

Skipper, never one to embrace rejection, continued to let his hands wander, and moved closer and closer to her on the bed.

"Skipper, I told you to cut it out. Now, you keep that up and I'm on my way home!"

It was an idle threat and they both knew it. She had enough money for the fare, but her dream of Hollywood stardom was not one to be easily squelched. Skipper, on the other hand, was not secure enough to test her. Aside from his physical attraction to her, he saw in Gertrude his chance to pluck the golden ring of fortune. With a little less persistence, he kept moving his hands toward her.

She bolted up and slapped him across the face. The fact that she was actually bigger than he, and possibly stronger, added to her courage. He took the blow without retaliation.

"Okay. If that's the way you feel about it, that's the way it'll be."

He turned away from her, quieted down, and attempted to fall asleep. Gertrude decided to accept the compromise. She turned the other way and before long the two combatants were slumbering. In this fashion, the issue was decided. Each night, Skipper would crawl into bed with her and she would voice no objections. Whenever he attempted any intimacies, however, he was immediately rebuffed. In a sense, he was "sleeping" with his dream girl. Gertrude, however, had retained her virtue and her independence without the risk of Skipper abandoning her for another protégée.

One morning, he left for work, telling her to busy herself about the apartment until he returned. She asked him to bring her a map of the city so that she could familiarize herself with the area. He agreed but cautioned her to be careful if she left the apartment. Actually, street crime was virtually unknown in those days, but he didn't want her meeting up with someone who might open her eyes to his own inadequacies. He wanted her to learn the facts of life his way. Unfortunately, it would have to be soon. He realized that he could keep her prisoner for only so long. Her demands came more abruptly than he had expected. She wanted to know when she was going to meet the producers he had told her about. What about her chances for an early audition? Where were his connections with the big studio bosses, the casting directors, the directors and production heads he had boasted of knowing? He stalled for as long as he could, then finally let her have the truth. The card he had flashed that night in Kentucky was a phony he had had printed in an arcade on Hollywood Boulevard. He did indeed know a lot of agents. He worked for them at the Jason Arnold office, in the mailroom. He went for coffee. He was the lowest paid "gofer" on the entire payroll.

She looked at him with hatred in her eyes. For the first time he heard her speak like a coal miner's daughter. "You liar! And for this shithouse you made me leave a good job in Kentucky where I was making three hundred dollars a week!"

"Now, honey, don't get excited," he said soothingly.

"Don't get excited? Don't get excited! Why you little sawed-off shrimp, you made me think you were going to make a movie star out of me. And you're nothing but a fucking gofer!"

He waited for her to calm down and then explained that his job did bring him into contact with some of the top men in the business. The Arnold office, recently moved from Sunset Boulevard to its present location on Beverly Drive, was a virtual mecca for every important writer, director, and producer in town. Even if the studios had their own list of stars under contract, it was at the Arnold office that they assembled to borrow talent from other studios and to negotiate for literary properties that would be made into feature films. If she would only be patient, only give him a reasonable amount of time, he'd get that interview or audition for her and the rest would be easy.

"Four weeks is enough time to see if you're serious," she answered coldly. "After that I move out and try on my own." These were strong words from a fifteen-year-old girl who had yet to visit a studio or even tour Beverly Hills on one of those commercial, star-gazing junkets. Gertrude Kolinski had grown up quickly.

During the next several weeks, as Skipper pondered his predicament and planned his moves, Gertrude started making her own exploration of the fabled city. She spent every morning reading *Silver Screen* and *Photoplay* to whet her appetite. Then she'd sally forth, finding her way to the studio gates, watching for the stars she'd read about entering or leaving following their day's filming, having luncheon at coffee shops near the studio lots, hoping to make contact with someone of influence. Once she actually faked her way into a studio casting office, only to be shown the door politely when it was learned that no agent had sent her for an interview.

At night, she insisted that Skipper show her the sights. Once, they had dinner at the Brown Derby; another time, at La Mer on the Sunset Strip. This was high living for a mailroom boy, but Skipper was intent on keeping her quiet and satisfied until he had time to make his move. He borrowed a convertible from a fellow worker who owed him a favor and they cruised the mansion-lined streets of Beverly Hills. This was the wonderland that she had read and dreamed about. She gasped in wondrous disbelief. People actually lived here; in West Virginia, they merely existed. If only one day she could afford this luxury, if only. She doubled her resolve that day. With or without Skipper, she'd find a way. She was Moses gazing at the Promised Land, determined never to return to wandering in the desert. Never.

She went shopping one day at a mini-market near the apartment and returned with a large bundle in her arms. Misjudging a step, she tumbled backwards, falling on what was an excuse for a lawn near their entranceway. The bag fell from her hands, oranges and apples rolling in every direction. Fortunately, she wasn't hurt. As she bent down to start collecting her purchases, a sensitive-looking young man, who seemed vaguely familiar, ran over to offer assistance.

"You okay?" he asked sincerely.

"Okay," she answered as she dusted herself off with as much dignity as the occasion allowed.

"Here, I'll help." He picked up part of the escaped fruits and vegetables and walked the few remaining yards to her stairway. "I'm Stan Marcus," he volunteered, "your neighbor from two doors away."

She looked at him critically. A quick judgment put his age at about twenty-five. He was tall, thinner than most men she knew, but carried himself without apology. A mop of dark brown curly hair topped an incredibly broad forehead, and sensitive deep brown eyes peered out at her through thick, tortoiseshell glasses.

He smiled pleasantly. "You've got a name, too?" he asked.

"Sure. Gertrude Kolinski."

"You don't look like Gertrude Kolinski."

"No. What do I look like?"

"I'm a writer. But I can't describe your looks. You are sensational-looking, just in case you didn't know it."

"And you're what my boyfriend would call a 'Hollywood wolf.'"

He laughed. "Hardly. But I wouldn't mind being one someday. I'm told they have all the fun. In the meantime, I'll just slave away at my writing."

She wasn't sure what prompted her to do so, but she sat down on the step, and he sat beside her. He was warm and obviously intelligent. It was an attractive combination.

"What are you writing?"

"Like everybody else in Hollywood, I'm writing scripts. Writing, so far, but not selling. It's tough to break in."

"Where do you come from?"

"Right." He laughed. "Everybody in Los Angeles comes from somewhere. No one is born here. I'm from New York. You?"

"West Virginia. Down near the Kentucky border."

"Not exactly my territory. They have any Jews down there?"

"Not many. I went to school with one Jewish kid once. His dad owned the local dry goods store. But they moved out. Not too popular with Polish and Italian Catholics. You Jewish?"

"Is the Pope Catholic?"

"You're Jewish. So what?"

"So put your things away and come over to my place and have a Coke. I just perfected a new recipe for the ice."

For the next two weeks, Gertrude and Stan Marcus spent more and more time together. She never mentioned him to Skipper because there seemed no reason to do so. He acted the perfect gentleman, never so much as trying to kiss her. She really felt no physical attraction to him, but the force of his intellect tugged at her with inexorable power. He had read everything. He had seen every movie, analyzed every play, experienced every work of art. She felt humbled in his presence. Then and there she became determined to be more than a beautiful ignoramus. Like civilized man bringing science to the aborigines, Stan Marcus sparked in Gertrude Kolinski a desire to improve herself.

He never asked her about Skipper or questioned the basis of their relationship. Apparently, Stan knew that such questions would only lead to a more serious alliance, and he seemed perfectly content with things the way they were. She would curl up on the sofa, concentrating on the latest book he had brought her while he banged away at the typewriter. Occasionally she would interrupt his thoughts to ask him a question about a puzzling passage, but she did her best to be as unobtrusive as possible. Once in a while he would interrupt her reading to try out a new scene, which he would read aloud dramatically, playing all the parts with great feeling. In doing so, he often belittled his own work.

"Don't do that," she remonstrated. "It's good."

"It stinks!" he would answer, and return to the typewriter.

They were drawn closer and closer together. Just looking at her incredible beauty was all the inspiration he needed. And when he finally got her to admit that she was only fifteen, he became certain that he would look and not touch. She, in turn, was entranced with his wisdom and sensitivity. Once, he brought her a battered paperback of Greek myths to read, including the story of Pygmalion.

"Hey," she joked, "that's you and me. I'm the statue and you're bringing me to life."

"Sounds like a Broadway musical," he replied. "Wait until someone calls George Bernard Shaw and gives him the idea." And then, of course, he had to tell her all about Shaw, and she promised to read *Major Barbara*.

Their idyllic relationship was shattered abruptly one day when Skipper returned unexpectedly from work and found them sharing a cup of coffee in his apartment. Never one for subtlety, Skipper drew the immediate conclusion that he was being cuckolded. He was rude and insolent. Stan Marcus didn't bother to embarrass him.

"Look, kiddo, your girlfriend and I have been reading and working together and that's all. No sex. Can you handle that?"

"A likely story."

"I can't make you believe it if you don't trust Gertrude. The fact is, she's a bright, beautiful young lady and it's a pleasure to be with her. Or weren't you aware of that?

Stan gathered his sweater and the new pages he had been reading to her and left. Gertrude decided that it would be best if there were no scene, so she made no protest. But she hated to see Stan Marcus walk out of her life. She had felt herself being drawn closer and closer to him during the past several weeks and was perplexed by the attraction. She had never known real love for a man, though she was convinced that more bells had to ring than she heard when alone with Stan Marcus. On the other hand, she found herself longing to be with him more each day. Could this be the kind of love one finds in a successful marriage? she wondered. Or was she merely confusing love with admiration and respect? It was difficult for a girl her age to sort it all out. Strangely, as Stan left she had the feeling that their paths would cross again.

She waited until he had negotiated the outside stairs, then turned on Skipper. "He's the nicest, brightest man I ever met, or maybe ever will meet. He taught me that I have more to offer than what you call 'tits and ass.' If it hadn't been for him, I'd have left you weeks ago. So don't be angry with Stan Marcus. Thank him. And, by the way, your four weeks were up two weeks ago. . . . When is it going to happen?"

"We're ready," he said with a victorious smile. "Sit down and I'll tell you all about it."

CHAPTER 4

March 1945

Manny Silverstein was in a rage. And hell knew no fury like Manny Silverstein inflamed. Continental Studio employees had learned to circle around him with what became known as the "mad dog" treatment when he was this upset.

In a sense, it was strange that Manny was not euphoric. The war was moving toward a successful conclusion. Shortages of film stock and materials for set building were ending. The big names of the industry were shedding their uniforms and marching home, emblazoned in patriotic glory. All the ersatz leading men, who had had field days while Gable and Stewart and Powers and Taylor had faced real danger in the shooting war, were suddenly being given their walking papers. The American public, wearied of death and killing, shortages and sacrifice, was pouring into neighborhood film tabernacles at an unprecedented pace. As an experiment, one theater manager had even shown an entire evening's worth of military training films. He sold out his house. His only problem occurred when one patron objected to three straight documentaries on the subject of venereal disease. The manager rudely returned his admission price.

Theater managers could afford to be independent. Sure, they were beginning to talk about the emergence of that little black box in the living room, but any man with half a brain could see that a six-by-nine-inch screen showing black-and-white pictures slightly out of focus could never compete with the Silver Screen.

With profits at an all-time high and a virtual torrent of features pouring forth from Hollywood, the future was rosy, the professionals sanguine.

Yet, Manny Silverstein was upset. Only that morning he had fired off a wire to his banking connections in New York that, in effect, told them to mind their own goddamn business. They had dared to suggest that the new super feature he was contemplating might exceed a two-million-dollar budget, dollars that might never be retrieved. Quickies and cheapies were the order of the day. Quality was an unwanted, uncalled-for luxury. His telegram was brief and to the point: "Don't tell me how to make pictures. I won't tell you how to rob banks."

Arguments with money sources were not at all disturbing to Manny. He thrived on confrontation and controversy. He was a scrapper by inclination and by training. He had got his first job vending hot dogs at a Coney Island food stand by knocking out his nearest competitor for the job with the blunt end of a claw hammer. Little did it matter that his victim was the same kid who had told him about the job in the first place. Manny Silverstein needed the job. His father had dropped dead at the reins of his peddler's wagon. His mother had four other kids to feed. He was fourteen, big and brawny for his age, and he desperately needed the job. So he chased three other kids away by brandishing a pocket knife, lied to two others, informing them that the job was already taken, and knocked out the last contender with a hammer lifted from a nearby carpenter's tool box. There never had been, and there never would be, any subtlety in Manny Silverstein's reasoning. He lived by one law alone: the law of expediency.

He worked at the hot dog stand for three weeks and by then he was his boss's number-one salesman. The other boys sold hot dogs. Manny hustled. He was always ready to push that extra bottle of Moxie, that side dish of kosher pickles. It was also true that though he outsold his fellow workers, he was not against a bit of personal appropriation. Nate Wiener, the "King of the Wieners," soon learned that every fifth nickel went into Manny's pocket.

"Hey, Manny," he said pleasantly one day, "it's okay to steal. But remember, I'm a partner, too. You get my joke?"

"What are you complaining about?" Manny asked with typical Silverstein logic. "You're doing more business than any other stand on the boardwalk." And that was true, thanks to Manny's aggressive selling.

Manny came back to work the next summer filled with the same energy but bored with being a subordinate.

"Hey, Nate, I got a great idea."

"So?"

"So what's in it for me if I tell you?"

"So what should be in it? A pip-squeak kid not dry behind the ears yet. You think maybe I should make you a partner?"

"Exactly what I had in mind," Manny answered.

And he was serious. He threatened to take his big idea to Bernie Frank, the "Prince of the Franks," unless Nate agreed to cut him in with a fifty-percent interest.

"Okay, so what's the big genius idea?"

"First you make me a partner. Then you learn."

It was done. In simple terms, Manny's idea was to take the food to the customers, instead of waiting for them to come to the stand. He fashioned a vacuum pack from an old milk jug, and a hot box from an old range, put straps on them and then hired a few husky football players to walk the beaches and peddle their wares. They were an immediate success. When competition reared its ugly head, Manny devised an immediate solution. More husky football players were hired to waylay the competing vendors and toss their merchandise into the surf. It worked like a charm. Soon, "Manny and Nate's"—formerly Nate Wiener, the "King of the Wieners"—had a virtual monopoly extending for five blocks of Coney Island beach. Bernie Frank, the "Prince of the Franks," retired to calmer waters.

By age seventeen, Manny Silverstein was sole proprietor of five food stands. He had long since bought Nate Wiener out and sent him to Florida and a peaceful retirement. Then one day he got an idea that made his touring-vendors scheme seem like small potatoes. The new nickelodeons were catching on. There was hardly a neighborhood without its movie palace, and tired workmen were saving their pennies to spend their nights squinting away at the flickering images. Why not, thought Manny, sell them candy and popcorn to eat while they watched? He approached the manager of the local movie house and suggested that more people would come to his show if they could enjoy themselves munching goodies during the shows. The manager played right into Manny's hands.

"I ain't got time to be a candy butcher."

"I do," Manny said, "and it won't cost you a cent!"

Within six months, Manny Silverstein was the candy-concession king of Canarsie. His brothers and sisters all got jobs, as did each of his friends. Once in a while he had to rough a kid up when he caught him stealing. That was all in a day's work for Manny, who by now needed one of Mr. Ford's horseless carriages to move around and collect his receipts. Amazingly, it wasn't until a full year later that one theater owner wised up and insisted upon a commission. Recognizing this as a dangerous trend, Manny nevertheless quieted the man by giving him a measly ten percent. He compensated for this, however, by raising his prices and never giving the theater owner an honest count. It was this basic philosophy that formed the cornerstone of Silverstein's Concessions. The business grew with incredible leaps and monumental bounds. It spread to Broadway when he opened stands in the lobbies of Manhattan theaters. Ball parks were next. Of course the wiener had been part of the baseball tradition for years. But Manny bought his way in by selling athletic field and team owners the message that they could make more money concentrating on their own businesses while his techniques would earn them more in commissions than they had ever earned alone. Besides, he argued successfully, now they didn't have to tie up capital in candy and beer stands; he would be taking all the capital risks himself. Amazingly, they bought his pitch.

At one point, he ran into competition from another concessionaire who tried to block his expansion. He used the same technique he had employed in the old days on the Coney Island beaches. His brother, Moe, knew a couple of toughs who were involved in the numbers racket. For a few hundred dollars, they placed several dozen well-designed stink bombs. They also left one unfortunate stubborn competitor with two broken legs. Soon, Silverstein's Concessions was unchallenged. It was really that simple.

In spite of it all, now that he was twenty-two and on his way to becoming a millionaire, Manny missed his days in the nickelodeons. Movies were becoming big, big business, and that's where his heart beat more furiously. When a small group of theaters that was trying to buck one of the larger, studio-owned chains ran into financial difficulties, it turned to Manny for a loan. He suggested a better plan. Let him buy in as a partner.

Bolstered with Silverstein capital, the company survived and even added a few units. But it soon became clear to Manny that it was no contest. Product was the key to a theater's success. Who could compete with a studio-owned house that was guaranteed a steady stream of films from Hollywood, while he had to bid for every nondescript picture that a few independents couldn't sell elsewhere? It was a dilemma. All of his money was now tied up in a chain of fourteen movie houses throughout New York City that he and his brothers owned. They were facing starvation from lack of product. The product emanated from California. Again with typically expedient Silverstein reasoning, he picked up stakes and headed for the Coast.

It was not to be an easy challenge. The film pioneers he found there all had their "hot dog" stories to tell. He wasn't the only one who had wielded a hammer or used the influence of shady characters. It was a tough group he tried to join. Eventually, he found a way. Financing, then as now, was always a problem for filmmakers, big and small. Manny Silverstein was one of the first to utilize Eastern banking connections to provide the funds for film production. He made a quick trip back to New York, borrowed $200,000 using his nickelodeons as security, returned to Hollywood, and turned out his first full-length feature. He used rented facilities in an area known as "Poverty Row" and found a few out-of-work New York actors, recently arrived in California to seek their fortune, who virtually paid him for the opportunity. His brother, Abe, joined him and traveled East to peddle the picture. Advance rentals paid the freight for the next picture, and the next and the next. Soon, the pump was primed and the cheapie flicks were being ground out by Silverstein Monographs at a rate of one a month. No longer did Silverstein Theaters in New York worry about product. Nor was there any need to give up thirty percent in distribution. Abe Silverstein became the president of Silverstein Sales and soon began distributing pictures for other independent producers. A smart young lawyer warned Manny one day that he might run into antitrust problems with the federal government.

"Look, Mr. Silverstein, why take a chance? 'Silverstein Monographs,' 'Silverstein Theaters,' 'Silverstein Sales.' Why blow a horn? Change the names. Let some government investigator find out for himself. Why help him?"

Thus, "Silverstein Monographs" became "Continental Studios." "Silverstein Sales" became "Feature Attractions, Ltd." "Silverstein Theaters" kept their name—Manny Silverstein was too much of an egomaniac to sacrifice everything. As proof of his appreciation, he fired the lawyer who had given him the advice. Manny never kept anyone close to him who could some day prove dangerous. Having devised the subterfuge, the young lawyer knew too much and had to be discharged. "The kid thinks too crooked," he explained. "We've got enough sharpshooters aboard without him."

Not surprisingly, the young lawyer needed the job desperately. He had a friend who was powerful in the film community call Manny and plead his case.

"He's a good kid. Smart. Loyal. Hell, what he told you to do was in your own best interests. Right?"

"Right," Manny answered. "And in my own best interests I decided to give him the gate. You like him? You hire him. I don't appreciate your telling me how to run my shop."

As so often happens in Hollywood, the young lawyer did get his job back. His sister was a beautiful model who was trying to break into the business. She camped outside of Manny Silverstein's office until he had to admit her. There was a convenient "resting area" adjacent to a side doorway where Manny could retire for rest and recreation. Three hours later, the young lady emerged, somewhat disheveled, with the firm promise of a screen test. Her brother was recalled to service the very next morning. Needless to add, he never made another constructive suggestion as long as he worked for Continental Studios.

Beautiful women had been Manny's weakness from the day he hawked his first hot dog in Coney Island. He had a habit of pursuing the most voluptuous customers at the stand with the same determination that characterized his business career. Generally, he ignored the golden bands on the fourth finger of their left hands. A lovely woman was fair prey regardless of marital status.

In Hollywood, Manny practiced his artful feminine predatory pursuit with ever-increasing efficiency. Rather handsome in a sexual way, prematurely gray and towering well over six feet, a stylish dresser who was instinctively tasteful in his attire, he cut an attractive figure whenever he entered a room. His own level of self-confidence was so enormous that it never occurred to him that women might not welcome his advances, no matter how unsolicited. Whenever there was talk of a husband being cuckolded, the usual reply would involve the "Silver Fox," and that meant Manny Silverstein.

To Manny, sex was a glorious game. Which was exactly why he was so outraged on this particular morning. One of his latest pictures had been rejected by Joseph Breen, head of the Motion Picture Production Code Office, the Motion Picture Association of America's self-regulating bureau. In an explanatory letter, Breen indicated what changes had to be made before a seal of approval could be granted.

"Did you ever hear such shit?" Manny raged. "The man must be a pansy, or something. He won't let my leading man use the word 'damn' when he falls out of bed. And he says it's too suggestive to have him and the leading lady say good night outside of adjoining hotel rooms. He says it's not permitted for anyone to say 'nuts to you' at that barroom brawl. The guy must be crazy! He wants a whole new redub in every one of those scenes."

"So we'll redub and *fahtig*," said the production head, who had been summoned to an emergency session along with the writer, director, and press agent for the feature.

"Sure, '*fahtig*' to you. It's like nothing if it costs me another twenty thousand."

"I don't like it either, but do you want to fight the MPAA? You can't win with that Eric Johnson in charge."

"Wait a minute," Manny said, his face lighting up. "What's that word, 'epurged,' 'unexpurged'?"

"Unexpurgated," advised the press agent.

"Exactly," Manny said. "We change the dubbing. Then we advertise, 'Wait till you see the unexpurgated version!' "

"But I thought Breen wouldn't pass it?" the press agent asked in amazement.

"Schmuck! Did I say he would? All I said was 'wait till you see the unexpurgated version.' That'll make them curious and they'll come."

He was right. The picture grossed far more than it should have, though it got generally horrible reviews.

Several weeks later, a conference to discuss the picture's promotion was interrupted by a ring on the intercom. Miss O'Brien, "Obie" to everybody at Continental, knew better than to interrupt Manny in conference. This had to be special.

"Yes, Obie?" Manny asked, impatience obvious in his tone of voice.

"Sorry to interrupt you, Mr. Silverstein, but it's Mickey Sklaroff from Jason Arnold. It's the third time he's called. He says he's taking the pullman to Chicago tonight and he was wondering if you'd have a drink with him at five. He says it's personal and very important."

"Tell him yes. I'll meet him at La Mer. Tell him he better talk fast. I gotta get home for dinner one night this week."

On that note, the conference ended. Mickey Sklaroff was one of the few agents that Manny Silverstein liked and, more importantly, trusted. Sklaroff, like Silverstein, was married; but, as he explained it, he wasn't a fanatic. This troubled Ike Feldman and the other top executives over at the Arnold office. Womanizing was all right in its own place, but you didn't flaunt it in front of the whole world. When it came to Sklaroff, even the top brass couldn't express too loud an objection. Mickey was undoubtedly the top "signer" in the agency. Others might handle their clients as well, but no one brought in new business like Mickey Sklaroff. It was obvious that he was ticketed for the agency's presidency. Anyone who could win Manny Silverstein's confidence could not be denied.

On several occasions, encouraged by Sklaroff's pleasant smile, Skipper Dawson had tarried when delivering mail to his office. Once, he even went so far as to engage Sklaroff in a conversation involving a soon-to-be-released picture that the agency had handled. Despite his pleasant demeanor, Sklaroff was tough; he was too busy to hear some pimply faced mailroom boy expound about show business. "You'd better push off, kid," he said brusquely. "You've got work to do and the other agents might be looking for important mail."

It was quite a letdown for Skipper, who thought that in friendly Mickey Sklaroff he might have found an advocate who would rescue him from his present humble position. He'd mistakenly assumed that Sklaroff's short stature made them natural allies. Other agents were constantly rude to him, so Sklaroff's words were nothing new. It was the disappointment, more than anything else, that affected Skipper's reaction. He could hardly control his temper. He vowed then that he would get his revenge. He remembered a bit of counsel his father had once given him. "Don't get mad," the elder Dawson had advised, "get even."

The incident with Mickey Sklaroff had occurred just before Skipper left for his two-week vacation, but the pain was still there every time he passed his office. He dropped off his mail one day and their eyes met. Neither one offered greetings. It was as if they were combatants in an undeclared war. Suddenly, Skipper smiled despite himself. An idea was forming in his brain that would enable him to "get even" and solve his problem with Gertrude.

Down the street from the office stood the palatial Beverly Wilton Hotel, with a full complement of conveniently located bars, restaurants, and luxurious suites. Once, running an errand for his boss in the mailroom, Skipper had cut through the hotel lobby to reach Wilshire Boulevard and had spotted Sklaroff and Manny Silverstein sharing a drink. He learned that they were very good friends. He, of course, was well aware of Sklaroff's reputation as a womanizer. It was common knowledge around Jason Arnold. What wasn't generally known was that Sklaroff was having an affair with the wife of the company's general counsel, Bert Nichols, who was considered a shoe-in for the board chairmanship once Ike Feldman retired. From a drinking buddy, Skipper learned that Sklaroff and Mrs. Nichols were rendezvousing at a hotel at Santa Monica beach. It was a gem that Skipper would put to excellent use.

He waited until late afternoon, when Mickey was working alone in his office, entered without invitation, and closed the door behind him. Sklaroff was startled.

"Who the hell invited you in? What do you want?"

"A favor," Skipper answered simply.

"I'm busy, kid. Beat it."

"It's not a very big favor."

"I don't care if it's so tiny you can't see it. Get out."

"Okay," Skipper answered matter-of-factly, "but Andrea Nichols is going to be very disappointed."

There was a very pregnant pause.

"What did you say?" Sklaroff asked in disbelief.

Now it was Skipper's turn to be tough.

"You know goddamned well what I said. I've known all about you and Mrs. Nichols for days. I've got a few pictures of the two of you at the Sands Hotel if you need convincing."

Sklaroff was stunned. "Okay," he said after a long beat, "what's your game?"

"It's simple. One word from me—one letter, pictures enclosed —to Mr. Nichols and you'll be out on your ass looking for a job. But I'll forget I even heard your name if you do me one favor.

I've got a client who is probably the most beautiful woman in the world. You've got a good friend who can make her career. I mean Manny Silverstein. Introduce them, and you get the pictures, negatives and all."

"You've got a client?" Sklaroff mocked. "Now I've heard everything!"

It was a Sklaroff miscalculation. Skipper was around his desk in a flash, had picked him up by the collar and was shaking him like a terrier punishing a sewer rat.

"Don't you laugh at me, you little mocky! I'll break your neck. I want that introduction and I want it by tomorrow night. You understand? Do you? Or do you want me to run down this hall and see Bert Nichols? Well, answer me!"

Mickey Sklaroff felt the wind leaving his lungs; he was flushed and turning purple when he finally gasped out his surrender.

"Okay, kid. Take it easy. Can't you take a joke? Sure I can introduce this girl to Manny Silverstein. What did you say her name was?"

"I didn't. Her name is Gertrude Kolinski. Here's her picture."

Mickey Sklaroff didn't laugh this time, though the name amused him. When he looked at the picture he could hardly believe his eyes.

"Christ, she *is* a beauty! And what a body. Are those boobs real?"

"I couldn't afford some good cheesecake. It's a lousy, cheap picture. She's even prettier than it shows. And she can sing, too."

"Hey, who's her agent? She got a manager?"

"She's got both. Me. I signed her weeks ago."

"You're a smart kid."

"Smarter than you think. Don't bullshit me about that introduction to Silverstein. I'd hate to squeal right here where I work."

Blackmail may not be good for the soul but it works ever so well under the proper circumstances. That very night, before leaving for Chicago, Mickey met with Silverstein. He didn't tell him every detail, but he got across the message that it was a matter of grave concern for him to arrange a meeting.

"Got your tit caught in the wringer again?" Manny joked.

"Not at all," Mickey answered. "This girl lives down the street from my aunt. I promised her."

"You're as full of shit as a Chanukah chicken." Manny laughed.

"But for an old friend, how can I refuse? After all, who arranged for that silent doctor the time I got that kid knocked up?"

"And the clap, three months later," Mickey reminded him.

"I'd almost forgotten about that *courva*. It was the last time I did it with a whore."

Three days later, conveniently arranged at the end of the working day when only Obie was left in the offices, Gertrude Kolinski was ushered into the palatial suite occupied by Manny Silverstein at the headquarters of Continental Studios. It was a moment to be recorded in the sometimes lurid, always fascinating, history of Hollywood.

CHAPTER 5

April 1945

Gertrude selected the flashiest gown she had taken from Sandy McNabb's wardrobe. It was green, emphasizing the emerald brilliance of her eyes, and cut down to the Mason-Dixon line, displaying a more than generous amplitude of luscious flesh. For good measure, it was too tight around the hips, advertising the roundness of her bottom. In short, it screamed sex from every seam. To Manny Silverstein, instinctively a man of sartorial good taste, it was somewhat of a turnoff. It was only after he took a long hard second look that he was stunned by her beauty. Himself a tall man, he always had been attracted to statuesque women. She looked very young, but seemed to carry herself with a confidence born of experience. She was intriguing and yet a bit pathetic in her whorish attire.

"Your name?" he asked, not inviting her to sit.

"Gertrude Kolinski," she answered simply.

"Where from? New York?"

"No. West Virginia. Down southwest near the Kentucky border."

Despite appearances, she was scared to death. Breathless. Skipper had warned her of Silverstein's power. She knew that he was one of the few studio heads who took chances on relative newcomers and backed them with his own money. And Skipper had let her in on the open secret concerning Silverstein's sexual proclivities. No need for surprises. That frightened her as much as the realization that she stood at the entranceway to the promised land and this imposing, self-confident man held the key. She tried to appear calm and concentrate at the same time. But it was a nearly impossible task. There was something about this Hollywood mogul that reminded her of Cass Kolinski.

Though she struggled to shut out the memory, her mind carried her back to a bitter cold, rainy Friday night in West Virginia. That afternoon, Gertrude had intercepted her father at the pay office and relieved him of most of his compensation, letting him keep just enough cash for a few drinks with his buddies at his usual hangout. He had then borrowed or cadged enough money to come home roaring drunk. The kids were asleep. Gertrude had waited up, enjoying a few quiet hours in front of the radio while she darned socks for the boys. As soon as Cass stumbled in, she realized that this was to be one of his meaner episodes. He started by demanding that she bring him the bottle of bourbon, which she kept hidden whenever possible.

"God damn it, bitch," he bellowed, "you're not my boss. Bring me that fuckin' bottle."

"Dad," Gertrude pleaded, "don't yell. You'll wake the kids up."

"I don't care," Cass screamed in defiance. "Let 'em learn what a mean bitch they've got for a sister."

It was then that he lunged for her. Gertrude jumped up and ran across the room, narrowly escaping his grasp. Despite his drunken state, Cass caromed around the room, lunging after her in sheer frustration. He finally cornered her and grabbed her arms when she tried to defend herself. She was no match for the powerful miner, who—even in a state of inebriation—could easily dominate a fourteen-year-old girl. He held her hands with one of his own, then backhanded her across the face again and again until she sank to her knees, crying pitifully.

Debby and Mary, who normally shared a large bed with Gertrude, were awakened by the commotion and came running into the parlor, screaming at the top of their lungs. This woke the boys up, too. Soon, all but the baby, who was now also awake and crying as if he were being stabbed, gathered in the parlor and pulled their father off of the inert form of Gertrude, who had simply stopped struggling. In shame now, Cass stumbled to his feet and cried remorsefully.

Gertrude wiped her eyes, straightened her hair and clothes, rose, and once again took command. "Go to bed, kids. Daddy'll be all right now. He just had too much to drink. He misses Mom, you know."

Her incredible calm worked miracles. The children stopped crying and headed back to bed. Only Debby asked if Gertrude would be all right.

"I'm okay. Don't worry. I can handle it," she said reassuringly.

That night, for the first time, she went to bed with her father. He made no sexual overtures but, rather, acted like a contrite child, cuddling up to her, sniffling his apologies and soon falling into a deep sleep. Gertrude soothed him, offered forgiveness; and shortly the two slept side by side. Cass seemed guilt-ridden the next day and was for all intents and purposes the model father. He offered to bathe the baby, hauled wood from the back yard, and even helped with the dishes. To everyone's amazement, he eschewed his normal Saturday-night trip to the tavern. Gertrude could not quite believe what was happening. There was a happiness in the Kolinski home that had been absent for months.

That night, he insisted that Gertrude sleep with him again. Partly out of affection and partly out of fear, she acquiesced. Again, Cass made no overt advances, kissing her on the cheek in a fatherly fashion and falling asleep quickly, like a well-fed baby. Actually, Gertrude enjoyed his body warmth. It was also a luxury to have half a bed to herself. The girls talked and moaned in their sleep, often rolling over on her and disturbing her much-needed rest.

It soon became a family ritual. Gertrude moved her few personal possessions into her father's room and slept in the same bed with him every night. She felt no real guilt at first. But it was a profound experience that would remain in her memory for the rest of her life.

The reminiscence ended suddenly, as if a projector bulb had burned out. She was back in Hollywood, facing Manny Silverstein, the man who could turn her dreams into accomplishments.

"And how long have you been out here?" he asked.

"Not long. A few weeks."

"Have you any training?"

"None." No need to lie. He'd get at the truth.

"I hear you can sing."

"A little. Enough to get by."

"You're modest. That will never get you anywhere in Hollywood."

"Would you like it better if I lied, Mr. Silverstein?"

"I don't know. Sometimes I lie. It depends."

He still had not invited her to sit down. His manner was cold. It was almost as if he had granted the interview to fulfill an obligation. Which, of course, he had. He turned to look out the window, apparently saw something that interested him, and continued to stare into space. There was a long, uncomfortable stretch of silence, which only added to Gertrude's discomfiture. Finally, he turned and spoke.

"What makes you want to be an actress?"

"What American girl don't want to be?"

"That's a lousy answer," he snapped. "Come here, kid, let me show you something."

He motioned for her to follow him to a low sofa, fronted by a coffee table on which there was a thick album surrounded by stacks of glossy pictures. She walked after him and he, for the first time, indicated that she should sit.

"Let me show you something."

He picked up the album and started riffling through its pages. It was filled with still shots of beautiful actresses. After he came to the last page, he dropped it unceremoniously, as if he had no respect for its contents, and picked up one of the stacks of glossies. Tossing them down like cards from a deck, he showed her every picture on the table. They were all pictures of glamorous, beautiful young women.

"See those pictures?" he asked rhetorically. "They all want to be stars. They're all beautiful. Some of them can even act. A lot of them have won beauty contests in their home states. All of them are desperate to be movie stars. They'll do anything, and I mean *anything,* to get on top. And do you know how many will make it? The answer is, 'none.' You want to know why?"

"Yes, Mr. Silverstein, I'd like to know why."

"For Christ's sake, stop calling me 'Mr. Silverstein.' I'm not that old."

"What should I call you then?" Gertrude asked simply.

"I haven't decided yet. In the meantime, don't call me anything. Just answer the questions."

It was at that moment that Gertrude knew she had passed

through those golden gates and was on her way. It wasn't what he said, but how he said it. And it was the way he was looking at her, drinking in her incredible beauty. She squared her shoulders and spoke with more assurance.

"Okay. Yes, I want to know why these beautiful ladies won't become stars."

"Because they lack a star quality. There's an old joke about a woman being asked why, if she can't dance, can't sing, and can't act, she wants to be in the show. And the answer is, because she wants to be a star. That's not as crazy as it sounds. A star is a person who stands in the middle of a big crowd and attracts everyone's eye. Oh, sure, it helps if she's beautiful. It helps if she can act or sing or dance or what the hell. But lots of people can do these things and do them well. One in a thousand—no, one in a million—has star quality. And it takes a genius to recognize it."

"You're a genius, Mr. . . . . Oops, I almost said it. You're a genius. Do I have it?"

There was a long, meaningful pause.

"I don't know, girlie. Maybe."

She sucked in her breath and took a chance.

"Don't call me 'girlie.' "

"No. What should I call you?" he asked with a smile.

"I haven't decided yet. In the meantime, don't call me anything. Just answer the question."

He laughed pleasantly. "Fair enough. The question is very tough. There's more to the story. If—and it's one hell of a big if —if you do have that star quality that everyone looks for, you have to be willing to give up everything else to cash in on it. You see, gir—Oops, I almost did it, too. You see, you can't be a little pregnant. Either you want to be a star, you want to live for it, breathe for it, screw for it, die for it, if necessary, or you're willing to be another picture in that album. You understand?"

"Of course I understand. Like my dad used to say, 'Only hungry fighters win championships.' It's the same, right?"

"The same thing. Now, take your clothes off. I want to see it all."

"Do I have to?" she asked hesitantly.

"Maybe you got something to hide?"

"That's not the reason."

"So what is?"

"I'm not used to running around naked with strange men."

"I'm not asking you to run around, and I ain't strange."

"You know what I mean. It's . . . we just met."

"You got a short memory. You know those pictures I just showed you? You remember what I said when you asked me about being a star? If you're afraid to undress in a closed office in front of a studio head, hell, you ain't got a chance out here. Like your pop said, you gotta be a hungry fighter. Now let's go. I can't take too much time."

Silverstein knew how to apply the pressure. He was enjoying every bit of this and hadn't the slightest intention of terminating the interview. Gertrude, on the other hand, instinctively knew that a little resistance would go a long way with this man, who obviously was accustomed to having his own way. In addition, the thought of whipping off all of her clothes on command was upsetting to a girl of fifteen fresh from the coal region of West Virginia.

She took a deep breath, considered the options, and finally decided to acquiesce. It might prove embarrassing but she was not unaware of her own beauty and the effect it would have on Silverstein. She rose, walked to the other side of the room, and slowly disrobed. She raised her long, graceful arms and, swaying rhythmically, slipped out of her dress. He watched her every move, astounded at her apparent sangfroid. Deliberately, she bent and rolled down her stockings, slipping out of her shoes and grasping the hose leg by leg to deposit on a nearby chair. She wore a small girdle, hardly necessary but there to help confine her curvaceous hips. It was off in a whisk. Now, there were only her panties and bra between her and the world. She turned to him, intercepting his gaze, and asked a direct question.

"These, too?"

"Those, too," he answered.

Now there was not a moment's hesitation. She was nude, facing him, exercising a tremendous power over this man, who not ten minutes before had filled her with fright. Without his asking, she assumed a series of model poses. Everyone during the war had seen the provocative stances of the pinup queens. Betty Grable and Chili Williams had kept a whole generation of America's fighting men frustrated enough to want to fight hard and end it all so that they could return to couple with that beautiful girl back home. Even back in West Virginia, Gertrude had mimicked the sultry beauties on cardboard. Now she went through her paces, dipping her knees, exaggerating the thrust of her hip, turning and gazing provocatively over her shoulder as she thrust her beauteous bottom in his direction. Silverstein drank it all in, calmly surveying her movements, frowning somewhat noncommittally as she continued to perform. Inside, he was churning, longing for the opportunity to bed her. But externally, he was the calm professional, examining a new prospect. He made no effort to stop her, letting her set the pace.

Finally, she stopped, facing him without shame or embarrassment. "Seen enough?"

He nodded his affirmation. Then he beckoned for her to approach him on the couch. She complied without hesitation. As she drew near, he rose to meet her.

"Take your clothes and follow me," he said, his voice husky with emotion.

She asked no questions, simply gathering her clothing from the chair on which it rested, and, slipping on her shoes, she followed him as he opened a side door and led her to his famous "resting area," which was so well publicized that even Skipper Dawson had warned her about it.

Once inside, he locked the door and faced her. "How old are you, kid?"

"Fifteen."

"You gotta be joking."

"I'm a very old fifteen."

He moved toward her, attempting to wrap her in his arms. She evaded his lunge nimbly and moved behind a chair. He followed her and again tried to grab her. Again she moved away, gracefully avoiding contact like a bull fighter performing a fluent high pass. She avoided him again as he charged a third time, determined to touch the beauty that had virtually hypnotized him. Now he felt deflated, like a junior high school Romeo striking out in his first romantic encounter. He paused, deciding that perhaps vocal persuasion might win the day.

"You're scared of me?"

"No. Not anymore."

"You don't like the way I look?"

"I think you're very handsome."

"You think I'm too old for you?"

"I don't go for young men. You're just right."

"So?"

"So, I'm not a whore. I came here because I want to be in movies. I was told you could help. After we start working, who knows what can happen?"

"You're a pretty good negotiator. You forget I've bargained with the toughest of them."

"I'm not bargaining. I'm telling you the truth. I'm not a whore. And don't grab for me like I'm a candy bar on the drugstore shelf. I've got feelings, too."

"What about my feelings? You think I'm made of wood?"

The question gave her the confidence to resist. Now he was bargaining, not grabbing. It made a big difference.

"I guess I know how you feel. Maybe I feel like that, too."

"So?"

She paused. She was running out of arguments, and she was attracted to this handsome man who could do so much for her career. Still, there was a louder voice within her that told her she must not succumb. Not so soon after meeting him.

"So. Like I said, Mr.—like I said, it's too soon."

He looked at her with new respect. This kid was not only beautiful and incredibly mature for her age, she was spunky as well. Hell, no young starlet, would-be or otherwise, had resisted his advances in as long as he could remember. That alone made her different. Well, if the prize was worth winning, he could wait. He wasn't some *pishika* kid out on his first date burning to get laid.

"Okay. Hurry up and get dressed. I want you to meet Obie."

"Obie?"

"Yes. She's my executive secretary. Has been for ten years. She's savvy. You'll see. Get dressed."

Five minutes later, they were seated comfortably in Silverstein's office, drinking iced Cokes and looking for all the world like old friends at a story conference.

"Obie," he asked, "you agree that 'Gertrude Kolinski's' gotta go?"

"Obviously. It would never fit in an ad. Besides, Polish names never make it out here."

"So whatta you hear? Lana, maybe? Trixie? Rina?"

"We already have a Lana out here. There's only one. Trixie sounds like a dog's name. Rina reminds me of colic. It nearly killed my old man."

"So? Any other ideas?"

Gertrude sat there, amused. It was like being present at your own birth and being old enough to understand the process.

"What about her own name? Gertrude. Gertrude is Trudy, right?"

"Trudy. Trudy." He sounded it a few times for size. "Trudy makes sense. It's catchy. No one's got a Trudy out here. I'll buy it."

"The second name is easy," Obie added with satisfaction. "Kolinski becomes Coles. Only we'll spell it with a *C*, not a *K*."

"Trudy Coles," Silverstein repeated with satisfaction. "Great. I like it. And as you say, it'll fit great in ads."

"And it's catchy, too," Obie added. "How do you like it, kid?"

"I was hoping you'd ask me," Gertrude answered. "Trudy Coles. It sorta sounds like me. Trudy Coles. I like it fine."

"Then it's agreed," Silverstein said. "Let's get the name registered with the Screen Actors Guild before someone else grabs it. Trudy Coles. I think it's great. How do you like the way she looks, Obie?"

"Stand up, kiddo," Obie commanded. "Do a few model turns for me, okay?"

Trudy obeyed.

"You're beautiful, but you have so much to learn I hardly know where to begin. For starters, get rid of that dress. Burn it. No self-respecting whore on Hollywood Boulevard would be caught dead in an outfit like that. It would make the police come running like a raid on a gaming house. Subtle, kiddo. Subtle. That's the way to win people's eyes. Not blatant, like that outfit."

"I like it," Trudy answered lamely.

"Gertrude the Polock liked it," Obie said cruelly. "Trudy Coles must learn to hate it. Take my advice. Burn it, kiddo."

"I will if you'll stop calling me 'kiddo.' "

"That's nice," Obie said in true admiration. "Trudy's got balls. I like that. Okay, I'm sorry. No more 'kiddo.' Trudy it is, from now on."

"What else?" Silverstein asked impatiently. It was obvious he relied fully on Obie's judgment when it came to female attire.

"The hair. It's all wrong."

"Blond, maybe?" Silverstein asked.

"No. Wrong again. This lady is no blonde. See that skin? It needs framing. Her dark hair is great. But we'll give it a little henna rinse to give it character."

"What's 'henna'?" Trudy asked innocently.

"Henna is red-brown."

"I hate red hair."

"So do I. Not red. Red-brown. It just gives your hair highlights that make the brown richer. You'll like it. Trust me."

"We gotta teach her to talk nice, too," Silverstein added. Apparently the matter of Trudy's tresses had been decided.

"She's gotta learn to walk and talk all over. We'll get her to Mollie Haines. She's the best coach in the business. Remember the job she did on Rita? A miracle, I tell you. But it won't be easy, Trudy, I can tell you that. She'll work your ass off. There'll be days when you'll wonder if it's all worth it."

"I'm not afraid of work, Miss Obie. Where I come from, work is all you do."

"There's work and there's work, Trudy," Silverstein interjected. "Out here, work is tougher than it looks. But it's like your pop said about the championship. You gotta be hungry and you gotta work if you wanna win."

She wished he would stop reminding her of Cass. "Just try me," Trudy said simply. "Try me."

Gazing at the satisfied look on Silverstein's face, Obie, ringwise as she was, supposed that he already had. He'd been robbing the cradle for years now. Hopefully, he wouldn't get in trouble.

There had never been any romance between them. She was a struggling milliner's assistant on Pico Boulevard when she'd met him just at the end of the Depression. He made a pass at her one night in a bar and they ended up drunk in some cheap hotel that had long ago been leveled to make room for an apartment house. It was a disaster. Somehow, though sex failed, they found there was great rapport between them. When he settled in, he called her. He paid her way through stenography school, and she had been his executive secretary ever since. She really had no life of her own. She was a Silverstein appendage. Tough, loyal, dependable. To know Manny Silverstein was to hear him say, "Tell Obie. She'll know what I want." Obie realized in a flash that Silverstein needed and wanted a new star. It wasn't difficult to recognize the possibilities in Trudy Coles. Having renamed her, Obie felt like a midwife assisting at a delivery. Hollywood had a way of recreating already living beings. This kid needed a hell of a lot of polish, but there was a diamond in that stone which could blind you with its brilliance. The still-unanswered question was whether Trudy Coles had the guts to take the burnishing. The process wasn't easy.

Silverstein's voice broke her reverie. "Call Mrs. Silverstein. Tell her I've got a dinner meeting and she shouldn't stay up. Take this kid to wardrobe and find something to replace this green *schmatta* she's wearing. Then book us a table at Chasen's. Say for about seven-thirty. I've still got some contracts to check out."

"Yes, Mr. Silverstein. I'll take care of everything."

Obie always did.

An hour and a half later, they were seated at one of the prime tables in one of Hollywood's most fashionable restaurants. A bowing and scraping head waiter had insisted that Dave Chasen himself would want to escort Manny and his date. Silverstein was known as a generous tipper. More importantly, though he was no Louis B. Mayer or Barney Balaban or Joe Schenck, he ran his own shop. Power was the key word in the world's film capital, and Silverstein had it and exercised it. His crudeness, his womanizing, his craftiness, his diabolical temper, all these were known. Yet they faded to nothingness in light of his courageous dedication to his trade. Silverstein was a picture maker. He wasn't afraid of the Foxes, the MGMs, the Warners, certainly not the Republics. He was Continental. He called the shots. He hired the talent. He picked the stories. He manufactured the stars. Silverstein, a wag once joked, should have been named "Silverscreen." Motion pictures were his life.

In days to come, Trudy Coles would grow accustomed to Romanoff's, the Brown Derby, Lucy's, the Polo Lounge, and all the other "in" spots that Hollywood gave birth to and which, in turn, gave birth to Hollywood. But this was the start of the magical sleigh ride and she would never forget it. Imagine, Gertrude Kolinski of Hubbardsville, West Virginia, dining with Manny Silverstein of Continental Studios! Could it really be only ten weeks since that train had puffed out of Charleston? She wished there was a picture she could mail to Helen Caputo. She'd never believe it! Frankly, she hardly believed it herself. Silverstein realized what she must be going through and for once his kinder instincts rose to the surface. He took over as guide and instructor.

"See that guy over there at the second table? The one in the white jacket? That's Jimmy Fiddler. A big-shot columnist. That's Cliff Work from Universal with him. Recognize that blonde at the next table? That's Marilyn Maxwell. And over there—in the corner—that's Vera-Ellen and Ann Miller. You wait. They'll all be asking for your autograph if you stick with it."

"Maybe you've got too much confidence in me, Manny." She had dropped the "Mr. Silverstein" routine following their session in the "resting area."

"Maybe I do. Maybe I don't. That's what makes this a fascinating game. Here comes our captain. Let me order for you. You like steak?"

"I like what you like."

What Manny Silverstein did not like was his first meeting with Skipper Dawson. Silverstein's genius was many-faceted. Among his talents was a determination not to underestimate his enemies. The moment he laid eyes on Skipper he knew he was no friend. He had arranged the meeting the very next day after the dinner at Chasen's. He had suggested that Trudy not be present. Instinctively, he felt he might have to throw his weight around and he didn't want her to witness any ugliness.

He intentionally kept Skipper waiting in his outer office for more than half an hour. He instructed Obie to treat him coolly, in an effort to throw him off-balance. He'd taken a peek at the man through a one-way mirror he had rigged in his office for just this purpose, and was shocked at his youth and apparent insignificance. Yet he was determined to gauge him after they met, not before. He'd been fooled before, sometimes overestimating people, sometimes doing just the opposite. The trick was to be alert at all times, like a hunter in the wildest of jungles. Hollywood was a jungle. One walked with caution if one wanted to survive.

Finally, he summoned his visitor in to the inner sanctum. He nodded coldly, pointed to a chair, and dispensed with any preliminary chitchat. "They tell me you got this Kolinski kid signed. Right?"

"That's right, Mr. Silverstein. For fifteen years."

"You an agent or a manager?"

"Both."

"That's gonna become illegal out here soon."

"Maybe. It's perfectly legal now."

"What are the terms of your deal?"

"That's Miss Kolinski's business. And mine. It's nobody else's concern."

"You're a pretty smart kid. You came in here asking me to give her a break. And when I ask a simple question, you get touchy."

"I'm not touchy, Mr. Silverstein. And I didn't come in here asking for anything. You sent for me. Right?"

"And who sent the girl to see me in the first place?"

"I think it was Mickey Sklaroff. He's such a good friend that he couldn't resist doing a favor for a friend and client of mine. Naturally, I didn't object."

"That's how it happened, eh?" Silverstein asked sarcastically.

"Just like that," the kid answered.

"Okay. Let's cut out the bullshit and get down to cases. The girl is very pretty. But she's a hillbilly if ever I saw one. Can't talk, can't walk, can't act. It'll take a lot of money and a lot of patience to turn that rough stone into a diamond brooch. I'm willing to gamble with her. But I'll be goddamned if I'm going to take the chance with you looking over my shoulder for fifteen years, raising the ante every time I make a score with her."

"What do you want me to do? Walk away like a nice fellow? You're not the only independent producer in Hollywood. And I could take her to one of the major studios and they'd sign her in ten seconds."

This kid was tough. He wouldn't be bluffed very easily. The days he'd spent eavesdropping at the Arnold office hadn't been wasted. There were a lot of beautiful girls out here but this one had an incredible dimension. Silverstein felt it. By God, he knew it. And Skipper Dawson knew he knew it. That's what made the going tough.

"That's easy to say. Just take her to Warners or MGM and see how far you get. Christ, Twentieth Century won't even let you by the front gate. Don't threaten me with that crap. You'll be damned lucky to get her in a Bible scene as an extra!"

"We're in no hurry, Mr. Silverstein. Gertrude is young. So am I. With fifteen years to maneuver, I can afford to take my good old time."

"Nobody knows what she'll look like in fifteen years. Those Polock broads age fast. In fifteen years her tits will touch her toes."

"If that's the case, I don't know why you want her."

Silverstein was beginning to lose control. Here was this pimple-faced errand boy, the low man at the Jason Arnold mailroom, matching him, the great Manny Silverstein, spade for spade. And the kid wasn't backing down either. Secretly he wished he had a couple of tough kids like this on his team. The agents wouldn't mash Continental's balls so easily then. He decided to try a more avuncular approach.

"Kid, look. No point in our fighting. We should be on the same team. You know the ropes. Just because a broad's got a cute ass and big tits, that's no guarantee she's going to be a star. Why don't you act sensible and make a deal?"

"So far I haven't heard any deal offered, Mr. Silverstein. All I hear is that I should back off and you should get her."

"Okay. Maybe you're right. I'll tell you what. I'll give you a special deal. I'll give you a thousand bucks, a thousand bucks cold cash. You tear up the contract and let me handle Gertrude in my way on my terms. You won't be sorry."

To Silverstein's amazement, Skipper Dawson rose with a smile.

"It's nice of you to give me your time, Mr. Silverstein. Someday, when Gertrude is the hottest property in this town, you'll be sorry you insulted my intelligence."

And he was gone without a backward turn.

Skipper Dawson was confident he had won the first round in his skirmish with the lofty Manny Silverstein. He might have, at that, but he hadn't reckoned with the anger that defeat always manufactured in Silverstein's breast. It was cold, cruel anger. Anger directed at revenge.

Four days later, on the occasion of his being ten minutes late for work, he was summoned to the personnel director's suite at the Arnold office and fired summarily. He wasn't even given a chance to explain. Next, he got a note from his landlord telling him that the rent had been doubled. One week later, he received a visit from the local morals squad officer, requesting information concerning his relationship to the young girl who seemed to be sharing his quarters. How old was she? Did she go to school? Where were her family and parents? No overt threats were made. Just an inquiry, you understand. He became aware that he was being tailed.

His money started running low, especially since he had Trudy to support as well as himself. He pondered his next move, certain that the trap was being tightened on Silverstein's orders. Unfortunately, he couldn't confide in Trudy. She'd hate him if she learned that he was standing between her and a movie career.

Trudy began to grow restive when no word came from Silverstein. Something told her that the lack of communication had its roots in Skipper Dawson. He had not told her about his meeting with Silverstein but it was the only conclusion that made any sense. Silverstein had told her he would see her in a few days. Now it was more than a week and not a word. She decided to cast her pride to the winds and call him. After three separate attempts, she finally got through to Obie. Obie could not have been colder, informing her that Mr. Silverstein had left for a few days' rest at Palm Springs. He never permitted her to give out his phone number to anyone. Just be patient, she advised. No doubt he would call her on his return. When he found the time, she added, striking the words slowly like anvils in the chorus from *Il Trovatore*.

The final blow fell when Skipper received a registered letter from the legal counsel to the Motion Picture Association of America informing him that they had received an anonymous telephone call claiming that he, a non-registered agent, had signed an aspiring actress to a long-term contract. Should he try to exercise it, he was informed, he would be prosecuted in the courts. Skipper wasn't clear as to his rights but there seemed no point in spending money for an attorney against the power of Manny Silverstein and Continental Studios. At least not yet. He went to his favorite neighborhood bar to have a beer and consider his options. It was a big mistake. He never remembered exactly how it started but somehow he got involved with a big thug who insisted he had flirted with the man's wife. He was lifted from his seat, smashed in the face, pushed up against the wall, and punched in the stomach until he fell to the floor unconscious. He came to several minutes later, bloodied and beaten, to find the tavern owner looking down on him with concern.

"Don't give them another chance at you, kid. Those guys are bad actors. I've seen them work before. They're bad actors. They'll kill you if you fight back."

Painfully, assisted by the proprietor, Skipper climbed to his feet. He dragged himself home, took a hot bath, and went to bed. He couldn't get up for two days. He couldn't prove anything of course. But it was all too clear that the whole campaign against him had been engineered by Silverstein.

Skipper Dawson was stubborn, too. But he was a pragmatist. If Silverstein wanted Gertrude's contract this badly it must be worth a lot to him. The trick was not to fight to the death but to capitalize on the opportunity for all it was worth. Otherwise, he would lose Gertrude anyway. She wouldn't be content hanging around forever.

He found a smooth-talking divorce lawyer whom many considered more handsome than any of the leading men in Hollywood, and who had dabbled in the entertainment business from time to time and was well known in studio circles. A meeting was arranged and Lance Rawlings agreed to represent him on a contingency basis for one-third of the settlement. Rawlings scheduled an immediate session with Silverstein. Although Manny didn't admit that he had had anything to do with Skipper's chain of misfortune, Rawlings lied back. He told him that a detective who was tailing his client had worked for his office in the past, owed him a host of favors, and for a few hundred dollars would be happy to testify to his knowledge of the whole unsavory scheme. Manny was sure the smooth-talking lawyer was lying, but he couldn't afford to take a chance. Besides, he had forced the kid to the conference table again and that was where he wanted him. The final settlement called for a payment of $12,000, $4,000 of which went to the attorney. In one area alone did Silverstein give in after he had fought like a tiger. Skipper retained, for life, two percent of Trudy Coles' gross earnings, a small percentage but one that would make him rich. Silverstein knew in the end that he would have little trouble getting Trudy to agree to the payments. What he wanted, and what he got, was Skipper's binding assurance that he would never again interfere in any way in Trudy Coles' career.

Three days later, Trudy received a call from the chief lawyer for Continental Studios. With a "friendly" attorney suggested by the studio representing her, she signed a one-year contract, with four additional one-year options to be exercised at their choice by the leaders of Continental Studios. Her pay: $300 a week, plus an apartment to be supplied by the studio, which she might be asked to share with another would-be starlet. Only then did she receive a congratulatory call from Silverstein. They celebrated by sharing a delightful dinner at Lucy's, then returning to Silverstein's office.

There was no point in asking why they had headed back toward the studios long after working hours. Only fifteen, and still a virgin, Gertrude understood only too clearly what was in store. Even if she had really wanted to resist, she was at a loss as to how to proceed. Manny Silverstein was too powerful an individual to take no for an answer even though she had been able to hold her ground in their first encounter. That, of course, was before he had done so much to launch her career. She stole a glance at him as their taxi moved through the silent city. He was hellishly attractive. But why did he remind her so much of her father?

Her mind moved in reverse gear to a Saturday night no more than six months ago, when Cass had come home from work and demanded that Gertrude bring him his bottle of bourbon. She couldn't refuse him a drink after his week of hard work. One drink led to another and soon he was slurring his words and weaving a bit, unsteady in his gait.

"Why don't you go to bed, Pop? You're tired," Gertrude had suggested.

"You join me," he answered simply.

Gertrude knew of no way to refuse. Once under the covers, he clasped her to him and kissed her brow with what seemed like unusual fervor. This was different from the paternal embraces of the past. Gertrude grew uncomfortable when she realized that he was holding her very tightly against his body. Without causing a commotion, she tried to pull away, but Cass was much too strong for her. He pulled her closer and closer. She became painfully aware that her father was aroused.

"Don't, Dad," she whispered. "This isn't right. Maybe we never go to church, but this is against God's law."

Cass gave no indication that any law mattered. He held her tightly, started rubbing furiously against her, and suddenly moaned as his body was wracked with spasms. After a few minutes, saying nothing, he got out of bed and visited the bathroom while Gertrude, in tears, terrified and confused, lay motionless. When he returned to bed several minutes later he seemed contented, and with a simple "good night" he was off to sleep. Gertrude cried silently and fell asleep, dreaming fitfully throughout the night.

"Hey, Trudy, what's wrong? You look like you just saw a ghost ten thousand miles away."

Gertrude snapped back to the present and tried to smile. They had reached the studios and Manny was dismissing the driver. Nodding to a night watchman at the main gate, he led the way via a circuitous route to the rear door of his office complex. Gertrude surmised only too accurately that he had taken this path on many occasions. He said nothing as they rode the elevator, traveled down the hall, and finally entered his suite. Then, predictably, he led the way to his "resting area." Wasting little time, he pulled her to him and nearly devoured her with his first kiss. Gertrude felt her young heart pounding as his tongue explored her lips and mouth. She struggled to gain control of her emotions, but it was a losing battle. Manny pulled her down beside him on a wide, luxurious divan, and his busy hands explored her marvelous young body.

"Please, Manny," she whispered. "I'm scared."

He paused to look at her. She was such an interesting mélange. On the one hand, tall and Junoesque, looking as sophisticated as any woman of the world; on the other, innocent and childlike, her emotions that of a callow adolescent.

"Scared?" he repeated. "What's to be scared about?"

"It's my first time. I'm still a virgin."

Whether Manny really believed her or whether the thought of introducing a beautiful, young neophyte to the wonders of lovemaking excited him, she would never know. But soon they were both lying side by side, their clothes abandoned on the carpeted floor, and he was covering her neck, her throat, her breasts, her luscious, round belly, and her stately thighs with a torrent of passionate kisses. Gently he forced his knee between her legs and was on top of her. There was a sharp pain as he entered her but it soon dissolved in the flow of excruciating, joyous passion. She was a woman now, having crossed that magic threshold to experience the bliss that only the act of love induces. She was lying in his arms, her mind a tangle of a thousand romantic thoughts when they were both jarred back to reality by the raucous ringing of Manny's private phone. Quickly he disengaged himself and moved toward his desk.

It was his wife, Tillie, who was growing a bit suspicious about so many night sessions away from home and hearth. "Finish your business and get home," she ordered. "No one has to hold meetings at eleven o'clock at night. Only monkey business goes on this late."

The iron-fisted mogul was no match for this tough lady. He apologized, explaining that he hadn't realized how late it was. He'd be home shortly. Trudy got the message. She dressed quickly, as did Silverstein, and he put her in a cab. It was Trudy's first encounter with the wife of a lover, and it disturbed her. The contrast between Silverstein the powerful film mogul and Silverstein the chastened husband was so obvious that it shocked her back to reality. Even though she didn't know Mrs. Silverstein, she feared that exposure might result in a terrible loss for him. Most telling was the thought that she was doing what she was doing for her own personal aggrandizement. In short, she saw herself suddenly as a whore selling herself to a married man who could further her career. It was an ugly picture, one that she was unable to shake for many days.

In later years, she came to accept the fact that infidelity was Hollywood's theme song. But on this night, she felt ashamed of the cheap role she was playing. She hardly said a word to Silverstein as the cab moved off, leaving him waving from the curb.

Skipper Dawson moved out of the apartment several days later, leaving Trudy several hundred dollars to meet upcoming bills, money that had been furnished by Continental. He explained that he felt guilty monopolizing her time and really was in no position now to help her career. Trudy realized that this wasn't the whole story, but she couldn't have cared less. The truth was that he bored her. They exchanged formal good-byes and he was gone.

CHAPTER 6

June 1945

There was no more significant year in American history than 1945. Two days after Skipper and Trudy separated, Franklin Delano Roosevelt, in the words of his wife, Eleanor, "slept away." Less than a month later, Dwight Eisenhower accepted the unconditional surrender of Germany at Rheims. The world entered the nuclear age at Hiroshima and Nagasaki during the first week in August. President Harry S. Truman announced the unconditional surrender of Japan on August 14. For Trudy Coles, all of these world-shaking events paled into nothingness compared to her meeting with Richie Stevens.

For six weeks following her dinner with Silverstein at Lucy's, she cooled her heels. An underling from the studio's costume department took her on a shopping tour, during which she was outfitted with an entirely new wardrobe. Pointedly, she was told that the studio would lay out the money for her personal clothing but that the funds would be recouped via weekly deductions from her salary. She was to be charged a nominal interest of three percent on the declining balance. She was moved to a small apartment on Rossmore Avenue near the El Royale Apartments, which housed a number of minor stars and studio executives. It was furnished quite luxuriously by West Virginia standards, and came complete with a roommate: another starlet, named Penny O'Neill, some fifteen years older than Trudy but a "starlet" nonetheless. Trudy was somewhat shocked on receiving a notification from Continental's accounting department informing her that, though her rent was free, she would be expected to pay for her share of the utilities and phone bills. Also, the cost for half the furniture and moving expenses had totaled $3,300. These, too, she would be expected to assume. One hundred additional dollars per week were to be subtracted from her pay envelope. The same minimum three-percent interest would be charged until the debt was erased. Trudy thus received her first lesson in "creative" studio accounting.

"Whatsamatter, kiddo?" Penny asked on seeing the look of consternation on Trudy's face while she pondered the effect on her pay envelope of all of these stated deductions.

"They take out for everything. Do you think I'll have enough left to live on?"

"I doubt it. Out here you need a benefactor."

"What's that?"

"A benefactor. A boyfriend, kiddo."

"You mean someone to keep you?" Trudy asked in shock.

"Call it what you want. Without my Mr. Landis I'd've starved two years ago. And forget clothes and vacations. Shit, without Lee Landis I'd be back in Bushkill Falls long, long ago. There's no free lunch in Hollywood, kiddo."

"Please call me Trudy. I hate 'kiddo.'"

"Sorry. But by me you're still wet behind the ears."

Penny O'Neill's story was identical to that of literally hundreds of aspiring actresses in every studio. Blessed with a lovely face and voluptuous body, she had worked in a small department store in the Pocono region of Pennsylvania until an opportunity to reach for the brass ring appeared. There was a look-alike beauty pageant in a neighboring resort, which she entered and won as a dead ringer for Lana Turner, the current Hollywood rage. One of the judges at the contest had been Lee Landis, an assistant director for Continental. He had been given the assignment as a reward for helping Manny Silverstein in a legal scrape with a young actress who had found herself in a family way after several encounters in the Silverstein "resting area." Through a connection, Landis had arranged for a discreet abortion. That didn't really guarantee him a career with Continental, but he was in line for a few fringe benefits. One was a trip to the Poconos, away from his wife and family, in the guise of supervising a talent hunt.

The moment he set eyes on Penny O'Neill, Lee Landis was spellbound. Although she was really too short for leading roles—she stood only five feet tall—she was soft and curvaceous and her glass-blue eyes shone from a face that boasted a cream-pure complexion and near-perfect features. It was a doll's face, lacking intelligence and character; but, together with the breathtakingly rounded bottom and architecturally perfect bosom, Penny was an eye-turner first class. She was just ring-wise enough to tease Landis and reject his initial quest for the birdie. This ploy resulted in a series of frantic calls to Continental, a promise of a screen test, and the hope of adding her name to the long list of extras who were used frequently in crowd scenes in virtually every feature Continental filmed. Landis was successful in moving her up to minor contractual status after about three months. After five years in Hollywood, Penny liked to joke that her biggest part called for her speaking one line: "You want it with sugar and cream or you like it black?" She had never had any illusions of becoming a big-time screen siren, and attended the early barrage of studio classes in half-step, marking herself as an also-ran in the very first round. She eventually fell in love with Lee Landis but really had no false impressions about his leaving his wife and marrying her after he made promises in that direction for two long years and never took the fatal step. She was like a beautiful, petrified butterfly, trapped in granite, awaiting the inevitable day when her beauty would fade and Landis would cut her adrift.

Still, she was not bitter; she enjoyed California and the friends she had made there, and looked forward with warm anticipation to the hours when Landis could steal away from his job and family and spend time in her company. Their physical attraction for one another had persisted, indeed grown warmer; and she admired his intelligence and, compared to hers, his superior intellect. Landis, similarly, had been loyal to her, and though he had given up any thoughts of legalizing their relationship, he felt responsible for her and was to be counted on whenever Penny had a real or imagined crisis.

Penny and Trudy became fast friends in the days that followed. Trudy had never had the luxury of having an older sister to turn to for advice and Penny assumed that role.

"I know you hate me calling you 'kiddo' but I *am* twice your age. So listen to me. Don't wear those shiny red and purple dresses. You're so beautiful you can hardly make yourself cheap and ugly, but you're working at it. Don't look like a hooker."

A good pupil and a natural imitator, Trudy learned how to improve her appearance rather than harm it. Penny was no purchaser of designer gowns, to be sure, but she did have an innate sense of style, and after five years in Hollywood she had learned the ropes. She was happy to share her knowledge with Trudy.

"You busy Saturday, kiddo?" she asked one evening when they were alone together. "Lee's got a friend visiting him from San Francisco. Lee wants to double-date. That's pretty special for him. Most of the time he wants to sneak me in and out of out-of-the-way restaurants 'cause he's afraid someone he knows will see us and squeal to his wife. Anyhow, I told him about you and he asked if you'd come along Saturday night."

"Why not? If you want me to."

"Sure. It's arranged."

Trudy took an immediate dislike to Lee Landis' friend. He tried to paw her immediately and every word out of his mouth made it obvious that he felt he was slumming with a couple of lowbrow chorus girls. Even Lee was annoyed, cutting the evening short and driving the girls home at an early hour.

"Well, that one was a real schmuck!" Penny said as soon as they were alone. "Sorry, kiddo."

"Forget it. It was fun to be out for a change."

Her only contact with Silverstein during this period was a phone call one day from Obie asking her to appear at the offices of Mollie Haines for a reading. She would be expected at ten o'clock the next morning. She dared to inquire concerning Mr. Silverstein's whereabouts and was informed curtly that he was back in New York for an extended stay. There was no exact information as to when he planned to terminate his current business trip. She would hear from him, Obie informed her, in due time. Please report promptly. Miss Haines had agreed to see her as a personal favor since her present schedule was overcrowded.

Wearing as simple a dress as she now had in her wardrobe, her hands dripping nervous perspiration, her voice husky with stage fright, Trudy was ushered into Mollie Haines' presence the next morning at precisely ten o'clock. An unsmiling lady, small and nondescript, greeted her coldly from behind a huge teak desk. She directed Trudy to seat herself in a straight-backed chair alongside of the desk, which somehow made Trudy feel more exposed than she would have behind the desk's protective shield.

"Tell me about yourself," Mollie Haines said without prelude.

"What do you want to know?" Trudy answered with an innocent question.

"Obviously, I'm not interested in when you menstruate or if you're constipated. I want to know about your work as a performer."

"Oh," Trudy said, completely shaken. "Well, I really only had one job. Back in West Virginia, or rather in Kentucky to be exact."

"No difference," she answered deprecatingly. "What did you do on the job?"

Mollie Haines was an exacting professional, who had served some of the greatest Hollywood actors of both sexes as personal drama coach. She knew, as did everyone else in the industry, of Silverstein's predilection for shapely nymphs. She resented serving as an excuse for his constant philandering, for too often he sent some talentless, buxom shopgirl to her on the pretense of starting a career in films. And too often, after bedding them down for a month or so, Silverstein refused even to accept their telephone calls. Since Mollie Haines had an annual coaching contract with Continental, it was difficult for her to refuse to play a part in these charades. Her mood on meeting Trudy reflected her assumption that this was just the latest in a long line of Silverstein's "sexploitations."

"I sang. In a café. It was called Sandy's Cafe."

"Oh, yes," Mollie answered sarcastically, "I've heard of it."

Despite her desperate nervousness, Trudy decided to fight back. She had learned to handle bullies long ago. "It's easy to be nasty to me now, Miss Haines. "I'm sure it makes you feel very big."

Somehow, Mollie Haines had not expected a spirited comeback from this obviously ingenuous girl. She paused and looked at her more critically. What she saw amazed her. This was really an outstanding beauty. And the anger in her incredibly green eyes made them shine like piercing, emerald beacons. She waited a dramatic beat, then apologized.

"I'm sorry, Miss Coles. It's been a bad week. I'm usually not known for rudeness. You were telling me about your singing."

The atmosphere was immediately relaxed. With the tension removed, Trudy felt it easier to be candid.

"Okay, I understand. The truth is that I'm not a very good singer at all. I sang a little in church. Then, I won a contest in a small tavern and got a job. A lot of lonesome soldiers thought I was pretty. I don't know if they even listened to me sing."

"So you came out here to be an actress?"

"Yes. I'm sure I couldn't be a big-time singer. But in a pinch, I can get by. And people tell me I'm graceful. So I guess I could learn to dance, too."

"You don't know how to use makeup, if you'll not be offended by the truth. But you are very, very beautiful, Miss Coles, and if you work hard and learn to read, who knows? This is the land where dreams come true."

"I'll keep dreaming, then," Trudy answered with a chuckle.

"You have a nice, melodious laugh. That's a good sign."

"Thank you."

The ice was obviously broken.

"Here's a long, narrative poem. It's kind of sad. It's about a country girl who falls in love with a convict. He's eventually tracked down by police, shot, and killed. It's called 'The Highwayman.' Look it over for a short time. I'll be back and then I want you to read it to me out loud. Now, don't be nervous. I'm an old pro and I know how difficult this can be. I just want to hear you read so I can tell where work is needed."

Trudy was near-paralyzed with fright. But she did her best, and as she got into the rhythm of the poem her reading improved.

"Not bad for a first morning," Mollie commented after Trudy had finished. "You'll be surprised yourself how much you'll improve as you work at it."

In her report to Silverstein, Mollie wrote:

> *This girl needs mountains of work. But there's a quality there, I believe, just waiting to be summoned out of the bottle. If you haven't done so yet, sign her is my advice.*

Two days later, Trudy received a surprise call and visit from Silverstein. It was a warm, humid California afternoon. He brought a bottle of chilled, white wine, which they drank in juice glasses in her small kitchen. They were in bed minutes later, and whether it was because of the wine or the loneliness, Trudy wasn't certain. It was the kind of passionate sex about which young girls dream. She couldn't get enough of him. Even the worldly Manny Silverstein was surprised.

"Hey, take it easy," he cautioned. "You'll wear me out in one session. Like the man says, 'Once a king, always a king. Once a night's enough.'"

"We haven't been together in weeks. I thought you were disappointed in me." She considered mentioning his wife but thought better of it.

"Disappointed in you? You gotta be kidding. I've been away. Busy. I've been thinking about you a good deal. Today I got a great note from Mollie Haines. She thinks you can make it. Big. How do you like that?"

"You're kidding me," she said, pouncing on him once again and burying his mouth with kisses.

He fought his way up for air. "Hey. Give me a break," he said, laughing. "No kidding. She says you got a long way to go. But she really thinks you can rise to the top of the bottle. Like cream. And she was impressed when you told her off, too. You got guts, kid. Not many women talk back to Mollie Haines and live to tell the tale. I can promise you that."

"I thought I did awful. I didn't think I had a chance."

They rose and showered. Then he told her about Richie Stevens. She had heard the name, of course, even during her short existence in Hollywood. Richie Stevens had worked first as a production assistant, then assistant director, and finally as a full-fledged director at both MGM and Warner's. He had spent a few years in New York as a successful leading man before coming to the Coast, enchanted with the growth of the film industry. He had soon given up acting, feeling more challenged on the other side of the camera. As his reputation for directing grew, he longed for the independence of the producer-director's role. Silverstein had given him that opportunity, promising him complete freedom in the selection of properties, the hiring of writers, and the selection of stars and supporting casts. He soon became the top creative force—under Silverstein to be sure—in the Continental Studio apparatus. He and Manny had had their difficulties, of course; and despite his elegant, effete appearance, it was rumored that, one night at a party, he had punched Manny in the jaw and propelled him into a swimming pool fully clothed. They had been on the outs for months. Finally a reconciliation was accomplished and their relationship had been on a more or less even keel for a period of more than a year. It was Richie Stevens, more than any other single person, Silverstein believed, who could guide Trudy into a successful career. Like Mollie Haines, Richie Stevens had had his own experiences with what he termed in his own badly immitative Yiddish, "Silverstein's *tsotzkillahs.*" It was only after a half hour of arguing that he had finally succumbed and agreed to see her.

"You'll see," Silverstein had prophesied, "this one is different. She's gonna be a big, big star."

"I'm sure she's got big, big boobs," Richie had replied skeptically.

"Maybe for you we'll get her to sand them down," Silverstein had answered angrily and banged down the phone.

Later, as she contemplated their first meeting, Trudy tried to reconstruct exactly what it was about the man that had impressed her so indelibly. First, she had had no preconceived image of what he looked like. Second, exactly as she had experienced with Mollie Haines, she had expected rejection, rudeness, and sarcasm. She was well aware that coming in under the blanket of Manny Silverstein's sponsorship also carried with it the implication of sexual promiscuity. She had made a few friends in the studio and had called them, seeking their impressions of Richie Stevens. What she had gotten was a picture of an aloof, noncommunicative man who acted as if the world was not good enough for him. As one of the more direct and less subtle of Trudy's acquaintances put it, "He thinks he pees olive oil." Another had indicated that he was known to scorn Manny Silverstein, and anyone he met who was "a front-office must" was doomed to face his animosity.

What none of them realized, however, was that, above all, Richie Stevens was a professional and a man with exquisite taste. He might not enjoy wasting time with a voluptuous neophyte who was Silverstein's latest roll in the hay, but he had trained himself to be objective when it came to sizing up talent. He was amazed when he caught his first glimpse of Trudy. She wore an understated outfit that emphasized her natural beauty. She was shy, tentative, and somewhat pathetic as she entered the room, not at all the brazen tart he had somehow expected. Her little girl's voice, as she said hello, was appealing, seductive, totally captivating. Even the thought of her in Silverstein's arms was anathema to Stevens.

He, on the other hand, was the handsomest, most appealing man she had ever seen. He rose from his desk to greet her, a briar pipe in his mouth, and gave her a smile that could have easily melted granite. He was extremely tall, standing well over six feet four inches, broad-shouldered yet trim and athletic. His hair, burnished gold in color, was carefully coiffed, with an abundance of neatly trimmed waves and ringlets. He moved with the rhythm and grace of a young antelope as he bounded forward to usher her in. His eyes, intelligent and piercingly blue, exuded a feeling of gentleness, yet suggested power and concentration when they focused in on any subject. His voice was deep and resonant. Trudy Coles was convinced that she would never meet a more attractive human being.

In contrast to her initial treatment by Mollie Haines, Trudy felt immediately in tune with Stevens. He was polite, understanding, considerate, and in no way gave her the impression, as so many male admirers she had encountered did, that his only goal was to see her nude. It wasn't that he seemed indifferent. As she later explained to a friend, Stevens made a woman feel like a woman, not a slab of meat. He invited her to have a seat, spent a few minutes talking about his own roots, indicating that he, too, had been born in a poor, rural Southern community. It was his way of putting her at ease. She appreciated his having taken the time to learn her background, because of—or probably in spite of—Silverstein's sponsorship.

For the next half hour, Stevens delved into Trudy Coles' inner being. Instead of asking her to read for him, he questioned her on subjects she could discuss intelligently. He asked about the coal mining region, her parents' background, her own interests at school, her friends, her aspirations, her experiences at the tavern where she had been discovered by Skipper Dawson. Everything she said seemed to intrigue him. Trudy felt herself growing in confidence, revealing all of her thoughts, holding little in reserve. The one subject he avoided was Manny Silverstein, referring to him only once, briefly, as "Mr. Silverstein, the head of our organization." If he harbored any animosity toward him, it was completely obscured; that, too, put Trudy at ease: after all, Silverstein was her benefactor.

Finally, he suggested that they stroll over to one of Continental's larger sound stages where the final scenes of a Western potboiler were being filmed. Then, after a reasonable stay, he took her to the screening room where a portion of the day's rushes were being viewed. From there, he led her to the laboratories, where mixing and developing were in progress, and finally to an audio studio, where sound was being matched to silent film. It was an entrancing experience for Trudy, who had not really had a behind-the-scenes view of the magic of movie making.

What Trudy did not realize, however, was that it was she who was being observed. Richie Stevens watched her every move, listened to every syllable she uttered, caught every nuance of her personality. Finally, at his suggestion, they returned to his office for a cup of tea and a candid discussion. In a few words he told her that she was probably the most beautiful "child" he had ever seen. He also felt that there was a power within her that shone in her face, an electricity that some day could come to the surface and light up the screen.

And then the bad news. He told her quite frankly that she was woefully unprepared for her career. The way she talked; the way she walked; the way she expressed herself; the way she dressed; her obvious ignorance about films, acting, dancing, singing; the entire spectrum of talents needed in Hollywood she had yet to learn. He would recommend to Silverstein a complete regimen of training if she, determined to make the grade, would commit herself to the drudgery required.

"Remember, Miss Coles," he said, "it's easy to say yes now. You're like a young girl gazing into a shop window loaded with chocolates. They seem to be beckoning. They're so enticing. Why not reach out and grab a handful? But I am Mephistopheles. I'm the devil who tells you that to get those sweets you're going to be forced to sell your soul to the god of work. Think about it! Work, work, work, from early morning to late at night with no time for relaxation, for fun, for love and romance. And if you do make the grade, there will be no real personal life to call your own. You'll belong to the masses, make no mistake about it. Show me a happily married, family oriented actress in Hollywood and I'll show you a lady who didn't make the grade. Is it all worth it? Is it really, Trudy?"

"I think it is," Trudy answered quietly.

And so the rebirth of Trudy Coles began. Under Stevens' tutelage she learned to speak, to read dramatic lines. He convinced Mollie Haines to take over that section of her education. She was sent to modeling school, and there taught to move with grace and poise. She was taught to harness her natural rhythms, to move with sexual magnetism, yet to avoid open displays of animal coarseness. Since she had interrupted her schooling and had no real knowledge of the world, Stevens insisted that she enroll as a freshman in the studio high school training program. When she balked, he reminded her of her pledge.

"Remember the chocolates, Miss Coles. Remember the devil. Remember that the gods are willing to sell anything, but the price they charge is hard work. I warned you. Work until you're bone-weary or quit this business."

She learned foreign languages, and her tutors were delighted to discover that she had a natural ear for imitation that made conversation in other tongues relatively easy. She had a good mind and a good memory, which would later be of great help to her in learning her lines. Throughout her career she would be known as a "quick study," a director's dream.

She was introduced to ballet and modern dance, and she loved it. Despite her height, she moved gracefully and easily with any partner. Here, too, she was a quick study. And she was strong. Hours of painful exercise, all manner of stretching and moving, were easy for her. She ached at times, but at fifteen one recuperates easily.

She was assigned to a singing teacher and here she encountered her greatest difficulty. Though she had a sweet little voice and could carry a tune, there was no resonance to her singing and, try as she might, in this area her development was slowest. Even at such an early stage in her training, the inevitable conclusion was reached that Trudy Coles would never be a singing star.

For six months, day in and day out, week in and week out, Trudy Coles studied. She saw little of Silverstein—it was as if he had shunned her. Then one day, unexpectedly, he called and suggested that they have a drink later that afternoon. Happily, she acquiesced.

"I missed you so much," she said innocently once they had been seated. "Why haven't you called?"

"I don't touch nuns," Silverstein explained simply. "You're a religious fanatic now in the church of Hollywood. I made a promise to Stevens. He told me that if I interfered with your life in any way, he'd give up on you. I can't afford to get him mad. Trudy, I need a star. I need one bad. And you're my prime candidate. Don't let me down."

Later, they went to bed, despite his excuses. It wasn't very good. The image of herself as a nun troubled Trudy. And the truth was, having met Richie Stevens, no other man attracted her. She had fallen in love at a single glance. It would take years before the effect of that moment would begin to wear thin. Silverstein, the sex machine, also functioned hesitantly. She suspected that he had another "protégée" but really couldn't be sure. Nor would she give him the satisfaction of asking. They fondled each other for some time, then kissed and gave it up as a bad job. There are moments like that and they were both aware of the futility of forcing the issue. Yet, in a strange way, Trudy was happy. She felt relieved of a certain burden. She knew that she could never really love Manny Silverstein. Apparently, he understood and was himself relieved. She had feared that there might someday be an angry parting. Now, that threat seemed to have been averted.

She found herself longing for a more personal relationship with Stevens. To date, though he showed professional interest in her career, he had avoided being alone with her in anything like a compromising situation. She tried to learn more about his personal life without in any way revealing her longing for him. She discovered that he had been married before but was currently on the loose thanks to a legal technicality. There was one lady he shepherded to important Hollywood functions, a female lawyer who worked with one of the competing studios. She was a handsome lady in her late forties, a widow whose husband had died at sea during one of the many convoy operations in the early days of the war. Trudy had once caught a glance of her in the studio cafeteria when Stevens unexpectedly showed up during the lunch hour. Most of the top executives ate in the executive dining room, and Stevens was no exception. Why he was there and why he was escorted by his friend was not clear. Trudy made it her business to catch his eye at one point and he nodded pleasantly. She got the distinct impression that he was talking about her then, because Stevens' companion turned around and gazed in her direction. Trudy, embarrassed, turned away and concentrated on her salad bowl. She had been gaining weight and the studio dietician had issued several warnings. She had learned that the camera added width to any face or body and film stars had to be on constant lookout against unneeded avoirdupois.

"Fat jockeys don't ride horses," the dietician said. "Fat actresses end up being dieticians. Ask me. I had a career once. Now look at me," she said, slapping her spreading hips. Chocolates, rich desserts, fried potatoes, all of the attractive junk foods that Trudy had gluttoned over as a child in West Virginia were now forsaken. It was one of many sacrifices that she was called upon to make in search of Jason's golden fleece of stardom. One day, after a particularly disappointing session with Mollie Haines in drama class, she returned to her apartment alone and despondent. Perhaps Richie Stevens was correct after all, she thought, as she curled up on the sofa with tomorrow's script spread on her lap. She had no friends, no family, no romance, actually no life beyond the constant battery of classes. A few of her fellow students interested her, but they were terribly immature despite the fact that many were older than she. One muscular weightlifter type asked if he could see her home one day, and, feeling guilty after a long ride, she invited him in for coffee. It was a terrible mistake. No sooner were they alone than he pounced on her and virtually wrestled her onto the sofa. It took all of her strength to repel him and escape. Glowering angrily she shouted, "You ever touch me again and I'll kick you in the balls." And she meant it. He never bothered her again.

She longed to spend time with Stevens, but she knew it was impossible. After hoping against hope that one day her phone would ring, she decided that she would take matters into her own hands. She called his secretary and asked for an appointment. He was on location, filming in Arizona, but was due back the following week. She left word for him to call her on his return. After waiting breathlessly, the call finally came and she was told to be at his office the following afternoon at four, following the completion of classes.

The next day's classes were tortuously long. She found herself checking the clock every fifteen minutes. She forgot her lines in drama class, flunked an exam on the history of the West, fell all over herself in ballet training, and generally sleep-walked through her assignments. But finally, classes were over and she found herself, exhilarated but breathless, approaching his office door.

Once inside, she was greeted by his secretary, who apologized for him but explained that he had faced a sudden script crisis and had to leave the office for the day. He was heading back to Arizona and would be gone for another week. He asked her to be patient; he would call her on his return.

She had great difficulty holding back the tears. Out of frustration, she went to a nearby pay phone and called Silverstein. A totally frigid Obie informed her that it was Mr. Silverstein's wedding anniversary. He and his wife had gone to Palm Springs for the week.

Trudy's loneliness was accentuated because she missed Penny's companionship. Penny had been away on location in the depths of South America, and it looked as if she would be gone for at least six more weeks. Lee had arranged for the fortunate casting since he, too, was assigned to the film. This would give them the luxury of nearly two months alone together with no need for subterfuge. Trudy had received one brief message via postcard. It read: *This is like being married. Only better.*

That night, desperate for companionship, she ate virtually no dinner, showered, put on one of her gaudier dresses, and headed for the excitement of Sunset Strip. Alone, she entered a small café where a hot jazz group was blasting away before an exuberant crowd. The maître d' seated her at a small booth near the front of the house, assuming that such a beauty would only be alone until joined by her date. The musicians were all black. The leader, on tenor sax, was ebony dark but his aquiline nose and sharp features differed dramatically from the more African features of his fellow instrumentalists. He spotted her immediately, turned in her direction, and seemed to concentrate all of his efforts on her behalf. His attentions were so obvious that others in the crowded room became aware of the byplay between the handsome black musician and the green-eyed, curvaceous beauty smiling encouragement to his advances. Because she'd had little dinner, the white wine she drank went immediately to her head; she felt herself losing all her inhibitions despite her awareness that she was being watched.

Trudy had never had any real contact with blacks, aside from a few laborers. The mixed Polish and Italian mining community she called home reeked with prejudice. In West Virginia and Kentucky there were no "blacks," only "niggers." They had their own little ramshackle church, their own grocery, their own barber and beauty shops, and—needless to say—their own funeral parlor. Actually, they were few in number and if they chose not to attend school, no one attempted to force them into classes. One shy studious black lad had been in Trudy's class but he was so blatantly ostracized that he'd soon dropped out and his family had moved North. Trudy had never given him the time of day.

Here in Hollywood, the picture was not much different. A few beautiful black ladies were employed by the studios, but even in the cases of stars like Lena Horne, they were treated like lovely animals who could take no part in the dramatic development of any script. Then, of course, there were the Stepin Fetchits and the Hattie McDaniels, portraying the good blacks who lived only to serve.

Malcolm Roberts, nicknamed "Mulch," was an Ethiopian college student who had come to California to attend UCLA on a scholarship provided by an international students' fund. He was quite well bred, his father having taught religion at one of the more respected secondary schools in Addis Ababa. He fell in love with the freedom of California and decided immediately that he would never return to his homeland. A talented musician, he formed a small jazz group while in college, and now, some three years after graduation, was making a fair living playing the many night spots that were springing up as the war drew to a close.

He approached Trudy's table when the set was over and smilingly made his pass: "Little lady, mind if I make a onesome a twosome?"

"Why not?" Trudy asked for want of a better reply.

He joined her each time his set was finished and she stayed until the room closed at three in the morning. She found him utterly charming, the first time in her recollection that a young man interested her. None of the old prejudices had the slightest effect on her, and his coal-black countenance and elegant speech intrigued her. Soon she was holding his hand, rubbing thighs under the table, laughing at his every joke. She was completely a victim of his charms. It was quite natural that when he drove her home in his Ford roadster, she invited him in.

They headed directly for the bedroom and she insisted on keeping the lights on; the contrast of their skin tones delighted her. He was lean and muscular, she soft and curvaceous. He was tall and so was she, but he towered above her by at least six inches. Her emerald eyes were piercing, but his, as black as coals, were even more penetrating. His breath was sweet, his kisses warm and tender. As they lay in bed, becoming aroused, she sneaked a glance in the direction of his manhood and whispered, "Not too big, Mulch. I'm not scared."

"Little lady," he crooned, "you've been hearing too many of those white boys' stories. We're not any bigger. We're just better."

He rolled her over and gently eased his frame on top of her, kissing her nose, her closed eyes, her ear lobes, and then gradually moving lower. He rolled his tongue around the areolas of her breasts for what seemed like endless minutes. His knee worked between her thighs, and he rode her gently up and down like a child on a heavenly seesaw. Then, finally, after she longed for him beyond description, he entered her. Moving in and out with gentle thrusts that sent her blood coursing madly through her veins, he whispered romantic messages of love into her ear. She hoped he would never stop. That, too, was his intention. It was more than fifteen minutes before they joined each other in violent orgasm, then lay back, only to regroup their energies.

They never slept that night, making love right through the dawn. At eight she rose, showered quickly, and made coffee for them both. When she reached the studio an hour later she felt completely invigorated, not in the slightest enervated by the night's activities.

Mulch Roberts filled Trudy's desperate need for companionship and she began spending more and more evenings in his company. It was generally on weekends that he stayed with her, because it quickly became obvious that she could not engage in endless sexual gymnastics without her work at the studio schools suffering. Despite his devotion to her, she knew that she could never love him fully. It wasn't a matter of his skin tones; it was his youth and her incredible longing for Richie Stevens that prevented a series of joyous experiences from maturing into a lasting and meaningful relationship.

Though she never knew who blew the whistle, one day she was summoned to Stevens' office during lunch hour. He was waiting for her, smoking the inevitable briar pipe and looking so painfully handsome that she struggled to hide her emotions. His face was stern, betraying not an iota of warmth.

"Sit down, Trudy," he commanded. "I've ordered us a salad so we can lunch and talk at the same time. I've got to be out of here by two for a story conference."

"A salad is just fine," she answered.

After they were served, he immobilized her with his dark azure eyes.

"Tell me about this black man you've been having an affair with."

"Who said that?" she responded weakly.

"Come off it, Trudy. Everybody knows about it. You don't think you could have an open interracial love affair in Hollywood without the world being aware of it, do you?"

"Just because he's black, doesn't make it dirty."

"I didn't say it was dirty. I will say that it will crush your career before it starts. Look, it's nice to grow beyond the prejudice we learned in the South, but there are limits even in this permissive society. Once the word spreads that you're in love with a black, you'll be taboo on every lot in this town."

"I didn't say I was in love with him. It's just that he makes me feel wanted. Ever since I started these classes, I've had no one to talk to, no friends, nothing but work and study night after night."

"I'm not interested in that," he snapped. "I warned you. You wanted this career, now you'll pay the price or it will go to someone else who does."

She could not believe how belligerent he was. His face was a stone mask, relentless and uncompromising. Could this be the same kind man for whom she felt such love?

"I've held to my part of the bargain, haven't I?"

"Perhaps. But the fight is just beginning. You've got a long way to go. Now say good-bye to this Ethiopian Romeo or I'll never talk to you again."

It was that simple. They ate the rest of their lunch in silence. He sent her off with a cold, formal good-bye. She excused herself from classes for the rest of the day, claiming a headache. At home, she spent the afternoon peering into nothingness, assessing her future. In the end she knew what decision she would make.

That evening, she called Mulch at the club and told him that she couldn't join him. She refused to explain. He called her the next evening and she cut him off before he could ask what was wrong. She begged him not to call again until she had time to get her thoughts arranged. She would call him when she was ready. Intensely proud, Mulch would not pursue her against her wishes

—and Trudy knew it. Their affair ended abruptly. She didn't see him again for many years. By that time she was a major star, he a cocaine freak playing odd jobs to keep body and soul together.

Two weeks later, without notice, Stevens called her at home and told her to skip classes the next day. She was going to shoot her first screen test in the morning. She slept fitfully that night, wondering if her moment had arrived.

CHAPTER 7

1945–1947

Trudy Coles had her screen test the next day and hardly needed to await its outcome. She was brilliant and she knew it. All of her months of pent-up emotion found their release in that fifteen minutes before the camera's inscrutable eye. She drew from powers within herself that she did not know existed. Everything she had learned in all of those long months of study came to the surface at the moment she needed them most. On several occasions she looked into the face of Richie Stevens, sitting rather noncommittally in a director's chair at camera left, and read his own amazement at her accomplishments. In one sequence, he asked her to perform a simple modern dance and she was convinced that no star had ever moved more gracefully. Next, she sang a song to the camera and her sweet little voice registered at its best. But it was in a torrid love scene that she really shone. Even the blasé cameramen, who had filmed thousands of romantic interludes, were impressed. They smiled knowingly to one another. Hollywood was constructed of legends like this; a star was being born before their eyes.

She saw the rushes together with Richie Stevens that afternoon as soon as the film was developed. He, too, was impressed.

"Trudy," he said, "I told you the gods would sell anything for work. Can you see what you've accomplished?"

"You helped, Mr. Stevens. I couldn't have done it without you guiding me."

"That's nice to hear. If and when you're a big star you'll remember only that you did it all by yourself. And, in a sense, you did."

She didn't know what to tell him. She wanted to say that it was her silent love for him that had made her persevere, had led her through the dark moments of doubt, the lonely nights, the solitary weekends when she longed to pick up the phone and call him but didn't have the nerve to follow through. She couldn't, however, because he gave her no opportunity to do so. He was supportive now, thrilled at her success, but there was always that cold wall of professionalism between them that seemed impervious to the possibility of any personal relationship. Besides, he made her feel like what she really was: a fifteen-year-old child in the treacherous garden of Hollywood. A worldly child, perhaps. A sexually active child to be sure. But still a child in the presence of a man of the world. What he could never understand, what she herself did not fully comprehend, was that it was the very gulf of age between them that made him so utterly attractive.

Manny Silverstein saw the test in his office the next morning. He was joyous beyond words. He thought he had spotted a beauty the first time she had crossed his office threshold, but what this fifteen-minute reel of film showed took even him by surprise. She was electrifying. She had that quality he had described to her in his office that afternoon when he showed her the stack of glossies of other beauties who would fail. She would take this city by storm and bring new riches to Continental Studios—of that he was certain. Manny Silverstein had hit the jackpot.

Her first screen role came in a frothy little love story in which she was called upon to portray the younger sister of the feminine lead. Her work was good, not great. Next she was cast as a young high school student who falls in love with her history professor. She was the second lead and her work was again passable. Stevens called in Mollie Haines and asked what was missing.

"Nothing is missing," Mollie responded. "Your own miscalculation is what is wrong. This is no high school kid. Oh, yes, she may be sixteen now but she's as old as your grandmother. That body is twenty-four; those eyes are as ancient as love. Take off the wraps. You'll see for yourself, Richie."

Two months later, after a return to the studio training ground, she was given a small spot in an adult film about the rise and fall of an ambitious politician. Trudy's cameo appearance called for her seducing him as he visited a small town on a speaking engagement. Of course, the heavy cloak of morality sprayed by the Breen office on every code-approved feature had to be reckoned with. All that could be shown of such a scene was the man and woman entering a hotel bedroom and his reaching for the clasps at the top of her dress. Trudy communicated the message that there would be no resistance. And when the camera flashed back to her post-orgasmic face, there was little doubt concerning exactly what had taken place. The scene sizzled and Trudy Coles' career was launched.

Stevens moved even more boldly in her next feature. It was still a small-budget potboiler, but now he cast her as a forsaken housewife who longed for the physical love of many eligible males. In the end, of course, the Hollywood code demanded that she pay the price. She spends her last years destitute after her husband, learning of her affairs, banishes her to the streets, forbidding her to see her children ever again. Corny it was, but it jerked tears in every theater that exhibited it. She caused a minor sensation and Hollywood scribes began to sit up and take notice. Louella Parsons mentioned her name first in her column in the *Los Angeles Examiner:* "That steaming beauty you spotted last week enjoying a coke with owner Milton Kreis at the Beverly Wilshire Drug Store was none other than Richie Stevens' new protégée, Trudy Coles."

Not to be outgunned, Hedda Hopper came back the next week with an equally intriguing item in the *Los Angeles Times.* Leading off with an intriguing note in "Hedda Hopper's Hollywood," she wrote: "They say she's only sixteen, but what red-blooded male wouldn't risk the Federal authorities for a date with Trudy Coles, the latest sensational find for Manny Silverstein's Continental Studios?"

To which Sidney Skolsky, always alert to the possibility of a plug for one of his favorite clients, Schwab's Drug Store, responded: "Sweet sixteen and never been missed! Guess who buys her cosmetics at Schwab's? Her name rhymes with 'poles' and her figure curves like Route 66!"

The mad, mad scenic railway ride had begun. Trudy tried to keep her head. She began to receive fan letters, mostly propositions from lovesick youths. The studio took over the chore of answering them for her. They enclosed a steamy shot of her in a tightly fitting bathing suit in every reply. As the build-up began, she spent more and more time with studio publicity experts. The war was ending, but the era of suggestive pinups had just begun in earnest. It was grueling work under the hottest photographic lights, but Trudy loved every moment of it. She didn't know the meaning of the word *narcissistic* even though she actually embodied it. She was photographed from every leering angle and she enjoyed paging through the results when the pictures were printed. She really had no need for mirrors in her apartment. She hung her pinups on every bare spot of wall. Walking into her bedroom was like being surrounded by a hall of mirrors. She wrote to her old friend Helen, in one of her few contacts with home: "They've taken a picture of my ass in so many ways that I'm beginning to think they like it better than my face. Hah!"

It was a beautiful ass, to be sure, and picturing it was just one small part of the Hollywood build-up. One day she was called in to Silverstein's office.

"Trudy, Trudy," a beaming Silverstein said, "you're gonna be a big, big star just like I told you. If . . . if . . ."

"If?" Trudy questioned, disappointed. Obviously, he felt she was not fulfilling her obligations.

"If," he echoed, "you are willing to give us that extra ounce of effort. You see, being a beautiful young actress isn't enough. It's like being dealt a poker hand with three aces and two kings. You gotta understand how to play it. You know what I mean?"

"Not really, Mr. Silverstein."

"Manny," he corrected.

"Not really, Manny," she mimicked obediently.

"You gotta be seen around town more. This burg is hungry for new stars. But they want to see them on the go in all the elegant places. It's part of what they call 'the mystique.'"

"I always attend all the studio parties, and go wherever the publicity department wants me to go, don't I?"

"You do and you don't. I understand you won't accept dates when the young male stars-to-be call you. They want to usher you around."

"They're kids, Manny. Why don't you call me?"

"Trudy, you gotta understand how it works. Now that you're a somebody, I'll be visible as hell taking you out. It'll be bad for you, too. Nobody hungers for a kid who hangs around with old farts like Manny Silverstein."

Trudy was convinced now that he had a new "protégée." The

one thing Manny Silverstein would never think of himself as was an "old fart."

"Now you gotta promise me you'll be cooperative."

"I'll try. But I need some sleep, too. There are classes every day, learning new scripts at night. A girl needs some rest."

"Time enough to rest when you're dead. You need action now."

So, the new social whirl started in earnest. The studio made most of the arrangements for her, mainly with actors from Continental. One evening she dined at Romanoff's, the next at Lucy's, then the Brown Derby. She was taken to screenings and sneak previews in Pasadena, Huntington Park, and far-off Santa Barbara.

One night, after viewing a particularly moving drama at the Pantages near Hollywood and Vine, she ended up drinking heavily with Rick Seymour, one of the town's more sophisticated and eligible bachelors. The studio had reserved a particularly important table for them at the Cricket Lounge in the Beverly Wilton Hotel, and Rick made the most of the opportunity by crooning love tunes into her ear at a volume level designed for all to hear. Though embarrassed at first, Trudy found her narcissism rising to the surface as all eyes focused on her table. They left as the last lights were being doused and ended up in one of the hotel's charming bungaloes, which Seymour had conveniently rented for the night. He was so drunk that he could not perform, which was fine with Trudy. It conveniently avoided the inevitable argument that she was determined not to lose. Halfway through the evening she had thought ahead to the moment when he would expect her to undress because he was an eligible bachelor too rich to think of her feelings, and because she had been tagged as an ambitious starlet who would happily screw her way up the ladder of success. Well, Mr. Rick Seymour—you with the two first names and celluloid personality—you were in for a surprise, she thought. Long before he believed he was seducing her by leading her to one of those oh-so-glamorous cabins, she had decided to show him a real strikeout, West Virginia style. In a way she was unhappy that he collapsed and made the job easier. She would have enjoyed telling him off.

After he snored off for the night, she poured a hot bath, carefully double-locking the bathroom door lest he suddenly come to and decide he was ready. As she luxuriated in the steaming, bubbly water, she reconsidered her willingness to obey each of Manny Silverstein's demands. Christ, working all day at the studio, studying scripts at night, taking classes in everything from body motion to foreign language pronunciation were heavy enough chores. Why did she have to display herself on the arms of half of the young whoremongers in Hollywood? What did she want from the likes of Rick Seymour?

As planned, their little romance was reported diligently in the local press. Both Hedda and Louella featured the story several days later. Silverstein smiled appreciatively when he read them. Now the kid is really trying, he thought. Those lucky bastards I've given her to. They should thank me!

Through it all, she hoped and hoped that Richie Stevens would see her as more than an aspiring actress. She sent him notes on the slightest provocation. She conveniently bumped into him whenever the opportunity presented itself. Finally, she thought she might have struck oil when he called and asked her if she would accompany him to the Academy Awards. She fairly screamed yes. She was surprised that he wasn't taking his lady lawyer friend, but apparently she was out of town. There was nothing in his manner to imply that this wasn't part of the usual studio build-up. To be seen on the arm of Richie Stevens on such a night was certain to be reported coast to coast. Still, she hoped she read more in his lines than he indicated.

Cinderella's evening at the ball was small potatoes compared to this night of festivities. The studio informed her that it was creating a special gown for her to wear for the ceremonies. Joyfully, she stood through three special fittings, and the results were smashing: a brilliant emerald green sheath that clung to her curvaceous hips and dipped daringly low in its décolletage, showing enough flesh to be banned by the Hays office. She was even issued a giant emerald pendant, which dangled on a gold chain and nestled in her milky bosom for all to ponder. The gem, though certainly an imitation, had to be returned after the ball. The dress, however, was a gift from the studio. Had she been charged for it with interest compounded, she would not have been terribly surprised. She'd learned that studio largesse was frequently merely a credit, but in this case she apparently was given a free ride.

She went to bed early the night before the great event. When Richie Stevens arrived in a limousine just before sunset the following evening, he gasped at her loveliness. She was as fresh and startingly beautiful as the most magnificent rosebud. He had brought her a corsage of white orchids, the first she had ever seen. Perched on her head, they capped her splendor like the crown jewels on the queen's tiara.

The crowds, pressing one against the other outside the Shrine Auditorium, screamed greetings to her as if she were the oldest of friends. Bathed in the warming glow of arc lights, she waved happily and smiled brightly for all assembled. She couldn't help but feel a surge of pride as she overheard one lady shout, "That's Trudy Coles. I saw her in *The Rise and Fall of McNulty*. They say she'll be the biggest star of them all."

The flashbulbs popped away merrily as they crossed the red carpet and entered the auditorium. Ring-wise Richie Stevens turned her this way and that, pausing for all of the news services and waving happily as if this, too, was his night supreme. Briefly and happily, Trudy thought of home. Wait until Pop and the kids saw this on their local newsreel! And Helen Caputo? She'd wet her drawers in envy. But the thoughts of West Virginia were fleet and passing. This was the new Trudy Coles.

Proudly, Richie Stevens led her to their assigned seats, strategically located near the raised podium for all to see. Trying her best to look nonchalant, Trudy nonetheless turned like every tourist to observe the gala gathering of celebrities. There was Clark Gable. And Myrna Loy. And Douglas Fairbanks, Jr. With him was a handsome man who looked terribly familiar. Of course, it was Errol Flynn! Imagine! As an avid reader of the fan magazines, Trudy recognized many of the great directors, such as Frank Capra and Robert Rossen and Cecil B. De Mille. Her eye identified Walter Wanger and Charles Vidor and Jerry Wald. It took no great expert to realize that that was Barbara Stanwyck sitting near Bette Davis, and not very far from Joan Crawford. If Hollywood had died that very night, heaven would have looked like this, its stars shining brightly.

The ceremonies were endless, but not for Trudy Coles. She loved every minute of them. She cheered madly when Fredric March and Olivia de Havilland won their Oscars. And when *The Best Years of Our Lives* was selected best picture she cried. The biggest emotional blitz was saved for double amputee Harold Russell, who beamed his little boy smile and, clutching his Oscar in his hooks, waved it skyward for all to see that a handicapped man had won a top award as the best supporting actor. Later that night she met William Wyler, the film's famous director; she swelled with pride when he mentioned that he had heard good things about her and hoped that someday she would work with him. And when the picture's co-star, Dana Andrews, left his table, sought her out, and asked her to dance, she thought she finally had climbed the mountain.

Following the festivities, there were a host of private parties, and apparently Richie Stevens was determined for her to attend them all. He was warm and friendly throughout the evening, treating her paternally, like a father taking his own daughter to the senior prom. She clung to him when they danced but there was never the slightest reaction or encouragement from him. She wondered if there was something she had done—or hadn't done —that never lighted his fuse. He was always warm and pleasant; but never passionate or sexually aggressive. She could not believe he didn't understand how stricken she was. She pondered a frank admission of her passionate love for him but thought better of it, and besides, he gave her no opening for such a confession.

The sun was just rising when they finally closed the last party and their limo approached her door. Despite her realization that it was a loser's tactic, she invited him in for coffee. Politely, he refused, explaining that, despite the celebration, he was due in the office at ten that morning. There was just enough time for a quick snooze, a shower and shave, and a change of clothes. And so, good night. The fairy tale ended with a fatherly peck on the cheek. Now, back to work.

Without a week's respite, she was assigned to another Continental ultralow-budget feature, this time playing a teenage runaway who joins a band of desperadoes planning a bank robbery. She becomes a gangster's moll who meets her death in a shootout with the FBI. It was hardly the stuff of which Academy Awards are born, but it did have one thing going for it. She was billed just under the title, her first emergence from anonymity, from the standpoint of credits. She soon learned that billing could be more important than money when climbing the filmland escarpment. Actresses would kill for above-the-title billing, yet submit meekly to cuts in pay or percentage deals that could never possibly pay off. The bigger the print, the more prominently the name was displayed, the hotter the career. It was as simple as that. Humility and Hollywood were oil and water. They just didn't mix.

She felt herself tiring as the mad social whirl continued and feature followed feature with barely a week between the completion of one and the start of another. And then, a new wrinkle was added. She received notification that she had been assigned to a feature at Republic Productions, a studio famous for its lack of high standards and often referred to as "Repulsive Productions." Once again, she was to play the gangster moll who meets a bloody death following a gunfight with the law. Manny Silverstein was elated to learn that Republic was so eager for her youthful sexuality that they would pay him $15,000 for a three-week shoot, an amount representing his entire commitment to her for the year.

Less than a month later she was back at Continental, involved in another potboiler as a young war bride whose husband never returns from action. Her scenes were mechanically conceived, routinely photographed, and unimaginatively directed. She had the feeling that she was moving back and forth like the blades of a windshield wiper but making no real progress. Disheartened, she sought an interview with Richie Stevens and expressed her disappointment. Only too knowledgeable about Continental techniques, he advised her to bide her time.

"After all," he argued, "you've only been in films for less than two years and look how far you've progressed. Which reminds me," he added, almost as an afterthought, "Obie asked me to tell you to be ready for shooting at Twentieth Century. They've got you on loan for six weeks for a new Western. I understand you'll be shooting on location in Arizona."

That at least represented a change in scene and a chance to learn how to ride a horse. It was painful work, but aided by youth and tenacity, Trudy mastered the art. But it could have been one of her bigger career mistakes. Westerns became her métier. She made three more in a row, one for Columbia, one for Fox, and another for her home studio. Unbeknownst to her, her loan-out fee had risen to $40,000 a feature. She still collected $300 a week, less deductions for past debts and ever-mounting interest. In her monthly letter to her sister, Debby, she described the black and blue marks on her posterior, which were nearly indelible from constant pounding. She also referred to the constant coughs that her exposure on the Western plains seemed to bring her. Shooting started at sunup; partying often continued to sunrise. There wasn't much time to build resistance. She hadn't had a real vacation since she came to Hollywood. It was just as Richie Stevens had forecast: work, work, work.

Her phone rang unexpectedly one night. It was Debby, calling from West Virginia, an extravagance she had indulged in only once before in the more than two years since Trudy had left home. Trudy broke in immediately and instructed the operator to reverse the charges.

"Hi, Debby, what a great surprise! Everything okay at home?"

Debby's tones were somber and foreboding. "No. Afraid not. It's Pop. He's got emphysema bad. Doc Obieski says he needs an operation bad. He says he might have lung cancer, too. I don't know what to do."

"Is Pop saying no to the operation?" Trudy asked.

"It's not that. It's the money. Doc O can't do it. Pop has to be taken to the university hospital at Morgantown."

"So?"

"So that costs twelve hundred bucks. Where are we gonna get money for that? I thought you could help."

"I can help, sure. But I don't have that kind of money. I just about cover my expenses out here."

"I thought maybe you were making a lot by now."

"No. I'm under contract on a minimum salary. You know I've got a lot of expenses, too. What about that money I left at the bank. Any of that left?"

"Gone a long time ago. The kids need clothes and Pop's medicines and all. Not a dime left."

"How much time is there? Until we figure out what to do?"

"Doc O says it's very serious. Right away, he says."

"What about the company?"

"I checked. Pop used up all his medical benefits two months ago. There's no more insurance. I asked the mine boss, Mr. Kunzig, for a loan. He laughed at me. Don't tell Pop. He didn't want me to ask. He's too proud."

"I won't. Look, Debby, I'll think of something. I'll call you back in a couple of days. Maybe less if I get a good idea."

Trudy couldn't sleep at all that night. She cried, her heart burdened with feelings of guilt. Maybe if she had stayed home this wouldn't have happened. Maybe Pop would have taken better care of himself. Maybe if she was still working at Sandy's Cafe there would have been plenty of money. Maybe. Maybe. Maybe. She thought about alternatives. Maybe if she quit, went home and asked Sandy for a job again, he'd lend her the money. That really made no sense at all and she realized it. Sandy's was a one-way street to oblivion. Here at least she was on her way. It would be a tougher and tougher fight as she climbed the ladder, but she was determined, and everyone thought she had a chance of making it, making it big. She owed it to her family; she owed it to herself to keep trying.

She thought of her father and, inevitably, of her love for him. It was painful to relive those months in bed, those months of rejection, her jealousy of Aggie Stephanik, but these thoughts would always be with her.

Aggie Stephanik. That was a name that had not crossed her mind in many months. As if it were yesterday, she remembered that Saturday night when, after long hours at a nearby tavern, Cass had come home with a visitor. It was Aggie Stephanik, a notorious local widow who had had her innings with virtually every willing male in town. They both were obviously drunk.

"You're sleeping with your sisters tonight," Cass told Gertrude imperiously.

She was too hurt to protest. Aggie merely smirked and treated her like an unwanted child. Quietly, she obeyed, going into the bedroom only long enough to recover her nightgown and toilet articles. The girls were already asleep but she managed to slide them over and make room for herself. She lay awake for hours, saddened, puzzled, resentful. Hearing Aggie cry out in ecstacy several times during the next several hours did not improve the situation.

She had struggled to bury the memory of Cass's relationship with Aggie and all of its obvious implications, and thought that she had succeeded. Now, the sad memory was bright and clear, adding to her sorrow.

The clock ticked loudly. She turned on the bedlamp; it was past three o'clock in the morning. Penny was still out. Lee Landis' wife was out of town visiting her parents, so they had a long night to howl. She cried again and wondered whom she was weeping for—her father, Debby and the kids, or maybe for her own feelings of grief, guilt, and frustration. Then, there was the reality of it all. To whom could she turn for the money? Her only hope was Manny Silverstein. She had seen very little of him lately and he was such a tough customer. But maybe he'd relent if she pleaded with him. Maybe she could threaten to break her contract now that he was apparently making money by lending out her services, though she didn't know how much. That wouldn't sit well with Manny. He was the one man who hated to be threatened. She had heard that a dozen times.

Her thoughts were interrupted by the arrival of Penny. She wasn't inviting Lee in because they had already been to a hotel room together, and Lee was afraid to be seen going in and out of a company-owned apartment in the early hours of the morning.

Trudy got up as soon as she heard Lee's car drive away. Her eyes were red from weeping, her face swollen. Penny was one of the few people she'd let see her in this state.

"What's the matter, kiddo?" Penny asked in alarm. "You sick or something?"

"Worse than that. It's my dad."

Trudy explained her dilemma. She had once, in a roundabout way, indicated to Penny that her relationship with her father had been a bit more than platonic. Penny was smart enough to fill in the gaps.

"Sit down. Make yourself a cup of tea and have a Scotch. No use getting sick. That won't help a fucking bit."

Trudy did as she was told, like an obedient child. She washed her face, put on some light makeup to bolster her spirits, and waited for her mentor to come up with some viable solution.

"I had one idea. . . ." Trudy began tentatively.

"Yeah?"

"Manny Silverstein. He likes me in more ways than one. Maybe he'd let me get an advance against future salary."

"Don't!" Penny commanded. "Whatever you do, don't go to Silverstein. He hates people who pound him for money. Even if he takes pity and lends it to you, he'll never let you forget it. Hell, you'll have no independence left for the rest of your working days at Continental."

"Maybe you're right. But I can't go to anybody else. I'd die before I'd ask Mr. Stevens."

"I'd go to Stevens before I'd go to Silverstein. But wait a minute," Penny said, brightening perceptibly, "I got an idea."

"What's that?"

"Lee Landis. He'll lend it to me when I tell him why we need it."

"I couldn't ask you to do that!" Trudy protested.

"You didn't ask. I volunteered. Now shut up and go to bed. You'll look like a hag tomorrow and they might can you on the set."

That's the way it happened. Lee Landis, though he wasn't delighted about selling stocks to raise the money, acquiesced when Penny insisted that it was an emergency. Cass was taken to Morgantown and the operation was successful. Trudy eventually returned the money. She would never forget Penny's kindness. In future years she would encounter many friends whom she called "The Hello and Good-bye People." There would never be anyone kinder than Penny O'Neill, and Trudy vowed to remember that fact.

She got in an argument with the studio brass when, upon returning to Continental, she learned that once again she was being loaned out to shoot another Western. The meeting with the head of assignment was terribly unpleasant. His name was Jerry Greenberg and he allegedly was a distant cousin of Manny Silverstein's. He had graduated from Harvard Law School, come West to practice law with a Los Angeles firm specializing in theatrical law, then moved into the business affairs department of his cousin's company. Now being groomed for a larger role, he had transferred into production and was charged with scheduling the studio's contract players. He handled the chore deftly, moving them in and out of features like a chess champion pushing crusading knights across the board.

"I'm tired, Mr. Greenberg," she said simply. "I need some time off to get rid of this cold. I feel terrible."

"I'm tired, too," he answered, without emotion. "You want rest, sell dresses."

"I've been assigned to nine pictures in eleven and a half months. I'm an actress, not a dray horse."

"Actresses act," was his simple logic. "You report to Republic tomorrow morning at six or you're on probation."

There was no appeal. She reported on time, but never finished the picture. The first scene was shot in a driving rain on a windswept Colorado cliff. The cold penetrated her bones. She coughed so much they couldn't record a word. She rose the next morning with a high fever, her chest so congested she could scarcely breathe. It was obvious to the local doctor who was summoned to examine her that she was suffering from pneumonia.

"Get this lady to a hospital and fast," he advised. "She's very sick and bound to get sicker. Maybe the new sulfa drugs can help her, but my feeling is she needs rest. She's obviously run down, exhausted I'd say. Her temperature is a hundred and three and seems to be climbing. Fortunately she's young and strong, but I wouldn't take any chances. She won't be ready to work again for weeks."

They rented a local ambulance and drove her home that same day. The studio doctor came to see her at her apartment and confirmed what the Colorado physician had diagnosed, double pneumonia. Despite her protests, she was sent to the hospital that same evening. Magnanimously, Continental Studios would pay her bills, assuming, of course, that there were no complications like major surgery. Routine hospital stays were adequately covered by company insurance. It was one of the perquisites that Manny Silverstein boasted about whenever extolling the virtues of his own benevolent despotism.

Impatient about the obvious interruption of her career, and foreign to the strange surroundings of hospital life, Trudy all the same welcomed the weeks of rest that were now forced upon her. Her attending physician summoned a famous internist to examine her. Her cough persisted despite the passage of time, and there was suspicion of incipient tuberculosis. Trudy recalled that several of her uncles had died of consumption, which at the time had been attributed to their lives in the mines. She couldn't help but wonder if she had inherited a family weakness for lung infection. The company physician who had treated her as a child had, on several occasions, reported suspicious chest sounds when she suffered upper respiratory distresses. He had warned her mother that the child needed plenty of rest and protection from dampness. It was the sort of advice emanating from the offices of most general practitioners, and mine mothers, accustomed to illness, paid it little heed.

Her recovery period was unusually slow. After three and a half weeks in the hospital, Trudy was released with a word of advice from the discharging physician: Don't rush back to work too quickly; you're a long way from complete recovery. During her hospital stay her normal weight of 118 had dropped precipitously to 105, leaving her pale and gaunt, yet somehow increasing her beauty. Her facial bone structure was now more clearly outlined; her deep green eyes shone with greater fervor. Interns who had no assignment on her floor somehow managed to stop by and check on her progress. When she was packing her few belongings in preparation for her departure, a whole retinue of medical men stopped by to say farewell. She had become a hospital celebrity without realizing it.

The one thing that saddened her the most was the realization that neither Silverstein nor Stevens had found the time to pay her a visit. They were both generous: fresh flowers arrived from the studio twice a week. Stevens sent a lovely card with a handwritten get-well message scribbled at the bottom. Obie phoned a few times on behalf of Silverstein. She received not a single in-person visit from her employers. Only Penny, good old reliable, loving Penny, found the time to visit her. She came whenever she was free from work, bringing flowers, candy, even "chicken soup," her way of describing a camouflaged bottle of Scotch.

"Look, my old man said it never killed anybody. And it sure makes you feel good after a couple of snorts."

Continental sent cards and flowers, nothing more. Apparently Hollywood had no time for the sick or maimed. More and more, it became apparent that Richie Stevens' analysis of the business was accurate. There was little room for—certainly no inclination for—caring.

After three more weeks at home, she received an inquiry from studio employment wondering when she would be ready for a new assignment. A brief reminder: Sick leave ran out in another week and her pay would be docked thereafter. She indicated that she was ready for work at once. She was called to Stevens' office the first day back. Her fluttering heart told her that his grip on her emotions had not loosened.

"Terribly sorry about your illness," Stevens said, puffing on the ever-present briar pipe, which contributed to his maddeningly attractive appearance. "I really wanted to come see you but the load of work here has been ungodly."

"I understand. Thank you for the flowers. I'm anxious to get back to work."

"Well, come here and sit down. Let's talk a spell. I had a long talk with Mr. Silverstein yesterday and he wants you to keep on with the Westerns. No one can really foretell in this crazy business what the best career moves are, but I feel obligated to tell you how I feel. I'm against it."

"Why?"

"Because you've done them. Again and again. I think it's time to move on."

"How do I do that?"

"You just refuse. The studio puts you on probation. Eventually the lawyers get in on the matter, they come to an agreement, and you leave Continental and seek work elsewhere. But it takes guts."

"And what happens to me if I don't get work?"

"I guess the answer is obvious. You give it your best and if you strike out, moving pictures aren't the only thing in life."

"They are for me. Now."

"Well, of course, I can only give you artistic advice. I'm not the best businessman in the world."

"Mr. Stevens, can't you talk to Mr. Silverstein for me?"

There was a long, pregnant pause.

"Trudy, maybe you don't understand Mr. Silverstein. I don't want to imply that there's anything evil about him. But he's a self-made man and somewhat of a pioneer in this business. Successful, self-made men don't like advice. He thinks you need a tremendous amount of experience and exposure before you try the big leagues. The more I insist, the less he'll listen, the more stubborn he will grow. It's either play it his way, or try another studio."

"That sums it up, I guess. I don't think I have a real choice. I'll play it the Silverstein way for the time being."

A month later, having regained most of her weight, she was completing another Western when she was summoned to Silverstein's office. Obie delivered his message. He and Mrs. Silverstein were entertaining at a small dinner party on Saturday night. There was a command performance demanding her appearance. She was to report to Agnes in the costume department, where a special gown was being prepared for her. Also, a visit to the head of hairdressing was essential. Mr. Silverstein wanted her to look her very best. There was no information as to the whys and wherefores of the party, or who was to attend. A limousine would pick her up at eight precisely and deliver her to the Silverstein home.

Throughout the remainder of the week, Trudy wondered if

this party had any special significance. There was no one to ask, and Obie just wasn't saying. She was flabbergasted when she visited wardrobe and saw the magnificent dress being prepared for her. And her head was to be crowned with a diamond tiara, real diamonds to be sure. Not to worry, they were heavily insured and all the gems were to be returned the following Monday morning. Otto, in the beauty salon, had created a special upswept hairdo for her that made her look heavenly. Even the blasé hairdressers "oohed and ahhed" in appreciation.

Mr. Silverstein's own chauffeur picked her up at the appointed hour. She had him make a few touristlike turns through the hills overlooking Sunset Boulevard, gaping at the incredible mansions set behind dog-guarded gates. Her visit to the Silversteins' was her first personal incursion into the opulence that symbolized the life of the movie moguls in those salad days of pre-television Hollywood. It was a mind-boggling experience. The magnificent plantings; the tree-lined paths; the huge, Olympic-sized, lighted swimming pool; the artwork and the sculpture garden; the marble floors; the silken curtains; the book-lined study; the outdoor and indoor bars; the trio playing classical music: Was this the life of luxury she had seen depicted in the fan magazines? It must be for real. For an instant her mind drifted back to the Kolinski home in West Virginia. It was an unpleasant thought and one she had learned to bury. Smilingly she accepted a glass of champagne and, with trepidation, her first caviar hors d'oeuvre. Happily, she loved the taste. A second glass of champagne helped settle her nerves but made her feel just a bit tipsy. She found herself giggling with a little extra spirit, egged on by her light-headedness.

She met Mrs. Silverstein for the first time and understood why Manny had virtually run home that night she had called at the office. She was only about five feet tall and her figure less than perfect, but she was in control and moved about among the small group of guests with the assurance of a rajah reviewing his elite troops.

"I hear Manny thinks you're going to be a big star," she said to Trudy, with just an edge of skepticism.

"I hope so," Trudy answered simply.

"Well, I've seen a lot of them come and go. I tell Manny only his wife stays put forever."

There were twelve for dinner, including the Silversteins. Now at last, Trudy thought she understood the rationale for her being invited. She was seated next to the only single male guest. He was a tall, handsome, dark-complexioned young man named Robert Wenger. The name meant nothing to Trudy, nor was she impressed by the immature actions and high-pitched voice of the youth who suggested she call him "Rob." "Everybody does," he explained. She was to learn later that week that Rob Wenger was the scion of the Wenger clan, Los Angeles' richest banking dynasty. His great-great-grandfather had come to California in a covered wagon, and opened a trading center after hitting it lucky on a gold strike. From merchandising he moved to banking and soon had eliminated virtually all of his competition. As the oldest son, Rob Wenger was destined to take over the reins of the banking chain that remained family-owned. The Wenger family was one of the few California sources for motion picture investment capital and accordingly was courted by all of the studio heads.

Somehow, Rob's father, despite his somewhat aristocratic nature, had taken a liking to Silverstein. He admired his courage and entrepreneurial spirit. He had taken chances with this New York Jew that even the Wall Street bankers had eschewed. To date, Silverstein had never let him down. Silverstein, in turn, had decided that if he could get young Rob to marry Trudy Coles he could accomplish two goals. First, he would have a much tighter rein on Wenger venture capital. Second, the publicity that would ensue would certainly launch Trudy Coles' career in style. The fact that Rob Wenger was building a reputation as a wild, carefree playboy who spent his energies chasing fast women in speedier cars was of little importance. Silverstein was in the business of making movies and moving stars around to suit his purpose. He was no save-the-world sociologist and never pretended to be one. After a few rolls in the hay with Trudy Coles, he reasoned, Rob Wenger wouldn't have the energy to chase women. Forget her magnificent looks; Trudy Coles in bed was a tigress on the loose. Too bad that Tillie had the instincts of a bloodhound. With or without Rob Wenger in the picture, he could use a little of that Trudy Coles himself.

Trudy found Rob Wenger waiting for her outside her apartment the very next day when she returned from filming. She was working on a little cheapie being filmed at the studio and was weary after a six A.M. start. Rob had been very attentive the night before, but hadn't mentioned calling on her so soon. Apparently, eligible bachelors in his class didn't bother with the niceties of Emily Post. She invited him in since there really was no way to avoid it without being rude. She tried to ease him out quickly, since she was quite exhausted from her day's filming, but, as she was to learn, Rob Wenger was not one to be put off when his own pleasures were involved. Finally, she came to the point.

"Rob, you'll really have to excuse me. Honest, I'm beat."

"Hell, it's only six o'clock. You haven't even had dinner yet."

"Oh, I just open a can of tuna or something simple like that. Got to watch my weight, you know."

"I'll watch it for you. You got the best figure I ever saw. Hey, I've got an idea."

"What's that?" Trudy asked warily.

"A real dinner. Where's your phone? I'll call the Brown Derby."

No amount of protesting on Trudy's part was effective. Rob simply would not take no for an answer. Soon they were in his Cadillac convertible heading for the restaurant. There, she was amused to find that he had a standing reservation, a table reserved in his name whether or not he chose to show up for dinner. The name "Wenger" was an "open sesame" to all of Los Angeles' "in spots."

They said good night at the door after Trudy explained that late hours were not possible for her while in the middle of shooting. She might just as well have been talking Russian as far as Rob was concerned. He was back the next afternoon, proudly cradling a small package that he insisted could only be presented to her within her apartment. It was an antique diamond bar pin, which even Trudy, as unsophisticated as she was, realized must have been worth thousands of dollars.

"Oh, I can't accept this," she protested. "We just met."

But she did, especially after Rob pretended he would flush it down the toilet if she didn't relent. This was but the first in a steady stream of gifts that he forced upon her. After a while, being human, she just accepted them routinely.

In a matter of weeks, she became Rob's steady date, a fact that Obie, having gleaned the information through the Hollywood grapevine, duly reported to Manny Silverstein.

"Doesn't surprise me," he said cynically. "What she's got he wants. What he's got she wants. It figures. And it ain't bad for us, either."

Alone at night, Trudy began to examine her feelings about the entire relationship. It was obvious that the film community considered Rob Wenger a person to be reckoned with. And that power rubbed off on her as his girlfriend. Her first taste of power was sweet to her palate. And the gifts—the diamond ring, the mink cape, the Ford roadster—who could deny the pleasure they brought? But what of Rob himself? He had a boyish charm and he was certainly good-looking, but he failed to touch her heart. Even though he was older than she by at least five years, she still thought of him as a boy. How could he compare to Richie Stevens? Or to Manny Silverstein? And, again, she thought of her father.

After weeks of protesting she ran out of excuses and they finally went to bed. Rob was so excited that he had an orgasm as soon as he entered her.

"Whoops, I'm sorry," he said, not too apologetically. "I guess the little fella is as excited about you as I am."

"No matter. There'll be another time," Trudy replied.

There was. Fifteen minutes later. And again a half hour after that. Trudy was certainly aroused but there was something missing. It wasn't a matter of lack of passion on his part, certainly, or, for that matter, her own lack of responsiveness. Rather, it was a lack of finesse. Rob Wenger approached sex the way he pursued food, drink, and play. There was never any thought of subtlety. You rushed to the bar, downed three Scotches on the rocks, then banged away at the brandy until your eyes were bloodshot. The gift of wealth had robbed him of the virtue of patience. He wanted it all and he wanted it quickly. That was the way he lived. That was the way he loved.

One night, after a bout of carousing, she refused to get in the car with him. It was obvious that his reactions were slowed, his speech blurred, his judgments affected. She had seen him drive in this condition before, swerving down the hairpin turns overlooking the city at breakneck speed, almost as if he were seeking disaster. To date the god of drunks had looked after him but on this night Trudy had a premonition of calamity.

"You'll kill us both. Let me drive," she argued.

"I'm fine. You're too nervous for a young girl. Nothing's going to happen with old Rob at the wheel."

"Suppose a cop stops us? You could go to jail."

"Me? That's a joke. Get in, for Christ's sake."

There was, fortunately, no accident. But they were stopped by the Beverly Hills police, who spotted their car weaving all over the road.

"Let's see your license, buddy," an angry cop demanded.

Rob fumbled around in the glove compartment and produced the necessary card.

"And the owner's card, too," the unsmiling officer added.

With both cards in his possession, the officer looked carefully at Rob, then went back to his own vehicle to confer with his partner. He was back in a few minutes to address Rob.

"Listen, Mr. Wenger. You'd better go a little easy on the juice when you're driving. You're gonna get hurt one day or kill somebody else. Now you keep it down to fifteen miles an hour and get home and sleep this thing off."

He was released with nothing more than a lecture. Apparently God, the Continental Congress, and the Wengers could do no wrong.

On occasion he snorted cocaine, but fortunately that was not one of his favorite pursuits. He invited Trudy to join him, but when she refused, he did not insist. He did persist in forcing her to smoke a weed he had learned about in Mexico and which he could acquire with relative ease. She found that smoking marijuana turned her on sexually and she came to like it. Many of the studio bigwigs had given up tobacco for this happier weed; the fact that Rob and his wild friends enjoyed it did not surprise her.

A big surprise awaited her, however, when he suggested that they spend a weekend together in a family cottage on the ocean at Malibu. She had been there once before when first meeting his parents. The elder Wengers treated her with limited warmth; not exactly rejection, but certainly not a warm welcome to the family bosom. Rob had explained that the family always looked upon newcomers with an air of skepticism, since there were so many fortune hunters plotting at entering their charmed circle. They did seem to warm up each time she met them again. Indeed, Mrs. Wenger had once invited her to a tea she was giving for her favorite charity. In a sense, they had accepted her as the probable bride of their eldest son. Mrs. Wenger did ask a few leading questions as to her parentage and background. Trudy finessed. She simply said she came from a small town in the East, her father was retired, her mother dead, and left it at that.

Arriving at the oceanfront cottage, Trudy was pleased to see a few cars parked on the lot before them. She had spent one solitary weekend with Rob in the mountains and he had simply drunk himself into oblivion the first three hours. He usually was more restrained with company even though his circle of wild, rich friends at times tended to encourage his escapades. Entering the home she was surprised to find only his best friend, Charles Twining, heir to a mining fortune, and three rather gaudily made-up women whom she had never met. Drinks were being passed around and, relaxed after the long drive from the city, she joined the fun. At the end of several hours of imbibing, it was time to shed inhibitions.

"It's show-and-tell time," Charlie announced, and the three giggling girls left the room. Charles had explained that the ladies were friends he had met in college, though they certainly didn't look like college girls to Trudy.

Five minutes later, the girls returned wearing little but smiles. They immediately went into their act, a female circus of sexual activities. Through the thick marijuana smoke that filled the room, Trudy witnessed acts she had never even imagined took place behind closed bedroom doors. Whether the girls were homosexuals or merely performing for commercial gain, they went at each other with gusto. At one point in the proceedings, Charlie was invited to join the fray, an invitation he hurriedly accepted. Trudy had to admit that she felt herself being turned on despite the fact that she found the demonstration degrading.

After another fifteen minutes, Rob rose, took her by the hand, and led her to one of the bedrooms. They undressed silently and jumped in bed. Stimulated by what they had seen, by a large amount of alcohol and marijuana, theirs was a wild coupling. After a few minutes' rest, he stood up, signaled for her to follow, and practically pulled her into the living room, where the orgy had continued unabated. As soon as she sat on the sofa, looking uncomfortably about her, two of the whores jumped up and surrounded her. Despite her resistance and protests, they forced her into a prone position while one sucked her breasts and the other spread her legs and started licking her vagina with undisguised relish. She hadn't the power to resist and, building to a climax she would not have considered possible, she came with a loud, explosive sigh while the others in the room cheered her madly.

The next morning, Trudy rose early and subjected herself to

a steaming shower that virtually burned her skin. Charles and his women friends had left. It was Sunday. Trudy made herself dark coffee and silently awaited Rob's arising. He slept away half the morning, and still she sat silently awaiting him. When he finally arose and entered the living room after showering she faced him solemnly.

"Rob, do you love me?" she asked.

"Honey, that's a crazy question. You know I do."

"I mean really love me. Not just enjoy fucking me?"

"I do that, too. But sure I love you. Why?"

"Last night. My body is human like yours. They made me come and act like an animal. I really hated it. If you ever take me to another orgy, I'll never see you again. Do you understand?"

"Honey, it was just wild fun. Don't make a big deal out of it. It's no federal case."

"It is to me, Rob. I don't need that kind of excitement in my life. I'd be happier, too, if you didn't drink so much. Some day you'll have an accident and kill yourself. Promise me you'll ease off."

"Of course, if you want me to I will," he answered obediently.

It was the first of many such meaningless promises he made in coming months. Two weeks later, the Malibu incident gone and hopefully forgotten, Rob Wenger, heir to the Wenger banking fortune, proposed to Trudy Coles, née Gertrude Kolinski, daughter of a destitute, semi-alcoholic, sexually perverted coal miner from West Virginia. Since she had not heard from Richie Stevens for months, she readily, yet with certain inner reservations, accepted.

The Wengers took over the main ballroom of the Ambassador for the festivities. The Beverly Wilton would have been classier, but they needed the biggest hall in town to house the social event of the season. One wag said that those not invited immediately gave up their leases, packed their belongings, and headed back East. Not to be invited to the Wenger-Coles wedding was tantamount to a dismissal notice from a major studio. There was not a working actor, director, writer, producer, or composer who was not invited. Leading politicians, banking executives, the cream of Los Angeles society attended en masse. It took two full moving vans just to cart away the wedding gifts.

At age seventeen, Trudy was possibly the most beautiful bride that Hollywood would ever see. The fact that she had elected not to invite any of her sisters or brothers—not to mention her father —to the wedding, and the more germane fact that the man she really loved was merely a pipe-smoking, elegantly charming guest at the festivities, were realities that she pushed into the inner recesses of her consciousness, determined not to allow them to surface and tarnish her day. She was marrying one of the richest, handsomest young bachelors in California, and she was on her way to becoming a movie star: that this had become a media event was partially attributable to her own career, not just to the status of the Wenger family.

BEAUTY AND THE BEST screamed the *Los Angeles Examiner.*

The L.A. *Times* headlined TRUDY AND ROB, AMERICA'S SWEETHEARTS.

But Silverstein said it best that night as he and Tillie prepared for bed.

"Pussy and Money! What a combination!"

CHAPTER 8

July 1948

It took the newlyweds twenty-two hours to fly to Miami, which included a four-hour layover in Chicago. Approximately two years before, Trudy had boarded the night bus from Hubbardsville to Charleston. No powers of imagination then would have enabled her to conjure up visions of herself sharing this magic carpet ride. Now, she was Mrs. Robert Wenger, wife of one of the richest young men in the country. And she was a budding Hollywood starlet to boot! Who could have foreseen such accomplishment in just two short years?

As she waited with Rob in the Miami airport for the plane to Puerto Rico she thought that, in a sense, she owed it all to a pimply faced, lying hustler named Skipper Dawson. She had not forgotten that Silverstein had been paying him a two-percent override on her salary, an obligation that she would have to assume once her current contract ran out. Still, fair was fair. Had he not urged her to take the chance, she might still be singing in Sandy's Cafe. The thought sickened her. The vision of a return to the life in Hubbardsville was enough to make her re-count her blessings.

The champagne-laced flight from Los Angeles had been a thrilling experience. At a few points, particularly over the Rockies, the plane had quaked violently. It was her first flight and that in itself was scary. But Rob had been most attentive. He had flown many times before and explained that turbulent air was quite common. Her only regret was that he had drunk so heavily during the journey. Visions of her father coming home polluted after his Saturday nights on the town returned to haunt her. She had promised herself that she would never marry a man who drank. That was before she had come to California and seen what life in the film colony was really like. Yet, she was determined that somehow she would help Rob Wenger control his problem.

There was also another fear nagging at the back of her brain. Rob seemed to love her so much, yet he was an inveterate flirt. Perhaps he didn't realize it, but she had overheard him exchanging intimacies with a voluptuous stewardess who seemed all too eager to serve them. She saw him surreptitiously hand her a note. When she questioned him about it with an attempt to seem casual he explained that the girl had once met his friend, Charlie Twining, and had asked for his phone number. She knew that Charlie was quite the man about town, but she really didn't swallow the explanation. Just some innocent flirtation, she told herself. She had said the same thing at one point during their wedding when she found Rob exchanging laughs with a buxom barmaid at the Ambassador. Well, at least he's attractive to other women, too, she had concluded.

After another three hours of waiting in the stifling terminal, they boarded a flight for San Juan, where they were scheduled to spend a month in the bridal suite of the Caribe Star Hotel. She had seen travel brochures on the wonders of the Caribbean but her grandest dreams were exceeded by the elegance and beauty that awaited them. Rob kept drinking throughout the five-hour flight from Miami, and by the time they reached their destination he was glassy-eyed. She took over, ordering a taxi to transport them from the steamy, overcrowded San Juan airport to their fairyland hotel suite. Even at seventeen, she was accustomed to assuming authority, and she realized that Rob was in no condition to make clear decisions.

Luckily, their luggage arrived without incident, porters quickly carted them to a waiting line of cabs, and in a few minutes they were at the hotel portico. She had to nudge Rob several times to keep him awake. They were shown to their suite without delay, and she threw open the curtains to breathe in the beauty of the sapphire waters of the tropics. It was spectacular, but she was tired after the long hours of travel and turned to Rob to suggest that they nap instead of heading for the beach. She found him already asleep, not even having taken the trouble to undress. Just as well, she thought. There would be plenty of time for sex in the long years to come.

When she awoke from her siesta she found herself alone. It was past five o'clock and there was a note from Rob: *Darling—Meet me at the Coconut Bar just alongside of the pool. Wear something casual. No one dresses until dark.*

For some strange reason, she resented waking up alone in a strange country on the first real day of her honeymoon. Perhaps she was being hypersensitive. The airline stewardess incident was still troubling her. She showered quickly, threw on a simple dirndl, and went looking for Rob. Quite predictably, she found him, drink in hand, talking to a long-limbed blonde, who seemed enraptured by his every word. Struggling to be nonchalant, she walked directly up to them and beamed a big hello. "So here's where my husband has been spending his honeymoon! Hi there!"

Seeming somewhat embarrassed, Rob introduced her to the lady he had been chatting with and immediately suggested that they invite her to join them for dinner, since she was alone on her vacation from New York. Obviously, he left Trudy little room for dissent. Their first night together at San Juan was spent with Rob dividing his attentions between Trudy and their new friend. Fortunately, the blonde was only there for a few more days. Trudy decided to express her displeasure when they were alone that night.

"Are you bored with me so soon?" she asked.

"Honey, what do you mean?"

"I think you know what I mean. It's the first real night of our honeymoon and you have to invite along some dumb blonde who I could care less about. Why don't you ask her to share the suite with us? After all, there is plenty of room."

"Jealous! Now I know why you have green eyes!" he said, reaching for her in an effort to defuse an argument.

She pulled away. "Green, blue or brown, makes no never mind. I'm not going to stand by and watch you flirt with every barmaid with big tits. You're a married man now. Act like one!"

If Rob Wenger knew how a married man should act on his honeymoon, his actions belied it. He spent his time drinking daiquiris by the pool during the day, Scotch by night, gambling to excess in the casino, and ogling every shapely female who strutted by.

"Why don't you take her to dinner?" Trudy asked angrily when he swiveled around to eye one overdeveloped cocktail waitress. "You seem more interested in her than in your wife. Remember, we are married."

"Come on, honey, grow up. I'm married, as the man says, but I'm not dead."

At night, he might as well have been. He was usually so drunk he fell asleep as soon as he lay down. One night, he reached for her in a halfhearted gesture that smacked more of duty than of passion.

"You don't have to prove anything to me," Trudy said.

"You know how you turn me on," Rob answered.

She excused herself to visit the bathroom, and when she returned Rob was sound asleep. She didn't try to wake him. She cried herself to sleep. If this was a taste of marriage, she wondered why couples ever stayed together for so many years. She vowed that neither wealth nor convention would force her to stay with a partner who had so little feeling for her as Rob Wenger was displaying on their honeymoon.

"Hey, I got a big, big idea," Rob said over his third Scotch one night in the company of another honeymooning couple whom he had invited to join them. "Let's play switchies tonight and we can all get together in the morning and report if we learned any new positions."

Trudy wasn't sure if he meant it or if this was just some clumsy joke. Even the other husband seemed somewhat shocked at the suggestion, and the dinner ended prematurely. Back in their suite, Trudy considered giving Rob a piece of her mind but thought better of it. He wouldn't have cared. And this was only the second week of their honeymoon, with a whole life before them!

Toward the end of the second week, Trudy heard herself being paged while they were breakfasting on the terrace. Rob had his face buried in a copy of the *Los Angeles Times,* which he had flown to him each morning. At first Trudy thought that she had erred and heard incorrectly, but the bellman persisted in calling for Mrs. Rob Wenger. She rose and walked hurriedly to meet him. He told her that they were holding an overseas call for her, a call from California. Trudy made arrangements to have the call transferred to their suite. Her heart beat in anticipation, fearful that a call at a time like this could only portend bad news. Who would want to reach her now, and to what avail? Everyone at the studio knew that she wasn't due back in California for another two weeks.

Fearfully, she raised the phone, waited with bated breath for the operator to acknowledge her, and, finally, after identifying herself and hearing the operator say in Spanish-accented English "Okay, California. Here is your party," she heard the voice on the other end of the line. She could have cried for joy. It was the mellow, cultured baritone of Richie Stevens that greeted her.

"I say, Trudy, is that you?"

"Yes, Mr. Stevens. I'm here. How are you? Is anything wrong?"

"Not a thing, my dear. How goes the honeymoon? Swimmingly, I'm sure."

"Great. Just great," Trudy lied, hoping against hope that her endless drama lessons stood her in good stead at a moment like this: no need to share her disappointment with the one man in the world for whom she hungered.

"Just as I expected! You must forgive me for invading your moment of joy, but I had to talk to you now and it could not await your return."

"Is anything wrong at the studio?"

"No. Not wrong. It's just that Manny Silverstein and I have reached an impasse. I'm tired of all the garbage we're turning out here at Continental and he won't let me out of my contract. So I've come up with another escape hatch. And you're going to play a part in my scheme. Intrigued?"

"Why, yes, of course. But I'm not sure I understand."

"You couldn't understand. I haven't told you enough yet. I told him that I want to make a three-million-dollar epic. I want to do a screen treatment based on the story of the Trojan War. Do you remember the story?"

"Not really. I know there's a wooden horse in there somewhere. I think we read about it in tenth grade just before I had to quit school when I came to California."

"Well, it's really a fascinating tale. Paris was the son of Priam, King of Troy. He fell in love with Helen, the wife of Menelaus, the King of Sparta. He either charmed or kidnapped her and took her home to Troy. The Greeks spent ten years trying to beat the Trojans in a war for revenge, but finally it took Ulysses to figure out how to capture the city. The Greek army hid in a big wooden horse that was placed outside the Trojan city walls. The dumb Trojans brought it inside the city, and the Greeks jumped out and killed everyone in sight."

"And who am I to play, the horse? Hah!"

"My dear, you are to play Helen, allegedly the most beautiful woman who ever lived. You're to be the lead! It'll be your first starring role!"

"What does Mr. Silverstein think about this idea?"

"He thinks I'm crazy. He is afraid that if I'm wrong, I'll bankrupt the studio. And, frankly, my dear, he thinks you're two years away from playing leads. He wants to put you in a thriller, then two more Westerns in which you get violated by drunken cowboys."

"This must be costing you a fortune. Can't we talk when I get home at the end of the month?"

"Don't worry about the call. I've made plenty of money for this studio and I'm calling from my office. No, it can't wait. I need you home right away. Silverstein says I can do it if I raise most of the money. And I've done that from MGM. They have a sound stage open, the script is ready, and I've made up my mind to direct. Silverstein gets ten percent off the top, then it's a fifty-fifty split all of the way. If we're right, we'll own this town."

"And if we're wrong?"

There was a long pause.

"I guess then we'll both be looking for jobs. Are you ready to take the chance? I am."

"I am, too," she answered without hesitation. "I'll leave for home first thing this afternoon if I can catch a plane."

Rob wasn't at the table when she got back. The waiter indicated that he had headed toward the pool. The area was deserted when she got there. Just a few waiters and pool boys getting ready for the day's activities. The sun always shone in San Juan, which meant no respite for the hotel's pool employees. She recognized one waiter who usually served their cabana.

"Pablo, have you seen my husband, Mr. Wenger?"

The waiter seemed distracted, even evasive when he answered. "I think maybe I see him go back to your rooms."

"No. I just left there. He must be somewhere around here."

Just then she thought she heard a giggle in their assigned cabana. Walking forward quickly, she pulled back the curtain.

Rob was inside with a curvaceous female guest they had met several nights before. They were both nude, holding each other's suits, and there were smeared cosmetics all over his face.

"You pig!" It was the only thing she could think to say. She turned on her heels and went straight to their suite. When Rob got there five minutes later, she was packing.

"Honey, let's not get excited. We were only playing."

"I couldn't care less. I'm going home. You stay and enjoy the rest of the honeymoon with your lady friends. You've been doing that for two weeks anyhow."

He tried to dissuade her, then, seeing it was hopeless, desisted.

"I'm going back to work," she said emotionlessly. "Mr. Stevens promised me a big role. You can come home when you're good and ready but I won't promise I'll be there for you."

Somewhat remorseful, Rob offered to leave with her, but she was adamant. She wanted to be alone for a while, alone to work and think. His parents had bought them a lovely home in the hills and she would head there for the time being. When he got back, they'd talk and see if either was interested in continuing the charade. She would pack only a few suitcases. He could bring the rest with him when he returned in a few weeks. Luckily, there were good connections to Miami and she hoped to be back in Hollywood in twenty-four hours. He didn't argue further. He helped her pack, took her to the airport, and they bade each other a tearless farewell.

Whatever the jungle drums are that transmit gossip in Hollywood, they worked ever so efficiently as soon as Trudy arrived in Los Angeles alone. A reporter, waiting at the airport for some celebrity due in from New York, saw her land and board a taxi without an escort. The calls from columnists started the moment she had unpacked. Hedda was on the phone, followed by Sidney and then Louella. My dear, they all gurgled, how nice to have you back so soon. We thought you weren't due back for another two weeks or so. And how is Mr. Wenger, might they ask?

Trudy Coles had worked it all out in her mind long before landing in Los Angeles. Rob had been called away on a tremendously important business trip; she had been offered a leading role in a giant epic that she was contractually forbidden to name. But they would be the very first to know, she promised.

Did they believe her? Who knew? Who really cared? As long as there was slop to fill their troughs no one really cared if it was true or manufactured. A whole new journalistic industry had been bred by the Hollywood glamor mechanism: the gossip column. The trick was to keep it churning. No one had visions of winning awards for accurate reporting. When they pressed her, she simply told them they would have to contact the studio publicity department for further information. Let the pros lie to the pros.

The filming of Richie Stevens' *Helen of Troy* started two days later. A portion was shot at an MGM sound stage, the balance on location in the foothills approaching Mount Whitney, just west of Sequoia National Park. It was a near-disaster from start to finish. There was a strike by the cameramen, which held up shooting for nearly three weeks. Heavy, unseasonal rains caused further delays. The leading man developed appendicitis and required emergency surgery, delaying the proceedings three more weeks. A truckload of film was mysteriously hijacked. The project went almost immediately over budget. MGM agreed to an advance. Then another. Then no more. Silverstein, wearing his usual "I told you so" leer, refused to ante up a single sou. At the eleventh hour, Stevens flew to New York and, on his own personal signature, got a Wall Street firm to make a $200,000 loan for fifty percent of his end of the profits. It was the usual story: last money in, first money out, the greatest leverage on its investment. But Stevens would not complain. This was the money that would see the picture through to its completion.

One evening, after shooting some clean-up shots at MGM, he invited Trudy to have dinner with him at his home. She accepted happily. Rob had returned long since but they were far from reconciled. She had really been too busy working to concentrate on her domestic problems. Rob and she merely coexisted. She went her way, he went his. Occasionally, they would dine together or appear in public if it was de rigueur. To the world, they were still those fabulous all-American sweethearts, the envy of every romantic. In reality, it was all what the French would call *trompe l'oeil,* merely an illusion designed to fool the eye. Those beaming smiles for the society cameramen, those quotations of joy from their luxurious love nest, all illusions to give the public what it wanted: a Hollywood fairytale in living color.

Stevens' houseboy served them an ice-cold salad, a rare, chilled white wine, a heavenly duck buried in cherries, and baked Alaska topped with fresh whipped cream along with pungent iced coffee. They sat alone by the pool watching the reflection of a full harvest moon. Soft Gershwin melodies played on the high-fidelity system. It was truly a moment to be cherished.

"I asked you here for one main purpose," he said.

"Yes?"

"To tell you how much I appreciate all you have done to stand by me these many difficult weeks. Without you, I wouldn't have finished this picture."

"That's just not true," she protested. "I worked. You paid me. That's all."

"That's all nonsense. You were wonderful and loyal and brilliant. You were the inspiration that held it all together."

He took her hand, pulling her to her feet, and held her in a warm embrace. Trudy's heart beat wildly. Now, she thought, at last the moment she had awaited so long was upon her. After a few seconds he released her and said, "I can't let myself be swept away. You're married. I'm more than twice your age. You're going to be a big, big star and I'll always believe that I played a part in your career."

Before she could mount a protest, he had summoned his Japanese houseboy.

"Please drive Miss Coles home," he said simply. "She has to be on set early tomorrow to finish her scenes."

Helen of Troy was finished two weeks later. Sneak previews in nearby California communities were very disappointing. The film wasn't bad; it just wasn't very good. It would receive moderate reviews, play around the country, and, with luck, retrieve its monumental investment. There would be no real profits, except those blotted up by the MGM and Continental accounting departments for prints, publicity, and distribution costs of every description. Even at a relatively early age, Hollywood mathematicians had learned to steal most effectively.

Stevens got enough of the box-office receipts back to pay off his debts. He and Silverstein were still friendly adversaries. Ostensibly, his position with the studio was secure. Manny Silverstein recognized his potential and was not about to scrap him—yet. He could not deny Stevens' accurate prediction, however.

Richie Stevens had prophesied that *Helen of Troy* would make Trudy Coles a great star. And he was nearly right. Though she was still looked upon by the skeptics as that girl with the green eyes and big boobs who couldn't really act, *Helen of Troy* made

Trudy Coles a force to be reckoned with. Her acting had improved to a point where no one in the cast outshone her. Her face had matured. Her Junoesque figure remained unequaled. Her self-assurance, her presence in every scene, was of starlike stature. She was no Sarah Bernhardt perhaps, nor Nazimova nor Judith Anderson. She was Trudy Coles. She stood on the threshold of Hollywood stardom. One had to be blind not to realize it.

CHAPTER 9

October 1948

Rob and Trudy Wenger spent the next four months living separately together. There were no open battles. There were no heart-to-heart talks. There was nothing. As soon as he had returned from the honeymoon, Rob moved his clothes into a guest bedroom. He needed no spectacular insight to realize that was what Trudy wanted, and in fact, that was what was indicated. Occasionally, they took their evening meals together, always at home, prepared by the cook whom Trudy had hired. On several occasions they were forced by convention to attend parties together. It was not clear whether anyone guessed that all was not well in their garden of love. On one occasion, Trudy received a message at the studio to please call Rob Wenger Senior at her convenience. She found time that afternoon during a break from filming. The father, it developed, was concerned about his son's drinking. He was gone from his office more than he was present, he frequently reeked of liquor, and his attention span was growing shorter and shorter. Was anything wrong, the senior Wenger inquired?

"I don't like his drinking, either," Trudy responded. "But I can't influence him at all. Maybe he'll listen to you."

Trudy never learned what, if anything, transpired when the two men discussed the problem. She was sure, however, that Rob had turned on the charm and assured his father that all was well and agreed to cut back on the drinking. She had sat through a similar conference concerning his senseless, madcap driving when they were engaged to be married. He had totaled two automobiles and received enough speeding citations to result in permanent cancellation of his driver's license. As usual, it was the "Wenger connection" that spared him. His worst penalty had been a thirty-day suspension that resulted only because four persons were seriously injured in an accident when Rob was driving in the wrong direction on a one-way street. Rob ignored the citation, never stopped driving, and scoffed at the police authorities who, he felt confident, would never touch him.

One evening, alone with a script that had to be memorized by the following day, Trudy decided to make one last attempt to reach a reconciliation. They had dined silently and Rob had spoken only to mention that he had been invited out for the evening, so he could not linger over coffee. When he came downstairs about an hour later, showered, shaved, and dressed to the nines, Trudy cornered him.

"Rob, I want to talk to you."

"Can't it wait for another time? I'm late now," he said impatiently.

"No, I want to talk now. It won't take long."

"Okay," he said petulantly and sat down across from her.

"Rob, what do you think is going to happen to our marriage? I didn't marry you to be an old maid."

"You're married to that goddamned studio. You don't give a damn about me. Right?"

"No, wrong. My career is very important. But I'm not Mrs. Continental. I'm Mrs. Wenger. We hardly talk at all. That's not my idea of marriage."

"You were the one who ran from the honeymoon. You were the one who flew back to L.A. because your darling fairy, Richie Stevens, phoned for you."

"Don't you dare call him a fairy! You're just jealous because he believes in me, that's all."

"I only know what everyone else in Hollywood seems to believe. But who cares? I wouldn't mind if he slept with a male hippo."

Trudy sucked in her breath. The thought of Stevens' sexual preference had crossed her mind once or twice, but only because he seemed so restrained in his treatment of her. And there was that recent night by his pool when she was certain that they would make love and didn't. It was just like Rob to throw out a red herring when the issue was his own behavior and not Richie Stevens' sexual predilections. It was his favorite, immature way to win an argument, but she wouldn't let him get away with it.

"Let's talk about us, our future. Mr. Stevens has nothing to do with us in this matter. You're out every night until God knows when, you're drunk half the time. I hear you stumbling up the steps like a bum. Your father is worried sick about you, do you know that?"

"Sure. I know he called you. I'm worried sick that he'll kill my mother if he doesn't stop chasing young starlets. But he doesn't want to talk about that. Only my drinking."

"Let your parents handle their problems. We've got our own. Do you want this to work? You told me once that you loved me so much you couldn't look at other women. Remember?"

"Yes, I remember. And I remember when you used to make love to me as if it mattered. Hell, on the honeymoon you were so cold and mechanical I had more fun jerking off."

"It seems to me that you did nothing but chase other women on our so-called honeymoon. You made me feel dirty, not like a beautiful bride."

"If you had been more responsive than a wooden surfboard maybe I wouldn't have chased. Sex is a two-way street, you know."

"Look, Rob, I'm not perfect. No one is. I did love you or I wouldn't have agreed to marry you. Especially after that orgy you set up at Malibu. I think I could love you again. I'm willing to try. But you have to want to. You have to try, too."

"I'd like to try again. Tomorrow, we'll go out to dinner just like the old times. I'll book us a table at Romanoff's. We'll do it alone. No friends. Just the two of us. Let's see if we can't get back to where this trouble started and make it work."

"What about tonight?"

"I'm meeting some guys on a business deal. I can't cancel this late."

She really didn't believe him but this was not the time to protest. He came home at a rather decent hour and gave no indication of being inebriated. He headed for his own room and she was glad he did so. She really wasn't ready to take him back into her bed as yet.

It seemed as if the talk had worked miracles. Rob actually tried to recapture what they both had felt for each other in those magical days of their courtship. He limited his nights with "the boys" to one night a week. He cut back on his drinking to a measurable degree. He went to work regularly, even causing his father to call Trudy again and thank her for her help. He was more attentive at parties. He still flirted now and then, but it seemed like innocent kid's stuff and never caused Trudy a moment of embarrassment. After a few weeks, Trudy suggested that he rejoin her in the bedroom. Happily, he accepted. There was a mad, impassioned reunion under the sheets. It was the best sex they had ever had, still not up to Trudy's dreams and aspirations, but given the framework within which they related one to the other, very good.

Trudy now felt she had it all, or almost all. A budding career; a rich, handsome, and attentive husband; beauty and good health —what more could she ask for? The treasure she wanted most of all, she now assumed was beyond her grasp. Perhaps her professional relationship with Richie Stevens would have to replace a romantic one. She hoped that she would learn to deal with that.

Occasionally, she would see Stevens in the studio, and he was always gracious and friendly. His failure with *Helen of Troy*—for the industry considered it such—was deflating, but his power at Continental seemed undiminished. Silverstein was too smart a campaigner to let the opportunity slip entirely. He added a bit of timely ridicule to his assertiveness. For example, they would be at a business conference discussing potential new projects. If Richie agreed with him, fine; if not, he was likely to shake his head and say with apparent pain for all to hear, "Ah, Richie, another of your *fecockta* cundrum ideas, right?" "Cundrum" was Manny's word for "condom," his crude way of referring to Richie's failure, since Trojan was the best known prophylactic on the market.

Stevens knew that his days of power at Continental were numbered. He would leave, when the right opportunity presented itself. He realized, of course, that hundreds of Silverstein's lackeys thought and said the same thing but never had the courage to jump off the gravy train. He hoped that he would be different.

He still had his differences with Silverstein in regard to Trudy Coles. One of the major studios, impressed with her work in *Helen of Troy,* wanted to borrow her for a new dramatic feature they were planning. They said that their budget would not permit them to pay more than $100,000 for her services. Since Silverstein was still paying her fifteen thousand a year, one would have thought that he would have jumped at the opportunity. Not Silverstein. He felt that he could get one hundred and fifty, and when they refused, he would not budge.

"Give the kid a break, Manny," Richie argued. You'll be making a killing and she'll be playing a role half the dames in Hollywood would kill for."

"Fuck half the dames in Hollywood and suck the other half," Manny answered angrily. "I'm not in the charity business. They'd bust my balls if they could. Now they'll pay or she won't play. As for the kid, she's moving fast enough for an eighteen-year-old *courva* from West Virginia." *Courva,* the Yiddish word for "whore," was one of Manny's favorites. He used it to describe every woman he ever met—except Tillie.

"It's not a question of how fast she has moved. She's ready to break out and when she does it will be great for Continental. Why impede her?"

"I'm saving her for another cundrum," Silverstein answered tersely. Richie knew better than to press the discussion further.

Strangely, though, Stevens thought he had won his point when three weeks later he was called in to Silverstein's office for an emergency conference. Silverstein was ecstatic, literally walking on the ceiling. Quite by coincidence, he had optioned a novel by a new American writer that had shot to the top of the best-seller list and was now being prominently mentioned to win a Pulitzer Prize. It was the story of two beautiful sisters, one of whom becomes America's leading actress. Her younger, shy but talented sister lives in her shadow until there is a showdown. The older woman, however, diabolically schemes to prevent her younger sibling from ever attaining her due, even though she herself has all that she wants from life. The one thing she will not abide is competition from her own sister. It was a powerful story with two excellent roles laden with dramatic possibilities. That afternoon, the head of Twentieth Century-Fox had called and proposed a joint venture. They would supply Hollywood's reigning superstar to play Andrea, the older sister. Silverstein could pick someone from his coterie to play Beth, the younger sister. Fox was willing to provide all of the financing. Silverstein would get fifty percent of the profits. It was an incredible offer. Marjorie Hansell was the hottest property in Hollywood; Fox had never permitted her to make a film for any other studio. With her on the marquee, the film was bound to succeed.

"And what about distribution?" Manny had asked greedily.

"Yours," came the reply, and the deal was made.

Silverstein offered Stevens a bonus of $25,000 if he would drop his current project and agree to direct *Loving Sisters*. Stevens had, as an inviolate part of his contract, the final word on what features he directed. And though Silverstein had little doubt as to what his choice would be, he threw in a clause allowing Stevens to select anyone available, and not under prohibitive contract, to play the part of the younger sister as further incentive. Stevens made his selection on the spot. Trudy, about to leave for Colorado and another quickie Western, was given a change of assignment. As a parting gesture, Silverstein patted Stevens on the back and said with a smile, "Let's not fuck it up. One wooden horse was enough for the Trojans. For you, too."

Loving Sisters was to be the most important film ever produced by Continental. The cast and director were announced at a specially arranged press party at the Beverly Wilton Hotel. And there, for the first time, Trudy Coles met Marjorie Hansell. It was an experience that would stay with her for the rest of her career.

News of a new Marjorie Hansell feature was always significant and the press turned out in droves for the announcement. The drinks flowed. The caviar was the finest. The mood was festive. The studio assigned Mark Walters, their most experienced press agent, to shepherd Trudy to the affair. He intentionally arranged for them to arrive early, knowing that Hansell would make her appearance at the last instant. The studio dressed her in her most revealing outfit. The photographers had a field day, and the more they drank the more adventurous they became in posing Trudy for their shots. Walters, normally in favor of a ton of cheesecake, became concerned that the pictures might prove too risqué for reproduction in syndicated papers.

"Hey, fellas," he pleaded, "take it easy. Miss Coles is a fine actress, not a stripper. Focus in on that face. That's where the money is."

He was wasting his breath. He might as well have asked a

swarm of bees to steer clear of the honey. There was more to Trudy Coles than a beautiful face. And truthfully, she was proud of her assets and enjoyed flaunting them for all to see. The posing didn't bother her a bit.

Suddenly, there was a hush in the room, almost as if someone had called for silence. The pushing and shoving stopped. The bartenders whispered their inquiries. And then Marjorie Hansell stalked in, followed by her own retinue of agents, managers, and assorted flunkies. She held her red head proudly, rolling her hips rhythmically and looking neither left nor right as she haughtily approached the table that had been set aside for her and Trudy. The crowd moved toward her magically, deserting Trudy in midpose. Hansell was the queen, and the queen had arrived.

Somewhat nonplussed by the degree of the upstaging, Walters rushed to Trudy's side, took her by the arm, and led her to the seat she had been assigned to occupy. Glancing menacingly in Trudy's direction, Marjorie Hansell, in the deep contralto that was her patented glory, stage-whispered loud enough for all assembled to hear, "And who, may I ask, is this child at the head table?"

Desperately trying to avoid an embarrassing situation, Walters moved in and said, "Miss Hansell, this is Trudy Coles, your co-star in *Loving Sisters.*"

It was an unfortunate selection of terms.

"Co-star? Co-star?" Marjorie Hansell roared. "I have no co-stars in my pictures. A Marjorie Hansell film needs no co-star!"

The press was eating it up. Striving to save the day, Mark Walters apologetically reneged.

"Of course not. I only meant that Miss Coles will be appearing as your younger sister in the picture."

Having clearly established her supremacy, Hansell was willing now to appear more gracious.

"Come here, child, let's have a look at you. My, you are a young beauty!"

Dutifully, Trudy left her seat and paid homage to the queen, a fact that did not fail to be noticed by all the press assembled. As one wag in his *Silver Screen* column put it:

> Hansell met Gretl yesterday at the Beverly Wilshire Hotel. This Gretl, better known as Trudy Coles, had better watch

out or she'll end up as a gingerbread cookie in the witch's oven!

Trudy, forewarned about Hansell's capriciousness, simply smiled sweetly, determined not to make a show. She had long since learned that one picked one's moments for revenge. Any show of temper now would be interpreted as a sign of weakness. Instead, measuring her words carefully, she answered, "Coming from a great beauty like you, Miss Hansell, that is a compliment. I've admired your pictures for years."

Even Marjorie Hansell wasn't sure whether there was sarcasm in those words, especially the reference to her veteran status, so she decided to ignore them for the moment. But she had the feeling that this curvaceous upstart was not going to be a pushover.

Trudy had seen Marjorie Hansell's fangs bared ever so plainly. In the next three months she was to feel them time and again. There was no indignity, no matter how small and petty, to which Hansell did not subject her. Whether it was a choice of dressing rooms, a selection of colors to be worn, a reading of lines that she insisted was amateurish, Marjorie Hansell demanded her due in ferocious terms. On several occasions, unable to bear the insults, Trudy rushed from the set in hysterics. That was exactly what Hansell wanted. Now that she was dangerously close to fifty, Marjorie Hansell deeply resented the rosebud beauty of an actress with obvious talents who would someday challenge her own reign.

Trudy lacked the maturity necessary to deal with her tormentor unaided. But Hansell had overlooked the presence of Richie Stevens, whose own experience with bitchy actresses was exceedingly well grounded. He knew that patience and perseverance would have its way. Nightly, he visited Trudy in her dressing room and calmed her nerves.

"There is only one effective way to fight her, Trudy. Do a better job than she can do. Don't slip to her level. You can't beat her at that game. Simply ignore her and do your best job. She'll know she's losing and give it up soon enough. You mark my words."

And to Hansell, he purposely pretended that he was not aware that her temper tantrums were anything but that—tantrums. He quieted her, comforted her, told her how well she was performing, and remained aloof from the pettiness of her squabbling. What Marjorie Hansell wanted was for Stevens to take sides with Trudy. Then she would revolt, demand that he be banned from the film, and insist that a new director be brought in to finish his work. Stevens was on to her game and would not give her the satisfaction of becoming the sacrificial goat. Instead, he gave her the Gandhi treatment, meeting her charges with passive resistance, pretending a neutrality that even she realized did not exist. Gradually, reluctantly, she gave up. After all, she reasoned, she was the queen. Why worry about an eighteen-year-old ingénue when she herself had the lead? Besides, as secure as she felt, there was the power of the Wenger clan. Why challenge them unnecessarily? Perhaps she was overplaying her hand. And Trudy did seem like a nice girl after all. She hadn't fought back like so many of the young bitches she'd played with.

Gradually, the heat subsided. The spirit of friendly tranquility that descended on the set was contagious. It brought out the best in everyone, and soon the word spread throughout the film community: great things were happening on Sound Stage Two. *Loving Sisters* was going to be a big, big hit!

The constant harassment from Marjorie Hansell and the challenge of playing a major role in the company of one of Hollywood's greatest stars took its toll on Trudy. She was exhausted by the time a studio limousine returned her to her Beverly Hills home each night. She had just enough energy to eat a light supper, shower, then fall into bed, script in hand, to learn her lines for the next day's shooting. She knew that she was not being attentive to Rob. But she was only human. Who had time for idle chatter or frenzied lovemaking when what she needed was rest and sleep? She really couldn't afford the heavy, dark rings under her eyes that invariably appeared when she did not get enough sleep. Rob did not complain visibly. On several occasions he seemed upset when she resisted his advances. She tried to explain that they would vacation together and that she would make it up to him as soon as the filming was completed. She really did not know at this point that the studio would insist that she take a three-week, nationwide publicity jaunt to drum up demand for the picture before it was released. Big pictures did not just happen by themselves. The public had to be told what it liked. And, there was no better "teller" than a sexy young beauty with big breasts.

Richie Stevens was a harsh taskmaster. He was certain he had a big winner on his hands and he was determined to wring out of it every drop of brilliance he knew it contained. Retakes were the order of the day. Whole sequences were shot again and again until they met Stevens' demanding standards of excellence. For once, Manny Silverstein stayed clear of the proceedings, not badgering him with cost and time overruns. After all, Twentieth Century-Fox was footing the bill. Let it take all year and then some. He could wait. There was a mammoth payoff just around the bend and Manny Silverstein could afford to be patient. What did it matter that the film was already two months late? Fox would be happy. He would be happy. They'd drown their tears running to the bank.

As the dreary work continued, Rob Wenger found time hanging heavy on his hands. Despite his efforts to be an obedient husband, he was human, too, after all. He started seeing his old friends more and more. Happy to have him along again, they outdid themselves trying to make him aware of all of the fun he had been missing. In a matter of weeks, it was back to the old days of heavy drinking, sniffing cocaine, partying into the wee hours of the morning. Trudy was not really aware of what was going on. She went to bed so early each night that she never knew if he went out or not. She was up at dawn; her call for makeup at the studio was six-thirty in the morning, and by that time Rob was sound asleep. Occasionally, she would look in on him in the morning and realize that the room smelled of drink. Yet, she could not complain too loudly, since she was not making herself available as wife and companion. She hoped the picture would be finished soon and they could take up again where they were just before the start of *Loving Sisters.*

His carousing did not escape Robert Wenger, Sr., however, who was again only too painfully aware that his son was ignoring his work and generally carrying on at the bank in a disgracefully irresponsible manner. One day he summoned his son into his private office.

"Rob, I'm disgusted with the way you are conducting yourself. You've become the laughing stock of this company."

"Well, why don't you fire me?" Rob asked insolently.

"I would if I thought it would do any good."

"No you wouldn't, Dad. You wouldn't do that because then the whole world would know what a fuck-up you have for a son. You couldn't stand that, could you?"

The father imperiously signaled that his son should take a chair. Rob refused, preferring to stand. He felt that this was the moment he had been awaiting these many years, the showdown when he would speak his piece without interference or interruption. He was tired of being the dutiful son who stood or sat at his daddy's whim.

"You have no right to complain to me. I've given you everything a person could want in life and all you do is dissipate and act like you had the breeding of a desert rat. You've been a disgrace to your mother and me ever since you outgrew your knee-pants."

"Yes, you sure have given me everything a person could want in life. Everything except the feeling that I amount to anything but a pile of horseshit! You sent me to Carlson Prep. Not because I wanted to go, but because that's where you went and you were such a hero. In every class, the teacher asked me, 'Are you the son of Robert Wenger? He was the best student I ever taught!' I tried out for the boxing team. The gym was plastered with pictures of you winning the Junior Golden Gloves. The coach told me fighting was not my thing. I tried out for football. When I dropped a few passes in the end zone that lost us an important game, the coach came over and asked me if I was sure I was the legitimate son of Robert Wenger. He told me maybe I'd better try the crocheting team! When I graduated in the bottom twenty-five percent of my class, you and Mom wouldn't even come to the commencement exercises. You were ashamed. The same thing happened at UCLA. That's why I dropped out after my freshman year. Then I joined the bank. All I ever got from everyone was how lucky I was to have you for a father. Did it ever occur to you that maybe I can't compete with you, the all-American genius?"

"Now, that's what I call a feeble excuse. You never tried to compete with me. How do you know you can't if you don't try? Forget about me. What about that beautiful girl you married? If you loved her you'd want her to be proud of you, right?"

"Who says I loved her? I married her to show you that I could do something. I tried to prove that the girl who was supposed to be the most beautiful girl in Hollywood could fall in love with me, Rob Wenger, Jr., everyone's major fuck-up. You like to sit there high and mighty, preaching to me about accomplishment and responsibility. You've made it with every starlet that comes down the pike. Maybe you're just jealous that I took one away from you, the man who can't be beat."

The two men glowered at each other, their anger lead-hot. Rob Wenger, Sr., thought that there was a chance that his son had heard about his romantic escapades. Somehow, he did not expect the information to be thrust at him face-to-face. He considered himself beyond reproach. Son or no son, he would not take this. His voice trembled with indignation. He paused before speaking, to control his temper. "I think you'd better clear out of here now and not return until you're ready to apologize."

"That'll be a cold day in July!" Rob answered, turning on his heels.

Far from having any constructive effect on him, the face-off gave Rob a feeling of freedom. Now at last he was free to do and act and be himself. He was beyond paternal lectures. He was beyond the need for parental acclaim. He was Rob Wenger, Jr. His own man. Screw the world! He'd do as he pleased when he pleased. As far as Trudy was concerned, she never had really loved him any more than he had really loved her. She was in love with being a movie star and with being the wife of the scion of one of California's richest families. She had the title now. What more did she need?

That night she told him that the studio was insisting that she go on a three-week publicity tour. She'd ask him to go along but they felt it was better for her image if the world didn't see her as a married woman. Stupid, wasn't it? she asked. Everyone knew she was Mrs. Robert Wenger, Jr. He assured her he understood. The truth was, he didn't care. He had neither the desire nor the intention of following her around the country while she made goo-goo eyes for the press.

Trudy's three-week publicity junket gave Rob freedom from all surveillance. He was drunk most of the time, seeking the constant companionship of the wild bunch he had temporarily left behind when he accepted the onerous title of "husband." One night, out with an obvious prostitute, he stopped for a nightcap at one of the private drinking clubs that was the current "in" place for Hollywood's beautiful people. Out of the corner of his eye he spotted Louella Parsons and he hoped she had not seen him. Of course, she had, and immediately became an uninvited guest at his table.

"Well, Rob Junior, how goes it with California's most handsome young husband?" she crooned.

"Fine. Just fine, Miss Parsons. How goes it with you?"

"Swimmingly. Swimmingly. And how are your parents?"

"The same."

"And your wife?" she asked, looking meaningfully at his woman of the evening.

"They tell me she's fine. She's on a publicity trip for three weeks. It's drum-beating time for *Loving Sisters.*"

"Yes, I heard.... And aren't you going to introduce me to your date?"

"This is Kate Raidy. Kate is my cousin from New York."

"Really!" Louella said in disbelief.

"Really!" Rob repeated. But he hadn't fooled Louella.

And so the word was out that all was not well in Hollywood's Garden of Eden. Rob didn't care. Although the studio had a clipping service, which supplied any and all publicity concerning their major stars, they managed to keep these ugly items away from Trudy so that she would not know she had been gossiped about in her absence.

A large, exciting party had been arranged for the night of Trudy's return. Silverstein and Fox were footing the bill jointly as a sort of reward for the cast, crew, and creative staff who had brought them such a gem as *Loving Sisters.* The party had been planned for weeks and Trudy had told Rob about it before she left for her junket. She explained how important a night it would be in her career. She insisted that he attend with her. A few key press people would be there but essentially the party was only for the family and friends of those who had been involved in the film. Trudy wanted Rob to be present to share the accolades with her. She hoped that it might kick off another honeymoon for them, since she had been promised a four-week vacation before starting another picture.

Trudy was somewhat let down when she arrived at Union Station that afternoon and did not find Rob waiting. Somehow she had conjured up an emotional rendezvous, kisses and hugs while the photographers shot away and vicariously shared their joy. Instead, only a small contingent was present, assigned by the studio to see to it that she got home safely. She hadn't even met the young courier from the press department who took her and her luggage in tow.

"Did you enjoy the trip, Miss Coles?" he asked.

"Sometimes. It was awfully tiring."

"Yes. I know. I've been out on them a number of times and they really can leave you dragging. But they're necessary."

"Perhaps."

They were the last words spoken before the limousine arrived at the Wenger home. Trudy's dampened spirits started to revive as visions of Rob awaiting her in a flower-filled living room, arms outstretched to receive her with an impassioned welcome, flashed through her head. Instead, she was in for another disappointment. The house was in semi-darkness. Only the night maid was present, Rob having given the entire staff the night off. She informed Trudy that Mr. Wenger had left home that afternoon, leaving word that he would not be available for the party but would see her when she got home. It was now six o'clock and the party was scheduled for eight. On the verge of tears, she considered not attending but knew that her absence would put a pall on the entire celebration. After a few moments' thought, she went to the phone and called Richie Stevens.

"Trudy," he bellowed warmly, "how nice to have you back in California. How was the trip?"

"Fine, Richie, fine. We got a mountain of press."

"Yes, of course, the studio clipping service has been supplying me with more daily copy than I have relatives. The pictures of you are great, and you seem to have handled yourself very well in the interviews. I loved that part about your looking on Marjorie Hansell as your real, long-lost sister. I hope those words didn't stick in your throat."

"Well, we did make peace at the end, you know. I don't bear grudges. . . . Richie, I wonder if you could pick me up?"

"Tonight?" he asked in surprise.

"Yes, tonight. Rob had to leave town on a business trip and I'd hate to attend unescorted."

"Of course. It'll be my delight. Pick you up at eight-fifteen. Stars don't arrive right on time."

The party was in full swing when they arrived at the hotel. The wine was flowing, the orchestra blaring away, and even the Fox executives were happily conversing with their opposite numbers from Continental. It was a true victory celebration—this was no time for partisan prejudices. Sneak previews of *Loving Sisters* had brought ecstatic reports; everyone was aware that this would be the picture of the year. It dripped with emotion and was bound to capture the public's fascination. Yes, it was money in the bank. There was already talk of a sequel.

Louella, always on the lookout for a hot gossip item, cornered Trudy as soon as she and Richie entered. "Darling, you look simply smashing! We were afraid you might not get back in time for the party."

"I never miss a party, Miss Parsons, if I can help it."

"So Rob tells me. We ran into each other just the other evening at Ripples. He was with that ever-so-attractive cousin of his from New York. You know the one I mean?"

"Of course. You mean Micky," Trudy answered without missing a beat.

"Funny, I thought he called her Kate."

"Kate is her middle name. They call her Micky."

"Of course," Louella answered as Richie Stevens pulled Trudy away from further pummeling.

"Let's have a drink at the bar, Trudy. Excuse us, Louella, but we're both parched. See you later."

Trudy was mortified. So he had returned to his philandering without even having the sense to avoid a public spot like Ripples! Even the amateur gossip columnists kept their field glasses focused on clubs like Ripples. At least he could have had the decency to be discreet. True, she hadn't been much of a companion for the last several months. But that did not excuse public whoring. One would think he had enough personal pride to try and protect the Wenger name even if he didn't care about her.

"Hey, Mr. Stevens, how about an intro to your friend?" They were at the bar now. Trudy turned to see a handsome, blond, athletic apparition beaming down at her. He was at least six feet four inches tall, with wavy blond hair that framed a heavily boned, perfectly formed face. He was so broad, Trudy thought at first glance, that certainly there were two of him. His smile was warm and winning, and in that one sentence of greeting, Trudy detected a deep Southern drawl that reminded her of folks back in West Virginia and Kentucky.

"Hello there, Jocko," Stevens answered pleasantly. "Glad to

see you. Of course we won't monopolize Miss Coles. Trudy Coles, this is Jocko Rachubinski, Hollywood's new golden boy."

"Howdy, ma'am," Jocko virtually shouted. "How about a dance?"

"Thank you, if Mr. Stevens doesn't mind."

"Of course not," Stevens answered diplomatically, and she was off to the dance floor.

After a few whirls about the floor, Jocko looked down and said, "I knew we two Polocks would hit it off just great!"

"You knew?" Trudy asked in surprise.

"Ma'am, you gotta be one to know one!"

Jocko Rachubinski, all-American fullback at the University of Alabama, had come to Hollywood three years before as a stunt man. His dynamic good looks made him an obvious candidate for romantic leads, so he was snatched up by Fox to join their studio cadre of young leading men. Everyone forecast a brilliant Hollywood career for Jocko, though it was rumored that he had better go easy on the elbow bending and carousing. Fox was urging him to drop the "Rachubinski" in favor of "Raines" but Jocko remained adamant. "Once a Polock, always a Polock," was his credo.

The electric attraction between these two handsome human beings was immediate. Despite his size, Jocko was featherlight on his feet and an excellent dancer, as was Trudy. Rob had never liked dancing; whenever they partied it was a cause of frustration for her that she could not join their friends on the dance floor. Jocko suffered from none of Rob's inner bitterness. His own father had deserted the family when he and his siblings were very young. Having worked his way through high school, he had won an athletic scholarship to college and his greatness on the gridiron won the loyal support of affluent alumni, who peppered him with expensive gifts, ignoring the requirements of amateur sports edicts. He had never really known want or experienced defeat. Here in Hollywood, he had more money and more beautiful women than he knew had existed back in Alabama. It was only natural for him to be joyous, and he radiated that exaltation wherever he went.

Urged on by Jocko, and eager to shake the depressing experience of her lonesome homecoming, Trudy drank more champagne than she ever had in one night. Pleasantly tipsy and taken with Jocko's company, she was soon unashamedly hugging and kissing him on the dance floor. Richie Stevens, feeling responsible for her, became uneasy as he watched Trudy veer increasingly out of control while Parsons took notes. When Jocko left Trudy temporarily to use the men's room, Richie cornered her as she was heading back to the bar for a refill.

"Trudy," he said softly, "don't you think you had better take it easy with the grape?"

"Champagne?" She laughed. "Why it's only bitter ginger ale. Jocko says the more you drink the less it gets in your way."

"Make that 'the less it gets in his way.' You know Parsons has been watching you all evening. So has Manny Silverstein. None of us wants you to make a fool of yourself."

The champagne was getting to Trudy now and she was angered by the advice. It was all the more upsetting coming from the man she really loved and who apparently had little desire for her. She struck back viciously.

"What's the matter, can't I have some fun, too? I've been working like a slave for six months to make your damn picture a big winner. What am I, a piece of meat? You're a user like the rest of them, Richie. Oh, I know. Mr. Richie Stevens, the big artistic director who believes in me. I've had a bellyfull of you and your advice. You don't really care for me, do you? I'm a meal ticket. You may be a little smoother than Silverstein. But you ride us all like horses, too. Now leave me alone. I want to have fun tonight!"

"Having problems, little lady?" It was Jocko back from the rest room.

"None at all," Trudy replied, fire in her eyes. "Mr. Stevens is just leaving."

Richie looked at them both, his face a mask of unhappiness. Then, slowly, he took his leave, not desiring to make a scene.

After a touch-up in the rest room, Trudy joined Jocko outside the hotel, where the beautiful people were busily involved in dropping off or claiming their cars. It was a typically glorious California night and the cool evening breezes had chased the morning's smog together with the afternoon's oppressive heat into another galaxy. Trudy breathed in deeply, savoring the heady perfume of gardenia plants rimming the driveway. This was the time to be young, the time to be fetching, the time to be joyous. Despite her resistance, Trudy felt her mood darkening as the cool air brought somber thoughts of a world that was not quite as filled with mirth as the script would have indicated.

For one, her angry words to Richie Stevens had left her feeling sad and petty. Instinctively, she felt that she could never escape the grip he held on her emotions. And he really had not deserved the chastisement she had dealt him. On reflection, she realized that it was Rob she really resented for deserting her in this hour of need. Desertion. It was a strange knife that cut both ways. Had she not, in a sense, deserted him by following the long, dreary hours of filming *Loving Sisters* with an extended publicity jaunt? He should never have flaunted his infidelity by appearing in public with some floozie. But she should have known him by now; leaving him dangling all of these long weeks was a gamble she took with open eyes.

Guilt was surging now, threatening to engulf her and destroy the evening. For a moment she considered changing her mind, returning to the party, and removing herself from the attractive nuisance known as Jocko Rachubinski.

"What's the matter, little lady, cat got your tongue?" It was Jocko, smiling down on her with that incredibly magnetic charm that could have melted fields of glaciers.

"Maybe. Maybe not."

"Not sure I get your drift."

"Not sure I do. It's just that what seemed like such a great idea five minutes ago seems to be souring."

"That's the trouble. You can't think too much about having fun. You just up and have it. Know what I mean? Soon as you try to dissect it like a frog on a lab table it loses its kick. I had my fill of that party. So did you. Come on over to my place and we'll live a little."

"It's that easy, is it?"

"You're damn right it is. Come on. I'll get us a cab."

Trudy hesitated. Strains of a pop song—*"This is my first affair, so please be kind"*—echoed in the chambers of her conscience. Well, hell, maybe Jocko was right. Rob was off somewhere with some little tart having a blast. Maybe this was her turn. Maybe once he learned that she was her own woman he'd respect her more.

"I'll come. Give me your address. But I want to leave alone."

They left in separate cabs, Trudy none too eager to advertise what she was about to do.

Jocko lived in a small ranch house in Bel Air, just north and west of Beverly Hills. He was waiting when she arrived. The lights were low, the hi-fi playing soft romantic tunes, the magic of the evening in complete control. They started dancing together closely, soon were aroused, and, as if by mutual consent, headed for his bedroom. They literally pulled their clothes from their bodies, so eager were they to make love. Soon, two healthy young animals, they were twisting and turning on the bed, making love for hours on end. Trudy suddenly realized that she had not had sex for almost two months and realized now how much she had missed it. Even her lovemaking with Rob in the months preceding the business-enforced hiatus had been only mildly satisfying. This was the tempestuous excitement she had craved. Only in her brief meetings with Mulch Roberts—and that seemed like centuries ago—had she enjoyed such sexual gratification. Jocko Rachubinski was, she decided, all-American in more fields than one. He was, for her, the lover par excellence. She was determined to make the experience as moving for him as it was for her.

"Polocks screw the best!" he murmured as he recovered from his fourth orgasm. The sun was up when he came for the seventh time.

Although she had difficulty explaining it to herself, Trudy felt not the slightest apprehension about returning home and facing a possibly bitter reaction from Rob. He had abandoned her in her hour of need, flaunted his lack of fidelity to their marriage, and now would have to face the consequences. She rose, showered, enjoyed a cup of coffee, then asked Jocko to summon a cab, rejecting his offer to drive her home. She reveled in the glory of the morning as the taxi, heading down toward Sunset Boulevard, circled above the fog that normally engulfed the city before noon. It was clear, cool, and beautiful. Her body felt absolutely splendid after the stimulation of the preceding hours. Even the champagne had worn off, without the hint of a hangover. She did not relish what lay ahead in her relationship with her husband, but at least there was a new lover on the horizon to bolster her spirits.

The street was quiet as the cab approached her address. As she paid the driver, she became aware that a strange vehicle was parked in the driveway, up toward the entrance to the home. She stepped from the cab, puzzled, and saw a police officer step from the parked car and move down the driveway to meet her.

"Mrs. Wenger?" he questioned hesitantly.

"Yes, I'm Mrs. Wenger," she answered with trepidation.

"I'm afraid I have some bad news for you."

"Yes?"

"There has been a terrible automobile accident. Your husband has been killed. He didn't suffer. He died instantly."

Trudy Coles, not yet nineteen, was a rich widow. But there would be the guilt to deal with for years to come.

CHAPTER 10

1949–1952

The four-week vacation that Continental had promised Trudy stretched into four months. Then six. Then eight. At first there was the funeral and usual period of mourning. Trudy didn't really miss Rob, yet there was the nagging feeling of guilt reminding her that she had been in bed enjoying herself with Jocko Rachubinski while her husband's broken and burned body was lying on the San Diego Freeway. His fiery death had been as predictable as her night with Jocko and, in a sense, equally justifiable. But psychological trauma is not a rational force and Trudy linked the two happenings in her subconscious. Perhaps if she had been with him more frequently, perhaps if she had been more attentive, then perhaps he would not have gone out on the town seeking to bury his pain in wild escapades.

Her in-laws were bitter and barely communicated with her while funeral arrangements were being made, or later at the funeral itself. They realized that their son had been no angel, of course, but they blamed Trudy for not bringing more love into his life and giving him greater incentive to accomplish something. Word of her carrying on with Jocko had reached them, though they were not aware that the police had had to wait four hours to inform her of the death. They also resented the fact that she was inheriting a home and more than a million dollars in assets after so brief and unsuccessful a marriage. They were as frustrated in their grief as they had been during Rob's lifetime.

Trudy was a handy scapegoat on whom to deposit their own guilt as parents who had failed.

Jocko, out of respect, waited several weeks before calling her, though he did send a huge bouquet of roses to the funeral. She had her maid inform him that she could not speak to him at the moment and would call back in time.

Richie Stevens paid her a sympathy call and there was a strange gulf between them. Nothing was said about her actions at the party, including the verbal attack prompted by his attempt to restrain her that night. She realized that she had few friends and no other supporters on the professional front besides Richie. Yet, there was definitely a schism between them, one that would have to be forded in years to come. She told him quite frankly that she was in no condition to face a new feature at the time. He advised rest and a vacation trip that would get her away from the Hollywood scene. She agreed to consider it. As he left, he took her hand, and gazing into her emerald-colored eyes, he said, "Trudy, you've had a rough setback, but you're young and sorrow passes. There is a brilliant career in motion pictures in front of you, if you want it. It'll take lots of work. It gets harder as you climb the ladder, not easier. But you can make it, if you want to."

"Right now I don't know what I want. I'm tired. I'm sad. I just want peace and quiet for a while. Then we'll see. Thank you for coming to see me, Mr. Stevens."

"Richie," he corrected.

"Today, 'Mr. Stevens' feels better," she answered simply, showing him politely to the door.

Several weeks later she was summoned to visit Manny Silverstein. It took a great effort to visit the studios, but she could think of no good reason to refuse. The meeting, as was Silverstein's custom, was arranged for the late afternoon when most other employees had gone home.

Obie was there, of course, and for the first and only time greeted her with quiet respect. "Sorry to hear about your loss, Trudy."

"Thank you."

Silverstein was strangely, uncharacteristically reserved when he greeted her. It was hard to look at Trudy without thinking about sex, despite the fact that she was wearing a simple, loose-fitting black dress. But on this occasion, even Manny, to whom most women were objects to be used and enjoyed, strove to treat her sensitively.

For Trudy, it was still difficult to look at Manny Silverstein without thinking about her father. They were so different, and yet, there it was, a comparison she couldn't block out no matter how she tried. Strange, she had been thinking more and more about Cass in recent weeks. She guessed that she would never get over the shock of his rejecting her in favor of Aggie. She thought back to the day she had actually gotten up enough nerve to voice her objections. It had been early one morning when the older kids were off to school and she was too tired to join them. Cass, still hungover from a night of carousing with Aggie, had been unable to make it to the mines.

"If you stopped seeing that woman maybe you'd stay sober."

"Maybe I'd drink more. Not much fun around this house, I can tell you."

She looked at him for a long time before replying, their eyes challenging each other to speak what they really felt.

"Fun? How much fun do I have? I can't even get a good night's rest when you bring her home and I gotta sleep with the kids."

He didn't answer. There was no question she hated Aggie, but she was afraid to probe for the real cause of her animosity. By mutual consent, the conversation ended.

"So, Trudy, how are you coming along?"

The question snapped her back to present realities. "Pretty good, Mr. Silverstein. It was quite a shock, you know."

"Oh, I'm sure it was. Life's like that, kid, take it from me. You're riding high, everything is coming your way, and all of a sudden you hit a bump and there's *tzuris* all around you. That means 'trouble,'" he explained.

"Yes, I know. He was so young. It's a pity he couldn't have lived to enjoy all the wonderful things he already had."

"And you among them," Silverstein added somewhat insincerely, remembering Trudy's actions at the party the night of the tragedy.

"Perhaps," was the only reply Trudy could muster.

Tillie was in New York and Silverstein asked if she would like to have dinner with him before returning home. She looked at him quizzically, trying to determine if this was an appropriate invitation from a concerned boss or merely Silverstein playing his usual role of the male animal wishing to take advantage of a sexual opportunity. But he had anticipated her thoughts.

"No strings attached. Just a quiet dinner at the Brown Derby."

Later, she was glad she had accepted, for never before, and never again, was she to feel so close to Silverstein and as understanding of his problems and the pressures he was subject to. He explained that even though *Loving Sisters* was bound to make Continental a lot of money, the industry as a whole was facing treacherous times. Television, that little black box in the living room that everyone had scoffed at, was now becoming a terrible threat. On Tuesday nights, even the finest restaurants in Los Angeles were deserted. Everyone was home watching Uncle Miltie on the "Texaco Star Theater." Fewer and fewer features were being made than had been made five years before. The ruling last year that movie studios had to rid themselves of all of their exhibition chains was another bitter pill that was rocking the whole industry. No big business, he explained, could survive without a constant flow of borrowed capital. Now, the money was harder and harder to come by. All of the big studio heads were being pressured to produce profits or resign. Profits in the last two years alone had dropped by thirty-five million dollars and were still descending. With TV growing rapidly, the future was dark indeed. What's more, the industry had taken an "ostrich head in the sand" attitude about television. Any movie studio that dared to sell the networks programming was deemed a traitor and was subject to boycott from exhibitors.

"That doesn't make any sense to me," Trudy interjected.

"Of course it doesn't," he said, "but these schmucks have been rich so long it has softened their brains. They see television as an enemy. I think it can save our asses. The more people rely on moving pictures for entertainment, the stronger our hand. You watch and see," he said with a friendly pat on her knee. "Now, let's talk about you. When are you coming back to work?"

"Not for some time, Manny. I need time to rest and think."

"Rest, maybe, but not think. What's there to think about? You're an actress. Actresses act. It's that simple. You don't act, you go stale. Worse, the public forgets about you. Before you know it, it's Trudy who? *Loving Sisters* is your start. Now, you gotta capitalize on it and move ahead. Pretty soon, they'll forget all about Marjorie Hansell and think only of Trudy Coles. You lay off long enough and you'll be 'that girl who played Marjorie Hansell's kid sister.' Take my advice. Besides, work is the best way to bury troubles. It's the best forgetting medicine there is. That's one reason I wanted to talk to you.

"I got a super-duper Western that's meant for the whole country. It's not the usual cowboys and Indians crap. It's got the perfect part for you. A wife of a sheriff who is killed takes over the job to finish his work and wipe out the baddies who knocked him off. You'll be great in it. How about it?"

"Manny, please. I'm not ready. Give me another few weeks."

"Okay. I got another idea. Tillie and I own an oceanfront apartment in Acapulco. No one uses it half the time. You take a friend, go down there for a month and get your head together. No cost. All on me. How about it?"

"That's a very attractive offer. Sure Tillie won't mind?"

"She'll be happy. She hates to waste money. When the apartment sits empty, Tillie feels she's wasting dough. Use it, *gezunderhait!* That means, use it in good health.

"Incidentally, I want you to know that I'm doubling your salary. I've made a lot of money with you and I want you to make more, too. I know you don't need it but that's not the point. What's fair is fair and fifteen thousand a year is a steal."

"I appreciate that, Manny."

"I only got one request. Don't tell that little putz, Dawson, about the raise. No reason I should double his two percent."

"I haven't seen or heard from him since the day I signed my contract. And I don't expect to."

He drove her home and left the car to see her to her door. Trudy hoped that his motive was politeness, nothing more. He paused, having helped her open the door with her key, looked at her questioningly, and then broke into a paternal smile.

"Just like I said before," he said. "No strings attached. Just a plain dinner with two friends. You got no worries with old Manny. I ain't some young stud in heat."

Trudy smiled. "I'm glad, Manny. It wouldn't be right for you or for me. It's nice for me to know that you're such a good friend."

Three days later, while she was still considering Silverstein's offer to use the apartment in Acapulco, she received another call from Jocko Rachubinski. This time she took the call. He invited her to have dinner with him that night at one of his favorite hangouts, the Cock 'n' Bull. After hesitating, she accepted. He offered to pick her up but she preferred meeting him at the restaurant. Somehow, she really couldn't explain why, she wasn't ready to have him that close to the house she and Rob Wenger had shared. It was irrational, certainly, but it was real to her.

He waited for her at the bar. She spotted him as soon as she entered the room, towering handsomely above all of the other customers and blasting away with his loud, booming baritone. When Jocko Rachubinski was in a room, everyone within hearing distance knew it. His was a command personality: vocally and physically he took charge of every situation. He polished off his drink and left the bar to greet her at the door.

"Trudy. You're even more beautiful than I remembered!"

Everyone in the room turned and had to agree. By now, almost everyone in Hollywood knew about Trudy Coles. She wondered if they would condemn her for having a festive dinner so soon after her husband's death. She still wore basic black, which only served to accentuate her beauty. Her own height was a good match for Jocko's. They were a striking, undeniably attractive duo. He suggested that they have a drink at the bar while waiting for their table.

It seemed like decades had passed since they had spent that wild night together. So much had changed and yet, as the French might say, the more things changed the more they stayed the same. Jocko was an incredibly attractive man and she felt the electricity he generated from across the room. Before long, she felt herself edging toward him, wanting the body contact it was so difficult for her to resist.

And yet, there was something eternally youthful about him that was, for her, a turnoff in other men. Sometimes she wondered if she would ever emerge from the web of paternal longing. She never consciously thought about her father. Yet, his influence seemed to hover about her whenever she was sexually aroused. Was this normal? she wondered. One day she would have to discuss the problem with someone more knowledgeable than she. All of the "in" people were now visiting one of the new class of psychiatrists who were springing up along Bedford Drive in Beverly Hills. One day, if she had the courage, she'd make the trip to "headshrinker's row" and seek solace in professional counseling. For the moment, she'd settle for doubt in the arms of Jocko Rachubinski.

As an actress, Trudy was accustomed to being stared at wherever she went. Far from resenting the attention, she enjoyed it. Still, when the headwaiter informed them that their table was ready, she felt overly self-conscious as many eyes followed them while they made their way from the bar to the dining area. She almost wished the evening were ending, for she was finding difficulty in finding the right words.

"So how's it going, Trudy?" he asked for the third time.

"Sometimes good. Sometimes not so good. With Rob and work both out of my life, there's a lot of empty time to kill."

"I would have called sooner, but—"

"I understand," she said, interrupting what sounded like an unnecessary apology. "I wasn't ready to see anybody yet."

"Trudy, I've got to say this and it's tough to say."

"Say what you want, Jocko. I can handle it."

"Well . . . well, it's just that I hope that what happened doesn't rub off on us. On our relationship, if you get my drift."

"Of course, I understand. But it's got to in a way."

"Why does it 'got to'?"

"We were in bed making love while my husband was lying dead on the freeway. I'm not saying that our marriage was ideal—far from it. If it had been, we'd have been together that night and I probably never would have met you or seen your home. But I'm human. I have feelings, feelings of guilt that just won't go away that easy."

"I understand," was his weak rejoinder.

They said very little to each other after that for, in reality, there was little more to say. The evening ended quietly. Jocko saw her home and made no effort to gain entrance. They both realized that Trudy was not ready for romance.

Patience was a Rachubinski virtue. He courted Trudy as slowly as a high school senior approaching the beauteous cheerleader he longed to escort to the senior prom. They dined together many times, took long rides into the California hills, engaged in discussions of their respective careers, and scrupulously avoided any discussion of the fateful night on which they first had met. Trudy gained more and more respect for this big hunk of masculinity, who on first meeting she had classified as little more than a handsome, macho gigolo. He was really an intelligent, sensitive creature, and she was more than grateful for his understanding of her own grief and jumbled emotions.

It was inevitable that the sexual attraction between them could not be bottled up forever. One night, as might have been predicted, he drove her to his home for the proverbial nightcap.

There was the usual, romantic musical accompaniment as one drink grew to three and at long last their inhibitions were banished in a passionate embrace.

"It's time now," he whispered, leading her toward the bedroom.

"No, Jocko. I'm really not ready for this."

"It's been months. He's dead now. We're full of life. How can we deny that fact forever?"

"Not forever. I'm just not ready."

He refused to take no for an answer. Soon, despite her objections, they were entwined in a naked embrace. He used every technique he knew to arouse her. But it was a futile effort. Trudy knew her body and the strong voice of her conscience. He tried again but it was to no avail.

"Please stop, Jocko. It's no good. I told you that."

"I guess I was fooling myself," he said deprecatingly. "I thought that we really meant something to each other. Obviously, we don't."

She sat up angrily and started to dress. "That's crap and you know it. Stop feeling sorry for yourself. I'm tired of that little-boy act. The lady doesn't want to yet. That's all there is to it. Now let's have some coffee before you take me home."

He obeyed. Gradually, they rewarmed to each other and the night ended pleasantly.

As she kissed him good night at her door, she smiled encouragingly. "My pain won't last forever. You'll see."

Jocko's patience paid off several nights later. This time it was Trudy who invited him into her home. Their coupling was warm and tender, not as madly uninhibited as on their first mating. But mature and warm and ever so moving. Their affection seemed to mount with every new meeting. They saw each other more and more frequently and on those rare occasions when Jocko was in demand at the studio, she realized how much she had come to depend on his love. He laughed when she complained that she resented their separations.

"Hell, honey," he joshed, "didn't your ole Polish mammy ever tell you that absence makes the heart grow fonder? I ain't goin' nowhere. Just gotta make a few bucks now and then, you know?"

"I'm the rich widow Wenger," she answered. "What's the use of having a lot of money if you can't share it with someone you love?"

And she meant it. She bought him fabulous gifts—a diamond watch, solid gold cuff links, crystal brandy snifters with matching decanter, alligator belts and shoes, and more and more. All he did was admire an item and it was his the next time he saw her.

"Hey, lady," he protested, "I'm a wage earner, too. Don't make me a kept man! But I'll love you for it."

He did. In more ways than one. Why should he deny her the pleasure of buying him gifts, he reasoned, when it seemed to bring Trudy so much pleasure? He explained it all to one of the starlets he dated on a few of the nights when he felt a change was needed from Trudy's constant companionship. He never really lied to Trudy about seeing other women. He just was certain not to volunteer the information. Whether or not she would object, he wasn't certain. Experience had taught him, however, that one of the subjects a man of the world did not discuss with a woman was his ongoing relationships with other women. That was not the way to make points.

At times, Trudy considered what her own reactions would be if she ever learned that Jocko was seeing other lovers. She told herself that she really would not care. Her relationship with Jocko was fun at a time when she needed some joy to help her glide over the ugliness and pain she had just experienced. So, in effect, she was using Jocko for her own purposes. Still, she was human; jealousy was as natural to her as it was to all. She wouldn't make the same mistake with Jocko that she made with Rob when she sensed competition. She would strike out offensively and claim him for her own when the time was ripe.

The opportunity arose sooner than she had imagined. At the beauty salon one day she was buried under a thick mud-pack and therefore incognito when a bitchy clerk for one of the literary agents sat down in the next chair. Before she could be cautioned, she let loose with a stream of gossip involving Jocko Rachubinski's affair with the wife of her boss's attorney.

"Here the old girl has been practically supporting him for two years and now she's learned that he's been seeing that Coles broad!"

There was a sudden hushed silence as the hairdresser madly signaled toward the unidentified customer sitting nearby.

Trudy decided not to discuss the matter with Jocko when they dined that night. It was information she could use without tipping her hand. The best plan, she judged, was to get him away for a while where she would have him to herself. That afternoon, before even meeting Jocko, she called Manny Silverstein.

"Manny, is that offer for the apartment in Acapulco still on? I'm ready to use it now. I could really go for a month in the sun."

"Great! Tillie and I are heading for New York. Then after two weeks of meetings with those *fecockta* bankers, we're heading for Nassau and a long vacation ourselves. Obie will make all the arrangements. Just live it up and don't even think about Manny Silverstein or Continental."

She broke the news to Jocko over dessert.

"We're going away for a month to Mexico. Tell your agent you need some rest. When we get back, I think you could use a new agent anyhow. If he gets mad, tell him to go fly a kite."

"Hey, that's kinda sudden. I got to have a few days to think it over."

"Like hell you do, Polock. In a few days you'll be sunning that beautiful ass of yours on the beaches of Acapulco. You say no to me and I take Manny Silverstein. It's his apartment anyhow."

"You do that and I grab Tillie. Looks to me as if she could use a good Polish lay."

"I'm betting on her. Pack your bag. We leave tomorrow evening at six. I've already made the reservations."

The phone rang the next morning as Trudy began her packing. Despite the interruption, she was delighted to hear from Penny O'Neill, from whom she hadn't heard in many months.

"Penny! How's my old rommate? Has someone replaced me yet?"

"I really don't know. I'm not in the apartment anymore."

"How come?" But Trudy could almost guess the answer.

"You want it long or you want it short?" Penny asked mechanically.

"Tell it like it is."

"Well, it started when this freshnik on the lot kept putting his hands all over me. I warned him three times but he wouldn't listen. So finally, I complained to Lee. The kid was only an assistant grip but his uncle was a big shot with the union. A big fight followed when Lee fired him. Luckily, Lee won out and the front office supported him. But that was just the beginning."

"What happened?"

"The kid knew about Lee and me so he arranged to call Rhoda, Lee's wife. There was a big scene and she threatened to divorce him and take the kids unless he severed all ties with you know who. Poor Lee really had no choice. We stopped seeing each other with the usual bullshit tears and regrets. Two months later, my contract expired and wasn't renewed. I got a polite notice to vacate the apartment."

"Where are you living?"

"Oh, I'm okay. I'm sharing a flat with Hildy Nolan. You remember her? From special effects?"

"Yes. Nice girl. Are you okay with dough?"

"Yeah, fine. That's not why I called. I just wanted you to know where I was in case you needed me. I'm back at my old racket, working at Bullock's. Men's furnishings, of all departments!"

"You'll be back in the business before you know it."

"No chance. Who the hell wants a thirty-three-year-old never-was whose tits are beginning to sag?"

"Stop putting yourself down. You're a beauty and you know it. Listen, I'm off for a few weeks' vacation in Mexico. We got to get together soon as I get back."

"Sure thing. Here's my new address and phone number. . . ."

Their apartment in Acapulco was elegant and situated with a clear view of the sea. They took many of their meals in informal dress on the outdoor terrace. Silverstein, not a piker when it came to luxurious living, had arranged for a chef and a maid to cater to their every whim. The bar was stocked with champagne and the finest liquors; the refrigerator was overflowing with delicacies. Jocko confided that he was sure he had died and awakened in heaven.

"And the angel they assigned to me is one sexy lady, let me tell you!"

Trudy, still smarting from the news she had learned at the beauty salon, thought of discussing the matter with Jocko one night while they were out on the town. They had been dancing under the moonlight to the tunes of one of the great Latin bands that were in vogue that year. The mambo was great fun when you knew how to dance without counting audibly, as so many Latins from Manhattan were wont to do. Jocko had just mentioned that he hoped the vacation would never end.

"How about the lawyer's wife? She'll miss you?" she asked more playfully than condemningly.

"Little pitchers have big ears," he replied.

"Oh, on the contrary. The news was practically screamed in my ears. They didn't have to be big to catch it at all."

They both had been drinking a bit more than usual and one could feel the tension rise as they somewhat sullenly returned to their table.

That night, for the first time since they had arrived in Mexico, they slept in separate beds. Trudy blamed a convenient headache; Jocko made no effort to dissuade her. She slept late, awakening to find the apartment deserted. Jocko was gone until noon, arriving with the explanation that he had been "visiting old friends." Since this was his first visit to Acapulco, it was rather an unlikely alibi. Trudy briefly considered pressing him on the point but decided to let it pass. They spent the rest of the day sitting on the terrace lapping up more sunshine. Jocko busied himself with a mystery novel and made little effort at conversation. Trudy suffered in silence, hoping that what she was experiencing would not ripen into a serious rift.

They dined out again that evening, but Jocko remained sulky, making little effort to bridge the chasm between them.

"We're really getting on each other's nerves, eh, Jocko?"

"Speak for yourself."

"Speak to myself might be more like it."

"You seem to have little trouble expressing yourself when something annoys you."

"And you seem to have pretty thin skin for that big, blond Polock act you like to play."

"It's not a question of the thickness of my skin."

"What is it then, Jocko?"

"It's the thickness of the chain you want to wrap around me."

"Oh, I see. I'm keeping you captive. Is that it?"

"Not yet. But I think you'd like to. And I like my freedom. So don't get any ideas. I'm not the marrying kind."

"You have one hell of a nerve! I've never even referred to marriage in all the months you've been seeing me. The truth is I'm not the marrying kind, either, if you know what I mean. And if I was—"

"If I *were,*" he said, nastily.

"Yes, Jocko, I know you went to college. I've read all those clippings about Jocko Rachubinski, the big-time all-American lover. What I was saying before you interrupted me was that if

I were going to get married, I don't even think you'd be a candidate. You're great as a stud, but next time, if there is a next time, I might just look for something more."

"Good. That's a big relief to me."

They finished their dinner in silence. After a while, Trudy began to regret that she had been so outspoken. Perhaps it had been tactless of her to repeat the beauty parlor gossip. It was also true that from their very first date, Jocko had made it quite plain that he was not interested in permanent alliances at this time in his life. He offered her fun, fun, fun. Nothing more. She decided that nothing was to be gained by starting a feud on this much-needed vacation. Right or wrong, she was determined to enjoy it. Just as she was reaching for the right word to say, she was startled by a seductive, feminine voice.

"Well, Jocko, what a coincidence!"

Trudy looked up to see a glamorous, dark-complexioned lady in her mid-forties smiling down on both of them. Jocko said nothing. He merely smiled sheepishly and pretended to be surprised.

"What's the matter, big boy, at a loss for words?"

Jocko laughed. He rose somewhat clumsily and said, "Hi, Gerta. What a surprise."

"I'm full of them, don't you remember?"

"I seem to. Trudy, this is Gerta Clurman. Trudy Coles."

"Charmed. Jocko has told me a lot about you, Miss Coles."

"I have a feeling I know something about you too," Trudy answered bitchily.

"Oh, so that's how it's going to be. What a pity. Jocko, don't just stand there with your teeth in your mouth. Ask me to dance or to sit down or to do something, for Christ's sake! Come, they're playing a heavenly mambo, and you must push me around that dance floor."

She took his hand and led him away from the table. Jocko made little effort to resist. Trudy, red with anger, watched for a few moments as Jocko and Greta bounced around the floor like Astaire and Rogers. It was an annoyingly long set and Jocko made no effort to return to the table prematurely. Instead, he laughed aloud and never even glanced back at where he had deserted Trudy. When the set ended, he and Gerta headed for the veranda bar that was crowding up with happy, beautiful people who were just starting the night's revelry.

Ashamed, angered, humiliated, Trudy decided that Jocko had left her little alternative but to get up and leave. Tears filling her eyes, she jumped up from the table, wrapped her shawl around her lovely shoulders, and headed for the door. She dashed up the steps, avoiding the eyes of the maître d'. Fortunately, there was a cab parked just across the street. Hailing the driver, she raced across to meet him. She never even saw the motorbike that at that moment came whirling around the corner. The bike driver was so startled that he could not react in time to avoid hitting her. There was a sickening thud as the speeding vehicle hit her, lifting her completely off her feet and tossing her body high in the air. She landed on her back in the center of the road, just yards from where the driver and motorcycle crashed into a car parked by the curb.

She lay there unconscious, blood pouring from a scalp wound as the taxi driver rushed to her aid. The driver of the ruined bike scrambled to his feet, pulled the damaged two-wheeler to an upright position, and, frightened beyond his wits, sped away. No expert at first aid, the driver lifted Trudy from the road and somehow dumped her into the back of his cab. He raced to the nearest hospital.

Trudy lay unconscious for twenty minutes, finally regaining her senses as she groaned from the pain. She opened her eyes to see a whole squadron of strange faces peering down at her. They were all garbed in white and for an insane moment she reasoned that she had died and was being inducted into some sort of angelic society. The pain brought her back to reality and she understood that they were doctors and nurses who were frantically tending to her medical needs. Although her reputation as an actress had not yet reached international status, by strange coincidence one of the doctors had seen *Loving Sisters* during a recent visit to Los Angeles and recognized Trudy immediately.

"Can you hear me, Miss Coles?" he whispered.

"Yes. I can hear. Where am I?"

"Bella Vista Hospital. The emergency ward. You've had a bad accident."

Trudy felt the needle in her arm, then happily sensed herself slipping into sedative-assisted Nirvana.

She awoke ten hours later, her leg in traction and pain radiating from every muscle. As her father would have said after one of his frequent Saturday-night barroom brawls, even her hair hurt. Her mind drifted back to the snowy mornings in West Virginia, when, after helping her mother with the breakfast dishes, she would plod through the snow on her way to school. The world seemed quiet then, draped in white. Here, too, everything was white, cool white, and the room was vacuum quiet.

The list of Trudy's fractures read like a freshman medical school manual in anatomy. She had compound fractures of the right leg and arm, three broken ribs, a punctured lung, and assorted cuts and abrasions. It was obvious to all that she was in for a long, long convalescence. A great deal of physiotherapy would be needed before she learned to use crutches, feed herself with one hand, slip into her clothes without assistance and finally recover normal use of both arms and legs. She listened sadly as this was carefully explained by Dr. Santos Samboro, the chief resident in surgery, who had recognized her from her last film.

"It will be very painful, I fear, Miss Coles. But time will have its cure and you will walk again just as you did before the accident. I'm happy to say that all of the swelling will go down, those blackened eyes will get better, and your lovely face will be as beautiful as ever."

"Thank you, Doctor," Trudy mumbled, not really feeling much gratitude at all as she contemplated the long months of confinement.

"Is it your wish to go back to the States? I think it's safe to say that you can be transferred after a one-week stay here."

"Can I go to my home?"

"Not directly, I'm afraid. You'll need at least one month in a Los Angeles hospital. Then perhaps you can be treated at home."

On the third day after her talk with Dr. Samboro, Trudy received her first visit from Jocko Rachubinski. It wasn't an easy meeting for either one of them. Jocko had rushed to the hospital the night Trudy was admitted, but she was too injured to have visitors. He left and sent her the largest bouquet he could find. Unfortunately, because of the heavy input of oxygen in the recovery room, floral bouquets were forbidden, and the flowers were distributed on three different wards before Trudy ever returned to her own private room. A nurse had informed her of this fact while she was still under the influence of sedatives, so she didn't remember.

"Trudy, I can't begin to tell you how sorry I am," he began lamely.

"Don't bother," was her reply, dipped in anger.

"I know you're mad. I don't blame you. But I never wanted you to get hurt. You can't blame me for that."

"There are worse hurts than being hit by a motorcycle."

"I didn't mean for you to get hurt either way."

"This isn't the time or the place to discuss that. I think you had better go. I'm tired and want to sleep."

He returned two days later, getting the same frigid reception. He tried to cheer her up by bringing headlines from the Los Angeles papers relating to her accident. She remained bitterly hostile.

"Mr. Silverstein once told me that the Los Angeles papers would write headlines about dog shit if they thought it would sell papers. I'm not impressed."

"Well, Silverstein is sure an authority on shit. He dishes out enough of it from that toilet of his he calls a studio. If you'll pardon the comparison."

"I think you'd better go now," Trudy said, glowering.

On his fourth visit, they reached somewhat of a truce. Trudy was not exactly friendly, but she accepted his offer to supervise her return to California. She really could not make it without assistance, and there seemed no point in summoning help from Los Angeles. Jocko made all of the necessary arrangements. On the eighth day of confinement, she was released from the hospital and taxied on a stretcher to the airport. There she was transferred to a charter flight to Los Angeles. Jocko had shamed Continental into picking up the tab for the emergency flight. An ambulance met them at the airport, and, screaming its way through heavy traffic, deposited her at Cedars of Lebanon Hospital, where physicians, alerted by the studio, were awaiting her arrival. Jocko bid her an embarrassed farewell once she was admitted. He knew and she knew that they would never see each other socially again.

Contrary to the Mexican doctor's prediction, she spent the next three months in the hospital and her next six months at home. It took that long for all of her bones to mend and her scars to fade. But the pain in her broken limbs would stay with her for years, reminding her on every damp day of being jilted in a Mexican restaurant by a man who had sworn his undying love through bursts of ecstatic passion.

The physical pain was severe at times but in no way a match

for the emotional stress. The long hours alone, striving to make some sense out of the sudden, destructive turn of events, was the worst part of it.

"Why?" she kept asking herself. "Why me?"

She had never been religious, or superstitious, yet now there was the unmistakable feeling that she must have, in some unknown way, contributed to her own ill luck. She began to examine and re-examine her young life. She rethought the relationship with her father. Had she been wrong to join him in bed? But she had not been the aggressor; he had taken her. And yet he *hadn't* taken her. He, her own father, the man who had challenged God's law and bedded down his own flesh and blood, he had finally rejected her. And for whom? For a worthless woman like Aggie Stephanik! Was there something about her that turned off her own father?

With Rob Wenger she had been less successful still. She, the brightest and most beautiful young starlet to hit the Hollywood scene in years, rejected by her own husband. Why, he had even ignored her and been unfaithful during their ill-fated honeymoon! Even when she had tried her best at a reconciliation she was able to establish emotional contact only in a limited and impermanent way. In the end, he virtually took his own life rather than spend the evening in her company. Why? Was she not being punished for wrongs unnamed perhaps, but still of her own doing?

She cried herself to sleep, falling into a deep dream that carried her back to her childhood. She saw her mother again, struggling to keep the family together in the face of her father's constant, chronic alcoholism.

As her dream took shape it hammered away at a familiar theme. She was the target of sexual pursuits by men who belittled her, raped her, scorned her. And there were always those who witnessed her distress but refused to help, calling her wanton and depraved. Her primary censor was her own mother.

"He was mine and you took him!"

"No. Not true," Trudy moaned piteously.

"In your heart, you know you wanted him. You betrayed me!"

She awoke, tearful, feverish, emotionally shattered.

The orthopedic staff at the hospital was puzzled. Her bones seemed healed; her spirit broken. She seemed to lack the desire for complete recovery.

"You simply must get some exercise, Miss Coles. Otherwise, your muscles will lose their strength. You might find yourself, I hate to say it, a cripple for life." It was Dr. Hans Braunstein, chief of orthopedics, who had taken a special interest in her case.

"Not to worry. I'll be okay in time."

"But we do worry about you, Miss Coles. Frankly your recovery is way behind schedule. You have to try, too. You must get up and walk around these corridors for an hour every day."

"It hurts, Doctor. And I'm still weak."

"I'm afraid you'll get weaker if you don't move around. Now I'm ordering a new medicine, sort of a tonic. But you must promise me to exercise or we'll have to order supervised rehabilitation. The patient without the will to get well, won't get well."

It was a long, tedious, uphill climb. Slowly, she began to cooperate and recover her strength. But there were always the bad dreams filled with guilt. Trudy had convinced herself that she, the captain of her own fate, had run aground because of her own sins.

CHAPTER 11

1951

While Trudy Coles lay in a hospital bed recovering from her accident, Manny Silverstein faced his own trial by fire. His two weeks in New York, which he blithely described to Trudy as a meeting with "those *fecockta* bankers," was really a first-round skirmish in a fight for survival. Never one to complain, Silverstein was a back-alley brawler who would go under before screaming for relief. He knew the minute he received a call from his brother, Abe, that it was bare-knuckle time.

"These putzes are screaming for your head, Manny. They want you on a plate like that Joe the Baptist."

"Fuck 'em. I couldn't care less. They want head, I'll get a hooker who serves head."

"Manny, stop with the jokes. This is s-e-r-i-o-u-s, serious. The guy over at Chase wants his money and all the other schmucks are following suit. They got this accountant from Price Watering says you can't run a business."

"Price Waterhouse."

"So? Isn't that what I said? This snotnose kid out of the Wharning School at Penn says he can show them where all the waste is going. He recommended a new studio head to watch the dollars and he says you should be put on pension. It'll be cheaper for the whole studio, he says."

"Before they put me on pension they'll have to whip me until

I'm dead. You and I started this goddamned business and the only one who replaces me in this job ain't born yet."

"Manny, I'm scared. It ain't like all the other times when you bullshitted us out of trouble. They mean business. I tell you there's blood in their eyes. They asked me when you're coming East. I told them next Purim. They didn't laugh. They want meetings now. I told them I'd call you."

"Tell them I'll be there next Wednesday. Tillie wants a vacation anyway. We'll tie the two together."

"But what are we going to tell them?"

"We'll tell them we'll take down their ideas and push them around."

"What the hell does that mean?"

"Abe, if I knew what it meant, do you think I'd tell those *fecockta* bankers? We'll tell them we're going to push it around and they'll think we're seriously considering their ideas. In the meantime, we'll do our thing and fuck them all. Then we'll have one big feature, make a couple of million bucks, and they'll be back pushing money on us and kissing our ass. You mark my word."

"Okay. But come loaded for a fight. It ain't gonna be easy this time. That kid from Penn's got them reading statements like kids in an alley reading *schmutzik* Joe Palooka story books."

"Calm down, Abe. If accountants could be businessmen they would be. For my money they can shove their profit and loss statements up their debit and credit assholes."

Despite his air of bravado, Manny Silverstein knew he was in deep, deep trouble. For the past few years, ever since the release of *Loving Sisters,* Continental had been running a bad-luck streak. Picture after picture started on a level of high hope only to be dashed into the red ink column through rising costs and the ever-expanding television monster. It was a condition that Continental shared with other studios. All was gloom and doom in Hollywood, and the trades were calling the situation "Götterdämmerung," the twilight of the filmland gods.

Indeed, the title was not inappropriate. Studio head after studio head was reported to be in deep trouble. Silverstein witnessed the impossible. The great Louis B. Mayer was being not too subtly eased from power. Rumor had it that Dore Schary, who had risen to the heights with so much intellectual promise, was fighting for his life. During the next few years, while Silverstein struggled to stay afloat, Nick Schenck would fall. Then Darryl Zanuck. Howard Hughes would back away to seek his millions and showgirls elsewhere. Cecil B. De Mille would die. Louis B. Mayer would try to climb the ladder again and fail. The good times had rolled and were gone. And one after the other, like dominoes, theaters were closing. The toughest managers, the men who had fought off extinction during the great Depression with bingo nights, free glasses, and barter ticketing, were trying the same techniques now and failing. And always it was the same excuse. Television.

Manny checked in at the Straford. He insisted upon his usual, rajah-like suite.

"Maybe you should take it easy this time," Abe suggested. "The first meeting is here tomorrow morning. Maybe you should show them we practice economy."

"That's the way we're going to lose this fight. You run scared, these goyim bastards will eat you alive. Abe and Manny Silverstein go first class. You tell room service for me I want the most expensive breakfast they got . . . go for broke or you'll end broke."

The first arrival was Hugo Reid, vice-president of New York Fidelity and head of its venture capital department. He was immediately followed by Lance Connors, his counterpart from the eastern division of National Indiana. Next came Marcus Stinson, leader of a consortium of Wall Street brokerage firms that had developed a heavy corporate investment business built around Hollywood's speculative capital needs. They had all grown fat during the late forties when film ventures threw off heavy profits. Now that the going was getting tougher and tougher they were reluctant to give back even a little of the gold they had mined.

"Gentlemen, gentlemen," Manny greeted them, with an effervescent smile, "what a pleasure to see you all together again. I've got just the wine to celebrate the occasion."

"It's a little early for celebration, Manny," Reid replied, eyeing the bubbly suspiciously. "We New Yorkers avoid anything stronger than a cola drink in the morning hours."

"My doc says cola is worse for you than lye. Tears up the stomach lining something awful. Here, try this champagne. The best you can get in the entire city of New York. No time's too early for the good things in life, right, Marcus? Right, Lance?"

They all accepted the glasses. Their eyes opened wide as waiters wheeled in trays of caviar, steaming scrambled eggs, hot rolls, sticky buns, and caldrons of steaming coffee. It took a strong man to resist the sumptuous repast and the pure Havana cigars that followed. All present found themselves relaxing as the delicacies hit their mark.

"So, gentlemen," Manny opened, sucking on his Havana and issuing a smooth stream of white smoke that seemed to engulf his entire face, "how's tricks in New York?"

"Things in New York seem okay. How are things in Hollywood?" Connors replied. "We don't like the signs of the times. We're especially concerned with figures you're putting out at Continental."

"Right!" added Stinson, joining the attack. "Since *Loving Sisters* you haven't even had the smell of a winner. And everything we read about television makes us feel pretty insecure on your line. You're into my firms alone for four million. Reid tells me that you owe him six. And there's another one and a half due Connors. You may owe more we don't even know about. Where is it all going to lead?"

"Now, gentlemen, I can't blame you for feeling itchy, but the answer is it is all going to lead to bigger profits. It's not the first time studios have had their bad luck streaks. But we always turn around and knock 'em dead with big, big winners. You tell me one serious loss you've had since financing our features."

"Manny, that was then. This is now," answered Reid angrily. "Hell, before TV was one thing. After, that's another story."

"Sure, as I was telling Abe just yesterday, TV is a challenge. But so was the talking pictures when we were all up to our kazoos in silents. We adjusted and bingo, the red ink disappeared."

"This is different, Manny. Hell, last Tuesday there weren't ten men in my dining club for dinner. How are you going to fight that competition? The interest on our loan by itself at three and a half percent will cost you half a year's profit. TV is just starting to spread like a great plague that will knock you filmmakers on your tails. What can you tell us that you can do that will be any more effective than the rest of the majors? They're all in deep trouble."

"I learned a long time ago to play my own hand. I really don't give a shit what the majors do. I know that Continental will weather the storm and come up smelling like roses. You guys are great with balance sheets. But you get scared at the first sign of winter."

Reid was the toughest and he spoke out first. He wasn't going to let this transplanted New York Jew-boy bully him.

"Listen, Silverstein," he said, dropping the "Manny" that he normally used. "Don't think you can turn it around against us. We've played that game with experts. Nothing scares New York Fidelity except welchers, big talkers who fail to repay their loans. Hell, if we didn't have guts we would never have lent you any money in the first place. Without our group Continental would be nothing but an empty lot today."

"That's right," said Connors, joining the chorus. "We've been looking at your statements for the past two years and they look like embezzlement alley. Christ, you've spent more money on 'Travel and Entertainment' than you've earned in five years. That apartment the company pays for in Acapulco. What's that for? Is that where you get your big-time ideas? Or is that where you Hollywood geniuses take your fancy women?"

"And that yacht at Malibu," Stinson said, jumping in with both feet. "Is that what we call 'executive prerogative'? Hell, we put up with your little indulgences when there was a chance to make money. But you're so deep in red ink, you may never climb out."

This was the holocaust that Abe had anticipated, and he began trembling with fear. Not so Manny Silverstein. He let them speak, not bothering to interrupt, smiling sardonic agreement. Then he jumped to his feet and did the "Silverstein Turn."

"Listen, you bastards," he fairly shouted, "now you listen to me. You're goddamned right I spend a lot of money. And I'm gonna keep on spending it as long as I'm boss at Continental. What the hell do you think I'm doing out there, playing penny ante like a fucking bank clerk? I'm playing an illusion game and illusions take balls and moxie, things which you pale-assed Eastern bankers never heard of. Don't give me that shit about yachts and vacation apartments. Where would you bastards be if it hadn't been for all the dough I made you for the past twelve years? You want me to run scared, get yourself another boy. I'll get that dough back to you just as soon as you give me the sign. Shit, there are four banks in L.A. right now who want my business. They'll buy you white-livered bastards out in a minute. But once you leave me, don't come sniffing around for peace treaties."

His voice had gradually risen to a pitch that made it heard a block away. His face was crimson with anger, the veins jutting out on the sides of his neck and throat. It was the Silverstein that terrorized disloyal employees. Now, of course, it was all an act for the benefit of the money changers, but it was effective. He strode across the room to where Reid was sitting and, grabbing him by the shirt, lifted him from his seat. Reid towered over him by at least four inches but he was frightened out of his wits by Silverstein's temper.

"And I don't like your tone with me, you hear? You think I can't tell how you feel about Jews? Well here is one Jew who ain't walking into that oven saluting and kissing your ass. You talk to me like a gentleman, you hear? You don't and I'll kick your ass right across Fifth Avenue so hard you'll look like a fuckin' baboon. Now all of you, clear the hell out of here. You'll get your goddamned blood money when I'm good and ready. Get out!"

Red-faced, the three money barons rose to their feet, attempted to regain their dignity, and walked out without comment. Abe was nearly hysterical. Once they were alone he attacked his brother.

"Manny, you crazy or something? Moe once told us, may he rest in peace, that you don't point a gun you can't shoot. What four other bankers? Shit, no bank in California will touch us with a twenty-foot pole. Now you went and kicked these guys out, how the hell you gonna keep afloat?"

But Manny was undisturbed. He was calmly pouring himself a big glass of iced champagne and picking on the remainder of the eggs and salmon that had been left behind.

"Be calm, will you, for Christ's sake? Moe also said, 'You lose your nerve, you lose your fight.' I got a plan. You watch how those anti-Semitic cocksuckers come running back."

Manny Silverstein never turned his back on a friend. He never broke a relationship once established. Left alone, he calmly walked to the phone and called his old friend Rocco Martucci, the same man who had helped him and his brothers out in the old days when he was fighting off competition that hindered the growth of Silverstein Concessions. In the intervening years he had seen Martucci and his cohorts less than a half dozen times. But whenever they came to Hollywood, it was Manny Silverstein who turned out the red carpet. He supplied them with women.

He got them free hotel suites. He saw that they were "comped" at all the best restaurants and night clubs. And when they faced serious trouble with the federal authorities and needed someone clean to help them launder money, Manny Silverstein was there to pave their way. He had never cashed his chips with them in all those years. Now it was time to call his marker. He knew he would not be refused, just as he knew that Reid and Friends were no match for the likes of Martucci and his cronies.

It worked like a charm. The next morning, just as he settled into his swivel chair to read *The Wall Street Journal,* Reid was informed by his secretary that an insistent customer was demanding a brief meeting with him.

"Tell him I'm busy, Miss Chandler. Tell him to phone for an appointment. We just don't let anyone off the street barge in here you know."

Miss Chandler believed in the power of the whisper and Reid got her message.

Leaning into the phone, she said in a hushed voice, "I tried to, Mr. Reid, but this man will not take no for an answer. He scares me. He just plumped down in the waiting room and told me that he'd sit there for three weeks if you won't see him. I don't like his looks. I'm scared, Mr. Reid."

"All right. Send him in. What did you say his name is?"

"He says it's Martucci. Rocco Martucci. He says you don't know him."

In a manner of speaking, Hugo Reid did not know Rocco Martucci personally, but there were few knowledgeable people in New York who hadn't heard about him. In the crime families that ruled the darker side of the city's commerce, Martucci had a reputation as an enforcer with a prodigious, violent temper. He wasted little time with subtlety once he faced the white-faced banker.

"I got a friend. His name is Manny Silverstein. He's a good man. Smart. Makes good pictures. He's owe you some dough. You bedda not bother him more right now. Else I can'ta be sure what's agonna happ to you and your kids. You *capisce?* Now you tella your buddies they gotta lay off too. You getta my point? Else, who knows, maybe they justa go for a nice long swim in the Hudson Riva."

"Mr. Martucci," Reid protested weakly, "I can't tell the others what to do. I can be patient, but I can't vouch for them."

"Yessa you can. You gotta speak for them too. Else you might getta your feet wet, too. *Capisce?*"

On that note the meeting ended. Reid thought of calling the police department, but knowing that the present administration had a "working agreement" with the underworld powers, he wasn't at all confident that he wouldn't be laying himself open to greater abuse. He decided to play it safe. He immediately phoned Connors and Stinson, suggesting an emergency luncheon. When they heard his story they all agreed that patience might be the appropriate course of action. They contacted Manny Silverstein and suggested another breakfast conference. Manny was warm and friendly and invited them to rejoin him the next morning.

Again they assembled and shared a sumptuous feast. Not a word of business was discussed until Manny raised the subject.

"The thing about television is that it can't give you the same kick as movies. There's a magic about a big screen that those little piss-ant black boxes can't create. But if we're smart, the thing to do is to play up the areas where they can't compete."

"Like?" asked Reid.

"Surrounding the audience in pictures. That's the thing of the future. Every big studio is into it now. The leader is using the name Cinerama. It takes three separate projectors and a special large screen. They're going to make their own features just for this process. And there are a bunch of competitors. Mike Todd is betting on something he calls 'Todd-AO.' Then there's Vista-Vision, 3-D, CinemaScope—you name it. They're all going to make the screen bigger and bigger so the customer feels like he's part of the story he's watching. Television can't do that."

"How does Continental fit into this?"

"Easy. I got a system that'll make the rest of them look sick. We call it Opta-Vision. We're not ready to release it yet because it's not quite ready. But when we do, hell, the others will come running to lease our patent."

"When will it be ready?"

"Soon. We do need some more development money. Not a hell of a lot, but some more."

"How much?" Reid asked cautiously.

"Not much. I'd say about two million."

"Two million? Are you crazy?"

"No. I'm conservative. This process will bring in millions. We got it from a Jewish physics professor who ran away from Hitler. He experimented with it in Germany back in the early thirties and I'm tellin' yuh it's the nuts. Nothing even looks like it. Hell, you put up a gorgeous broad on that screen and with this process you think she's puttin' her duff on your lap. Every viewer will think he's the one making love."

"And suppose we extend ourselves and give you the money. What's in it for us? Besides interest, I mean."

"You get double interest—seven percent—and twenty-five percent of the net. We've formed a separate corporation called Opta-Vision International. Frieshoff—he's the inventor—owns half, Continental owns half. We'll give you half our interest and first money back. How can you miss?"

In the end, they gave him the money. Big screen, three-dimensional techniques eventually went by the wayside and no one even bothered to tote up how much money was squandered. It really didn't matter to Manny Silverstein. There was no German Jew named Frieshoff working with him. There was no Opta-Vision International. He formed the corporation immediately, or at least told his lawyers by long-distance phone to do so, just as soon as the breakfast meeting ended. The important fact was that by the time he had returned to Hollywood, the two million dollars was resting in Continental bank accounts, granting him breathing space and the opportunity to continue the fight for survival. Manny Silverstein, street fighter extraordinaire, had done it again. But the struggle was far from over.

What he needed now was the big feature that would turn the tide in his favor. With all of Hollywood facing starvation, with more and more money being placed into television, the odds were strictly against him. That didn't dissuade Manny Silverstein. He had faced hard times before and come out on top. It was time for a master stroke, a feature so profitable that the whole town would sit up and take notice. The man who could bring him such a hit was Richie Stevens. The sex goddess he needed was Trudy Coles. She still hadn't had the ultimate hit that would catapult her to stardom. The time was now.

CHAPTER 12

1951

While Manny Silverstein was fighting for survival in his struggle with the Eastern bankers, another warrior in the theatrical maelstrom was taking his lumps. His name was Larry Hocker, a tall, thin stringbean of a man who had but one all-consuming passion, the Broadway theater. Physically unattractive, not particularly prepossessing as a personality, Larry Hocker had substituted sweat for talent and had scaled the heights as a producer at a very young age.

And it all happened almost by accident. Working as a messenger in a small Wall Street brokerage firm, Larry had been befriended by a sixty-year-old bachelor named Barney Stilson. Tight with a buck, Barney loved the excitement of Broadway but didn't enjoy the costs involved in taking a date. Instead, he invited Larry, whom he didn't have to entertain lavishly. Once Larry was exposed to the magic of live theater, nothing else could satisfy him. Another soul had been bitten by the Broadway bug.

Barney took him to Lindy's after a show one night and he sat in awe as the out-of-work actors and Broadway press agents traded gossip about the current theatrical scene. It didn't really matter that many of them who spoke *ex cathedra* had their facts all twisted and boasted of knowledge that was far from accurate. The fact was that they were immersed in the land of magic—theater, where every girl was a raving beauty and even beanpoles like Larry Hocker could find their dreams fulfilled. One specific dream was named Marianne Fuller, a plumpish farm girl out of Minnesota who, having won a local beauty contest in Duluth, came to Manhattan to seek her fortune and, after sixteen months of near-starvation, found her way into a chorus line on Broadway.

"She's lookin' at you kid. Go over and say hello," Barney urged between bites of a corned beef, cole slaw, and Russian dressing special. "You gotta have a little nerve in this life if you're gonna make it."

Fearfully, Larry rose and walked over to the neighboring table, where Marianne was carefully examining the menu.

"I liked you in the show tonight," he tried for openers.

"Thanks. Fact is I didn't sing tonight. I have a raw throat and the stage manager gave me the night off."

"Hot tea with honey. It's the best remedy."

On this fragile note, a love affair had its origin. Twenty-seven-year-old Larry Hocker, a virgin, spent the night in Marianne's small, West Side apartment. He saw her regularly for a year and a half until she decided to pack New York in and return to her home in the Midwest. But through her he was introduced to the backstage magic that even Barney Stilson had never penetrated. He got to watch shows from the wings of stages, met agents and aspiring stars, even traveled to Boston to view out-of-town try-outs; and, having taken two courses in theater production and stage direction at The New School, finally landed a job as an assistant stage manager, thereby earning a coveted Equity card. It was a terrible Off-Broadway show that only lasted about a week. But Larry Hocker was prouder than Helen Hayes in her first starring role. He was a working professional now and the world of theater was his to conquer. He said good-bye to Wall Street that same week.

Within a year he had produced his first play. It was a fragile little romance that a fellow Marianne had introduced him to had written while working as standby for a star in one of the current hits. Larry loved the story the first time he read it, and as the author worked and reworked it he liked it even more. It was perfect for a younger audience in one of the many little Off-Off-Broadway houses that were springing up like weeds. He figured he could launch it for less than $10,000, with a small reserve for advertising. Now, if only he could find the $10,000.

He remembered something someone had said down on Wall

Street when floating a small bond issue. "It's easier to find a hundred people with ten dollars than ten people with a hundred dollars." It was the secret of Larry Hocker's early success as an entepreneur.

Larry found that it took a lot of $250 investors to make up the needed $10,000. But finally, after months of constant effort, he found them. Larry made another discovery in his quest for funds. It took more than effort. What was required was a bit of creative imagination.

"Hey, Larry, I thought you told me that show was supposed to open in April," a prospective investor said to him one day in late August.

"It was—originally. I postponed it because I didn't like the rewrites. Now, it's ready and it's perfect."

No matter how outrageous your story might be, say it with conviction and wrap it in the magic of the theater, search long and diligently enough, and you'd eventually find a fish biting.

Love in a Co-op, as the play was titled, proved to be as good as Larry had thought. There were no Pulitzer Prize nominations on their way, but the show was poignant, charming, and amazingly well done. Larry worked around the clock, serving not only as producer, but as press agent and general manager as well. He succeeded in convincing two second-string critics from major newspapers to review the show on opening night. He had met them in the early days at Lindy's, and since they had no assignments that night, they succumbed to his pleas.

"No strings attached, for sure, Charlie," he told the man from the *Daily News*. "You'll call it as you see it."

"You can bet your ass on that," Charlie responded.

Both men genuinely enjoyed the show and wrote glowing reviews. Word of mouth was good, too. People kept coming and enjoying themselves. In seven weeks, the show earned enough to enable Larry to return one hundred percent of his investment to every backer. Then he started sharing dollar for dollar under the standard limited partnership arrangement. Larry Hocker's very first show earned him $23,000 and he came within a gnat's hair of selling the movie rights for $50,000. His career as a producer had been launched in style.

Luck, like bananas, comes in bunches. Three months later Larry found another property he liked, this one a farce with serious overtones. He held an audition, well attended by many of his former backers and their friends, who were green with envy because they had missed out on the first bonanza. He rented a small auditorium in the Edison Hotel in the theater district for the reading and enlisted the help of several out-of-work actors to perform all of the parts. He even splurged for a few bottles of booze and dry mixes of chips and nuts. He wanted everyone to feel happy and the liquor created greater euphoria. When everyone had heard the show and was ready to be taken, he called them to order and made the pitch.

"I'm really very grateful that you all thought enough of my project to show up tonight. Obviously, we're not at all interested in raising funds now. We just wanted you to hear and enjoy and ask any questions you might have."

"When is the show coming off, Larry?" asked one of his friends, who was serving as a shill and charged with the responsibility of getting the questions started.

"Oh, pretty soon. No point in sitting on a hot potato."

"You taking this one straight to Broadway?"

"Maybe. Certainly to Off-Broadway. None of that off-off stuff for this one."

"Larry"—this again from a shill—"is it true that *Love in a Co-op* made a hundred grand on a ten thou investment?"

"Well," said Larry, smiling, "a lot of my partners here tonight might not want anybody to know how much income they earned, so I'd rather not talk numbers. I think you can appreciate that. Now, who's for another drink?"

Actually, each investor had gotten his money back, and had enjoyed a profit measuring two and a half times what he had invested. They were too naive to realize that the $100,000 figure was bandied about at Larry's request.

No one has ever been able to explain the magic Indian drumbeat that tells the world that a theatrical hit is on its way. People just seem to sense when a show has good vibrations and they line up for tickets the day the box office opens. *Losers Weepers*, Larry Hocker's new show, had strong word of mouth before it even opened at the Pearl, one of the larger Off-Broadway houses, with a seating capacity of just under five hundred. A week of previews were just about sold out. Ronnie Slater, the star, had worked in a few movies in the mid-forties. She was far from the star Larry had promised his backers, but she was a competent comedienne with a recognizable name. With business humming, no one complained.

Once again working as his own press agent, Larry managed to get some fairly well-known critics to cover the opening. No one raved, but no one panned it either. They all said it was "good entertainment," the kind of show that helps you forget the cares of the day. Larry took a three-hundred-line ad in *The New York Times* three days later, quoting and misquoting to serve his purpose. It was fairly unusual in those days for Off-Broadway shows to spend that kind of money on quote ads, but Larry believed in blowing bugles. In this case he was right. Lines continued to get longer and longer at the box office, and he had retrieved the cost of the ad five times over before the week was out.

It took Larry Hocker four more years and a string of mild successes, marred by a few failures, to make it to Broadway. His first Broadway show was a serious melodrama that the critics enjoyed. It failed to please audiences, however, and its life was destined to be terminated rather quickly. Larry worked like a demon, promoting theater parties, offering group discounts, spreading "twofers," those little bits of pasteboard entitling the bearer to two tickets for the price of one. It was exhausting, challenging toil for Larry, but he loved it. And he succeeded in extending the show's life for three more months. It never earned a cent. But he was able to return ninety percent of his backers' money. That seemed to satisfy just about everybody.

The night the show closed, Larry walked home with Barney Stilson, who had raised $40,000 of the capital.

"Sorry, Barney. Afraid I let you down this time."

"Forget it, kid. Who's counting? You can't win 'em all. You gave us one hell of a ride for our money."

Larry's next show, his first musical on Broadway, brought in a gusher. He had never dealt with so many diverse elements, so many creative people each pulling in different directions. But he kept his cool and instinctively knew just when to exercise his power as producer and when to give in, in seeming surrender to superior forces. He knew from experience exactly what he was doing. This time he hired a top-flight Broadway press agent and the best advertising specialist in the field he could find. He still felt that a producer's major challenge was to "sell" the show and he met with his advisors every morning in a half-hour strategy session. He was at the theater every night making sure that the show always looked sparkling fresh and never down at the heels and shoddy. Not only was the show a smash hit, turning a $30,000 profit every week, but there was immediate interest in a movie sale. As a "producer's fee," Larry got one and a half percent of the gross, approximately $2,000 a week. He got another $500 a week as a "cash office charge" to run his office. And once his backers had received back an amount of money equal to their $500,000 investment, he was earning $15,000 a week more! Fantastic! This was what show business was all about.

He opened an office right in the heart of the theater district, being careful to have it decorated in the latest vogue. He drove a Cadillac, or rather had one driven for him by a liveried chauffer. He did his best to forget his roots. Calls from old friends and early investors turned him off. Even Barney Stilson had trouble getting through to him.

"That schmuck again?" he roared at his secretary. "Tell him I'm in conference. Tell him I'm at the bank. Tell him anything you want but don't put him through. Christ, I can't spend my life talking to a bunch of old farts when I've got scripts to read!"

He might have been able to play his game without interruption if every show he touched was a hit. King Midas lived only in legend and Larry Hocker was riding for a fall. It came in the form of his next show, a musical capitalized at just under $1 million. It died in three performances. Larry had to chip in $40,000 of his own funds to meet the costs of dumping the sets, storing the costumes, and paying off advertising debts.

Suddenly, he wasn't such a glamor boy on the rialto. The best tables at the Plaza, at the Pierre, and at Sardi's seemed suddenly occupied when he arrived. Even his old friend, the maître d' at "21," seemed to greet him a little less enthusiastically. He received a few polite reminders from several restaurants where he dined regularly that his bill was about thirty days overdue.

The kids were getting older and his wife Millie, a former chorus girl, was more demanding every day. His savings were beginning to run frighteningly low as living costs kept skyrocketing.

"You already have two fur coats. What in the hell do you need with a full-length mink with a hood attachment?"

"You want me to look like a pauper's wife, is that what you want?"

"Eight thousand dollars for a coat ain't exactly cheap, you know."

"No. But you are. Is it my fault if you haven't had a winner for years? Maybe you ought to get out of this crazy business and try a legitimate job. My cousin Herbie never got beyond tenth grade and he's making a bundle in real estate."

"I don't know my ass from first base about real estate. Have a little faith in me for a change. That might help."

"I've got faith. That's why I bought this coat."

He returned to his office determined to glean a winner from the pile of scripts that were waiting on his side table. He read assiduously for the next three weeks and finally found what he liked, a simple, single-set comedy with only four characters. Musicals were growing out of hand these days. Hell, even this show would cost at least $300,000 to mount.

He found what he expected when he started raising the money. Money was tight. The market had dropped precipitously and all the high rollers were tightening their belts. Besides, his last debacle had burned quite a few of his cadre of backers and they were not eager to answer the phone when he called.

"Hey, Marty, Larry Hocker here. I'm gonna make you rich."

"Larry, do me a favor. Just let me stay rich. No more show deals for me. Sorry."

Or again: "Hi, Stan. How's Tracy? Still as pretty as ever?"

"Yes, thanks. She's a freshman at Radcliffe. Costs a hell of a lot of dough to keep her there. Nothing left over for being an angel, if that's why you called."

Larry stayed at it, working ten hours a day on the phone, and finally the pledges started trickling in. It took him almost four months to raise the money and even then there was more than a twenty percent fallout when he distributed the partnership papers. It was back to the phones for three more weeks before he was fully, legitimately capitalized. Larry Hocker knew he was playing with scared dice. He simply had to win this time or he might never get another turn.

He knew he was in trouble from the day of the first rehearsal. The script, which had seemed so hilarious in the quiet of his office, was a big dud when read on stage. The casting was bad. The scenic designer insisted that he couldn't get the effects he wanted on his limited budget. The director, the man who, in the last analysis, can make or break a show, had somehow lost interest in the project. The Boston tryout was a disaster. The show was losing $50,000 a week. He fired the director and hired another one. The author hated the new man and threatened to walk out if another line was changed.

Money problems were severe. Larry received a call from Chuck Henry, his general manager.

"Things are grim, boss. We've been out of dough for four days. I gotta make payroll tomorrow."

"How much?" Larry asked, fearful of the answer.

"Thirty-eight thousand. Minimum."

"Ouch!"

"And, boss. You'll need at least a hundred more if we're to reach New York."

Pledging a large portion of the securities in his safety deposit vault, Larry borrowed $50,000. He'd just have to put off his creditors for a while and hope that the show got great notices.

It didn't. It was bombed by the critics and there wasn't even a trickle at the box office. He had to close the show after its fourth performance. Actors Equity, the performers' union, took money out of the show's posted bond to pay the actors for the final weeks' work. The debts he owed exceeded $125,000. And he was tapped out.

The glorious ride of Larry Hocker had ground to a sickening halt. It would take all of his ingenuity and all of his energy to climb aboard again.

CHAPTER 13

1952

Manny Silverstein's plans to create the super feature with Trudy Coles as star were destined to be rudely frustrated. Although he cut short his projected vacation in Nassau to return to Hollywood, much to Tillie's annoyance, even he could not cope with broken bones.

"So what's the rush to get back?" Tillie asked. "You promised us both a month in the sun. The goddamn business will wait."

"You run the house. Let me run the business. I faked these *fecockta* bankers out of two million and I got to put it to work fast. You like nice things? Furs? Big cars? Diamonds? Well, Tillie Schultz, somebody has to earn the dough to pay for them. The sun will wait. Besides, Dr. Schwartz says too much sun leads to cancer. He's a smart man."

"There's plenty of sun in Hollywood, Manny. And there's all kinds of cancer out there, too. You keep working round the clock like a horse, you'll drop dead one of these days, you wait and see."

"You don't know your ass from your elbow about horses. Besides, if I drop dead I won't see anything. Now, here's your going-home present."

Manny Silverstein was no fool. That afternoon he had rushed out and visited Cartier's. Tillie had a ten-carat diamond brooch to glow over all the way back to California. Of course, Manny had bought it on credit. Somehow, he'd find the money to pay the bill when it arrived. Or, maybe, six months later. Three days after his arrival in California, word reached him that Trudy had suffered a serious accident.

"My luck!" he complained to Obie. "Just when I get the dough and the inspiration to make it all click, that dumb Polock has to go and get herself banged up by a motorcycle. Who told her to ride that goddamned thing anyway?"

"She didn't ride it. She was hit by one as she left a restaurant. Maybe you think like Jane and Tarzan she should have grabbed a vine and swung away."

"Never mind the wise-ass remarks, Obie. Sometimes I think I let you get away with too much around here. You ain't a vice-president, you know."

Obie had heard it all many times before. Manny Silverstein was in trouble. That's when he lashed out at everyone around him, friend and foe alike. The best thing now was to let him simmer.

"I'm sorry, Mr. Silverstein, I really am. But you like the kid. Let's hope she'll be all right soon and can get back to work like nothing ever happened."

"Let's hope," Manny mimicked and, trudging into his inner office, slammed the door behind him with such temper that screws leaped forth from several of the hinges. Obie calmly made a note to have the door repaired. It wasn't the first or the last time that her idol would wreak damage as release from his frustrations.

The following day, Manny received a message that Mickey Sklaroff wanted to lunch with him at the earliest opportunity. It was a matter of great importance.

"What's that little putz got up his sleeve?" Manny grumbled when Obie brought him the message. "When an agent says it's important, you can bet your ass it's important to him, not to you."

"I can tell him you're too busy," Obie suggested.

"No. He'll just keep at it. He's one little schmuck who won't take no for an answer."

"I'll set it up at Chasen's. One-thirty tomorrow? Okay?"

"Okay. Okay, already. I guess I gotta eat anyhow. At least Sklaroff picks up the tab."

"So, Mr. Playboy, any more office boys catch you with your tit in the wringer? Maybe you'd have been better off if you were born with ten pricks and one finger instead of the other way around."

They were seated in their usual quiet spot at Chasen's, and

Mickey took it as a good sign that Manny was ribbing him at the outset of their meeting: when Silverstein was not in a receptive mood, he didn't kid around. Sklaroff decided to give him more rope.

"And since when did you become a Catholic priest? The first time I ever heard your name mentioned a man told me he knew you'd fuck anything from a hot stovepipe to a goat's ass. Now, all of a sudden, you got religious? Half the broads in Hollywood will have to go into mourning. Only in your case, they'll sit shiva in a whorehouse."

"That's a good place, as good as any." Manny laughed. "If you're going to be in mourning you might as well do it in a nice quiet place where all of your friends will feel at home."

The drinks were served and dinner ordered without a word from Mickey as to the purpose of their meeting. Manny Silverstein realized that what Mickey wanted must be very important to him; otherwise, he would have blurted it out as soon as they met. Now, it was obvious that he was picking his moment, waiting until the atmosphere was just right. Manny decided to bide his time; no need to give an agent a break by helping him along. Finally, after appetizers and entrees were served and as coffee and dessert time approached, Mickey felt the timing was right.

"By the way, I wanted to talk to you about a project."

"No shit!" Manny replied, smiling like a cat that had just devoured a mouse.

"This one can be big. Very big. I brought it to you first."

"That means that MGM, Fox, and Universal all said no, right?"

"I wouldn't pull a trick like that on you, Manny. You're too smart. When I say first look, I mean first look."

"And what is it that I'm getting first look at?"

"Who is it," Mickey corrected. "We just signed a new client, a writer. His name is Stan Marcus. He's been around a couple of years, banging his head against a wall at Warner's. You know what Jack thinks about writers. He calls them 'schmucks with Underwoods.' Stan was working eight, ten hours a day, writing and rewriting scenes, most of which never even got to be filmed. They had him working in a cubicle six feet by six feet, like a goddamn prisoner in a cell. If he didn't grind out four thousand words a day, they'd jump all over him and threaten to send him back East."

"So what's so terrible about that?" Manny asked. "You think

because he went to college he deserves some sort of cushy job making forty thousand a year? Writers are a dime a dozen."

"Not this writer. He's terrific. I know the business and I tell you he's the most creative guy I've met. And he's got a hell of a commercial sense as well."

"Now, you said something. Commercial I like. Creative, I don't give a crap."

But he did. Manny Silverstein liked to maintain the façade of the crass producer who thought only in terms of cost and bottom line. Deep inside, however, there was an ingrained recognition of talent and respect for creative genius. It was something which he tried to shield, especially from the world of agents.

"Commercial and creative, Manny, don't have to fight each other. Sometimes, they make good bedfellows. And when the combination is right, you really have something. That's why I'm here to talk to you about Stan Marcus."

"So talk."

"Like I said, he's been around the track enough to know a filly from a gelding. Jack Warner realizes that and has him signed to a long-term contract. Stan wants out in the worst way. But it would take a big hunk of dough to buy back his contract."

"So what am I? The head of the parole board?"

"Don't be so fucking impatient. Let me explain it all before you go chopping my head off."

"When I chop you'll know it. Your head will bounce on the street. All I said was, why should I want to rescue this writer schmuck from Jack Warner? It's his problem."

"Right. But here's the point. Marcus has got a script he's written on his own time. He's documented it so that Jack Warner can never say he pirated it or wrote it on company time. I read it and I tell you it's the best story I've read in the fifteen years I've been out here. Whoever buys that script and produces it, has got to make millions. Marcus will be the talk of the business and so will Continental."

"And how do I get the script? Buy back the kid's contract from Warner's, right?"

"Right. It's that simple. You free Stan Marcus, you buy the script dirt cheap."

"I gotta buy the script, too? Being a lifeguard ain't enough?"

"That's the deal. It's a steal."

"Like how much? Assuming I like the script . . . no, wait a minute. First you gotta tell me what's the script about. And how many zillion is it going to cost to produce?"

"You know *Madame Bovary* by Flaubert? That's a classic."

"Don't tell me you're going to sell me on another *fecockta Helen of Troy* like Richie Stevens? I like modern stories. People watch television now and the news breaks every minute. They want things now, not yesterday."

"You miss the point, Manny. Here's a chance to beat television where it can't compete. *Madame Bovary* is a story about a woman who thumbs her nose at society and satisfies her sexual needs just the way you do. In the end, she's caught and pays a terrible price. But Flaubert lived in the early nineteenth century. Marcus has written a story suggestive of *Madame Bovary* but different. His heroine gets caught, gets punished—that will satisfy the Breen office—but in the end says screw you world, it's my body and if I want to fuck, I'll fuck. She goes off to start another life, with no regrets and no looking back. You can't tell this story on television. Only on the big screen."

Manny Silverstein was impressed. He himself was enough of an instinctive genius to realize that Mickey Sklaroff was speaking great professional truths. He was also clever enough to pretend not to be moved.

"I can read this piece of dreck?"

"What do you think I've got in this envelope, a couple of dirty shirts?"

Manny Silverstein read *Mrs. Donovan's Defeat* the next night. He read it again, the following morning, phoning Obie to explain that he was taking the morning off, an almost unheard-of procedure for Silverstein. He spent the afternoon reading *Madame Bovary*, which he had heard of but never read. He returned home after lunch and read Marcus' script again. He was convinced that, for once, an agent had spoken the truth. Without shame or pretense, he called Sklaroff late in the afternoon. That night they were back at Chasen's.

"Here's your script."

"You didn't like it?" Mickey asked in amazement.

"No. I didn't like it."

"Well, that's why they make chocolate and vanilla."

"I loved it."

"That's better. You want to buy it?"

"Just because I loved it that don't mean I buy. Everything's got a price. How much?"

Now the real jousting began.

"It'll take fifty thousand to buy back the Warner contract. Another fifty gets you full rights to the script."

"A hundred thousand dollars? You outta your fuckin' mind?"

"It's a steal. And now I'm talking to you *emess*, Manny. The truth, so help me. You let this fall through your hands, *you're* out of your fucking mind. I can sell this five times till Sunday. Every studio in town would jump at the deal. And you know it!"

"I'll pay twenty-five thousand. Not a cent more. Ten to get the kid out of his Warner's contract. Fifteen for the script."

"That kind of robbery you won't pull. But I've got a way for you to meet me in the middle."

"Tell me."

"First, let's talk stars. Who plays Mrs. Donovan?"

It was an old technique. Get the buyer red-hot, panting to buy, then back off and let him dangle. It almost always worked, the perfect way to close a deal.

"What the hell's that got to do with the price of potatoes?" Manny barked.

"Plenty. Marcus has got a hot property. The Arnold office believes in him and wants this script to launch a great career. The star who plays the role is very, very important."

"I thought you said this script was so great that I could play the role in drag and it still would make millions. Now, all of a sudden, it's the star who is gonna make it happen. You better get your story straight."

"Listen, Manny, for the first and last time, let's be straight with each other. No more agent-versus-producer shit. Okay? Okay?"

"Okay," Manny grumbled.

"This is a great script. It can make millions. But like any great script, it can be screwed up. It needs a special director and a sensitive, beautiful actress. That's why, above all, I came to you. This is a perfect story for Richie Stevens to handle. It also screams for Trudy Coles. You agree?"

"I agree."

"Then let's stop horse-shitting each other and make a deal. I know that Trudy is recuperating. But she'll mend, she's young. I understand her face wasn't harmed a bit. It'll take a couple of months to free Stan from Warner's. And he's still not completely satisfied with the script. He needs a month or two more for rewrites. You need the time to organize the team. Marcus believes that this picture should be filmed in the south of France."

"Why in the hell do we have to go to the expense of overseas filming?"

"Because he thinks that a French flavor is needed to remind people of Bovary, and to show the contrast of modern thinking and modern morality. Which isn't really a contrast at all. That's the point. We're all still bigots and the people with the balls to stand up to society are few and far between. Besides, the French government is very cooperative and will actually invest in the film. With an international cast, you'll have a great shot at winning an international market. It all makes sense."

In the end, a deal was struck that night at Chasen's. Manny Silverstein agreed to buy back the Marcus contract for $35,000. He would pay another $35,000 for the script, plus five percent of net profits after recoupment. It proved to be a very expensive deal for Silverstein, but at heart, Manny was a riverboat gambler.

A serious problem arose from an unexpected source. Marcus, of course, knew all about the reputation of Manny Silverstein, but had been partially convinced by Mickey that much of it was unfair, based on industry jealousy of Manny's accomplishments as a loner swimming in a sea of great white sharks. Stan was so eager to escape from the Warner yoke, and so determined to find a backer for *Mrs. Donovan's Defeat,* that he was practically ready for an alliance with Count Dracula. Still, he wasn't ready for the treatment he received during his first confrontation with his new boss.

Manny had had a terrible night, starting with an enervating spat with Tillie and followed by a nerve-splitting headache that kept him awake until four in the morning. He arose to find that the stock market had dipped sharply, wiping out all of his loose cash accumulated during a six-month rising market. At the office, he found a note from Obie explaining that a cousin of hers in Seattle had died during the night and that she had rushed off for the funeral. Without Obie to protect him, he was unable to ward off a surprise visit from an aggressive starlet he had been bedding down for the past winter and who had been promised a featured role in his next picture in return for her favors—a promise that was never fulfilled. Could things be worse in one morning?

In addition, without Obie's prodding, Manny hadn't checked his appointment book and had completely forgotten that he had agreed to a meeting with Stan Marcus. Unfortunately, Mickey Sklaroff was in Palm Springs with another client, and couldn't attend. Had he been present, the rendezvous might have gone more smoothly.

"Who in the hell is this?" Silverstein barked, at his hog-calling best, frightening Obie's temporary replacement beyond recall. "Don't you know better than to come barging in here without knocking?"

"But Mr. Silverstein," the girl said tearfully, "I did knock. I knocked three times."

"Next time knock four. And wait till I answer. Don't you come in here with some bill collector before I say I'm ready."

"Mr. Silverstein," Marcus started to protest, "I thought—"

That was as far as he got.

"You shut up! When I want to hear from you, I'll let you know. All I need is another Philadelphia lawyer in here to screw up my morning. You get back to your desk now," he added, turning his attention again to the secretary. She scurried to safety, happy to leave Silverstein's presence at any cost. Marcus just stayed behind and held his ground. Normally a gentle man, his hackles were raised by the obvious bad manners and bullying tactics that Silverstein favored.

"Well, what do you want?" Silverstein said, turning his full face on Marcus in the hope of further harassing an unknown, potential enemy.

"I don't want anything, Mr. Silverstein. Mickey Sklaroff told me that you wanted to meet me and discuss my script for *Mrs. Donovan's Defeat*. I've been waiting out there for twenty-five minutes. The meeting was set for ten sharp." He stared back at Silverstein with a defiant air.

"Oh, you're too important to be kept waiting, is that it?"

"I'm not important at all, Mr. Silverstein. I just don't like being treated like a dish rag. That's why I left Warner's. Mickey Sklaroff told me that deep down inside you're one hell of a guy, despite what everybody in the industry says about you. But if this is a sample of how you treat people, I may never dig down that deep. I may not be a big-time studio head but I've got my pride. You want to cancel the deal on my contract, cancel it."

Manny Silverstein loved independent people. They just didn't live very long in his organization. He was half-tempted to tell Marcus to start walking, but there was a voice within him, a voice seldom heard or acknowledged, that told him to sue for peace.

"Listen, Marcus, let's not get off to a bad start. I've had a terrible morning and I'm a little jumpy. Come here and sit down. What did you say your first name was?"

"I didn't. It's on the contract you signed. My name is Stanley. Friends call me Stan."

"Okay. We're going to be friends. I'll call you Stan. You call me Manny."

"Silverstein feels better for the time being. But thanks for the gesture. Soon as it feels right, I'll call you Manny."

They were seated now, Manny behind his desk, Stan Marcus on the easy chair that fronted it. Determined to erase the ugliness that had characterized their meeting, Manny offered Marcus a cigar, his best Havanas, which Stan promptly refused. Manny lit his own, puffed luxuriously, and eyed his newest acquisition.

"I read your script. Twice. Terrific. You got it, kid."

"Thank you. You've got it now, and with a little luck we'll both make a hell of a lot of money. All I need is a bit of support and the opportunity to prove myself."

"You'll get both from me. But I hope you won't get sore if I make a little suggestion here and there."

"I'm used to criticism. Anything special in mind, Mr. Silverstein?"

"Yeh. The way your story begins. I don't think it grabs you like it should. You got this broad walking to work and she sees this guy standing on a stoop. She likes his looks, right? Before he even has a chance to start following her and make a pass, she walks over to him and practically grabs him by the cock. It makes her cheap. It makes her brazen. No sympathy from the audience, you know what I mean?"

"Yes. I know. But that's the way Mrs. Donovan is. That's the whole point. She acts. She doesn't react. She's a puncher, not a counter-puncher. That's the whole point of her character. She doesn't care what others think. If it feels good she does it. That's the part that society isn't quite ready to accept."

"Well, I still think it would be better if we got into it gradually. Another thing. Three scenes later we see the boss she works for make a pass at her. According to your instructions, he's a big, handsome fellow with a lot of money and a lot of savvy. Yet Mrs. Donovan tells him to fuck off. If she's so bent on getting laid, why does she say no to a guy who can really make a good life for her?"

"The point is that she isn't a whore. She's not selling anything. She doesn't feel attracted to her boss, so the answer is no. The whole point of my story is that here is a modern woman who follows her own tastes wherever they lead. She thumbs her nose at convention and doesn't worry about the consequences. You want her to think the way you do, Mr. Silverstein? That's okay for some women, but not for Mrs. Donovan."

"Okay. She doesn't like her boss, so she won't put out for him. But what happens when we meet her husband in the next scene? I was expecting some little sawed-off runt with a pecker an eighth of an inch long. You got him described as a great big, handsome Irish cop who has as much sex appeal as she does. Fact is, he's getting plenty on the side, too. What is more, you say she likes him. If she likes him, if he's good to her, if he makes a living, if he's pretty good in the kip, why is she running around like some cheap *courva,* some cheap whore, playing diddly with anyone who catches her eye?"

Stan Marcus was determined to keep his temper. He had come to the meeting expecting the worst. When he met Silverstein he knew why. But once the initial explosion had died down, he felt he had established his independence and all would be smooth sailing. Now it was obvious that Silverstein was trying to take his script and rewrite it according to his own conceptions. That he would not accept. He decided to restrain himself despite the temptation to re-establish his independence.

"Look, Mr. Silverstein, try to understand this—"

It was a bad phrase to use and Stan knew it the moment the words left his lips. Silverstein was too tough a man to be patronized. No one talked down to Manny Silverstein.

"Don't you talk to me as if I'm some sort of idiot with half a brain. I understand everything you say. Maybe more. Remember I've been in this business since before you got dry behind your ears. Maybe it's you who don't understand. It's your script, but it's my money. You wanna write just what you wanna write without listening to anybody's ideas but your own, fine. Help yourself to two million bucks from the nearest bank and *fahtig.* Write what you want. But now you work for me and I got ideas, too. If not, I'd still be selling hot dogs in Coney Island."

Silverstein was really getting wound up now, the heat of the morning's crises having taken their hold. The thought of this young upstart of a writer, who had the nerve to stand up to him, the great Manny Silverstein, and who was rejecting out of hand every idea he gave him, was too much to take. He'd better end the meeting now or there never would be peace between them.

"You better clear out now, Marcus. We'll talk some more in a couple of days when we've both had some time to think about what we've been talking about. You report to Nat Jacobs. He's our story department head and he's expecting you. He'll assign you an office, get you a secretary, and like that. I'll see you in a couple of days."

On this stand-off note, the meeting ended. But there was the ominous hint of fireworks yet to be exploded. Only the tenacious finesse of Mickey Sklaroff would succeed in defusing them. He worked on Stan Marcus first.

"Stan, you want to have the opportunity to use your creative genius? Back it up with a little common sense. You don't tell a man like Manny Silverstein he's wrong on every idea he brings you. You thank him, mull them over, then you do what you want. After all, you're not exactly George Bernard Shaw yet. Don't bang your head against mountains, move around them. Sidestep like a good boxer. Why go toe-to-toe with a Manny Silverstein in the first round?"

"Maybe you're right. But I can't have him telling me how to write. These are my ideas and *Mrs. Donovan's Defeat* is the best script I've ever done. I've got to fight for it."

"Fine. Fight. But pick your round. Don't go blowing it the first time you step in the ring with a heavyweight champ."

And this was his pitch to Manny Silverstein:

"Manny, you want a hack writer who kisses your ass every time you drop your pants? Then why buy a Stan Marcus? Genius doesn't sit behind every typewriter. And genius doesn't want to hear the first time you meet him that everything he's written is assbackwards. Wait a while. He'll come around. I even think now he's ready to change some of those scenes. He told me that he thought you were a pretty brilliant guy. He just didn't enjoy being pushed around on a first meeting. The kid's got guts."

The agent won his point. After all, he had nothing to lose. All he had to do was make peace, and he'd sacrifice anything, especially the truth, to accomplish that. The next time Silverstein and

Marcus met, he, the great negotiator was present. The subject of the script changes never even came up for discussion. Mickey Sklaroff saw to that. By the meeting after that, the changes didn't seem all that important to Silverstein. Marcus, at Mickey's urging, volunteered that he was contemplating a new opening scene, one that wouldn't give away Mrs. Donovan's character so blatantly.

"I've been thinking, Mr. Silverstein, maybe you're right. The audience may be led to believe that our lady is a whore and that's all wrong."

" 'Manny,' " Silverstein corrected, beaming.

" 'Manny,' " Marcus repeated.

Now, Richie Stevens was the next hurdle. The schism between Manny Silverstein and Richie Stevens had never been really mended since the days of *Helen of Troy*. Stevens did his work, made good money, acquiesced to Silverstein's demands when they were relatively reasonable, but, overall, insisted on his strict independence when it came to selecting projects. He had the right to seek outside financing when Silverstein and he could not agree on a proposed feature film. Several times he had left the Continental fold, each time scoring a mild success but not yet breaking through with a mammoth blockbuster. When approached by Silverstein on *Mrs. Donovan's Defeat,* he was less than enthusiastic. He agreed to read it first before entering any meaningful debate about abandoning his present project. Silverstein easily forecast the result. Stevens loved it. Yet, he had his reservations.

"It's a wonderful script, to be sure. But who is this Stan Marcus? I don't work well with new writers. Creating a script in the quiet of your office is one thing. But scripts aren't written, they're rewritten. Out in the field when the going is tough and tempers are raging like mad. That takes a real pro, not some young genius."

"Marcus is not so young," Manny countered. "And he's been around the track. You're going to like him more than I do."

"I'll reserve judgment."

"Guess who the script screams for? For Mrs. Donovan."

"If you're talking about Trudy, she's hurt. I don't know if she'll ever work again. I saw her last week and she's still in deep pain. She's also depressed as hell, dangerously so. She talks about being bad luck, to herself and to everybody she comes in contact with. I didn't like the sound of it."

"Go see her. Tell her we can't start this picture for four months. Let her read it. Take Marcus to meet her. Who knows? Maybe she'll fall for him on first sight. The way I hated him the first time I met him."

The reunion of Trudy Coles and Stan Marcus was something so emotional that Richie Stevens felt out of place. Stan, remembering her as Gertrude Kolinski, never connected the name Trudy Coles with that beautiful young girl he had met seven years ago in a run-down apartment she shared with a pimply faced mailroom boy. She, in turn, had completely shuttered their relationship from her mind and it wasn't until Stan was ushered into her living room by Richie Stevens that the name Stan Marcus sounded a loud, clarion call. They looked at each other in wonder, then fell into each other's arms for a warm embrace.

"Hey, there, easy," Trudy cautioned. "The ribs aren't completely healed yet. On second thought, break them again. It's better this way than on a Mexican street."

After Richie was informed of their former friendship, they sat down to a quiet discussion. Trudy was still depressed, uncertain as to whether or not she was willing to reassume the rigors of facing the cameras. After much urging, and mainly because of her respect for Stan Marcus, she agreed to read his script. They met again several days later. Trudy, predictably, was enthralled with what she had read.

"But I don't think I'll be well enough for months," she protested.

"We won't start filming for four or five months," Richie argued.

From the moment that Trudy laid eyes on Stan Marcus she knew that she was going to accept the assignment. It was strange how, after seven long years, she could still recapture her dichotomous feelings for this sensitive, gentlemanly writer. She had made no effort to recontact him after their stormy separation in Skipper Dawson's apartment. Frankly, she had felt that she really wasn't good enough for him. His mind was so complex, so fully developed beyond her own, that she had considered herself fortunate to bask in his glory. She also felt that if he had desired to continue the relationship, he would have found a way to recontact her.

She stole a glance at him now as he engaged in a brief, sidebar conference with Richie Stevens. The years had been good to him. Maturity had brought him greater dignity. He carried himself with increased authority. Yet, he was always kind and gentlemanly. She remembered how as a callow teenager she had wondered if she could ever fall in love with someone so intellectually lofty as Stan Marcus. And as she looked at him today, she still wondered.

When Richie reported back to Manny Silverstein he had a new surprise up his sleeve.

"She'll do it," he said simply.

"Great," Manny replied.

"Not so great. Trudy Coles is possibly the most beautiful woman who has ever worked in Hollywood. And she has natural talent. But face it, Manny, she's no great shakes yet as an actress. Besides, she'll have been sidelined almost a year before the cameras start rolling. This is a master script. This could be a classic feature, one that will be talked about as long as feature films are made. If you want me to direct it, I want your promise that we won't start filming until Trudy Coles is ready."

"And that means what?" Manny asked.

"It means that I will insist that she start training all over again, as if she never heard of Hollywood and never made a picture before."

"Okay. We'll get Mollie Haines into the act again and let her repolish the kid."

"No. She's grown beyond Mollie Haines. I want Sophie Thurston if we can get her."

"That old dyke?"

" 'That old dyke,' as you so delicately phrase it. I couldn't care less if her sexual proclivities leaned toward one-armed Armenian paper hangers with scabies. She's the best drama coach Hollywood or Broadway has ever bred. I want Sophie Thurston to make an actress out of Trudy Coles before the cameras start rolling on *Mrs. Donovan's Defeat.*"

"And how long is that gonna take?"

"I don't have the faintest idea. But if you see me as director, we'll wait."

"You got it. Now let's make it work."

CHAPTER 14

1953

After nearly a year of professional inactivity, Trudy Coles was back at work. She had accepted Richie Stevens' terms: a rigorous retraining period under the direction of Sophie Thurston, a legendary name in the business allegedly responsible for the success of a whole galaxy of stars. Reportedly, she turned down more clients than she accepted. Even though she had great respect for Stevens and had liked what she had seen of Trudy's performance in *Loving Sisters*, she accepted her client only provisionally. She would try working with her for a week or so and test the waters. If there was chemistry between them, if she found Trudy an apt pupil, then she would be willing to complete the training program.

"And how long do you expect the training to take?" Richie asked.

"It's hard to say. Maybe three months, maybe four. A lot depends on her. You know how I work. I start right from the beginning, wiping out all former concepts of walking, dancing, acting, emoting. Then I work with fresh clay."

"I understand. Do your best work with her. The stakes are very high."

Even Trudy, fully briefed by Stevens on what to expect, was taken aback that first morning when she walked into Thurston's studio. She was a half hour late, having had trouble locating its offbeat location in an older section of the city.

"I'm only a three-minute walk from Union Station," Thurston remarked condemningly. "Any cab driver could have shown the way. Let's not be late again. There's too much work ahead of us."

Sophie Thurston was one of the tallest women Trudy had ever met, probably well over six feet without shoes. She was lean and hard, with not a curve to her body. If she had breasts, they were so tightly strapped to her torso as to make them invisible. Her hair was steel gray, cut short in a mannish bob that spoke more of the Clara Bow twenties than the postwar fifties. She wore black —coal black—in every garment and every detail. A tight-fitting, long-sleeved jersey covered her upper body, giving way to snug man-tailored slacks that fit tightly in the crotch, reminding Trudy of the gays she had seen cruising the bars on Hollywood Boulevard. Instead of attempting to disguise her height, she wore high-heeled black pumps that made her seem taller still. Her face was deeply lined; "culture creases" by her definition. Trudy learned later that they were probably the result of overextended exposure to the California sun. Her eyes, also steel gray, were piercing and belittling. They made an odd contrast to the emerald green of Trudy's own spectacular orbs. Actually, in every detail they were, in a physical sense, diametrically antithetical. Only the fact that Trudy was also tall cast any similarity between them.

Having sized each other up from that first exchange of glances, work began immediately.

"Walk back and forth across the room a few times," Sophie commanded.

Trudy complied, walking rather self-consciously despite her former model training.

"You still limp? Is that from the accident or is it a natural gait?"

"It's from the accident. I'm still in pain. Sometimes I limp more than others. I walked at least eight blocks trying to find your studio and I'm tired I guess."

"We'll take care of that with lots of exercises. I don't like the way your ass shifts side to side. That can be corrected. One can be sexy without being obvious."

"I don't do it to be obvious. It's my natural walk."

"We'll correct that. Also, I'm going to teach you how to speak. That girlish, breathless quality might work fine in Westerns and B movies, but a great actress must talk with depth and resonance that commands everyone's attention. That, too, can be corrected, if you are willing to work."

"That's why I'm here," Trudy snapped churlishly.

"No need for temper. There will be time enough for that when the going really gets tough."

They worked steadily for the next three hours until, finally, Sophie signaled a break. Trudy was exhausted but determined not to ask for a respite on the first day of training. She knew that a battle of wills was being waged on this, the initial day of encounter with the Spartan Sophie Thurston. Not a word was spoken about lunch until Sophie broached the subject.

"I took the liberty of preparing a lunch for us here in the dining room. It's not much, but it will do the job. If you don't mind my saying so, you've got to lose about ten pounds. We don't want you jiggling in front of the cameras."

Trudy merely nodded in response. She had never thought of herself as a "jiggler," though she realized that she had put on a few pounds during these many months of inactivity. Lunch was about what she expected: Cold gazpacho soup, rye crisps, and a California salad. There was a small, tasty fruit salad for dessert, washed down with iced herb tea. All in all it was very refreshing. Trudy could not help recalling the lunch she packed for her father when he went into the mines: two or three ham sandwiches, the thick Polish bread greased with lard. An apple or banana plus a thick slab of apple pie. Hot, creamy coffee filled the old thermos bottle that had been in the family for years. No doubt Cass Kolinski would have starved to death on luncheons prepared by Sophie Thurston.

The rest of the day was reserved for reading and speech training. Sophie was determined to block out all colloquialisms and nasalities that marked Trudy Coles as the product of West Virginia. Although Trudy had succeeded in adopting more sophisticated tones, the roots were still there demanding to be heard.

"We can eliminate them," Sophie said, "if—"

"I know," Trudy interrupted, "if I am willing to work."

For the first time that day, the women shared a laugh. The ice was broken. After five successive days of uninterrupted labor, Sophie Thurston was satisfied that she wanted to continue the relationship. There was much hidden talent in this gorgeous creature and she was determined to expose it. Sophie was now involved with Trudy Coles and she struggled to keep their relationship on a professional basis. Nonetheless, it was she who originated the call to Richie Stevens.

"I thought you might want an interim report."

"I do if it is encouraging."

"It is. She works hard and shows great promise. She even does her homework when I give her assignments. There's a long trail for her to travel but I have no doubt she'll make it. I know you and that monster Manny Silverstein are eager to start filming but I can't really say how soon she'll be ready. I'd guess it will be closer to four months than three. But I really can't tell yet. She may surprise us."

"Not that 'a e i o u' stuff again," she protested one day. "Hell, I did that with Mollie Haines seven or eight years ago."

"Vowel habits are like bowel habits," Sophie responded. "You have to keep them open every day. Sometimes you sound as if you're squeezing them out; as if you're constipated. O O O," she sang out, "make it ring like Big Ben."

At home one night, practicing readings to develop vocal strength and clearer enunciation, Trudy was interrupted by a phone call.

"Who is it, Maria?"

"He won't say. He just says he's an old friend. I forgot to tell you he called twice yesterday when you were at class and said he'd call back. He sounds awful nice, Miss Coles."

"Nice or not, he's interrupted my train of thought. I guess I might as well take it if you're sure he's not some salesman."

"I don't think so. He says he's an old friend."

Curious, Trudy picked up the phone.

"This is Trudy. Who's my old friend?"

"Not really that old."

Trudy sucked in her breath as she recognized the deep, sexy voice of Jocko Rachubinski.

"Oh, it's you. Need a reference for a new girlfriend?"

Jocko laughed good-naturedly. "Good line. And I deserved that!"

"No shit! What is it, Jocko? What do you want? You're interrupting my work."

"Look, Trudy. I don't blame your being mad. I acted like a complete heel. But I didn't want you to be hurt and I won't go through life feeling guilty about the accident. Give me a break."

"The accident is old news. It's history now. I really would like to know why you're calling me."

"I can't say on the phone. Can I see you somewhere? Even if it's only for a half hour?"

"Anything we have to say to each other can be said on the phone. Now either out with it or I'm hanging up. Which is it?"

"I can't discuss it on the phone. After all we meant to each other it seems like thirty minutes isn't too much to ask."

"In my thinking it's a hell of a lot too much. Good-bye."

And she banged down the receiver. The call unnerved her, completely disturbing her professional concentration. She tried to return to her script, hated the way she sounded, switched to a classical play Sophie had asked her to read, couldn't get into it, and finally gave it up as a bad job. She spent a restless night and woke with a splitting headache. Over coffee, as she struggled to regain her equilibrium, she kept returning to the conversation and admitting to herself that Jocko had aroused her curiosity. What in the hell had he wanted that required a face-to-face meeting? She wished she could have dismissed the incident from her mind more readily. The best way to accomplish this was by throwing herself into her work. At rehearsal, Sophie complimented her on her progress.

"You're marvelous this morning, Trudy. Must have worked hard practicing last night."

"The usual. Just feel right today."

No mention of the phone call, of course, or the morning headache.

As the days stretched into weeks and the weeks into a month, Trudy became aware that Sophie was growing ever warmer in her attitude to her star pupil. Of course, Trudy reasoned, she had been so forbidding and cold at first that any human kindness would stand out in stark contrast. There were really no overt familiarities taken, just an awareness on Trudy's part that Sophie was staring at her more directly, examining her perhaps with a more personal intensity. It was obvious to even a neophyte that Sophie Thurston was not the marrying type. Yet, Trudy was not one to absorb gossip. She had heard too many Hollywood tales that proved themselves completely without merit.

On a given Friday, Sophie made an unusual suggestion. There was a new play in town and since there was little good live theater in Los Angeles, a city devoted to film, she suggested that they attend together. Trudy saw no reason to refuse. "We'll have supper at Romanoff's and then see the show. I'll book the table and reserve the tickets," Sophie said, in her usual take-charge manner.

The dinner was delightful and the play a gem. When Sophie suggested that they stop off at her apartment for a nightcap, Trudy saw no reason to object. After all, they were alone so many hours a day, another hour couldn't hurt. Besides, Trudy had grown to respect Sophie's intellect and was eager to listen to the older woman's analysis of the play they had just seen.

Sophie drank a little more heavily than Trudy had ever seen her do before, but after all, Trudy thought, this was Saturday night and Sophie never lost control. They spoke for more than an hour and aside from filling Trudy's glass more regularly than was needed, all was enjoyable. Even the slight kiss on the forehead seemed natural enough as they parted at the door after Sophie had insisted on summoning a cab.

It developed into a ritual. Since Trudy was in training and not seeing anyone socially, she had her weekend evenings free. It was stimulating to see movies and shows with Sophie as willing escort. Still smarting from the Jocko Rachubinski rebuff, Trudy was just as happy to avoid those dating alliances that inevitably led to the bedroom. Even the fact that they were seen in public with growing regularity caused little talk. Everyone knew that Trudy was in training for a great feature. Besides, her carryings-on with Silverstein, Rachubinski, her late husband, Rob Wenger, and a whole list of eligible males with whom she had been seen in public hardly marked her as a potential homosexual. There were suspicions aplenty, but no one actually knew what Sophie's proclivities were, since she had always been very discreet. The majority opinion was that she was asexual, a woman who really had no interest in sex in any form. That was the image that Sophie wanted and one she managed to maintain.

The following week, Sophie made an unusual suggestion. In light of her Trojan dedication to her profession, it was all the more surprising.

"What about a brief vacation from training?" she asked as she and Trudy sipped a glass of iced tea between vocal exercises. "I have a small villa in Palm Springs and I thought we might motor down there for the weekend. Ever been to Palm Springs?"

"Not really. We flew over it once and someone pointed it out; 'an oasis in the California desert,' he called it. But I've never been there. Is it nice?"

" 'Nice' is hardly the adequate description. It's pure heaven. I just hope they don't build it up to the point where every Tom, Dick, and Harry uses it for a get-away. It's thinly populated now, and the heat of that desert sun is really therapeutic. I bought this little place on a hunch about three years ago and I just love it. You'll love it, too. We have a small pool, a great garden, and the greatest slice of privacy in the entire town. We sunbathe nude behind a blossom-covered wall that stretches eight feet high. We can drive down Friday after lunch and come back Sunday night. Unless you have other plans . . ."

"Well, Sophie, I must admit I'm shocked. I thought that you were more like the Seven Dwarfs. You know, 'we work, work, work, work, work the whole day long.' I think I missed a couple of 'works' there but you get the idea. I have no plans. It sounds great to me."

"Good, then. It's decided. Now, let's work, work, work, work, to make up for the time we plan to lose."

Sophie picked Trudy up at her home Friday, as arranged, and they drove down to Palm Springs in her Cadillac convertible. The weather, as usual in California, was most cooperative. A slight breeze and azure skies brought the promise of a near-perfect weekend.

"You must really love this place. I never think I've seen you so happy," Trudy said.

"I do. And it's nice to have such an apt pupil for company," Sophie answered.

They arrived in time for a late afternoon swim, which was tremendously refreshing after their hours on the road. The hideaway was as charming as Trudy suspected it would be. It wasn't very large, just three bedrooms and baths, a spacious, cathedral-ceilinged living room/dining room combination, a flower-decked veranda, and a garden containing a small swimming pool. The view of the desert and the snow-capped mountains towering in the distance was enchanting.

Sophie suggested a pre-dinner nap and, feeling herself growing drowsy after the sun and water, Trudy happily accepted. She heard a gentle tap on her bedroom door several hours later as she awoke feeling marvelously rested.

"Time to dress for drinks and supper," Sophie whispered. "We'll have a few guests for cocktails but nothing auspicious, so dress informally."

Promptly at six, the guests started arriving, all tanned and lean, California-style. It was apparent almost immediately to Trudy that they were an odd assortment. Single men, single women, no couples at all, yet all friendly and casual, apparently determined to make Trudy feel welcome.

Billie Perkins, an athletic-looking lady in her middle years who arrived toting a tennis racket and still garbed in white tennis shorts, spoke out in a deep, almost masculine voice.

"Well, at long last we get to meet Sophie's prize pupil! She's been promising to bring you down here for weeks. Sometimes we thought she was just conjuring you up from her fantasies. But here you are and just as beautiful as she said."

"I don't know what to say." Trudy laughed. "I like being beautiful but I don't want to seem conceited. I guess I wouldn't be working in Hollywood if I hadn't inherited some looks from my folks. But, believe me, Billie, powder and paint help a heap."

"You see? I told you she was modest," Sophie said, beaming. "How about another round of drinks? Then we'll all be beautiful . . . or at least it won't make any difference one way or the other."

The cocktail hour ended as promptly as it had begun. By seven-thirty, every guest left, thanking Sophie profusely and urging Trudy to join them more often.

"Say, I'd love to," Trudy replied charmingly.

Sophie prepared a cold supper while Trudy napped, but she suggested that they first sit out on the veranda and watch the sun set behind the mountains to the west. She insisted that they sip some more cold wine, and Trudy was in no mood to resist. They both were quite tired. Trudy found herself fighting to stay awake. They retired by ten o'clock, Sophie bidding her a rather formal good night and suggesting that she lock her bedroom door before going to sleep.

"There's practically no crimes of violence out here but I like to play it safe. You can never tell when someone might slip in here in the middle of the night." The thought unnerved Trudy a bit, but she thought little of it once she was in bed behind locked doors.

After an early breakfast, they went for a long walk through the neighborhood, returning to the villa as the sun bore down with desert intensity. A swim was in order, but first Sophie insisted that they try some iced champagne she had received as a gift from one of the major studios.

"I'm not sure I'm up to alcohol at this hour of the day," Trudy protested mildly.

"My dear, champagne isn't alcohol. It's ambrosia," Sophia corrected. She was already handing Trudy a filled glass. Trudy sipped it and it did taste heavenly. She was amazed herself when she held her glass out for a refill five minutes later. The third glass seemed even more enticing.

"Now for a swim!" Sophie suddenly announced. "And this is the time to shed warm clothing and inhibitions."

To Trudy's amazement, Sophie stood up in a flash, dropped her sun dress; then, pulling down her panties over long, muscular legs, moved to the pool and dived in. Trudy tried to be discreet, but she had seen immediately why Sophie needed no brassiere. She was as flat and as hard as a man. Her hips were completely curveless, her torso square and erect like a well-trained athlete's. Strange, thought Trudy, the effect is not unattractive.

Sophie, a strong swimmer, moved up and down the pool with rhythmic, muscular strokes. She was supporting herself now by holding to the pool's upper ledge, urging Trudy to join her.

"Come on in. It's great once you get your clothes off and your blood pumping. It's completely private here. Jump in."

Accustomed to taking orders from the older woman for so many weeks, Trudy mechanically complied. In a jiffy, she, too, was nude and splashing up and down the pool.

"How does it feel?"

"Great. Simply great. I've been away from 'skinny-dipping' since I was eight years old but it's still fun."

Cautiously, Sophie swam toward her. She grabbed a bottle of suntan lotion from the ledge of the pool and opened the cap.

"Turn around. Your back is beginning to burn."

Trudy complied. She felt the cool fragrances of the menthol-laced lotion spread on her back as Sophie slowly, sensuously rubbed her shoulders, then the small of her back, and finally, to her amazement, her hips and the exposed portion of her buttocks. They were standing now in the lower end of the pool. The fiercely beating sun, the cool refreshing water, the glow of the champagne, and the sensuous and gentle rubbing of Sophie's expert technique were too powerful a combination to resist. When Sophie started rubbing her hips and thighs, she giggled and tried to squirm away but Sophie had already encircled her waist with one powerful arm and continued the rubbing with rhythmic regularity. To her amazement, she felt herself being sexually aroused. She wanted to resist, but somehow could not find the strength to do so.

"That's really enough," she protested weakly as Sophie continued to rub and rub, growing ever more intimate. She had inserted her knee between Trudy's thighs and was actually bouncing her up and down gently, as the buoyancy of the water aided her cause. Trudy felt the strong, muscular thigh riding up and down between her own softer limbs, the friction on her now-aroused vagina increasing with each bounce.

"Please don't," she pleaded softly as Sophie's free hand grasped her breast, stroking her nipple deftly with a determined thumb. She knew now that resistance was beyond her as she felt the sexual urge within her rising beyond her control. She moaned almost pitifully as Sophie's other hand, now free of the suntan lotion, which she had tossed on the lawn, gently stroked her vagina. She was near the peak now, aiding Sophie by moving up and down in the shallow water. And then it happened. She came with such violence that she was sure her muffled scream was heard high in the distant mountains. Sophie spun her around now like a child, burning her lips with a fierce, almost angry kiss, burying her tongue so deeply in Trudy's mouth that they both had trouble breathing.

Trudy had a new lover now and was off on a strange and perplexing adventure.

"Come, darling, let's get out of the sun," Sophie whispered. Trudy was too shocked at what she just had experienced to think of resistance.

They were by the side of the pool now, Sophie busy rubbing her down with a luxuriously fluffy terry-cloth beach towel. Her strokes were strong, yet gentle, and Trudy found her sexual excitement level rising again.

"Now, you dry me," Sophie commanded and, dutifully, Trudy complied, rubbing the taller woman dry and permitting her hand to be guided between Sophie's legs, which caused her to purr in catlike ecstacy.

Snatching the towel from Trudy, Sophie now wrapped it around her like a huge belt, pulling them both together in a fierce, bearish hug. Taking Trudy gently by the back of the head, she pulled her face down on her own blood-gorged nipple, which Trudy obligingly sucked with little enthusiasm. But as the rubbery button grew hard and incredibly extended, Trudy found herself being turned on once again and responded accordingly. Needing no instruction now, she placed her index finger in Sophie's moistened cleft and massaged her first gently, then with greater force, as the older woman's passion mounted to a screaming climax. Again they kissed, a hard, passionate exchange of affection.

"This is more fun lying down," Sophie whispered, and they headed for the bedroom.

"I'm not sure I can handle this," Trudy complained. But she did. Two hours later it was Sophie who suggested a nap.

They did little else but make love the rest of the weekend. Trudy, making no moral judgments, was amazed at how pleasurable the entire experience had been and why she had never before felt the slightest inclination toward a homosexual alliance. The fact that she had had no sexual activity for more than a year certainly contributed to her being so easily aroused. The sun, the water, the beauty of the surroundings, and the champagne had all been factors. Yet, truthfully, she had hardly resisted at all. And once she and Sophie were in bed, she herself had been just as active, just as responsive, just as aggressive as her seducer.

Certainly her respect for the older woman had also been an important element in her ready compliance. The truth was, however, that she never had been forceful about resisting sexual advances. Her father; Manny Silverstein; her late husband; Mulch Roberts, her black lover; Jocko Rachubinski; the young actors who carted her about at Silverstein's insistence; she had willingly made love to them all. There was an inner loneliness that was comforted by the act of love. She never had knowingly used her magnificent assets for personal gain. She was bright enough to realize, of course, that men longed for her and that once she acquiesced she had them in her power, at least for a while. That was not, however, her motivation in agreeing to the act of lovemaking. She just found it so satisfying that it was difficult to refuse.

Now, Sophie Thurston had opened a whole new direction in her life. It was amazing, in a sense, but she had no regrets. The one man she really wanted all of these years had resisted her. Unwittingly, perhaps, he had brought her a far more willing partner.

They were back in Los Angeles Sunday night and a simple kiss good night stated with obvious clarity that here different ground rules applied. They were training again at the usual time on Monday morning. There was not an iota of embarrassment exhibited by either of them and they were as formal to each other as if the weekend, filled with ecstatic lovemaking, had never occurred. When Trudy was sloppy in her diction, Sophie was as harsh and forceful in her correction as ever. When Trudy forgot lines that her tutor had commanded her to commit to memory, Sophie was far from understanding. When Trudy failed to please in exercise or dance activity, Sophie was there to reprimand her. Trudy asked for no quarter and was offered none.

Her struggle to attain professional perfection was burdened on several occasions by additional calls from Jocko. Each time, she either refused to take his calls or, when she did, was cold and curt and even threatened to speak to an attorney if he persisted in bothering her. Each time he would plead for a simple half hour of face-to-face conversation, insisting that if she met with him just that once he would pledge never to trouble her again. There really was no one she could turn to for advice. Finally, reluctantly, she agreed to seeing him at her home on an evening when she would make certain that Maria was present. She had considered having him meet her at Sophie Thurston's after work, but thought better of it on obvious grounds. She hadn't tested Sophie on that basis but she wasn't in a mood to determine if Sophie was a jealous lover. She saw no point in raising the question when a romance with Jocko was the furthest thing from her mind.

He showed up promptly as arranged, carrying a huge bouquet of American Beauty roses and looking as if he had spent a whole day grooming himself for the rendezvous.

"Who are these for?" Trudy asked disinterestedly. "Someone died?"

"No," Jocko answered calmly, refusing to join the issue. "They're for you. You always loved roses."

"Okay, thanks. Maria," she called out, happy to emphasize the point that they were chaperoned. If renewed romance was in Jocko's plans, she wanted to nip that thought in the bud right from the start. "Here, Maria, please put these in a tall vase."

Maria obediently took the flowers and was gone, as Trudy led the way into the living room and indicated a seat for Jocko. She placed herself safely on a single easy chair across the room.

"So, Jocko?" she asked in a businesslike fashion.

"I came to apologize," he said lamely.

"We've been all through that. Repeating empty words doesn't make them fuller."

"Doesn't," Jocko repeated with a smile. "That's one thing you learned from me."

"Yes, I remember. Jocko is the college Jock. A in English."

"Yep, A in English. Z in human relations. Trudy, I can't stop thinking about you and me and what a stupid ass I was. I came to beg for another chance."

"It's about a thousand years too late now, Jocko. It wasn't just the lawyer's wife, whatever her name was. Or the accident. Or the shame of being abandoned that night."

"Then what the hell was it? I made a mistake. You make mistakes, don't you? Everybody does. Even murderers are paroled after they pay their penance. I know neither of us is a practicing Catholic. But the Church realized thousands of years ago that people want to atone for their sins. That's what confession and absolution are all about."

"I'm no priest. There are sins and there are sins. It was your dishonesty that turned me off."

"And if I give you my word never to lie to you again? Couldn't you turn it back on?"

"Never. The truth is, Jocko, that as much as I loved you, once it ended I lost all taste for you. I can't say I hate you, but I did for a while. What took the place of hate was an emptiness. I have no interest in you, no feelings for you; nothing. You're a big zero in my life. I don't think of you warmly or otherwise. I just don't think about you and I don't want to think about you. Understand? You're a big cipher insofar as I'm concerned."

Jocko winced. "They're pretty tough words, Trudy."

"You bet your ass they are. And they come from a tough, West Virginia broad who has survived out here in this world full of sharks like you because she's tough. . . . Now, please leave, and I suggest you lose my phone number. If you ever call me again, I swear I'll call the police and report that you're bothering me."

Jocko got the point. He rose swiftly, made no effort at saying good night, and left quietly. Trudy watched the door shut behind him with relief. She had hoped she'd have the strength to tell him off and it had been easy. His first call had disturbed her, digging up exciting memories of a past romance. She knew it was a mistake to see him just as she understood that he really had nothing new or specific to tell her. She went through with the meeting mainly to test her own resolve. And she had passed the test with flying colors. Jocko Rachubinski was a dead issue in her life. For once, she had exercised her own determination. She neither needed nor wanted him, and had she had any inner doubts, the face-to-face rendezvous had clinched the point. Good-bye, Jocko, and good riddance.

On weekends, almost without invitation, Trudy packed her bag and she and Sophie were off to the glorious escape offered by Palm Springs. It was always the same; sun, water, mountains, and violent lovemaking without inhibition. They returned to the city Sunday nights, weary yet with renewed energy for the week ahead. One time Trudy received a phone call from an actor she once had had a brief affair with, a man she really had admired.

"Sorry, Chuck," she replied with little hesitation. "I've accepted another invitation this weekend. I'm off to Palm Springs."

"By the way," he asked, "how is it going with Sophie Thurston?"

Apparently the Hollywood gossip mill was primed and working overtime. Trudy didn't really care.

"A tough lady. But a hell of a coach! Thanks, Chuck, call again when you find time."

CHAPTER 15

1954

Five months to the day after Trudy had first hesitantly entered Sophie Thurston's studio, the cast of *Mrs. Donovan's Defeat* flew from Los Angeles to New York and then to Paris. From there they motorcaded to Avignon in Provence, an ancient walled city situated on the Rhône River not far from where it emptied into the Mediterranean. Normally a bit standoffish, the townspeople were so curious about the rich Americans who had come to film a motion picture in their back yard that they lined the streets when the company arrived. Richie Stevens had had the foresight to arrange a gala party in the center of the town to which everyone who wanted to attend was invited. The party, hardly provided for in the tight budget, paid great future dividends. It was a smashing success and the townspeople of Avignon took the *Donovan* company to their bosom.

At the last moment, Sophie Thurston had called Stevens and invited herself on the trip.

"My dear lady," Stevens cautioned, "Manny Silverstein is tight with a dollar. He paid handsomely for four months of lessons. And it took a lot of arguing on my part to get him to agree to that. I can hardly hear him agreeing to send you to Europe."

"He is and always was a cheap bastard," Sophie replied. "But I'm not asking for a salary. This gal is wonderful but she needs someone to keep her on her toes throughout the filming. Tell you what. You tell Silverstein that if he pays the fare one way, I'll work for free and also pay my way back. This picture is bound to be a sensation and I want to be part of it."

Richie's suspicions were aroused, of course, but the important thing was that Sophie would be a great help. And if there were some hanky-panky going on, at least it would keep Trudy out of the reach of some oversexed, overamorous Frenchman. He spoke to Manny Silverstein about it the next morning.

"Christ, what am I running, a caravan for dykes? You think I should spring for another fare?"

"Of course. We're lucky to get her. The best coach in the business and she'll work for free. I might even use her on some other members of the cast. To me it's inexpensive insurance."

"Okay. But if my old lady and I come to visit, better keep her off Tillie!"

"Why not let Tillie decide for herself? Good. I'll call Sophie Thurston and tell her it's a go."

The company, with cameramen, electricians, grips, actors, administrators, and all, numbered thirty-three. They were joined by an almost equal number of French technicians, who were to work on the film as part of the deal required by the French government in return for putting up a large portion of the capital and providing living quarters for all involved. It was a small, bilingual army Richie headed. He was thankful for his own fluency in French as well as for the fact that most of the natives had studied English in school. There were enough problems without the need for facing a Tower of Babel when the cameras started rolling. Trudy was housed in a lovely small villa on the outskirts of town. A French maid, Nicole, was assigned as her assistant and dresser; she also slept in the same home, which was bound to create a problem insofar as Sophie was concerned. Trudy was too excited to let this be a problem at the moment. She was happy that Sophie had decided to come along, but she had more serious considerations on her mind than lovemaking.

Although there were a number of featured male players cast in the story who would have affairs with Trudy as Mrs. Donovan, the climax of the film centered about her torrid mating with Maurice Beaulieu, a Parisian attorney who was spending a vacation in Avignon. The part was played by the internationally famed French movie star, Louis Marchand. Marchand, whose career had peaked a number of years before, resented the fact that so much attention was being afforded an actress who had yet to prove her salt. But what really irked him was that, in person, Trudy resisted his advances. Few indeed were the women who said no to Marchand, but to Trudy Coles he was just another aging leading man who touched up his hair to hide the gray, wore a corset to bind his expanding paunch, and ate just a little too much garlic to make love scenes pleasant. Actually, she found his obvious attempt to bed her down a bit amusing. He had invited her to share a cold lunch in the trailer that served as his star's dressing room. She found him garbed in a silk robe over virtually nothing, a fact which became apparent when he bent to pour white wine that he insisted was the best France had to offer. Trudy, no neophyte when it came to resisting male advances, decided to play the scene for the humor it contained.

"Louis, my pet, you'll catch the death of cold from that air conditioning if you don't put on some decent clothes."

"But this robe is quite adequate, my sweet."

"The robe is fine, Louis, but your balls will freeze if you don't put on some underclothes."

It was difficult to be romantic after such a start. Still, he tried. He came on stronger and stronger as the meal progressed. Trudy was just as determined to be uncooperative. Finally, she decided to make a stand.

"Louis, I really don't know what you have heard about me but I don't jump in and out of bed with three men at the same time. At the moment, I have a lover. If you want to be my friend, you must think of me as a fellow worker who respects your talent very much but will not become your bedmate. Is it a deal?"

Louis Marchand, far too self-centered to accept the idea that a woman could respond negatively to his advances, smiled in defeat but sought an explanation.

"Is it then that Thurston woman, as it is rumored?"

"That, my dear Louis Marchand, you will never know."

Stymied, Marchand decided to accept his defeat philosophically.

"Well, so be it. Righteous are they who do not kiss and tell. So we shall be friends."

That evening, in the villa where she was housed, Trudy dined with Sophie, as had become her custom. Dismissing Nicole, who was delighted to have an evening to spend with her boyfriend in town, Trudy and Sophie made love for the first time in more than a week.

"I really missed you, every inch of this beautiful body," Sophie cooed as she kissed every exposed inch of Trudy's person. "I had visions of that old goat, Marchand, trying to ravage you at lunch today, and that was hard to take."

"Mmmm, mustn't be jealous," Trudy whispered. "We have our moments together that no one can take from us. You know I like men, too. I can't change that any more than you can change the way you are. You've promised me so many times that you will love me as I am."

"Words come easy in passion, Trudy. Jealousy is a monster that is almost impossible to control."

"Remember that sign on Manny Silverstein's desk? 'The impossible things we do first; the difficult later.' Well, you can control anything you want to control."

Fending off the likes of Louis Marchand had been easy, and keeping Sophie in line was readily accomplished; but stilling her own longing for Richie Stevens was Trudy's most difficult assignment. Now that she was working with him again, watching him control the flow of international talent, observing him overcome the daily string of technical difficulties that seemed inevitable in a project of this size, she gained new respect for his abilities. There was no one who could be more inspiring for her and she found herself performing at a level that she did not know was possible. The coaching of Sophie Thurston helped. The inspirational script by Stan Marcus was a plus. The talented cast that had been assembled to support her was an undeniable advantage. But it was Richie Stevens—coaxing, suggesting, demanding—who brought out her ultimate talents. Whether the picture would make money or not she couldn't prophesy, but she was certain that she would be recognized as a real star once this hit the theaters. If only the money held out, to permit completion; if only. Hardly schooled in theater economics as she was, it was obvious to everyone connected with the filming process that they were running far above budget. When Silverstein arrived on the set unannounced, there was little doubt as to what had prompted his trip.

White-faced, he cornered Richie Stevens in his director's trailer. Manny Silverstein enraged was a frightening adversary.

"You out to bankrupt my whole company, is that it?" he barked for starters.

"That's so ridiculous I won't even answer it," Richie replied, determined to keep his own temper.

"Ridiculous my ass! We agreed to set the budget at three million dollars. That's not counting the three hundred thou and facilities the frogs are throwing in for their part of the capital. Then you call me and say things aren't so hotsy-totsy and you need a hundred thousand more. So I agree. Now the accountants tell me we're up to two million two and the goddamned picture is one-half finished. I saw the rushes in New York last night. I don't know what the hell is so goddamned expensive anyhow. I don't see any mob scenes, I don't see any tornadoes. I don't see any hurricanes. All I see is a line of guys knocking off Trudy Coles while her husband is off somewhere working for a living and playing with his putz."

"I don't waste money. I'm looking for the best this cast has to offer. And if I have to shoot a scene eighteen times, I'm going to do it to bring you the biggest money maker Continental Studios ever had or ever dreamed of. Do you understand that?"

Despite his resolution to hold his emotions in tow, Richie Stevens had difficulty keeping his internal thermometer from soaring.

"Do you want me to resign from the picture, is that what you want? I won't fight you. Bring in one of the schlock directors who grind out that pile of crap that Hollywood is famous for. I mean it, Manny. You begged me to do this picture. You told me that you had never read a script like this. And you know what? You were right. And Marcus is great under stress, too. He comes up with changes as quickly as anyone I ever worked with, and good changes at that. Goddamn it, Manny, I know I'm over budget but I can't help it. Now go back to New York and let me work. Go to those banker friends of yours and tell them they'll soon be able to retire. So will you, Manny, so help me."

There was a long, thoughtful pause. Manny Silverstein was not accustomed to losing too many arguments. Yet, he was smart enough to know that Richie Stevens was handling inspired material. He rose, touched Stevens on the knee, and made one of his few concession speeches.

"Okay, already. Get off the soapbox. Make the picture good the way you know how. All I ask is that I don't get to see it in prison because I can't meet my debts."

"I promise you. You'll see parts of it at the Academy Awards banquet. This time, I want you on stage getting that little golden statue and not watching others win."

As he angled for the door, Manny turned and questioned Richie about the star he had helped create.

"What about the old dyke? Is she causing any trouble? I'm afraid if we let her hang around too long she'll eat Trudy right out of the picture. We got too big an investment in that kid to see her disappear down somebody's throat."

"Don't worry, Trudy can take care of herself. And the truth is that Sophie Thurston has been a big help. I've got her working with half of the cast."

Having withstood the Silverstein attack, Richie turned his attention to artistic matters that troubled him. He had great respect for Stan Marcus, but there were times when he felt that Stan just didn't push hard enough to attain perfection. As great as was the rapport between them, he knew that Stan was sensitive and had to be led, not driven. He picked a moment when the writer seemed amenable to criticism.

"I read that post-accident scene again last night, Stan."

"Like it?"

"It's pretty fair."

"So? Does it play?"

Stevens paused momentarily, choosing his words with great care.

"The truth is, I don't think it works. I think you're capable of better writing."

"For Christ's sakes," Stan protested, "I've written that goddamned scene eight times already. You've got my best. There's no more juice in my lemon."

"Stan," Richie answered calmly, "I really don't care if we've redone it eight, eighteen, or eighty times. We stop counting when it's right. You know and I know there's a miss here somewhere. How can Mrs. Donovan watch her present lover get killed by an out-of-control car and then just move into bed the next night with his best friend? It's not natural."

"She can do it because that's what Mrs. Donovan is, a hedonist who fulfills her sexual needs no matter what happens around her. She isn't Mary Poppins, you know. She's Lisa Donovan."

"I know her name and I know she doesn't carry any bumbershoot. But we have to make the audience sympathize with her, not think of her as some heartless slut who is determined to fornicate her way to ecstatic bliss."

"We've been over this ground a thousand times. I just don't know how to make it seem righter."

"Try, Stan, try. You'll find a way."

That afternoon, excitedly, Stan Marcus virtually interrupted the filming of a key scene as he rushed onto the field where Richie Stevens was working.

"Richie, I've got it. I've got it. You'll love it, so help me. Wait till you read what I've got."

The sequence was perfect now as Stan had recreated it. Richie Stevens beamed in approval as he read the words.

"You see? I told you you could do it. It's perfect now. Lisa gets her wish but the audience feels she's entitled. Right after supper I want you to work on it with Trudy. She'll bitch a bit about being tired but I'll see that she sleeps late tomorrow. I really don't need her on the set until much before noon. You can coach her in the role until you think she's got the flavor you're looking for with the new words. I'll do the rest before the shoot on camera."

Nicole had prepared a seafood salad, fresh fruit, and white wine for supper. Trudy, once she had acquiesced to Richie's demands, insisted that Stan Marcus share it with her. Hardly able to contain himself until he heard Trudy read what he now considered one of the film's best scenes, Stan wolfed down his food like a starving refugee from war-torn Korea. Amused by his enthusiasm, Trudy laughed.

"Hey, Marcus," she joked, "come up for air or you're liable to choke. I promise no boogey man is going to grab that food out of your mouth before you swallow it."

"Who cares? I want food for thought, not for calories. We've got a whole new scene to learn and I promised Richie you would be letter-perfect in it by tomorrow."

"Relax. I will be. I promise."

Eventually, the meal was over, the table cleared, and Nicole excused for the night. They moved out onto a screened veranda, where the song of crickets and the smell of jasmine created almost too perfect a background for serious work. But Trudy had promised, and once she read the new lines for the first time, she realized that she was privileged to utter such perfect dialogue.

Stan read all the other parts, which he knew by heart, but it really didn't detract from the magic of the scene. This was Trudy's scene from start to finish and she took to it so quickly that even Stan was dumbfounded.

"Christ," he said in amazement, "I've heard of quick studies but you're too much. You know the lines after a single reading. Where the hell did you learn to memorize so quickly? There's got to be a memory trick there somewhere."

"There's no trick to it at all. The lines flow. You're the genius in this case. I'm just a parrot."

"Parrots aren't modest. Besides, I've got the parrot nose and the Jewish heritage to prove it. Come on, I want to hear you read it through one more time."

Trudy wasn't satisfied with one more reading. She rehearsed the entire scene at least a dozen times more, until each word was part of her, each line as natural as words she would speak in everyday conversation. They heard a nearby church bell toll eleven o'clock before they were through.

"How about one for the road?" Trudy asked. "You've sure earned it. I've got some velvety brandy that will put you in a sleeping mood."

"No poor writer ever thinks of refusing booze."

The brandy was everything Trudy had promised and more. If she had substituted the word "romantic" for "sleeping" her prophecy would have been more accurate. Soon she found herself sitting closer and closer to Stan, until the inevitable occurred and they were locked in a passionate embrace.

"We've been waiting for this a lot of years," Stan whispered.

"I know. I wondered even way back then if you found me attractive. God, you were a gentleman!"

"Gentleman, hell! I was a coward. You were just a baby. I didn't want to go to jail. Now, I'm ready to face a firing squad. Kiss me again!"

Their lovemaking grew more and more passionate as the brandy hit its mark. Stan had waited many years to possess her, but once on his way he was not about to pause for deep reflection. Trudy, who hadn't felt the heat of a man's embrace for nearly two years, had neither the power nor the inclination to resist him. Funny, she thought in a brief introspective moment, could this be the man I'm really destined to love? As a youngster she had been terribly taken with him. His restraint through the many hours they had been alone had convinced her that her feelings were not requited. So she had sublimated her sexual attraction for him and substituted feelings of respect, admiration, and gratitude. Now, she was really confused.

"Not here on the porch," she whispered. "Let's go to bed."

They did. It was lovely. Warm and caring. Soft caresses and mingled cries of delight. Slowly building passion egged on by the joy of first discovery.

They awoke cuddled in each other's arms. They watched the sun rise sharply over the horizon, toasted each other with stingingly hot coffee, frolicked in the impish pleasure of a joint shower; then, wrapped in heavy, terry cloth towels to ward off the chill of morning breezes, sat in wondrous silence to reconsider the bliss they had discovered.

Then, suddenly, it happened. Like an angry God invading Paradise, the door flew open and a wrathful Sophie Thurston entered, staring daggers at them both.

"So this is how the new words are learned! I'm sure Mr. Stevens will be happy to learn that his star and his hack writer have spent the night making passionate love."

Stan Marcus was nonplussed. He resented being called a hack and yet felt that any defense would just give credence to Sophie's accusation. Not so Trudy Coles. She was outraged, pure and simple. During the last several weeks, Sophie's monopolistic demands had begun to wear on her nerves. She still felt great affection for the older woman, and on those few occasions when they found the time and privacy to make love she felt some of the old excitement still present. But Trudy Coles was not about to allow someone to own her, body and soul. The more time she spent with Sophie, the more wearisome became the tutor's demanding attentions. That Sophie would have the effrontery to break into her home was something she could not—and would not—accept.

"How dare you come charging in here like some police officer telling me how I should conduct myself! And on Mr. Marcus' behalf, I resent you daring to call him a hack."

"I dare come here for a lot of reasons. And you know all of them. We'll start by saying that Continental Studios has charged me with the responsibility of getting the best performance out of you that is possible. I don't shirk my responsibilities like you do!"

"And that's what brought you bursting into my home, responsibility?"

"Yes, responsibility. You may have an alley-cat outlook on life, but I give full value when someone charges me with a job to get done."

"You're not the director of this film, Richie Stevens is. When he starts complaining, maybe then I'll start listening. Stan, I hate to ask you to do this, but you had better leave. Sophie and I have some personal matters to thrash out."

"Sure. No sweat. I'll be out in a few minutes. Just want to collect my scripts."

There were an awkward few minutes of silence until Stan Marcus left, with a self-conscious good-bye to Trudy and no communication at all with Sophie Thurston. The argument started anew a few moments after the ladies were alone.

"So this is your idea of love? I'm a prisoner. You snoop around and watch me like I'm some prized pet that can't be left off a leash."

"Trudy, you know how much I love you. Don't try to hurt me unnecessarily."

"That's not my idea of love. We've had a great time together and you showed me a side of myself I didn't know was there. But that's ending now. It can't last forever and it's stupid of you to think it will."

"Are you trying to tell me that you're tired of me, tired of our love?"

"I'm telling you how it is. We had fun together. We had great times and I grew from a young girl to a mature woman. Now I'm grown and it's time to move on. That's it."

"Oh, so you just toss me aside like an old boot that's sprung a leak. I'm not needed anymore. So out I go."

"I wish you could hear yourself. You've got everything anyone would kill for. I can't feel sorry for you. And you're getting a little tiresome, chasing after me and trying to hold me back."

"Hold you back? Hold you back? Why, if it weren't for me you'd still be some little bit player doing class B movies!"

"That's a lie and you know it! I've been a featured player—if not a star—ever since *Loving Sisters*. Just because Richie wanted me to sharpen up my skills doesn't mean that I have to be grateful to you for the rest of my life."

Sophie approached Trudy and attempted to cradle her in her arms.

"Trudy, this is really very stupid of us both. I admit I was wrong in bursting in here unannounced. Now you admit that it can't end this way for either of us. After all we have meant to each other it can't end with an angry spat."

There was something about Sophie's words that made Trudy angrier still. Once she stepped down and, in effect, pleaded for understanding, Trudy found that she had lost all respect for her. It was the tutor's mantle that had held them together; once it was shed, there was nothing left to maintain the relationship.

"Don't plead with me, Sophie. It's over now and I have to move on with my life. I'm thankful to you for your professional help. I'm certainly going to remember all of the affection we shared. But today's episode convinces me it's time to move on. Please go back to the States and let me finish the film."

There was a long, tension-filled silence. Sophie made a sincere effort to control herself, but it was hopeless. Her insatiable love for Trudy was so deep that she knew it could never be replaced. She also knew that begging and pleading would accomplish little. Hope dwindled; white, hot anger replaced it.

"You bitch! You whore! You've squeezed me dry like an old orange and now you toss the rind away because it has no more use to you? Is that it?"

"I think you had better go now. I have to get ready for work."

"Just like that?"

"Just like that. Now, leave. Please leave."

Sophie's wrath was violent. There was a small glass figurine on the coffee table in front of her. In one swift motion she picked it up, screamed "Ungrateful bitch!" and tossed it directly at Trudy's head. Only a basic instinct for survival guided Trudy's movement. She ducked at the final second and watched the figurine whistle over her head, crashing into a full-length mirror behind her. Sophie rushed at Trudy, grabbing her by the hair, and the two women scratched at each other's faces like two alley cats. Trudy kicked out in self-defense, turning her head from side to side in order to avoid the strikes of the other woman. Sophie screamed in pain as one of Trudy's kicks found its mark in her abdomen. The two combatants were rolling around the floor, breathlessly cursing each other as bitter hatred took over and the battle grew hotter.

Perhaps it was premonition, perhaps it was luck; but at that moment Stan Marcus returned, feeling a latent uneasiness about having left Trudy alone with the obviously angered, foresaken lover. Stan had no doubts about the true relationship between Trudy and the aging talent coach. He rushed at the pair when he discovered them rolling around the floor, and pulled them apart, raising Trudy to her feet.

"Are you all right, Trudy?" he asked simply.

"I'll be okay. Get that bitch out of here."

Actually, aside from a few welts and bruises, Trudy's face had been miraculously spared. Makeup would conceal the sore spots from the camera. Sophie's dress was torn, her eye blackened, and her hair pulled out in ugly clumps. Half gasping for breath, half crying, she straightened her clothes and headed for the door. Just before exiting she turned to Trudy. Speaking in barely controlled fury, she said, "Bitch! You'll pay for this!"

The door slammed and she was gone. Trudy went to the bathroom to assess the damage while Stan went to the phone and called Richie Stevens.

"Trudy's had a bit of a mishap. She won't be ready for the morning's shooting."

"What happened?" Richie asked.

"Can't talk now. She'll need at least three hours of rest but I don't think it's too serious. Reset the cast call for one o'clock. I'll stay with her until then. And I suggest you leave us alone."

"As you say."

They were on the set four hours later, Trudy looking none the worse for wear. They were readying a close-up of Trudy, as Mrs. Donovan, emerging from a passionate rendezvous with her neighbor's husband. No one saw Sophie stealthily approach from behind the central camera station. All were too busy fulfilling their duties to see her pull a small pistol from her purse, raise it calmly, and fire three shots directly at Trudy. The sudden explosions were deafening. Trudy fell as two bullets struck her. An alert cameraman nearby smothered Sophie with a body tackle and wrestled her to the ground. A cacophony of frightened screams filled the air.

"Call a doctor!"

"Get an ambulance!"

"My God, I think she's killed her!"

"Cover her with a blanket. It prevents shock."

Then suddenly, as Stan Marcus and Richie Stevens rushed to the fallen star's side, an eerie calm overtook the set. Actors and technicians alike were too stunned to cry out any further. Trudy, half-conscious and bleeding profusely, was silently weeping in pain.

An ambulance arrived on the scene. Accompanied by Marcus and Stevens, Trudy was driven to the nearest hospital. After what seemed like endless hours in the emergency room, a smiling surgeon emerged with the news.

"She is a very lucky lady, *messieurs*. Only flesh wounds, nothing more. One in the upper thigh, the other in the right arm near the shoulder. Profuse bleeding, true. But she is receiving transfusions and should be fine. Both bullets have been removed. By tomorrow, maybe the next day, she will be able to receive you both."

"How long will she be hospitalized, Doctor?" Richie asked, immediately ashamed at the callousness of his own question.

"A week. Ten days. Who can say for sure? She is young. She will recover quickly. But there is shock to be considered, so let us not rush her."

"Of course," Richie said in mortification. "She will have all the time she needs. And, Doctor, we are very grateful to you—*très reconnaissant*—for your consideration."

"But, of course. It is my duty, *monsieur*."

Soon, a very formal and unsmiling inspector of detectives was on the scene questioning the cause and perpetrator of the shooting.

"*Vous êtes Monsieur le Directeur?*" he asked Richie.

"*Parlez-vous anglais?*" Richie asked, hoping to duck intricate questioning by claiming a language barrier.

"Quite well, *monsieur*. I had the pleasure to spend two years in your country while training at the FBI headquarters in Washington. You may speak English. No problem. Now tell me, how did this unfortunate incident happen?"

Taking the inspector by the elbow and leading him to an outer alcove, where they could speak in privacy, Stevens tried his hand at international diplomacy.

"A mistake, Mr. Inspector, a mistake, nothing more. Some fool substituted live bullets for blanks in a gun that was featured in this morning's scene. We have taken steps to punish the man and send him back to America immediately. He is beside himself in grief because of the error. But there was no malice intended."

"A mistake, *Monsieur le Directeur,* a mistake?" the inspector asked in shocked disbelief, his raised eyebrows evidence of his doubting of Stevens' explanation. "But my men have told me they hear this was a woman, an angry ex-lover, who has wounded Miss Coles and nearly taken her life."

Richie Stevens' years in front of and behind the camera served him well. "A lover's quarrel?" he asked, laughing uproariously at his own question. *"Monsieur l'Inspecteur,* this is ridiculous. Merely an error, I assure you."

"And what of the stories that this crime is the work of some crazy woman?"

"Monsieur l'Inspecteur, I am sure you are aware of how ugly rumors crop up. People love to gossip, no? I am sure you understand the importance of your not acting in such a way as to arouse ugly publicity. This picture is important to France as well. Your government has a big investment in its success. My company will not forget you if you handle this with delicacy. Miss Coles will be well soon and you will be rewarded for your discretion. I'm sure you could use a nice car like the one we are using in our filming and which we will not need to take back to America."

The inspector got the point.

"All right, *monsieur,* as you wish. But you must sign a release stating that the gendarmes offered their assistance and that you insisted on terminating the investigation, that you have refused to prosecute. If Miss Coles does not recover this must rest on your head, not on mine."

"Thank you, Inspector. She'll be fine in no time. We are very grateful for your wisdom in treating this accident with such mature sensitivity. We shall also make certain to express our government's thanks to your supervisors for your professional attitude."

"Alors, it is settled. Call me if I can be of further assistance."

Though it had been possible to buy silent acquiescence from the French police, the American press was not to be denied. Before the hour was out, word had leaked across the ocean and reporters were pounding on the doors. It all shaped up as one of the juiciest scandals Hollywood had bred in years. Every columnist, every radio announcer, every red-dog journal in the States, blared out the news. The beauteous Trudy Coles had been shot right on the set and there were ugly rumors.

Stevens was hardly back in his hotel room before the phone started jangling. He had little doubt as to the caller. For years he had marveled at Manny Silverstein's ability to sniff out the news before it even hit the papers. He had planned to call him first, in self-defense if for no other reason. But Silverstein was on the trans-Atlantic phone as soon as the first rumor hit the air.

"Jesus Christ!" he fumed. "The only thing that hasn't hit this picture is an epidemic of syphilis. I knew it was a mistake to bring that old woman eater along but you, Mr. Director Maven, had to insist. It's a wonder you didn't want to put parts of the Trojan cundrum in the story and really fuck it up."

"Are we going back to that old chestnut?" Stevens asked wearily. "I thought by now you might have gotten tired of those old jokes that weren't so funny the first time."

"Funny! Funny! And what the hell's so funny about Continental going down the tubes? I got three calls from Reid this week threatening to call back their demand loan if we don't finish this picture. He says Stinson and Connors are beside themselves and he's losing control of the situation. Even the mention of Rocco Martucci doesn't bother them. They've hired some strong-arm guys of their own to deal with him. That's what they tell me."

"They're bluffing, that's all."

"Okay. So now you're a psychologist, too. I got a call from my bank here reminding me that the next payment on their notes will be due in twenty days and they're warning me they want no shit. Now try and call that a bluff."

"Look, Manny, this call is surely costing a fortune and it isn't accomplishing a thing. I want this picture packed up in the can as much as you do. But my star has a couple of bullet wounds to heal. I'll finish all the scenes I can without her. I'll shoot around her. I'll dismiss everyone not connected with the scenes we need to finish. Now we have to face facts. We're going to be delayed another three weeks. We're going to need at least two hundred thousand more. Maybe, two-fifty. I have made friends with the assistant minister of culture and he has promised me at least one-third of the money as a loan from the French Central Bank. He's seen some of the rushes and he's more excited than I am about the picture's prospects. Now stop wasting a lot of energy on me and go out and dig up some more money. We'll need it for certain but this picture will earn it back in two weeks or less."

"Just like that. Another hundred and fifty thou."

"Yes, just like that. And one more thing, Manny."

"Yes?"

"We're three thousand miles apart. But I swear the next time you throw up *Helen of Troy* to me I'm going to take a plane home at my expense and shove the entire ten reels up your ass. Now, good-bye."

CHAPTER 16

1955

Young bodies heal with amazing speed. Trudy was on her feet again in three days and out of the hospital before the week ended. She was weak, but rest, mild exercise, and medication performed incredible feats. Fortunately, the wounds had been superficial and would leave only surface scars, easily camouflaged. Trudy returned to the set in four weeks, determined to finish the film. Even Richie Stevens watched in wonderment as the girl-child now grown to maturity reached heights of professionalism even he thought she might never attain. Like a juggernaut charging down a mountainside, the film rushed to completion, actually finishing ahead of schedule.

There was a gala party after the last scenes were put to bed, to which everyone connected with the filming was invited. A quiet joy pervaded the atmosphere. Then, three nights later, after rough cutting had been completed, there was an informal screening of the final sequences that had been shot after Trudy returned to work. Those privileged to watch were rapturous in their words of praise. Richie was now convinced that once he returned to the more sophisticated laboratories in Hollywood he'd piece together a feature so powerful that it would be mentioned whenever filmmakers gathered to discuss that magic city's greatest accomplishments.

Stan Marcus was somewhat less enthusiastic. Whether it was a feeling of guilt, or simply the natural weariness that blends with depression when one completes a task, no one could say. Trudy cornered him one afternoon as they were both returning to their residences following the completion of a day's filming.

"Hey, Marcus, you got the blahs?" she asked.

"Not really. Just tired, I guess."

"You've been avoiding me as if I had leprosy. Anything wrong?"

"I still haven't recovered from that Thurston mess. I keep thinking maybe I helped it happen."

Trudy stopped dead in her tracks and faced him.

"Sophie and I were heading for a breakup for months and months. You provided a convenient excuse but, believe me, it would have happened one way or the other."

"I still can't get over that vicious look in her eyes. How in the hell could she have tried to kill you?"

"Luckily, she didn't. And you really saved my life twice, once in the house and again when the shots rang out. I'll never forget that."

She leaned close and kissed him gently on the cheek. Stan made no effort to respond. He smiled wanly and said, "I'm happy one of us can be so philosophical about attempted murder."

"Oh, shit, Stan, save the tears for a soap opera. Come on over, I'll mix you a drink."

But Marcus refused.

Four days later the film was completed. Stan didn't remain to share in the celebration. He left Trudy a simple note saying that he had to rush back to Hollywood for conferences on a new feature he had been commissioned to write. He hoped to see her back in California.

Trudy's return to the States was not all that she had hoped. Taking Richie Stevens' advice, she flew to Boston, hoping thereby to avoid a confrontation with the press. There was an obvious tie-in between Air France's publicity department and American columnists, for a whole battery of cameramen was waiting when the plane touched down at Logan Airport. In order to avoid attention, Trudy had traveled with only one maid and no studio attendees, who might have protected her. She was manhandled and surrounded even before she could enter the passenger terminal. Facing the inevitable, she held a brief press conference right on the runway.

"Any bad wounds, Miss Coles?"

"Why did she do it?"

"Are you going to press attempted murder charges now that you're home?"

Trudy Coles had been around the track enough times now to handle the challenge. She smiled, signaled for silence, and then handled herself with such sangfroid that even she was amazed.

"Listen, guys, it's very simple. Some dumb jerk put the wrong bullets in the pistol and I got winged twice. I'd show you where but I don't want anyone here being sued for divorce. I lost a lot of blood, but that was the long and short of it. I'm fine and I'm pressing no charges against someone who made an innocent mistake."

"Yeah," asked one non-believer, "where's Sophie Thurston? We heard she did it."

"Miss Thurston wasn't even in Avignon when the accident happened. Whoever tells you otherwise speaks lies. Now, boys, you'll have to forgive me."

With that, she threw a kiss, and took her leave with royal aplomb, sashaying to a waiting limousine and leaving the press corps behind.

Trudy returned to California and rented a small cottage on the Rincon, a scenic beach on the Pacific coastline not far from Santa Barbara. Accompanied only by a single maid, she spent the next several months "baking out," as she liked to term it. Her phone number was guarded and her only communications were with Richie Stevens, who called occasionally to keep her posted on the progress of the final editing. She heard nothing from Stan Marcus. There were regular flowers from a nearby shop sent by Manny Silverstein, but he, too, respected her privacy and desire for seclusion. She was bone weary and needed sun and rest. Gradually, she felt herself regaining her strength.

Richie Stevens insisted that only he and a few technicians view the film as it was nurtured to conclusion. On occasion he would permit Manny to see a scene here and there, but refused to permit him to see longer segments.

"Jesus Christ!" Manny bellowed. "Is it that lousy? Who the hell brought the money into this project? For two years I've been kissing ass for those *fecockta* New York bankers and now you won't even let me see my own property!"

"All in due time," Richie answered calmly, not one to be bullied or moved.

Finally, all was finished. The sound had been blended, the special effects completed, and unnecessary scenes left on the cutting-room floor. The studio's major screening room was reserved for the fateful night of first exposure. Only a few guests were invited, the selected list being carefully reviewed by Manny and Richie both and then culled once again by Continental's chief of protocol. Connors, Reid, and Stinson flew in from New York. A few key exhibitors who represented larger chains were recipients of mysterious calls, inviting them to visit Continental for a special sneak preview. Actually, it was one of Hollywood's worst-kept secrets, but efforts to restrict the first viewers were successful. Hedda, Louella, Sidney, and Jimmy all got word from their favorite pipelines but they could not beg, borrow, or steal an invitation. Only one person received an invitation and refused. Trudy Coles insisted that she would wait for the news in her Pacific hideaway.

As the auditorium slipped into darkness, a near-religious silence settled over the audience. The economic future of an entire company, and the hopes and aspirations of thousands of people, rode in the balance. Although those present wanted the picture to be a hit, it was their very real need for success that might have blemished their judgment. But no, there could be no mistake here. From the credits to Trudy's final words, "Whore I may be in your eyes, but my body and soul are my own," the viewers were genuinely moved. A hush ensued as the screen faded and the house lights were gradually brought up. At first, all were silent. Then suddenly there was a hum, applause, and expressions of wholehearted enthusiasm. Manny Silverstein actually hugged Richie Stevens and whispered in his ear, "Cundrum." Now Richie could bear the teasing. Messrs. Stinson, Reid, and Connors were, of course, beaming with unbridled joy.

"Manny," they shouted, "we knew you could do it."

Too old a campaigner to ruin a moment of triumph, Manny responded simply, "I'm not sure I did."

Richie suddenly remembered Trudy, huddled by the phone in her Pacific retreat. He rushed to his office, dialed her number, and when she answered he said simply, "Hello, star."

Trudy guessed the rest.

"Good, bad, or indifferent?" she asked, merely seeking reassurance.

"There are not enough superlatives to describe it. It's all we hoped and dreamed for. One week after this film is shown for the first time you will be the biggest star in Hollywood. You can bank on it."

After a brief conference with his top marketing experts, Manny Silverstein decided on a joint East-West premiere. Then, as soon as the film gathered the reviews and word of mouth he was certain it would receive, he planned a simultaneous release in two hundred picture houses across the country. Trudy would attend the opening in New York, Richie would be in Los Angeles, and the press department would beat the drums in both cities. No expense would be spared in an effort to make the release of *Mrs. Donovan's Defeat* a happening of mammoth proportions. It was all as predictable, and every bit as corny, as the exploitation of hundreds of other Hollywood features. The difference this time was that the product was so magnificent. Every viewer left the theater more elevated spiritually than when he had entered. Richie Stevens had been, if anything, modest in his evaluation of the picture. It simply broke all records wherever it was shown. Manny Silverstein was beside himself with joy.

"I knew that broad was going to be a big star the first time I saw her," he boasted to Obie. "Didn't I tell you that?"

"You did. But I think the first time you saw her, you couldn't take your eyes off of her boobs. I'm not sure stardom was the foremost thing on your mind."

"Someday I'm gonna fire you, Obie, so help me. What other secretary would have the nerve to call her boss a sex maniac?"

"I didn't call. I just thought."

Obie knew her playful banter would not be taken too seriously. When Manny was playing a hot hand she could say just about anything. Fortunately, the new hit would bring such a merry flow of cash into Continental's coffers that she could feel free to jest for months and months to come.

At Silverstein's insistence, Trudy agreed to a coast-to-coast publicity junket in support of the picture. It was a triumphant journey. Whatever city she entered, the populace seemed to be awaiting her. There were street parades, city hall ceremonies, critics' luncheons, newspaper features, radio and television interviews, and as many publicity stunts as the press representatives traveling with her cared to arrange. Interestingly enough, the shooting incident in France was all but forgotten. Trudy Coles was a household word. Trudy Coles was a giant celebrity. Trudy Coles was a star. And she loved every minute of it.

"Can you make one more TV show this afternoon?" she was asked by Corky Fierman, the studio's key press agent, who had chief responsibility for the entire junket. "I know it's been a long day and we have to show for that chamber of commerce banquet at eight tonight."

"Sure we can make it. And one after that, too, if there is one."

"You're great, Trudy. I wish all the ladies were as easy to work with as you are. Hell, my life would be a bed of roses."

"Look, Corky," Trudy said quite openly, "I've wanted to be a star for a long time. Where I come from a movie star is someone who really doesn't exist in real life. She's just some goddess up there on celluloid. My mom died in childbirth when I was just a kid. I've known what it's like to be hungry. I've known what it's like to be lonely. Now, I can have it all and I'm not going to louse it up. I'm going to squeeze all the juice out of this star thing I can get. And then some. You understand?"

"Sure, I understand. But the great thing is that you do, too. When the momentum's with you, play it big."

The trip had been scheduled for three weeks. But after ten days, the picture was reporting such fantastic grosses in every major city that further promotion seemed unnecessary. After conferring with his bosses in Los Angeles, who in turn won the approval of Manny Silverstein, Fierman brought Trudy the news.

"Mission accomplished. We're calling it quits. California, here we come!"

"What about Boise? What about Pocatello?" Trudy questioned.

"To hell with 'em. Manny S. says we're to pack it in. There isn't a city in the U.S. where this film isn't playing to capacity. I understand they've added two more showings a day at Radio City. And still, they say, the lines stretch all the way to Fifth Avenue and back. No need for further drum beating. We've got it made!"

"Just when I was getting accustomed to living out of a suitcase!" Trudy complained mockingly.

"Suitcase, my armpit!" Corky replied. "You've got more luggage than the entire United States Army on field maneuvers."

"Well, it's been fun while it's lasted."

"That it has. But there's a certain little gal on Wilshire Boulevard who's destined to spend an awful lot of time in bed for the next several weeks. So we might as well move it."

It suddenly occurred to Trudy that for the foreseeable future there was no one in California to share her joy. Now that the affair with Sophie Thurston had ended in such an ugly fashion, she felt a natural reluctance to get deeply involved on an emotional level with any one person. In retrospect, she felt that though her coupling with Sophie had been exciting, her heterosexual needs were stronger still. She wondered how many other women could find satisfaction in bed with members of either sex. She imagined that there were many who hadn't the strength to fight society and admit their cravings even to themselves. Maybe, she thought, she was lucky not to be bound by convention. Still, there was nothing like the comfort of being made love to by a caring male. Caring, that was the key word. And her own caring for Richie Stevens had not abated through all the months of stress they had both survived.

Now there was the new emotional involvement with mysterious Stan Marcus. That night before the Sophie Thurston attack she felt as if she was at long last being swept away by a man for whom she felt both admiration and sexual attraction. Somehow, though she was at a loss to explain it, she felt that Marcus loved her more deeply than he allowed himself to express. Was he the man who would sweep her off her feet and bring her the kind of lasting love that every woman craves? It was strange even to her that she could contemplate a love affair with Stan when all the while she longed for a signal from Richie Stevens. Well, she reasoned, one could not have everything in life. Here she was about to attain giant stardom and she was still dreaming of love like a schoolgirl.

Still, in spite of finding herself riding the crest of professional accomplishment, she could not but envy the simple, joyous anticipation that Corky was obviously savoring. He was going home to someone he loved and who loved him as well. A simple emotion, perhaps, but a beautiful one, Trudy thought. For her, home was where she slept. Aside from a few servants, there was no one who had missed her and no one she really missed either. She saddened, and found herself thinking of home—home in West Virginia. She hadn't been back since that ancient day when she and Skipper Dawson had slipped away on the night bus to

Charleston. She hadn't spoken to any of her family in nearly four months. She did send money home whenever the spirit moved her. She received an occasional letter from Debby, who was now married and pregnant with her second child. Dad had finally married Aggie Stephanik, according to Debby's last note. But he was still drinking heavily and too sick to spend many days in the mines. Trudy decided to call Debby.

"Oh, I'm glad the message got through," Debby exclaimed as soon as she picked up the call.

"What message?" Trudy asked, perplexed.

"To call me. I've been trying to get through to you for three days. I'd almost given up."

"Wouldn't the studio give you my number?"

"You've got to be kidding. They treated me like I was some nutty autograph hound. I begged and begged but all they said was they'd give you the message. Anyway, I've got bad news. Pop died."

"When?" Trudy asked, shocked.

"Tuesday night. In bed. He'd been awful sick for weeks but wouldn't even see a doctor. Aggie was with him in the end."

"When is the funeral?"

"I've been waiting for you. Can you get home?"

"Of course. I'll fly out first thing tomorrow morning. I think I can connect with Charleston. I'll hire a car and driver from there. We can hold the funeral Sunday morning if that's okay with you. What about money?"

"We'll need some. Otherwise it's a plain pine box and no real service."

"Give him the best. Spend as much as it takes."

Trudy's return to Hubbardsville was exceedingly painful. She could not believe that she had ever been part of a life so mean, so ugly, so devoid of inspiration. Wherever she went, people gaped at her, not in friendliness, but with a sort of jaundiced envy. She tried not to flaunt her wealth and success, but even in her less spectacular clothing she was as conspicuous among them as the proverbial whore in church. Debby, almost three years her junior, looked like her older sister, the cares and struggles for survival having aged her prematurely. Debby's husband, Clyde, also a miner, stared at her with obvious contempt. Brothers Billy and Steve seemed like distant strangers. Mary, now in her late teens, tried her best in a futile effort to be friendly. Bobbie, aged eleven, asked a few questions about Hopalong Cassidy, then moved off to safer ground. She exchanged a few stilted words with her old friend, Helen Caputo, but it was obvious that both of them were ill at ease.

She left town as soon as the funeral was over. She had a lonely, four-hour wait at the Charleston airport, then boarded a plane for Chicago, where she would catch the night plane to Los Angeles. She arrived in the city red-eyed and depressed. Now, as never before, she realized why one can't go home again.

CHAPTER 17

Life at the top was sweet for Trudy, yet somehow unfulfilling. After five months of rest, interrupted only by an occasional television guest appearance, Manny Silverstein started turning the screws again, urging her to go back to work. Trudy was just as determined to wait. After the incredible triumph of *Mrs. Donovan's Defeat,* which was bound to win its share of Oscars, she was reluctant to follow it up with some insignificant piece of trash. Richie Stevens urged her to turn down any script offered by Continental that didn't match the standard of excellence she had just achieved.

"Remember, Trudy," he told her over a drink at the Cricket Lounge, "Manny is your friend when it suits his own needs. But he's the original economic man, moved only by, and in the direction of, the big buck. He'll have you back doing two-bit Westerns if you let him."

"I think you're being a little unfair. Manny is my friend. Without him we would never have finished *Mrs. Donovan.*"

"You let that gratitude get in the way of your judgment and you are lost, lady. Don't work until you find the right property."

Obviously annoyed by what he considered to be Trudy's naïveté, Richie summoned the maître d' and requested his check. Trudy found her phone ringing when he dropped her off and, predictably, it was Manny on the line. He suggested lunch the next day at Chasen's.

"What did you think of that great script I sent you to read?" he asked as soon as they were settled at their table. All eyes were focused on them. Though Trudy was reveling in her new star status, she found it somewhat disconcerting.

"Can't I have a drink first before we talk business?"

"Drink and talk. There's no reason we can't do both."

"Okay. So you want to know the truth. I thought it was a piece of plain shit. You know I couldn't do that after *Mrs. Donovan.*"

"Why not? You'd've grabbed it last year."

"Maybe I've learned a hell of a lot since then. It stinks. So did the last three you sent me. Why can't you get Stan Marcus to write us another one?"

"Because the ungrateful skinny prick found an out and broke our contract. He's working for Mayer on a big blockbuster that's going to be filmed in Russia. Fuck him and fuck those commies, too."

"I guess you're not the only one who likes caviar, Manny. Order me another drink, will you, I'm dry as a bone."

She received a call from the studio one afternoon and was certain it was from Manny. She was wrong. An unfamiliar male voice was on the line.

"Miss Coles, this is Lee Landis. We met years ago. Remember, I was a friend of Penny O'Neill."

"Yes, I remember. Not that good a friend if I remember right. Didn't you dump her and have her evicted from her apartment?"

"That's not the way it happened at all, Miss Coles. I'm sure Penny never said that."

"She was too proud, too much of a lady. What do you want with me, Mr. Landis?"

"It's about Penny. We haven't seen each other in years, but I do keep tabs on her. She became an alcoholic. I hear she's in Milton Sanitorium, drying out. She refuses to take my calls."

"Where is Milton Sanatorium?"

"It's in Marina del Rey. About a half hour's drive. I thought maybe—"

But she cut him off abruptly.

"I'm not really interested in what you thought. Thank you for calling me. I'll find her."

The drive to Marina del Rey took much longer than anticipated. Even though Los Angeles' freeway madness had not yet reached its peak, vehicular traffic was heavy. The extra time gave Trudy room for thoughts of guilt. She hadn't seen Penny more than a half dozen times in the past five years. For a while, after Trudy had left the apartment and married, they were regular chums. The years had taken their toll. As Trudy had matured and moved onward and upward in her career, she'd found less and less in common with the woman who had meant so much to her in her early days at Continental. Even Penny seemed somewhat embarrassed in their most recent rendezvous. There really was not much to say after they had exchanged initial greetings.

Trudy calculated that with twelve years flown by since the day they met, Penny would be middle-aged, forty-two at her last birthday. Even that calculation was poor preparation for what she saw when she reached the private hospital and had Penny ushered in to meet her. She was led in by a masculine attendant obviously selected more for his physical strength than for his sensitivity. He seemed bored to death with his job and only perked up a bit when he realized that his ward's visitor was a famous movie personality. Penny, now prematurely gray and emaciatingly thin, was hardly recognizable. The fire in her eyes had been extinguished. She had little or no expression and her voice was dim and lifeless. Even her greeting to Trudy was cold and emotionless.

"How did you find me?" she asked.

"Lee Landis called me. I would have been here sooner if I had known."

"My friend Charlotte must have called him. I asked her not to. I'm in good hands here. They'll see that I die sober."

Nothing that Trudy could say had any effect on Penny. She invited her to come live with her when she was ready to be discharged.

"I'm alone now, you know. I'd enjoy the company."

Penny smiled wanly and thanked her. "We'll see."

That was her only response. After an uncomfortable thirty minutes, the maximum time permitted for visitations, Trudy said good-bye, promising to visit again soon. Before leaving, she had a word with the institution's director. Although it was a rather run-down private hospital for alcoholics, many of the patients were state-supported. In Penny's case, she was about to lose her private room because her own meager resources were running low and state aid provided only for ward residence. The director was surprisingly sympathetic, but financial facts were financial facts and could not be ignored.

"I want Miss O'Neill to have a private room, the best one you can find that's unoccupied. I also want her to have a private attendant. That guy who brought her in scares me. He looks like he should be guarding escaped murderers, not a lady who drinks."

"He can't help his looks, Miss Coles, but we can easily transfer Miss O'Neill to another floor and arrange for a new, female attendant."

"I'd appreciate that."

He hesitated, as if reluctant to bring up the matter of expenses.

"There is, of course, the matter of costs."

"I'll pay them. Here, I'm leaving you a check for a thousand dollars," she said, reaching into her purse for her checkbook. "And here is my private number at home, for your use only. I want you to call me, if you will, if she doesn't make normal progress."

Then, looking into his eyes with the emerald greens that had made her famous, and pausing for dramatic effect, she said, "Miss O'Neill is the kindest person I ever met. I want her to have the finest care possible."

"We'll do our best, Miss Coles, that I promise you."

Trudy returned to her home deeply depressed. Somehow, the experience strengthened her resolve to fight for her own career goals.

After Trudy had turned down eight consecutive offers, Manny started getting angry. He vented his spleen one afternoon on Obie, who could find no escape from his wrath.

"Why the cheap little hooker from West Virginia! Christ, when she first started she would have kissed my ass for films like the ones she's turning down. Now, all of a sudden, she's playing star with me. Well, fuck her! She turns down one more and she's on suspension. I won't give her a feature for the next five years. And if anyone else tries to bust my contract, I'll go all the way to the Supreme Court."

The next script deserved to be turned down, but just to be sure, Trudy consulted with Richie.

"Same old crap that Continental has been turning out since Manny started in the business. Tell him to shove it. You're too big a star now to appear in this kind of garbage."

Trudy returned the script to Manny's office with a terse note:

> Sorry, old man. I'm busy fumigating the house after reading this. Let's try again.

Manny swung into action. A formal notice from the head of production informed her that she was on suspension. Until she agreed to appear in at least one of the ten scripts she had turned down, there would be no salary or expenses forthcoming from Continental's pay office. In addition, she would be hearing from their chief counsel. She did. Two days later, she received a registered letter informing her that she was in direct violation of her contractual obligations. An injunction was being sought to prevent her from working for any other Hollywood studio. Trudy was a little scared, but more angered, by the legal threat. She got into her car and drove directly to Continental's main gate. She was stopped by the guard on duty.

"Sorry, Miss Coles, but we've been instructed to bar you from the lot as long as you're on probation. Mr. Silverstein's orders. Sorry."

"Well, hell, I'm on my way to see him now."

"Sorry. Orders are orders. Only Mr. Silverstein can change them. Maybe you'd better get in touch with him directly."

Furious, Trudy drove home with such temper that she ran a red light on Santa Monica Boulevard, only to be whistled to a stop by an angry cop.

"Where the hell do you think you're going? House on fire or something?"

"Sorry, officer. It's been a bad day."

"Ain't you Trudy Coles? I loved you in *Mrs. Whatshername's Defeat.*"

"Thanks. I'll be more careful next time."

"I'm sure you will," he said, pulling his pad from an inner pocket and writing out a summons. "This'll cost you ten bucks. No exceptions, even for movie stars."

Trudy remained on suspension for six months. She wouldn't call Manny and she was shunned by other studio executives. The word was out—propelled by Manny, of course—that her success had gone to her head. She was too much trouble to handle, despite her recent, brilliant success. Knowing Manny's terrible temper, no other studio wanted to incur his wrath when he was having a tiff with one of his stars. In the long run, the boys with the decision-making power had to stick together. It was the law of the Hollywood jungle.

Not having many friends, Trudy found time hanging heavily on her hands. She read a lot. She started playing tennis and hated it. She gave golf a whirl and found it just as boring. She found herself drinking a lot more than when she first had come to town. The image of her father coming home stinking drunk on payday had served as a preventive. But that was long ago and Dad was dead now. The whiskey made her feel warm inside and wanted. It did add to her weight problems, but she had always been able to shed the extra pounds quickly when she had to face the cameras. Who knew if, and when, that would happen again?

She realized suddenly that she was lonely, lonely for the love of a man. But she was a star now; the eligible bachelors were afraid to call. Besides, she was on the Hollywood shit list and those who had their own careers to think about worried that association with an outcast might not be good for their own professional futures. Richie Stevens had no real quarrel with Continental Studios, so he was off and working again. Although he seldom called, she did get a brief note from the Yucatan, where he was on location, urging her to keep a stiff upper lip and hold out for the picture she really wanted. He was sure that, sooner or later, Manny Silverstein would back down.

Great! thought Trudy. He's working and happy. I'm unemployed and all alone. It's easy for him to send me notes telling me to be brave.

That night, unaccompanied, and buffered by two stiff martinis, she headed for one of the newer, less formal restaurants in Westwood where the Hollywood set was known to be congregating. No town in America is quicker to establish the "in" place and swifter to abandon it in favor of the restaurant down the block three months later. The maître d', a former captain at the Brown Derby, greeted her warmly.

"Miss Coles, so nice to see you. What a pleasure!" He showed her to a conspicuous table and neatly pocketed the ten-dollar bill she crushed in his hand. Trudy looked around self-consciously and recognized a number of the young actors who were hanging around the bar looking for a connection. She ordered a drink although she knew she really didn't need one. It made her feel better, less self-conscious about being alone on a night when everyone around her seemed to be joyously pursuing romantic activity.

"Mind if I join you, Trudy? Or are you waiting for someone?"

It was Bill Peters, ex-actor, ex-agent, ex-personal manager, ex-everything. A steel-gray, handsome man in his late fifties, Peters had lined his coffers by marrying a succession of rich, elderly women, fleecing them, then forcing them to divorce him. Trudy had met him at a number of Hollywood parties, reacted to him as one does to a cobra, but had never actually exchanged more than a few perfunctory words with him. Tonight, however, was no night to be particular.

"No, Bill. Just waiting for dinner. Can I buy you a drink?"

"Drinking is what it is all about."

Despite the fact that Trudy had been building a tolerance for gin these many lonely months, five martinis before dinner were a bit much. By the time the food arrived, she was bombed and picked at it with little interest. Bill Peters, however, had paced himself. Since he knew she would be paying the check, he ate with complete abandon.

"Let's get out of here and have some fun," he suggested, and Trudy was in no condition to refuse.

He supported her as they left the restaurant, and but for his control she certainly would have stumbled and fell. Once in his car, she mumbled something about wanting to go home, but he easily persuaded her that the night was young. She revived in the night air as he drove toward the center of Los Angeles and then headed for what was obviously the slum district.

"What's this all about, Bill?" she questioned more in curiosity than anger.

"Big party. You'll love it."

He parked the car and helped her out, leading the way to a store that was obviously devoid of merchandise. He knocked on the door and Trudy thought she could hear the faint sound of rock and roll emanating from somewhere within the premises. A large, ebony-skinned Negro answered the door.

"Hi there, Mr. Pete, what you all got in drag?"

"Hi there yourself, Bumble Bee. I got me a woman, can't you see?"

"Sure enough and she is a jim-dandy! That'll be two biggies, if you please. That covers everything. We got the real dream wagon stuff tonight."

"Sure nice to know you trust me, Bumble Bee," Bill said as he reached into his wallet and handed over $200.

"As the man says, 'In God We Trust—all others pay cash.' Enter and climb the golden flight to happy land."

Three sets of heavy curtains, obviously hung to mask the sound of revelry within, were brushed aside by Bumble Bee to reveal a steep set of stairs leading to an apartment above the notions store that served only to conceal the establishment's real function. Though Trudy had recovered from the heavy drinking at dinner, she had a bit of trouble negotiating the stairs, even with Bill pushing gently from behind. The top of the stairs as well was blocked by heavy drapes, which Bill, having visited here many times before, easily separated to gain entrance. Another flight of stairs faced them and they climbed again to the third floor. Here the landing was concealed by a locked door.

Bill knocked sharply three times and the door opened to reveal a dimly lit room encompassing the entire length of the premises. The floors were covered with what appeared to be rich Oriental rugs but were actually cheap reproductions. The lights were very dim and it took a few moments before Trudy's eyes adjusted to the darkness. Couples were seated on the rug-covered floor against the walls, surrounding a small polished area on which a few men and women were dancing. A small jazz combo seated on a low platform beat out a muted accompaniment. Bill led Trudy to a far corner of the room, where there was space for them to settle down against the wall.

Trudy could see much more clearly now. The crowd was racially mixed, with whites, Chicanos, and Negroes in approximately equal numbers. The musicians were black, as were the waitresses, one of whom approached them almost instantly.

"Hi there, Mr. Pete, ain't seen you for a coon's age. You gone high hat on us poor darkies?"

The question, more rhetorical than not, was asked with a musical lilt that barely masked the girl's sarcasm. She was a great beauty, with a body more naked than covered by the skimpy costume that did little to cheapen her appearance. Trudy immediately suspected that the girl and Bill had a relationship beyond the obvious one of waitress and client.

"Well, Trix, a man can stand just so much of this high living. He's got to dry out once in a while. What do you suggest might be right for the occasion?"

"You just let matters rest with little ol' Trix."

She left, but returned immediately holding two cigarettes. She lit them skillfully in her own mouth, then proffered them to Trudy and Bill. Trudy had smoked grass on rare occasions but it usually gave her a bad headache and little lift. However, under the present circumstances she could hardly refuse.

"And a bottle of gin to wash it down, please," Bill requested.

About twenty minutes later, Trix returned, carrying a small silver spoon laden with fine white powder. Trudy had been to many Hollywood parties where cocaine was sniffed freely, but she had never tried it herself. By the time Bill placed the spoon under her nose she was so far gone it would never have occurred to her to refuse, even if she had wanted to. The heavy load of gin had left her senses paralyzed. The marijuana had carried her eighteen feet high, to a point where she imagined herself floating effortlessly, like someone beyond the pull of gravity. She seemed to have lost all feeling in her extremities, yet the more she drank and the more she smoked, the better she felt. Now, gingerly at first, she inhaled the happy dust for the first time. It burned her nostrils not unpleasantly.

Strangely, the coke brought her a sense of physical power, returning feeling to her limbs and creating an aura of bodily well-being. When another loaded spoon was offered her, she paused, took another sniff, and suddenly felt herself laughing beyond control. She struggled to her feet, pulled Bill up beside her, and, clinging to his arm, stumbled unsteadily to the dance floor. It was as if all the weariness of the evening had left her and like a Greek, dancing to mask his personal tragedy, she had to dance to give vent to her feelings of exhaltation.

At five in the morning, Bumble Bee, never one to ask a happy client to leave, suggested that tomorrow was another day and he was sure they would still be in business.

"Party pooper!" Trudy giggled and, attached to Bill like a postage stamp, she headed for the door.

Negotiating the two flights of steps was no easy task after her first night of drinking, smoking, and snorting, but the theory that there is a God who looks after the inebriated must be valid. They landed safely at the bottom and emerged into the cool, Los Angeles night air. She felt simply wonderful.

As they headed for Bill's car, Trudy spotted a dark figure moving toward them from the shadows of an adjacent building. The man was smiling pleasantly and was in no way frightening. He wore a soft felt fedora, which he pulled from his head, and, bending in a low bow, he said, "Mornin' folks."

"Good morning," Bill answered gruffly. "What do you want?"

"Just a little bread, Mr. Dude. I sure could use a fix. How about it, little momma?"

The voice, the phrase, the posture, all combined to wrench Trudy back to reality. She knew this man, or at least she once knew him. He smiled pleasantly but made no attempt to establish any bridge over the chasm that now separated them. It was clearly Mulch Roberts, her Ethiopian Romeo of yesteryear. His eyes were glazed over, his entire demeanor warped almost beyond recognition. His tattered suit was stark evidence of his recent failures as a musician. Trudy reached into her purse and pulled out a hundred-dollar bill. Mulch took it eagerly, bowed in appreciation, and was gone.

"Take me home, at once!" Trudy commanded. She was stone sober now, as if all the liquor and narcotics had been drained from her in one terrifying microsecond. From time to time she had been curious about what had happened to Mulch. Since they traveled in different worlds it was not unusual that their paths hadn't crossed. She wondered why he had never attempted to recontact her as her career soared. No doubt his intense personal pride explained it. Once she turned her back on him it was not like Mulch Roberts to plead for a reconciliation. Yet, to see him so obviously destroyed as a man was a bitter experience, one that would haunt her for months to come.

Bill Peters' efforts to spend the night with Trudy were in vain. She blamed a splitting headache, but he suspected it had something to do with the black beggar whom she had so generously rewarded. No need to press, Bill thought, there would be plenty of other nights. And there were. Bill Peters and Trudy Coles became a twosome in a matter of weeks. Since he had no visible manner of employment, he was always available to her. It came at a time when she was desperate for companionship. It mattered not that the $200 he had laid out for admission that first night at

Bumble Bee's palace of joy was the last money he spent when they were together. Money was one of the few things Trudy had plenty of, and she soon accepted the fact that Bill Peters, pimp without portfolio, was a man whom women supported.

It was a little embarrassing at first. Bill always had a convenient excuse as to why he was without adequate funds. But after a few dates and a few nights spent together, the charade was unnecessary. Trudy found it more expedient to load Bill with money at the beginning of the evening rather than to demonstrate to the world that she was paying the bills at the moment the waiter presented the check. Actually, she fooled no one.

Gigolos of one description or another were as old in Hollywood as prostitutes. Bill Peters had been around a long time and there wasn't a maître d' worth his salt who didn't know him for what he was. The only unusual aspect was Trudy's age and beauty; he usually preyed on older women who couldn't do better. Bill Peters was one of the first in line in the "go and catch a falling star" game. He performed well. Handsome, debonair, witty, and well groomed (thanks to some of his more generous benefactors), he always gave his women their money's worth. And he made it a point to concentrate on one "client" at a time, so there were seldom angry separations.

Trudy knew all this, half from gossip, half from instinct, but it didn't faze her. Bill made her feel good, physically and mentally, at a time when her spirits had been sagging. He was hardly the passionate young lover; but experience with women can go a long way to balance the absence of youthful fire. Also, Trudy felt comfortable with Bill Peters. There was no risk and no thoughts of a permanent attachment. Most of all, Bill lived life to the hilt. There were no lectures, no admonitions. They drank and smoked and sniffed cocaine until they slipped into near-oblivion. They made love whenever the spirit moved them.

Trudy's mirror reflected her dissipation; unusual dark circles were forming permanently under those incredible green eyes, but what did it matter? There were no cameras to face, no scripts to study, no deadlines to meet. Trudy was living the life of a sybarite and almost enjoying it. Deep down, of course, there were those nagging feelings telling her that her career was stalled. Still, she agreed with Richie Stevens that she could not allow Manny Silverstein to foist just any role on her shoulders. It was a dilemma complicated because Richie never showed any interest in her as a person, apparently concerned only with her professional career.

The weeks rolled into months and still the celebrating continued. She realized that she was running through a lot of money, especially since while on suspension there was no income from Continental Studios. What's more, there was talk of their suing her and that would require expensive legal representation. Still, she had inherited a large sum of money when Rob was killed and at this time of her life Bill Peters' company seemed very important to her.

One night, after a particularly heavy session with Bill at Bumble Bee's, she lost consciousness. She had fainted several times before, but this night they had great difficulty reviving her. She came to after the last customer had gone home, and Bill managed to half carry, half drag her into his car. Bumble Bee protested that maybe they ought to lay low for a few weeks, since he didn't relish any trouble with the authorities. Bill opened her purse, removed $300, and crushed it into Bumble Bee's hand.

"Well now, Mr. Pete, I catch your message. The lady seems just fine to me. See you tomorrow when the sun sets."

But she wasn't "just fine," and the next morning Trudy could barely get out of bed. She usually rose about eleven, started with a shot of vodka, awakened herself with a swim in her pool; then, after a small breakfast, sunned away the early part of the day. This morning, she found the Los Angeles smog too difficult to inhale, had a miserable headache, was nauseated, and found her heart beating with unusual intensity. When she headed for the pool, she lost her balance, fell heavily against a large vase, shattering it in a thousand pieces, and just avoided cutting herself severely among the scattered shards. Her housemaid came running and helped her to her feet.

"Call Dr. Goldberg. Find out if he can see me this afternoon."

Dr. Stanton Goldberg, one of Beverly Hills' rising young internists, had been Trudy's doctor for a number of years. Originally, she had met him as an intern during her stay in the hospital after she had collapsed making the Western in Colorado. Entranced with the fact that his patient was a real, live movie actress on her way to stardom, Goldberg had been overly solicitous during her illness. Later, having completed his internship, he opened an office in downtown Los Angeles and had met Trudy one night at a concert. She became his patient and watched his popularity soar, his fees rise abruptly, and his office move to Beverly Hills. Their relationship had always been very warm, more like caring friends than doctor and patient.

Goldberg was alarmed when he saw Trudy that day. His expression revealed his concern.

"See a ghost, Doctor?" Trudy joked.

"Not quite. But you don't look like the Trudy Coles I know, if I may be frank."

He was more alarmed after examining her carefully. Inviting her into an inner conference office that he kept for just such sessions, he decided to lay it on the line.

"Trudy, I'm not some Beverly Hills opportunist merely waiting until I can become a plastic surgeon and coin dough. I care about you and I must voice my honest concern. You've been abusing yourself to a point where I think you're about to endanger your health permanently. You're twenty pounds underweight, your blood pressure at 180 over 120 is dangerously high, your coloring is bad, your mucuous membranes look as if they're the remains of a forest fire that swept through your nose, and I don't like some of the sounds in your chest. You had better let up or you're in for real trouble."

"You sound like young Dr. Kildare."

"This is no joke. I'm going to prescribe medicine and assorted vitamins. But what you really need is plenty of rest, mild exercise, and a vacation from booze and that stuff you're sniffing. I can't give it to you any straighter than that."

"Okay. I get the message."

For a week, Trudy kept more regular hours and insisted that she and Bill spend quiet evenings at home. Evenings at home were bad for Bill Peters in many ways. Soon he had influenced Trudy to head out for an evening of excitement, which, quite frankly, she had missed. In another few days they were back on the old bandwagon, and the nightly dissipation resumed. There were occasional fainting spells, more lost weight, almost persistent headaches; but, despite them, Trudy hadn't the strength to resist. On several occasions, Dr. Goldberg called to find out how she was getting along, and asked her to return to his office for a follow-up visit, but he was unsuccessful. Trudy avoided speaking to him, telling her housemaid to pass the word that she was just fine and to thank the doctor for his interest.

Meanwhile, Bumble Bee was having his own problems: police raids. One Saturday night when the entire club was loaded with customers and the smell of grass was thick, three busloads of uniformed cops swooped down on the establishment and arrested everyone in sight. Trudy Coles and Bill Peters were among them. It was not a terribly traumatic experience for Trudy; she was so stoned she hardly remembered what had occurred. Fortunately, Bill had been arrested before and knew the ropes. A payoff to one of the arresting officers bought him the right to use a phone immediately. Within an hour, one of the town's more influential attorneys, who specialized in handling matters involving the movie clan, had gotten both free on bail. But there was no way to avoid a future hearing.

The next morning, suffering a terrible hangover but now informed of all that had transpired, Trudy put through a long-distance call to Richie Stevens, who was on location in the south of France. Stevens was terribly sympathetic but really at a loss for advice to give her. He, himself, was in the final stages of filming and really not in a position to think clearly about this kind of emergency. He wished her luck and embarrassedly cut off the conversation. A half hour later, Trudy received a call from Continental's legal department. They understood she was in trouble and wished to help. No mention was made of Manny Silverstein, and Trudy could never decide in her own mind whether it was kindness or a desire to protect an asset that motivated him. It really didn't matter. The studio took over her legal defense. She was acquitted without a formal hearing on some trumped-up technicality. Peters got off, too, but not quite as easily. His legal bill was $5,000, which Trudy reluctantly paid.

Within a month, Trudy, who refused to meet Peters socially again, had dried out. She went on a strict regimen of exercise and diet and regained the lost weight. Her blood pressure returned to normal, her chest sounds cleared up, and she made the necessary professional decision. She called Manny and he accepted her call.

"Manny, I surrender."

"I knew you would. You're too smart not to."

She was back at work shortly, grinding out picture after picture, like a hamster on a treadmill.

CHAPTER 18

1965

Trudy Coles realized her life's ambition at the age of thirty-five. She married Richie Stevens.

It all happened quite suddenly. One day, resting between features and preparing for yet another overseas assignment, she received a call from Antoine, his latest in a series of male secretaries. Mr. Stevens requested the pleasure of her company. They met for lunch in a quiet little French bistro in Westwood.

"I've been worrying about you," Richie said for openers.

"Worrying about me? For whatever reason?"

"It's hard to say. We both had such promise in *Mrs. Donovan*. What the hell happened to us?"

"Everything. I'm making more money than the whole town I was born in. You're one of the busiest directors in Hollywood, always on call, always in demand. Manny Silverstein is growing old and rich and still screwing every starlet who falls into his net. What more can one expect of this business?"

"Lots more. Christ, this town not only has surrendered to television, it's outstepping it in the race to produce shit."

"Shit is what it's all about."

"Not necessarily. I thought when the new independent producers took over it would all be different. But it's more of the same. The big studios may have taken their names off the masthead, but they still own the equipment and they still call the shots."

"Funny thing, all these egghead production chiefs may know

more about modern art and social causes, but I'll take the old-time mugs like Manny. Hell, they know how to make pictures."

"I'm glad someone does. I'm tired out. I haven't had a fresh, new idea in years. Maybe it's time I took off for the Himalayas and backpacked my way to the top with a Sherpa guide."

"Maybe it's time we both took off and had a little fun."

It started as an innocent joke, but the idea took hold. Three days later, having pleasantly bullied Manny Silverstein into allowing her a three-month vacation, Trudy joined Richie on a pleasure trip to Europe. By the time they reached New York they were sharing a bedroom. It was sweet, though hardly exciting. Trudy blamed the lack of passion on the fact that, for too many years, she had dreamed of being Richie Stevens' lover. This had to result in some sort of letdown, a condition that would soon reverse itself.

By the time they reached London they were like an old married couple, bedding down regularly but seldom engaging in sex. Two weeks later, in Paris, Trudy awoke to the realization that Richie Stevens would never really love her. He was sweet, considerate, debonair, sophisticated, knowing, and delightful company. Yet, the fact was that they were better friends than impassioned lovers. She really couldn't understand why.

"Richie, what's wrong with us? Is it me?"

"Wrong? What's wrong? Aren't you having fun?"

"Fun, yes. Educational experiences, yes. I've been to so many churches I could preach a sermon. I've visited so many art galleries I could paint a picture. But I'm talking about us. You and me. Can't you see and feel that something is missing?"

"Not really. Trudy, I'm fifty-three. You're thirty-five. We aren't kids on a sexual binge for the first time."

"Sex doesn't wear out like an old boot. If we turned each other on, we'd never think of age."

"You've been reading too many *Silver Screen* romances," he said, clucking her under the chin. "Now come on. Get dressed or we'll miss the show."

Two weeks before their intended return to the States, Trudy confirmed a suspicion. She was pregnant. At first, she hesitated telling Richie. Then, on more mature consideration, she broke the news, hoping that it might bring them closer together.

"Great," he said with little enthusiasm. "We'll get married just as soon as we reach California."

"I'll get an abortion if you want me to."

"You'll get no such thing. You'll get a wedding band like every other respectable married woman."

"Frankly," she said with a smile, "I was hoping you'd say that. At least we'll save on the honeymoon. We've just had it."

They were married in a simple ceremony at Richie Stevens' palatial Beverly Hills home. Only a few intimate friends were invited. Trudy made a point of inviting Stan Marcus, whom she hadn't seen in months, but he begged off with what she thought was a rather weak excuse. Manny Silverstein, quite predictably, was best man. Afterward, as they sipped champagne around the pool, they found each other alone and able to converse.

"Well, well, it finally happened. The guy I thought you wanted from the beginning you now got."

"Forever, Manny. Forever."

"Forever, my dear West Virginia *tzotzkillah*, is one hell of a long time. In Hollywood, forever is maybe five years. With luck, ten."

"Bite your tongue, you old cynic. In West Virginia we fuck around a lot. But we marry forever. And I've got real news for you. I'm pregnant."

"What took so long? You've been married ten minutes."

"I'm shy, I guess. Only about two months. We'd better do that picture we planned right away before I start to show."

"You feel up to it? It can wait till the kid is born."

"I'm up to it. My wedding present from my groom is that he has to go on location in a couple of days on an independent production for Jerry Wald. They're old friends and Richie made him a promise before we went on our trip."

"Okay. We'll get the team together. We'll probably shoot right here in California so you won't have to make any long trips."

"I'm tough. Don't treat me with kid gloves. Be the real son of a bitch of a Manny Silverstein I've come to love."

"You got it. We start next Monday."

Trudy finished the picture in four months and was just beginning to show enough to have made further shooting very difficult. She was recalled for some reshooting about three weeks later and the director used every trick in his book to hide her bulgings. Meanwhile, life at home was very lonely with Richie gone most of the time finishing his own picture for Wald. Although her pregnancy had been amazingly easy at first, she was having more and more stress as the months wore on. She tired easily, had difficulty digesting her food, and generally felt herself praying that what had started pleasantly but was developing into an ordeal would soon be over.

She was alone at night, still three weeks before term, when she awoke with violent cramps. When her pain started coming every twenty minutes, she called her doctor. He ordered her into the hospital at once and her real agony began. All in all, she was in active labor for fourteen hours. Just when her obstetricians were about to begin a cesarian, she delivered. Belinda Stevens, weighing a scant six pounds, came into the world fighting for breath. Sickly and undersized, she wailed piteously while Trudy, at last relieved of excruciating pain, wondered if so painful a beginning could ever lead to joy for mother or daughter. Informed by wire that he was a father, Richie Stevens was exuberant. He sent a roomful of flowers. Trudy spent most of her time giving orchids to passing nurses. Although she was quite capable of nursing the baby, she had no desire to do so.

"Elsie can do the job," she told the doctor. "All of my family was bottle-fed. I'm not one to change things."

They brought the baby to her every four hours for her feeding. Trudy marveled at her own detachment. The baby obviously looked like a sweated-down version of Richie. It was difficult for Trudy to absorb the idea that she, too, had helped create this young life. She was tender to the baby but hardly overwhelmed by maternal instinct. As soon as she was capable of leaving the maternity floor, she wanted to return to her own home. She, the nurse, and the baby arrived home just as Richie's plane touched down at Los Angeles International Airport. He rushed home filled with joyous expectation.

From the moment Richie Stevens first laid his eyes on his daughter Belinda, he fell madly in love. The joys of parenthood had evaded him for many, many years. But now he had a beautiful baby girl who looked like his mirror image. From the moment the baby stared at him with seeming recognition, his heart melted. There could be no question here. Belinda Stevens was her daddy's girl.

The thought of being a mother was not one that Trudy had anticipated with any degree of longing. Suddenly, without any prior planning, she had discovered she was pregnant. She'd been very happy at the time, for it enabled her to attain her long-held ambition of becoming Mrs. Richie Stevens. But in the months that followed, pregnancy had become really more of an inconvenience than a blissful state of expectation. In a sense, the painful delivery was a foreshadowing of things to come. Once home from the hospital, Trudy had little interest in rearing a daughter. It was not that the child displeased her. It was simply that motherhood as such was not something that brought her joy. Besides, from the very first moment that Richie looked upon the child with such adoration, Trudy knew instinctively that the baby would separate them rather than bring them together.

She found it troubling that the joys of motherhood seemed to escape her. Even with her limited experience, she had encountered friends and relatives whose very being had been enhanced by the addition of a baby to their households. The Hollywood gossip columns had carried a number of articles about the Stevenses' new arrival and Richie read them over and over as if to savor every drop of joy.

"What's the big deal?" Trudy asked skeptically. "People have been screwing and babies have been coming into this world since Adam and Eve's time. It really doesn't take a hell of a lot of talent."

"Sex is one thing," Richie answered quietly, "but parenthood is quite another. There are people who would give their eyeteeth for a baby. You've got a beautiful daughter, yet you act as if she is just another acquisition. You ought to be ashamed to talk that way."

"Well I'm not. That's the way I feel and I'm not ashamed."

Ashamed, no. Troubled, yes. Trudy envied Richie's obvious delight in holding little Belinda. She loved the baby, of course. But love on her terms was no match for her husband's exaltation. While having her hair done, she ran into one of her friends, Betty Carden, a fellow actress in the Continental camp.

"Trudy, you look absolutely radiant! So that's what motherhood does for you!"

"No, that's what this beauty parlor does for you if you hang around long enough."

"I hear the baby is gorgeous. You and Richie must be going off your nuts!"

"Richie and I are very happy, of course. How go things with the great Manny Silverstein? Devoured any young chicks lately?"

Trudy had changed the subject abruptly because she realized

that the answers for herself did not parallel those for her husband. Richie was, in Betty's terms, "going off his nut" over Belinda. She was only relatively happy, and she wondered why. She thought for a while that it might trace back to her being the head of a household in West Virginia at the callow age of fourteen. Motherhood there meant long, long hours of maternal chores while trying to fend off an overamorous father and attempting to meet the meager requirements of schooling. It had been no bed of roses, to be sure. She wondered if subconsciously the robe of motherhood was bringing these buried memories to the surface.

From the very beginning, Trudy entrusted the rearing of Belinda to hired help. She worked feverishly to regain her figure, spending three and four hours a day in gymnasiums and exercise salons to return to her prenatal weight. After three months she was pestering Manny for another assignment.

"Hey, I'm glad you're hot to trot. But don't you think you'd better spend some more time with the kid?"

" 'The kid', as you call her, has more company than Elsa Maxwell. What her mother needs is the company of mature people to remind her that she is still a woman. When is my next picture, Manny?"

"What about Richie? Does he want you back in harness so soon?"

"Richie has his career. I have mine. He's about to leave for conferences in New York and may be gone two weeks. He knows I love my work."

Four weeks later, Trudy left for shooting in Portugal. Occasionally, she called home to find out how the baby was doing. Once assured that all was well with little Belinda, she lost interest until the next call. Richie had accepted an assignment in Buenos Aires, and it troubled him that the baby was left in the care of a nurse. He called every night and was terribly disturbed at reports of the slightest indisposition. He vowed never to leave the country again if Trudy was not in Los Angeles. That night he phoned Trudy on location.

"When will your film be finished?" he asked.

"Another four to six weeks, I think. Why do you ask?"

"I'm worried about Belinda."

"Is anything wrong? I called several days ago and Agnes assured me that she's okay."

"Agnes. Agnes is a paid nurse. She isn't the child's mother."

"Neither are you. Stop worrying."

"Trudy, I'm serious. You've brought a life into this world. There is an obligation to care for it."

"So did you."

"I know. And it seems to me I'm more concerned than you are."

"We're both working professionals. I never promised to give up my career because of the baby."

"It's not a question of promises."

"What is it a question of?"

"Attitude. Love. It seems to me you would rather be off somewhere making films than seeing to it that your child is raised properly."

"This isn't the subject for a trans-Atlantic call. We'll talk about it when I get home."

In the years that followed there were many such calls and an equal number of discussions. The truth was that Trudy had no desire to be a mother. It was truer still that, from the very beginning of her life, Belinda Stevens was her daddy's pet and she was the very joy of his existence. Trudy's comings and goings seemed of little consequence to Belinda, who grew up expecting that her mother was off somewhere working. Her father's absences from the home, however, caused her real sadness. In order to spend more time with the child, Richie moved his office and his secretary from Wilshire Boulevard into an expanded cabana near the swimming pool. In that way he was generally available to comfort her and supervise her activities when Trudy was away.

Although Trudy and Richie seldom quarreled, it was obvious to even the most casual observer that their love had cooled. Neither one of them could have given an explanation for their emotional divergence. It was simply a fact of life that in their earlier days only their respective careers had interested them. Now that Richie was busy with his own projects as an independent producer, he had little time for, and less interest in, Trudy as a professional.

He never stated it in so many words but it was his opinion that Trudy had sold out, had become a meaningless pawn in the hands of Manny Silverstein. His desires for her to accomplish more with her art had been ignored. Therefore, he had no responsibility for the balance of her career. He knew that Trudy would always find work, but he believed that she would never really be recognized as a first-class leading lady. True, his own accomplishments since *Mrs. Donovan* had disappointed many, including himself, but at least he still had aspirations. Trudy was apparently willing to grind out the kind of class B pictures that were typical of what had become Hollywood's mindless sixties. Thus, the pattern of their lives was fixed: Trudy away on location, making a bad movie; Richie at home, planning production of what he hoped would be his Academy Award sensation; little Belinda, tottering in her father's garden, happy to be near the person who was both her surrogate mother and her father.

When the baby was two years old, Trudy spent four weeks at home awaiting reassignment. Belinda was hardly aware that this beautiful lady who flitted in and out of her life was the woman she was to call Mother. Agnes was still employed and she was the woman to whom the child related. More important, there was Daddy, always there with a kiss, a hug, and another delightful present.

Trudy and Richie no longer shared a bedroom. It was a move prompted by the fact that Richie had great trouble sleeping and insisted that the slightest movement on Trudy's part awakened him for the night. Trudy readily complied. They rarely, if ever, made love anyhow. When they did it was a perfunctory act, one which neither of them really enjoyed but engaged in as a somewhat routine reaffirmation of their legal state. In her absence, Richie had supervised an extensive enlargement of the home's cabana area. In addition to his office, there was a bedroom for himself and rather small living quarters for Marcel, his current male secretary. He spent most of his time there, only returning to the main house to dress and have his meals.

One steaming night in mid-July, when the temperature in California had risen to 103°, the air conditioning failed because the city's power sources were overburdened by the massive demand for electricity. Even with all windows open and with the cool night breezes, Trudy had difficulty sleeping. She awoke about one in the morning, sweating profusely and somehow feeling like a lonely stranger in her own home. She decided impetuously that an early morning swim in the cool waters of the pool might be just the tonic she needed to induce sleep. Slipping into a bathing suit and wrapping herself in a silken robe, she moved downstairs silently so as not to arouse Agnes and the sleeping

Belinda. Carefully opening and shutting the patio doors, she was happy to discover that the lights around the pool were still on, indicating that perhaps Richie had not yet retired.

She felt reassured when she heard quiet speech echoing through the garden as she headed for the cabana area. She couldn't make out the meaning of what was being said, but it was obvious that Marcel also was still awake, since she recognized both his voice and Richie's. Somehow she relished the idea of them both being awake, since the prospects of a solo swim were not that appetizing. She hoped that she could convince Richie to join her in the pool. She made no effort to silence her footsteps, assuming that they would hear her approach. She didn't think Richie would object to her interrupting their work at this late hour. She was convinced that he worked too hard for his own good and an hour of pleasant recreation was certainly in order.

Had she not been overcome by the shock of her discovery, Trudy would have pulled away before being discovered. As she entered the pool area, she found her husband and his secretary entwined in each other's arms, naked, in the throes of passionate love. All of the whispers and innuendos of the past came rushing back.

Aware that they were not alone, the lovers suddenly looked up. Marcel jumped to his feet and ran toward his room. Richie, striving to preserve his dignity, rose slowly and covered himself with a towel. Determined to maintain control, he spoke firmly.

"It would be nice if you had had the courtesy to let us know you were coming. Or do I select my words inappropriately?"

Trudy said nothing. She stared at him for at least thirty seconds, then, suddenly bursting into tears, turned on her heels and rushed back to the house. She climbed the stairs quickly, locked her bedroom door behind her, and buried her head in her pillow, crying away the remainder of the night. She arose early, phoned to cancel an appointment at the hairdresser and a later fitting at Continental, ordered breakfast to be brought to her room by the cook, and spent the morning behind locked doors trying to decide upon an appropriate course of action. When Richie knocked at the door to gain admittance, she quietly told him to leave, whispering that she wished to be alone before facing him again. She urged him not to create a disturbance, which would only upset Belinda and the rest of the household.

Several hours later, she was sufficiently in control to make a move. She phoned Manny Silverstein's office and explained to Obie that she simply had to see him at once on an urgent matter. He agreed to cancel a morning conference. She left for his office within a half hour, insisting on driving herself and refusing an offer from Carlos, the combination butler-chauffeur who served the entire household. She could not face meaningless chitchat this morning, despite her apparent composure.

"I caught them. Richie and his secretary, Marcel. Right by the pool like a couple of dogs in heat."

Manny looked at her for a few moments, choosing his words carefully before responding. He couldn't believe that a woman so knowing in the ways of the world could be so blind to obvious facts in her own life.

"Trudy, deep down inside, are you really surprised?"

"Of course. Shocked is more like it. How would you feel if you came home and found Tillie going down on the housemaid? Would you be surprised?"

"With Tillie, yes. With Richie, no. I thought you always knew he was AC/DC. Hell, that's been a given in Hollywood for years. Nobody really cares about that anymore. If a guy likes guys, he likes guys. If he likes broads, he likes broads. If he likes both, hell, he's in luck. He's never going to be lonely."

"Don't make bad jokes while my guts are on fire, Manny."

"It's not a joke. It's a fact. Richie Stevens has gone both ways for so many years I can't remember. I was sure you knew that. The day you were married, when we chatted by the pool and you said it was forever, I thought you were making a sort of pledge to yourself that you would turn the other way and make it work. How could you have ignored all the symptoms? You think that long line of *faygeleh* secretaries was a mistake? Come on, Trudy, face facts."

"Now I see. Then I didn't. I loved that man from the very first time you sent me to him for a reading. Now, there's nothing left."

"It don't have to be that way, kiddo. You just keep right on with your life as if you never saw that show at the swimming pool. Pretty soon the pain becomes a dull ache, then even the ache disappears. He goes his way; you go yours. Once in a while you meet and go to bed together. The world doesn't have to know all your *tzuris*. You're an actress. So act as if everything is jake."

"You really think it's that easy?"

"Of course not. But it's possible. You love the guy so much

you'll take him with all his faults. And if he just happens to swing with those sweet young guys, what's the difference? At least he ain't going to get one of them pregnant."

"Me either. Never again."

Trudy's talk with Manny Silverstein drew to a close on a painful note, but it did help to clarify her own thinking.

"It seems to me that people in glass houses ought to take baths in the cellar, as the man says."

"What's that supposed to mean?"

"It means that not too many years ago there was a bull dyke named Sophie Thurston. I never peeped into anybody's bedroom but there was plenty of talk around town about a certain les and her newest chicken. You two were thick as thieves for a couple of years. Remember?"

There was a long pause and Trudy decided to stonewall Silverstein without any unnecessary admissions of guilt.

"It seems to me that your studio sent me to Sophie Thurston. Just because we were good friends doesn't mean we were lovers."

"That's right. And just because a man looks like a duck, walks like a duck, quacks like a duck, and has only other ducks for friends doesn't mean he's a duck. But until he grows fur, most people think he's a duck."

"So?"

"So forget what you saw. Go home and try to rebuild the nest. It can be done, believe me. Tillie caught me five times and threatened to leave every time. But in the end we built a pretty good life together."

Trudy went home and tried to make a fresh start. That night she had a long talk with Richie and did her best to speak with candor and clarity. To his credit, he did likewise. He admitted to numerous affairs with members of both sexes but agreed to sever all ties with Marcel if she found the situation so unpleasant. He was as good as his word, giving Marcel his walking papers the very next morning.

One week later, he actually visited Trudy in bed and they enjoyed the most passionate sexual coupling since getting married. They started dining together regularly, were seen together in public, and even shared the joys of Belinda's upbringing for the very first time as a team effort. Trudy did her best to believe that trouble was behind them, just as Manny had said it could be.

Then it happened. There was an unexpected police raid on a homosexual bar in West Hollywood and fifteen noted filmmakers, Richie among them, were captured in the police net. It took a king's ransom in bribes and legal fees to protect their various reputations and to keep names out of the Hollywood gossip magazines. Richie, of course, insisted on his total innocence. He was just sharing a drink with a fellow worker, he said, when disaster struck. The fellow worker, it developed, was none other than Marcel, whom he had secretly rehired under another name. Trudy found this out from one of the other "wronged women" whose husband also was trapped. She blurted out the fact that both men had been sharing Marcel's affection for many months, and that Richie had once contracted a mild venereal infection from him. Now Trudy understood the two-month period when Richie had refrained from sharing her bed, and his visits to the doctor, which he assured her were merely precautionary. It was all obvious in retrospect, just like the time she first found him and Marcel wrapped in each other's arms at the pool.

For the next several years, Trudy forgot how to laugh. She started drinking heavily, refused to work, and started going out singly and with male companions with not even the slightest pretense of innocence. She sought out Bill Peters again, despite the fact that she knew he was dangerous company. Bill Peters liked to party and if ever a woman needed a blast of partying, that was Trudy Coles. It wasn't a case of Richie Stevens suddenly finding out that his wife was keeping company; the whole city knew it. Trudy would have invited Peters to pick her up at home had it not been for Belinda. She still felt affection for the child in a detached sort of way. It was just that she had nothing to say to her. Trudy was Belinda's mother in a biological sense only. She had no interest in nursery schools, trips to the zoo, children's theater and ballet, or any of the other childhood delights that Richie visited upon his daughter.

When Belinda was four years old, Richie planned a gala birthday bash that would set even Hollywood back on its heels. Every child of every prominent studio executive, every scion of every star and director, was invited to attend. Members of the Barnum and Bailey Circus were flown in from San Francisco, where they were scheduled to appear. All of the grounds of the Stevens' mansion were decorated like scenes from *Alice in Wonderland.* The pièce de résistance was a ten-foot-tall white rabbit made of marshmallow held in shape by frosted meringue. Planning for the party went on for weeks. Trudy, in one of their few cordial exchanges, promised faithfully to be present for the long-heralded celebration.

The night before the party, she and Peters went bar-hopping to all the latest "in" watering holes. They had taken to using cocaine again and by the time midnight rolled around, Trudy was drugged beyond recall. Half-conscious of her surroundings, she spent the night drinking even more heavily and rolling around in Bill Peters' bed. She finally drifted off to sleep at daybreak, awakening with a sickening headache at half-past noon.

"My God," she moaned, "today's the party!"

"What party?" Peters responded blearily. "Haven't we had enough partying for one night?"

"Belinda. It's her birthday. I promised Richie I'd be there and help with all of the kids. I gave my word."

Even a cold shower failed to sweep away all the cobwebs. Bill tried his best but was too hungover to make much sense. He could hardly keep in his lane after he valiantly agreed to drive Trudy home. They arrived when all of the children were already at lunch, joyfully gorging themselves on ice cream and cake. Trudy tried to retain her composure as Richie met her icily at the dining room door.

"So you've finally made it! Nice of you to remember!"

"Richie, I'm sorry. Truly sorry. Let me go up to my room and get the present I've bought for Belinda."

"Mommy, I already have enough presents," the child said sadly, clinging to her father's leg.

"Darling, you go back to the party. Not nice to leave your guests alone," Richie advised.

Then he turned on Trudy. Now they were alone.

"You are nothing but a drunken whore. You no more deserve the title of "mother" than any broken-down hooker on Hollywood Boulevard. You're a disgrace to yourself and to our industry. I want you out of this house. Out today. I won't have you corrupting our daughter. And as you leave, take a good look at yourself in the full-length mirror. You're over the hill. No one wants you, a once-promising, forty-year-old derelict. You're through in every sense of the word!"

Trudy was too shaken to fight back. Painfully, she climbed the stairs and—with little help from the hired hands, all of whom loved and sympathized with Richie—packed a few belongings and moved to the Beverly Wilton Hotel.

Months of costly and painful legal wrangling followed. In the end, Richie won permanent custody of Belinda; Trudy won occasional visitation rights.

CHAPTER 19

1969

Eased by mutual consent, a California divorce followed swiftly. Trudy was alone now, free from all surveillance, unfettered in what appeared to neutral observers to be a drive toward self-destruction. The keynote in her life-style was excess; nothing was done in moderation. She was drinking now at a furious clip. She virtually rinsed her mouth with champagne in the morning, fighting off the discomfort and pain of perpetual hangovers. And always, there was cocaine.

She ate less and less solid food, only to overcompensate by increasing her caloric intake in liquid form. At least the booze, she rationalized, brought her some solace from the pain and loneliness of her present situation.

"I'm a slob, right, Bill?" she asked Peters one night as, together, they stumbled drunkenly through the Wilton lobby. "Just a skinny, sloppy Polock, right?"

"You're still great-looking, my pet," he answered, practically in an incoherent stupor. "But maybe you could cut down on your eating a bit. You know the camera adds about ten pounds."

"Shit, if I ate less I'd die! That what you want? Who in the hell would be around to pay your bills then?"

"Now let's not get nasty, pet. Let's go up to the suite for another drink. Who loves a fat broad anyhow?"

"Right. I don't give a damn!"

But she did. She was as vain as any other movie actress and

what she saw in the mirror distressed her. Then she started experimenting with other drugs. She started with small doses of amphetamines, which not only reduced her craving for food further, but had the delightful side effect of lifting her spirits as well, fighting off the gray clouds of depression that had been closing in on her for months. Effective for a few days, the drugs soon lost their potency. The obvious answer was an increased dosage. Again the results were encouraging, but once again she soon found need for larger and larger amounts of the drugs. Then came the side effects. She was virtually walking on the ceiling, even after a heavy bout of drinking. She found it virtually impossible to sleep, relying some nights on as little as two or three hours of complete rest. With the sleeplessness came more depression, and with the depression came the need for still more amphetamines.

Bill Peters, who had lived with similar crises in the past, had a simple remedy: pills to make her sleep. So she entered the barbiturate forest. Tuinal, Seconal, Phenobarbital, Nembutal; all stood ready to aid her in the struggle for a night of blessed rest. Sometimes she had trouble finding these new "friends," but with lots of money there is always a way. In later months, as she struggled to reconstruct the pathetic history of this turbulent period in her life, Trudy had no clear recollection of what had transpired. It wasn't even a question of seeking enjoyment. She was a mechanical woman, rising in pain after drug-induced sleep, downing amphetamines to curb her ever-present longing for food, drinking with breakfast to steady her nerves, more liquor at lunch and dinner, and still more to end the night, followed by barbiturates to make her sleep.

She received a note in the mail from a woman named Rona Petersen, a name completely unfamiliar to her. The writer requested a face-to-face meeting on "a personal matter of extreme importance." Although she hadn't the foggiest idea of Miss Petersen's identity, she did recognize several names listed as references, names that were generally well known in Hollywood social circles. She could have called a few of them, but because of her recent fall from grace—the story of her being tossed out by Richie Stevens had been rich grist for the Hollywood gossip mills—she decided to meet the woman without checking. After all, it was one meeting. What harm could be done?

As arranged, they met in the lobby of the Wilton one afternoon. Petersen was thin, gray, and pale, her face the apparent reflection of much suffering. She was a woman approximately sixty years of age. They selected a deserted corner and Rona Petersen got down to cases almost immediately.

"Thank you for meeting me, Miss Coles. I'm Bill Peters' sister. Petersen is really his name, too. He shortened it when he moved out here to try his hand at acting, not that he ever had much success at it."

"A lot of people try and fail, Miss Petersen."

"Oh, I know that. I had aspirations myself once. You'd never guess it from the way I look today."

Rona Petersen looked directly into Trudy's eyes, subconsciously hoping for some expression of denial. Trudy was not about to lie. It was really difficult for her to picture Rona Petersen as a beautiful young starlet.

"Bill has never mentioned a sister, or any family, for that matter."

"We haven't seen him for years. There are three of us. My sister and I take care of our mother, who is eighty-three. Bill and I used to be close. He was very good to us all. Whenever he had extra money, he always sent us some. Then, the usual family squabble occurred—I don't even remember what it was about—and he broke off the ties. I read about him in the columns once in a while. One time we crossed paths in a department store, but he just looked the other way, even though I was sure he had seen me."

"I don't want to be rude, Miss Petersen, but I have an appointment coming up. What is it that you wanted to talk to me about? I really can't serve as peacemaker between you and Bill, if that's why you wrote to me."

"Of course you can't. I understand that. Besides, it's a family matter and not for outsiders."

Trudy admired the woman's sense of dignity. She obviously wasn't here to fall on her knees and beg.

"Then what is it?"

"I received a call the other day from Dr. Randolph O'Malley. He's been our physician for years, practically a member of the family. He knows that you and Bill have been seeing a lot of each other. As a matter of fact, we all knew that. There aren't many secrets about movie stars that don't make the rounds. He ran into Bill at a restaurant and was alarmed to see how he looks. I don't know if you know this, Miss Coles, but Bill is a very sick man. He's had three coronaries and he's suffered from angina for years. Dr. O'Malley took one look at him and was so alarmed he called me. It's so obvious that Bill's been ignoring his health that the doctor says his life is in jeopardy. He tried to talk to him, even called his apartment, but was unable to reach Bill. He left messages, which Bill wouldn't return. So he called me. I can't talk to my brother; he won't even pick up my calls. I thought maybe you could talk to him."

"I think it's nice of you to try and help your brother, especially since you two are on the outs. How old is Bill?"

"Nearly sixty."

"You think a man that age can be led like a child? I mean if he seems so determined to destroy himself, how can I change that?"

"You could try."

"Yes, I could. And I will. But frankly, I'm not too optimistic. Bill is headstrong. Strong in more ways than one. The fact is, *he* takes care of *me.* Maybe you should persist in seeing him. Or have the doctor give him another call. I'm not sure I can help."

"I knew it was an outside chance, but I hope you don't resent my seeing you."

"No. I'm sorry that you're worried. But maybe it's not as bad as it seems. Doctors sometimes exaggerate, you know."

"Not in this case . . . well, thank you. I do have one more favor to ask."

"Yes?"

"Don't ever tell Bill that we met and talked. He's a very proud man and if he learns that I spoke to you, he'll never talk to me again. He doesn't want anyone to know that he's been sick."

"I promise not to say a word. And if I can, well, maybe I will try to hold him back a little."

"Thank you, Miss Coles. My mother, sister, and I would be very grateful." With that Rona rose and, without further comment, was gone.

As the rounds of drinking, carousing, and pill popping gained momentum, Trudy felt her spirit ebbing, her strength weakening, her desire for survival depleting. Yet, somewhere deep within her there was a voice calling for her to resist and fight for her life. Truly worried about her failing state of health, she turned herself in at a local private hospital where her physician had connections. He would have preferred Cedars-Sinai Medical

Center, with its state-of-the-art facilities, but there was always the problem of avoiding the glaring spotlight of the motion picture press. The institution selected, one of many such hideaways where the movie set sought treatment away from the inquiring eyes of the gossip columnists, was at least capable of reaching a reliable diagnosis.

After a series of exhaustive tests, her own doctor was summoned to discuss the results in a one-on-one face-off.

"Miss Coles," Dr. Goldberg began tentatively, "I really am at a loss as to how to impress you with the seriousness of this situation."

"Don't pull punches, Doctor, I'm a big girl. Say it like it is. Is it cancer or something like that?"

"No. Nothing like that. It's more like suicide. You've been dissipating so long and so continuously that your body is being pushed to the limit. You keep it up and you'll end in a sanatorium, or worse. Your blood pressure is screamingly high again. Your heartbeat is muffled and your heart rate is dangerously elevated. You are, Miss Coles, some twenty to thirty pounds underweight. Your blood count is seriously unbalanced. You're anemic from loss of red cells. I could go on and on. But the fact is that unless you take immediate steps to live a saner life, you will not live to be forty-five."

"Hey, don't make it worse than it is. I'm only forty next month."

"When I first started treating you I told my friends that you were the most beautiful woman I had ever seen. Now—and you can vent your spleen on me if you wish—you are forty going on sixty-five."

Trudy rose in anger. No two-bit doctor was going to tell her how to live her life. It was hers to do with as she saw fit. Hell, she came from West Virginia Polock stock. Drinking was a natural talent for her. She'd watch her diet, gain a bit of weight, and show them all what beauty was.

She went back to the hotel and was passing through the lobby when the manager approached her and invited her into his office.

"Miss Coles, I really don't know how to say this," he began sheepishly.

"Say what, Mr. Hansforth?" she asked officiously.

"We've had a number of complaints recently from some of our other permanent residents."

"Complaints?" Trudy asked innocently.

Hansforth answered formally, hardening now to his task. "Complaints about the noise you and Mr. Peters are making late at night. You've been making a spectacle of yourselves, bouncing through our lobby like drunken sailors on a binge. Last week you two had a fight and were throwing things around the suite until two in the morning. I need hardly remind you that Mr. Peters is not even registered at the Beverly Wilton."

"Mr. Peters is my guest. I pay you two thousand dollars a month to live here. I can have a visitor now and then."

"Of course you can. But you can't be destructive or disturb our other guests. We're proud of the Wilton, Miss Coles, and we can't have someone destroying our good reputation."

It was too ignominious an experience to cope with properly. This little snit of a paid executive, daring to tell Trudy Coles how to act.

"Fine, Mr. Hansforth. I'm giving notice now. I'll be moving by the first of the month."

"As you see fit. You may leave sooner if you wish. We'll rebate the full balance for unoccupied time."

So, thought, Trudy, another squeamish rat had jumped ship. Well, screw him, too. There were plenty of other hotels in Beverly Hills. And at $2,000 a month she was hardly a charity case. Life would go on without the Goldbergs and the Hansforths of this world. What she needed was a stiff drink, and a nice hot shower. Then she and Bill could go out on the town. Tonight, above all, she needed to have fun.

Another gate crashed shut several mornings later. She received word by formal correspondence that her contract with Continental had expired and that they had no intention of seeking renewal. The notification was signed by some insignificant lawyer in the studio's business affairs department. Not even the courtesy of a note or call from Manny Silverstein.

"Manny, what the hell is this?" she demanded, having forced her way uninvited into his office an hour after receiving the letter.

"What is what, Trudy?"

"This goddamned notice. You're firing me? After all the dough I've made for you and this fucking studio? You send me a cold-turkey notice and expect me to take it lying down?"

"Look, Trudy," he said, motioning impatiently for her to sit.

"Anybody else busts her way in here, I ring a bell and have them thrown out on their ass. You, I tell the truth. You're washed up. You look like hell. You're the laughing stock of this business. Hell, you haven't made a good flick in five years. You can't even cut the grade B shit I've been charitably casting you in. You're maybe forty pounds underweight. You've got rings under your eyes that could qualify for boxing pictures. You think I'm crazy or something? I should ask for more punishment and re-sign you?"

It suddenly occurred to Trudy that showing belligerence, especially with a tough old horse like Manny Silverstein, would get her nothing. Here was a man who fought back below the belt. Better to practice her feminine wiles. Pausing for dramatic effect, straightening her dress seductively, she moved to his side with her most disarming smile. Reaching down deliberately, she patted his crotch.

"I bet our old friend here would re-sign me in a minute."

Manny looked neither shocked nor amused. He was clearly disgusted. Pushing her aside, he glared at her with anger, snapping, "Cut the shit! I wouldn't fuck you now with Buster Keaton's dick, and he's dead!"

Tears came to Trudy's eyes. She hadn't expected this kind of rejection. Over these many years she and Manny Silverstein had had their differences. Yet, in the end, she'd always considered him a sincere friend, the man who, above all, had been responsible for her career. She drew back, looked at him in deep sorrow, and fought for meaningful words.

"Like Caesar said, you, too, Manny? From you I expected more."

"Why? You're no better, no different than the rest. As soon as you made a little dough you tried to push me around, turning down just about every film I offered you. You never stopped to think that it was Manny Silverstein who saw possibilities in your career first. Manny Silverstein was the one who pushed that little schmuck of an agent down the tubes and bought back your contract. Manny Silverstein invested money in your training and never asked for a penny in return. Manny Silverstein didn't even lay a glove on you once you showed me that it was that *faygeleh* of a Stevens you thought was better than me. Now, you're nothing but a bum and a tramp and you think I'm gonna play dead because you play with my balls. I don't need my knob polished that bad, lady. And, let me tell you, I'm the only one in this town who would call you that—a *lady*. Now I'm busy and late for a meeting. Get your ass out of here before I toss you out!"

Shocked, eyes red with crying, Trudy whirled and headed for the door. She rushed down the path toward the studio's main gate, hailed a passing cab, and asked to be driven to her hotel. Once inside the suite, she double-locked the door and popped open a full bottle of champagne that was iced in the refrigerator, pouring herself a large glass.

Glass in hand, she moved into the bedroom to hang up her clothes and seek the solace of a hot bath. She never reached the tub. There, sprawled on the floor in the doorway between the bedroom and bath, lay the prostrate body of Bill Peters, his sightless eyes open and staring toward the ceiling. She touched his forehead lightly; it was cold as ice. Gingerly, fighting back the tears, she placed her ear on his chest. Nothing. It was obvious that he was dead and probably had been for several hours. There really was no need to call a doctor. Bill Peters had apparently suffered the heart attack that his sister, Rona, had warned about. Now there was more guilt to bear. And she was alone. Bill Peters was dead; she hadn't communicated with her family in West Virginia for months; her own daughter spurned her. Her husband preferred the physical company of a man; her long-time mentor and employer had turned his back on her; her doctor had rejected her; even the hotel where she had spent so many thousands of dollars had demanded that she move. Her first husband had faced a fiery death in a blind effort to escape her. Lovers like Jocko Rachubinski and Bill Peters had deserted her, for so, in her grief, did she construe Bill's death. She felt physically sick as never before in her life and her career was apparently at an end. What was the point of it all?

She reached for an unopened bottle of Scotch and started drinking without benefit of a glass. By the time she was halfway through the bottle, her mind, already out of focus because of the drugs in her system, shifted into neutral, losing all sense of reality. Then, perhaps because she felt so alone, she stumbled across the room and turned on the television. She couldn't believe her eyes. What an irony! The Academy Awards ceremony had just begun. Vaguely she calculated that fourteen years ago she thought she might win an award for *Mrs. Donovan's Defeat,* but that had never materialized. Since then, her path had been downward. Winning an Oscar seemed like an incredible, impossible dream.

She kept drinking, striving to keep up with what was going on at the Awards show, but really comprehending very little. Then, she decided on her course of action as she drained the last drop from the bottle. Having called the police, she left the suite, leaving Bill's body as she had found it.

How she managed to leave the hotel, find a cab, and get to the Dorothy Chandler Pavilion, she would never recall. How she bluffed her way past the doorman was an even greater mystery. But there she was with the entire industry and all of America watching. They had just presented the award for cinematography and the recipient had made his unnecessarily long acceptance speech.

"Hey, wait a minute," she shouted as she stumbled down the aisle and onto the stage.

A guard who was about to intercept her thought better of it when he recognized her as Trudy Coles, thinking perhaps that this was part of the planned diversion from the seriousness of the Awards ceremonies.

And now she was at the podium as the hushed crowd became aware of the horror of the occasion. The television director, just having completed a commercial segment, was reluctant to run three more commercials so quickly. Hypnotized, mesmerized, he kept the cameras focused on Trudy for all America to join in her shame.

"I'm the late Trudy Coles," she mumbled in an alcoholic stupor. The room grew silent as the tuxedo- and gown-bedecked celebrities watched in awe.

"You remember me. I was supposed to win one of these little gold bastards but you all screwed me. Yes, I'm drunk but I know what I'm saying. You all think I'm through. But don't be smug. Your turn will come too. . . ."

She never said another word. Two husky security men grabbed her and pulled her from the microphone. Their timing was perfect. She had just slipped into unconsciousness.

CHAPTER 20

1970

Reynolds Sanatorium, situated on the edge of San Bernardino National Forest, was a combination mental asylum and convalescent home where the very rich and very famous Hollywood celebrities were sent to regain control of their lives. Owned and operated by a consortium of reputable Los Angeles psychiatrists, it was the sort of institution where conscientious physicians could send their distinguished patients with confidence. No one could recall the accurate origin of the name "Reynolds," but it was rumored that the founding physician chain-smoked Camel cigarettes and chose the moniker to give the institution a further degree of anonymity, since the clientele never were proud of their residency. Wags termed it "Palm Springs Annex" because of its proximity to Hollywood's desert playground.

It was to Reynolds Sanatorium that Dr. Stanton Goldberg more or less committed Trudy Coles when he found her lying semiconscious in the emergency ward of Cedars-Sinai Medical Center. He had rushed to the hospital without being summoned after seeing the dreadful scene on television. He came despite his recent altercation with his once-beautiful client, for obviously this was no time to stand on professional ceremony. Gradually regaining consciousness, Trudy was grateful for his loyalty.

"Forgive me," she kept mumbling.

He squeezed her hand in return and, having determined that her vital signs were relatively stable, he ordered her stomach pumped, not certain of what she had consumed in addition to the liquor.

Her spirits, once it became apparent to her that she would survive, remained low. Like a child looking for parental comfort at a moment of deep stress, she turned to Goldberg for support. When he insisted that she must avail herself of professional psychiatric help for the immediate future, she readily accepted.

"But for how long, Dr. Goldberg, for how long?"

"That depends on you, Miss Coles. Maybe six weeks, maybe six months, maybe even a year. But you must dry out, emotionally as well as physically, or there is no hope. I'll speak to my good friend, Milton Gordon, who runs Reynolds Sanatorium. He was a classmate of mine in medical school. He's very bright and very caring. He's the top man at Reynolds and I'd trust my mother there. You'll have to sign the admission papers but I urge you to be cooperative. It's the only way for you to recover completely and return to work. I assume that is your goal. Incidentally, do you think we should speak to Mr. Stevens about this?"

"Believe me, he doesn't care. Of course I'll sign and be cooperative. If you're nice enough to want me to live, why should I object? Christ knows why I deserve it."

"Everyone deserves to live. Start there. Then remember all of the pleasure you have brought into the lives of so many people these many years. That's reason enough to get well."

Her first few weeks in the lovely suburbs of San Bernardino were not easy ones. She was watched carefully. Her particular "keeper" was a burly nurse from the cornfields of Iowa who outweighed her by fifty pounds. Margaret Knudsen stood at least six feet tall, her waist measured thirty-seven around, and her breasts were shaped like twin peaks of the Himalayas. Her deep auburn hair was pulled back in a huge bun. She absolutely never smiled. Her job was to control unruly patients; few were courageous enough to test their strength against hers. Rumor had it that, once, an ex-matinee idol, consigned to Reynolds to dry out after months of overindulgence with liquor, had grabbed her from behind one night with amorous intent. She had allegedly tossed him aside with such ferocity that he broke his arm crashing into the nearest wall. She showed little or no compassion, as her reaction to the incident revealed: "You grab my ass one more time, you'll have a broken leg too."

No one attempted to discipline her. Her amorous patient

called her "Miss Knudsen" from that day on. Despite her attitude, Trudy found this big bear of a woman amusing.

"Miss Knudsen," she asked one morning, "don't you ever smile?"

"Not much to laugh about around here."

"Maybe not. But you'll never have any fun in life if you go around frowning all of the time. You make me sad just looking at you."

"Sorry about that, Miss Coles. Don't look."

All of Trudy's own clothing had been removed from the room and she had been issued simple hospital smocks in a variety of primary colors. No high-heeled shoes were permitted. Indoors she wore soft woolen slippers. Crepe-soled walking shoes were issued later, when she was permitted to walk outside on the lovely, manicured hospital lawns. She was then compelled to take, accompanied by the ever-present Miss Knudsen, a three-mile walk every morning before breakfast and a shorter, brisker walk before dinner. She came to welcome these excursions into the nearby woods even though it was traumatic at first to be seen by strangers in hospital garb. When she expressed her shame to Margaret, the stolid nurse answered, "There is no shame in being sick. Only not trying to get well is a sin. That's the way I see it."

"Of course, you're right," Trudy acknowledged.

Her diet consisted of simple, carefully measured natural foods. Red meat was taboo. So were artificial flavorings, sugar, and salt. The food was terribly bland, but somehow, as she gained weight and began to feel better, Trudy learned to enjoy it. There was very little in the way of recreation aside from visits to the hospital's well-stocked library. Once a month, on Saturday nights, there was a social get-together with other patients and staff. Ice cream and cake were the highlights of the evening.

Dr. Milton Gordon was exactly as Stanton Goldberg had described him. He took Trudy under his wing and met with her regularly three times a week. At first she found herself resisting his attempts to probe into her past experiences. She got the feeling that there was a certain prurient pleasure he experienced in chatting about her past relationships with men. Frankly, she resented this and told him so.

"Why do you have to know how long it takes me to have an orgasm, Dr. Gordon? Are we shooting for the world's record?"

"Why do you think I want to know?"

"I don't have the faintest idea."

"I have to know many intimate things about you if you expect me to help you, Miss Coles. But if a question embarrasses you, there is no compulsion to answer."

She remembered hearing that patients sometimes were known to fall in love with their psychiatrists. Dr. Gordon—tall, lean, dark, pipe-smoking, and incredibly handsome—would have been an easy man to fall in love with under these circumstances. Yet she knew this was not to happen.

Though her physical condition improved rapidly and she was regaining her mature beauty, she was still deeply depressed. Being held virtual prisoner in an institution populated by many patients far sicker than she was did not help the situation. She began to long for her freedom, to be obsessed with it. Thoughts of trying to escape crossed her mind, but it was obvious that there was no place to escape to. She decided to discuss this openly with Dr. Gordon.

"Don't you think it's time we thought about my going home?" she asked him during one of their friendlier sessions.

"Do you think you really are ready for that?" he asked in response.

"Dr. Gordon, why do you always answer my questions with other questions?"

"So that you can ask still further questions and in that way think through all of your problems. But I'll break the rules of the game and answer your last question. It is too soon to think about going home. When there is little question that you are ready and eager to face the stresses of your life, we'll talk about it."

"And when will that be?"

"Only you can answer that question, Trudy," he replied.

In order to avert the constant boredom occasioned by her confinement, Trudy began to spend much of her free time in the hospital library. She had always immensely enjoyed reading, ever since being introduced to the magic of books by Stan Marcus. But time had been limited because of the demands of her career. Now a whole new world opened before her as she started reading current best-sellers and then gradually dipped into the classics. It was a mind-boggling experience and she looked forward to those hours each day when she could feel the intellectual growth that only reading can bring. Since she had to be with her at all times, Maggie Knudsen would sit beside her, reading her own choices. Frequently they would stop and discuss what they had read in hushed tones so as not to disturb the other patients who were in the library at the same time. There was an older, grumpy gentleman recently admitted to the sanatorium who usually sat in one corner of the room, immersed in his reading. He never even acknowledged Trudy's existence. One afternoon, as Maggie and Trudy were chatting away in what they thought were quiet tones, he slammed his book shut and stomped over to where they were sitting.

"Don't you give a damn about anybody else but yourselves?" he asked angrily. "How in the hell do you expect me to concentrate if you gab away like a couple of magpies? Please shut up!"

With that he marched back to his seat, not waiting for an answer, looked gloweringly at Trudy, then returned to his reading. Nonplussed beyond description, Trudy turned to Knudsen and, again attempting to keep her voice low, asked, "Who the hell is that? Boy, does he think he's important!"

"He is," Maggie replied. "That's Leonard Rush. He's head of the economics department at the University of California. You know his name. He won the Nobel Prize about ten years ago. He's here because of a terrible drinking problem, and he hates being here. Come on, let's go out for a walk. We've read enough for the day."

Trudy was fascinated. Though no intellectual, to be sure, she knew enough to stand in awe of a man who actually had won the Nobel Prize. And to think that she had interrupted his reading! It really was kind of funny. She saw him every day after their original, angry encounter, but Rush never so much as nodded his recognition. As a test, Trudy smiled at him several times when their gazes met, but he looked through her icily. The Nobel Prize, Trudy concluded humorously, was not awarded in recognition of friendly demeanor.

It became a challenge: somehow, she would get him to speak to her. Her opportunity arose four weeks later at the monthly social gathering of staff and patients. Rush was sitting glumly, staring off into space, looking altogether like an angry boy being forced to attend mass on a Sunday morning when he would rather have been sleeping. There was an empty seat beside him and Trudy, now well on the road to personal recovery, decided to test her luck. She broke off a meaningless conversation with a fellow patient about the newest films being released by the major studios, and walked directly to where Rush was sitting.

"If I promise not to interrupt your concentration, Dr. Rush, will you let me sit beside you? You seem to be the only one in the room more bored than I am."

Rush looked at her intently, then with little enthusiasm granted his permission. "I don't own this prison, you know, I'm just an inmate like you. What's your offense? You an alcoholic, too?"

She sat beside him and laughed. "Worse. I drank. I snorted. I caroused. I even overdosed. Here they're trying to convince me that I should want to live and suffer."

"And are they being successful?"

"Well, let's say things are looking up. Incidentally, I'm Trudy Coles, Dr. Rush."

"I know who you are. I knew that time I unloaded on you and your keeper. You're very beautiful. But even the Mona Lisa keeps quiet in libraries."

What started as small talk at an embarrassing social gathering of patients grew into one of the most moving relationships in Trudy's life. Rush was some fifteen years her senior, shorter than she by at least two inches, gray, and balding; and he had a nervous tic that twisted his entire face sideways. He was unschooled in the kind of surface sophistication that passed for Hollywood chic. But when it came to true worldliness, Leonard Rush was a bottomless pit of knowledge. There was no fact, no matter how remote, which seemed to have escaped his incredibly facile mind. His field of concentration was the economic causes of world revolution, but there was no area in the social sciences where his penetrating intellect had not invaded. Since modern economics required an intimate knowledge of higher mathematics, he had delved deeply into current mathematical theory. And the advent of the computer age, just at the dawning point, fascinated him beyond description. In order to keep abreast of world developments in his field, he had taught himself to read in more than eight languages, including Russian and Chinese. True, English had become the international language of science, but he felt more comfortable reading scientific papers in their mother tongues without having to rely on the whims of translators. His knowledge of the arts, music, sculpture, modern and classical painting, the theater, even the world of motion pictures, was astounding. In addition to his awe-inspiring mental prowess, he was a great conversationalist, always eager to hear what his companion had to say and not intent on parading his own knowledge before giving the other man a chance to express himself. Finally, he had a magnificent sense of humor, which seemed to color everything he said.

At first, they began to greet each other with more warmth. Next, they managed to sit beside each other at mealtime. Then they started sharing their daily walks, each with a chaperon, of course, as required by the rules of the sanatorium. Several times Trudy spoke to her companion and asked to be permitted to join Rush alone.

"Maggie," she questioned, "don't you think it's high time you trusted me alone for a change?"

"You tired of me, Miss Coles?"

"I like you very much, Maggie, even if you still don't know how to smile. But I'm past forty now. I'd like to have an hour to myself."

"I thought it was Dr. Rush you wanted to be with."

"It is. I never met a more fascinating man. I don't enjoy the feeling that the two of us have to be watched like two teenagers in love who might hop into the sack if their parents turn away."

"Speak to Dr. Gordon. He makes the rules."

Trudy did just that the next time she was alone with the psychiatrist.

"I don't think it's a very good idea just yet. As a matter of fact, I don't think it's a very good idea at any time."

"And why not?"

"Because you are still depressed, though you don't admit it. And Dr. Rush has not overcome his drinking problem. So if you two were alone and something untoward happened, it would cause a major setback for both of you. We never encourage emotional alliances here at Reynolds. Please accept that fact."

She settled for a platonic relationship and somehow found this more exciting, more stimulating, than any past alliance. Rush, in turn, though obviously taken with her, seemed happy to play the Pygmalion game, bringing knowledge to his already beautifully sculpted companion. Even though Trudy had left school before earning a high school diploma, she had a healthy intellectual curiosity and was motivated by a burning desire to improve herself. He started her on a reading regimen that would have discouraged a less ardent student.

"Here's a book that is not too difficult to understand. But if you get stuck, just ask questions. Don't be embarrassed."

"Don't worry. I'll ask plenty."

He started her off with Robert Heilbroner's *The Worldly Philosophers*, subtitled *The Lives, Times and Ideals of Great Economic Thinkers.*

"Any questions?" he asked with a smile after she had finished it. "Anything you don't understand?"

"Only everything. But I think I hear the music."

"You reading along, too, Miss Knudsen?"

"Dr. Rush, I don't believe in economists. If you men are so bright how come we keep having depressions?"

"Good question. I'll think about it," he answered with a laugh. "As for you, Trudy, here's some basics to wade through." He handed her Adam Smith's *Wealth of Nations* and Thorston Veblen's *The Theory of the Leisure Class.*

She read these slowly and carefully and, to her own amazement, actually understood what she read. She tried to discuss several controversial passages, but Rush refused.

"Read more. Understand more. Then we'll argue. Now it's like discussing art with someone who has made his first visit to the Museum of Modern Art in New York. I'm not being arrogant; just realistic."

After she had waded through *The General Theory* by John Maynard Keynes and a series of articles by Harvard's John Kenneth Galbraith, Rush was willing to accept her queries.

"All of these men think that if you do what's best in terms of economic theory, in the long run everybody ends up best. I can't agree."

"No. Why not?"

"Well, let's say that it's not economical to make shoes in Podunk, Idaho, but rather to raise potatoes. And let's say it's not economical to raise potatoes in Tipperary, Ireland, but rather to make shoes."

"The only thing I know about Tipperary is that it's a long way there."

"Len, I'm serious. What happens to all of those out-of-work people while they are trying to shift away from the jobs they know and find work in factories or farms that may not exist?"

"They starve."

"They starve. And that's your answer as one of the world's best economists?"

"Why do you think I drink?"

"You like the taste?"

"Now who is being serious? I drink because it depresses me to realize that modern man may not be able to solve his own economic dilemmas. We live in the short run. Economic truths reveal themselves in the long run. In between there's a lot of suffering. You understand?"

"Not completely. But I'll think about it."

"When you've got it all figured out, tell me. I'll nominate you for a Nobel Prize."

They laughed their way through the next month and it soon became apparent to both of them that they were in love. It was the strangest of all attractions; the tall beauty from West Virginia by way of Hollywood and the short, balding, unattractive, neurotic Jewish scholar from the Bronx by way of the University of California. For those who claimed that opposites attract, here was proof in living technicolor. Finally, facing the inevitable, Dr. Gordon granted them their freedom and they had many hours to spend in each other's company. They started peering into each other's pasts.

"Len, tell me about your wife. You've been here three months and she's never come for a visit."

"She's asked to. But Dr. Seltzer agrees with me that she's one cause of my alcoholism. Your Dr. Gordon concurs, from what they tell me."

"Don't you miss her?"

"At times. I'm fifty-five but not without my sexual needs. Maggie Knudsen is beginning to look good to me."

"Besides that. You've been married for nearly thirty years. You've got two grown children. All of that had to mean something for you."

"It did. It does. But Shirley turned left when I turned right about twenty-five years ago. And I don't mean politically. We just fell out of love, if we were ever really in love in the first place. She was a bright girl, daughter of one of New York's leading attorneys. Everyone felt that the brain my parents handed me meant that I'd be a big winner. She and her folks apparently agreed. When we fell out of love, we started fighting. And the fighting grew worse as the years ran by. When I took to the juice she was terribly unsympathetic. Matter of fact, the last letter I got from her father before he died warned me that if I didn't straighten out—the words are his—he'd see to it that Shirley got a divorce, got full custody of the kids, and took every goddamned cent I had ever saved. It made me mad. It was so unknowing that it made me drink more. I was too hungover to attend his funeral."

"Didn't all that liquor affect your work?"

"Of course. It affected my work, my home life, my self-esteem, my everything. But maybe that's why I started drinking in the first place. You see, Trudy, once you accomplish your life's ambition—and I was Nobel laureate at the age of forty-two—you start thinking that it wasn't all that important after all. You ask yourself, 'Is this really what I fought for?' Then you start getting scared as you realize that there are hundreds of young guys coming up who are as bright as, and now hungrier than, you are. Then that fear feeds on itself. And you start telling yourself that if winning the Nobel Prize isn't very important, then nothing in life really is worth a hoot and a holler. So you get depressed and since you're too much of a coward to end your life, you start drinking heavily."

Later, when the moment was right, he asked about her life. As objectively as she could, she told him of events leading to that fateful day at the Academy Awards when she had disgraced herself in full view of the entire nation.

"Well, here we are," he jested, "an alcoholic and a self-destructive exhibitionist, in love at Dr. Gordon's desert hideaway."

"That's all behind us," she responded.

"Let's hope for the best. Now about that *Marx, Engels Reader* I asked you to study . . ."

The inevitable occurred two nights later when, sipping coffee at the end of another boring day, they found themselves alone. They had just been discussing an obscure passage on Marxian theory when Trudy made her move.

"You know I'm tired of being the pupil. I've got something I want to teach you."

Taking Rush firmly by the hand, she led him stealthily into her nearby bedroom, closing the door quietly behind them. They were immediately in each other's arms in an embrace so intense, so filled with longing, that it blotted out all sense of reality. Months of desire, months of restrained emotion, months of pain and doubt about the future, all found their bombastic release in that first violent kiss. Once upon each other, there was not enough energy in the world to pull them apart.

Gasping for breath and crying with joy, they tore each other's clothes from their bodies and without pause charged into bed. Their coupling was so inevitable, so totally predictable, that nothing could have restrained them. They were two animals thirsting for each other.

"Here and here and here," he murmured as his lips found every luscious curve of her femininity. And when he plunged his tongue into her wettened crevice, she moaned in ecstacy, whispering, "More and more and more." Then, in turn, she took his stiffened member into her mouth and sucked with such frenzy that he felt his blood pressure soar beyond control, and believed that death at such a moment would indeed be heavenly. When finally he tore himself away and entered her, she moaned again in ecstatic fulfilment. She pulled him into herself and together they ground away in maddening tempo.

When it was over, he lay upon her, too spent to remove himself, too joyous to think of retreat. Together they descended from their sexual Olympus, as the pace of their heartbeats slowly, somewhat regretfully, returned to normal. For every human adult there is one moment of unrestrained lovemaking that transcends all others. Trudy Coles and Leonard Rush had had their moment in the sun.

They found Dr. Rush unconscious three days later. By his side was an empty bottle of Scotch that he had drunk in one continuous swallow. Investigation by the authorities at Reynolds quickly revealed that a new employee on the kitchen staff had happily accepted a $100 bribe to smuggle in the liquor at Rush's request. Having abstained from all alcohol for months, his system was in no condition to withstand the jolt of such a shock.

When he finally regained consciousness, he was surly, disoriented, and uncooperative. It took several muscular attendants to control him. He finally was restrained in a tub of warm water, given some medically prescribed sedatives, and secured to his bed, where he slept soundly for fourteen hours. When he arose, he was morose and uncommunicative.

Trudy, having heard of the problem, requested permission to see him. It was denied. She insisted on seeing Dr. Gordon but was told that he was not on the premises and not expected to return for the better part of a week. She suspected that the story was concocted for her benefit. She asked to see Rush's physician, Dr. Theodore Seltzer, whom she had seen attending other patients that very day. He, too, was unavailable, but sent word that if she were seeking permission to see Dr. Rush this could not and would not be granted. He was to be alone under observation for the next several days.

Trudy was beside herself and thought of forcing her way into his room on one pretext or another. She appealed to Maggie Knudsen, her only real friend at the sanatorium. Maggie used some pretext to gain admission to Rush's room but found him sullen and drowsy from additional sedation. She whispered to him that Miss Coles sent her fondest regards, but he simply stared back with little apparent reaction, leaving her in doubt as to whether he heard what she had said. In no way did he indicate that he wanted to see Trudy Coles.

A long three weeks went by before Trudy was permitted to speak to him again. When they finally met before retiring one evening, he was a different man entirely, a spiritual ghost of the Leonard Rush who had become so important a part of her life. The fire had fled his soul. His eyes were glazed, his demeanor listless.

"I missed you. Terribly," Trudy said sadly.

"Don't. I'm not worth it."

"Why? Why did you do it? Tell me," she pleaded.

"Why do I always do it? Because I'm scared. I couldn't face the threat of responsibility that our relationship carried with it. Love may be great for you; for me it's too heavy a burden. Forget me. I tell you I'm a loser."

"That's ridiculous and you know it! I've been through the same things you're facing. I'm making it. You can, too."

"I'm not you. I don't want to make it. Please leave me alone. Go find yourself a husband who's a real man."

There was little now to keep Trudy at Reynolds except the vague hope that Leonard Rush would recover and reconsider his decision. She decided to discuss the situation with Dr. Gordon.

"I guess you were right about Dr. Rush," she began apologetically. "I guess we should not have seen each other alone."

"Do you really think so?" Gordon asked.

"Dr. Gordon, you'll never get over that damn habit of asking me questions, will you?"

"It would seem that now you are asking a question," he replied with a smile.

"Maybe so. Anyhow, I really think so, not because of me but

because of what it apparently has done to him. He tells me that he just can't stand the weight of a love affair."

"That's quite consistent with his diagnosis."

"Dr. Gordon, believe me, I'm no angel. But I really love and admire that man. I'm not what one would describe as a sexually deprived female. I loved—correction, I love—him for his brain, not his body. Now what do I do?"

"That's up to you. I'd say you have your life under control now. It's time to test the water outside of the sanatorium. I really am ready to release you any time you say the word. I wrote to Dr. Goldberg to that effect last week."

"Thank you for all you have done. I think I'm ready, too. I'll miss Reynolds. Never thought I'd say that. I'll miss Maggie Knudsen, even if I can't get her to smile. I'll miss Dr. Rush, too. But maybe that's the real test."

CHAPTER 21

1971

Trudy Coles had been an actress for twenty-six years. She became a superstar almost by accident. Having returned from Reynolds, she rented a small home on Alpine Drive in the foothills overlooking Sunset Boulevard. It felt good to be free again after a year as a patient-prisoner. With only a part-time maid to help with the cleaning, she settled into a housewife's routine and was overjoyed to find that she didn't miss the excitement she had once experienced in this same environment. What's more, she found that now at last she could bridge the gap and befriend her own daughter.

Her daughter was six now, already on her way toward becoming another raving beauty. Richie was more attentive to the child than ever, and though he harbored no secret affection for Trudy, he was a man of compassion. He phoned Trudy once he had heard that she was home and suggested that they meet for lunch. She was delighted to discover that he planned to bring Belinda with him. After a warm and tender reunion, Trudy asked for permission to see her child on a regular basis. Richie readily agreed. From then on, mother and daughter became good friends, though they could never be as close as Belinda was to her father. Trudy accepted this as inevitable, under the circumstances.

One of Trudy's happily assumed responsibilities was driving

Belinda to ballet class in Santa Monica every Saturday morning, when Richie normally was involved in story conferences. One morning, she was walking Belinda down the pathway leading to the dance studio when she bumped into a man she hadn't seen in many years. His name was Monte Rubin, and he had been a close friend of Stan Marcus. He hadn't shared Stan's success as a writer and had turned to directing, where he made an immediate score. Soon afterward, as the role of the director continued to rise in the Hollywood hierarchy, he was given a lofty perch with one of the major studios and had a remarkable string of successful films to his credit. He moved to yet another studio and, though there were temporary setbacks, the course of his career moved steadily upward. In a matter of ten years, he had become one of the most influential independent directors in television and motion pictures.

Trudy and he had met on a number of occasions, but since Rubin lived an unusually normal married life, their paths did not cross often either socially or professionally. At the moment of this chance meeting, Trudy was rather amazed at how gracefully the tall, gaunt director had aged. His hair was silver gray; he sported an equally silver Vandyke beard; his figure was hard and lean; his visage leather-tanned by the California sun. He greeted Trudy warmly and suggested that they have coffee at a nearby restaurant while they waited for their future Pavlovas to finish class.

Settled in a booth with steaming cups of coffee in front of them, the talk turned to business almost immediately.

"I know you won't believe me, but I just mentioned your name this morning."

"I don't. Why for God's sake?"

"You remember my wife, Betty? She's my strong right arm when it comes to casting. Matter of fact, she's thinking of opening a casting service here in Hollywood. She knows just about every actor and actress who holds a card."

"I understand that's getting to be a good business."

"If. *If* you know your stuff, and *if* you have the right entree to the studios. . . . At any rate, we're doing a new film and it was Betty who suggested that you would be perfect for the lead. She's been one of your fans since *Mrs. Donovan's Defeat.* Never could understand why that flick didn't win an armful of Oscars."

"Neither could I. Anyhow, I haven't acted in so many years I don't know if I could even face a camera. You'd probably go over budget just on makeup. The lines are so deep now you could hide a string of pearls in them."

"We call them character lines. The part calls for someone in her middle to late thirties who finds out that her husband, an allegedly respectable physician, not only is carrying on with his receptionist, but is actually plotting to have his wife killed so that his way to philandering will be eased. She fights him tooth and nail, and, in the end, the receptionist and she team up to send him to jail. But there's a hell of a lot of tension in between. It's a super part. Incidentally, who's your agent?"

"What's that?" Trudy asked with a laugh. "I guess Jason Arnold. They represented me once."

"I'll call them in the morning. Sid Keyes is a good friend."

"I like him, too. But after you see me work again, I doubt if you'll still think he's such a good friend."

Filming on *Prescription Murder* began the next week. From the moment the first camera rolled, it was obvious that a big hit was in the making. Trudy loved working with Monte Rubin. He was sensitive, creative, well-organized, and tough. One did one's best for him or paid the consequences. Trudy found herself performing at a level that even she didn't believe possible. Within two weeks, word leaked out that here was a new Trudy Coles, mature and lovely, devoted to her work and deeply motivated. Rubin complimented her just enough to let her know that she was appreciated. But on those rare occasions when her work was not near-perfect, he was a harsh taskmaster, insisting that they shoot again and again until he had it right.

"Wow! They should call you Monte Legree," she jested half in earnest one day when he had made her repeat a single take eighteen times.

"That's what it's all about, sister," he retorted without a smile. "I get paid to find perfection. I really have no stomach for mediocrity." Again, there wasn't the slightest hint of a smile.

Smiles came in torrents, however, in early March when the Academy of Motion Picture Arts and Sciences announced its nominations for the 1971 Oscars. As many had predicted, Trudy received a nomination for best actress, Monte Rubin for best director, and *Prescription Murder* was a highly acclaimed nominee for the best picture of the year. And what a year it was! *The French Connection, A Clockwork Orange, Nicholas and Alexan-*

dra, The Last Picture Show, and *Fiddler on the Roof* were the other contenders. William Friedkin, Peter Bogdanovich, John Schlesinger, Stanley Kubrick, and Norman Jewison were Monte's competitors. And Trudy had to contend with the likes of Jane Fonda, Julie Christie, Glenda Jackson, Vanessa Redgrave, and Janet Suzmen. It was mind-boggling and somewhat difficult to breathe in such rarefied atmosphere. Trudy tried to tell herself that she was a seasoned professional who belonged in the company her nomination had put her in. Even so, for the impoverished coal miner's daughter from West Virginia, an Oscar nomination was almost too hot to handle. Monte Rubin, by contrast, took his nomination in stride.

"Oscar, schmoscar, a *bee gezundt!*" he joked.

"What's that supposed to mean?" Trudy asked.

"It means 'as long as you feel good.' "

"Well, it feels good to be nominated but it will feel a hell of a lot better if we win."

"We won't."

"That's confidence for you. If you don't feel it, you won't win it, as my old man used to say. And he could really pick horses."

"Horses ain't Hollywood, as my old man used to say."

"Why don't we have a chance?"

"Money. It's that simple. *Prescription Murder* is an independent production released by Paramount. The other contenders are all studio properties and the big guys won't let a stone remain unturned to win. They'll pour millions into promotion because they know what a win can mean at the box office. Even though George Scott turned down his Oscar last year, the fact that the picture was selected as the year's best nearly doubled its gross. It happens every year and this one won't be an exception. I think it's a miracle that we were nominated at all."

"Well, this fat lassie isn't giving up. I'm going to ride down Wilshire Boulevard on a white horse in my altogether like Lady Godiva just to let people know I'm in the running. And if there are any points for fat asses, hell, I'm a shoo-in."

As Monte had predicted, as the big day approached studio flacks worked triple time just to glean an extra column mention. Pictures that hadn't really caught on were released in major markets in the hope that their nominations would be enhanced by public support. Monte squeezed $100,000 out of Paramount for an advertising campaign in the trades, on radio and television, and for a flashy reopening in Los Angeles. But it was just a peanut whistle compared to the blasts for *The Last Picture Show, A Clockwork Orange,* and *The French Connection.*

Monte's pessimism had its effect on Trudy, despite her determination to put on a brave front. The more she read about Fonda, the more she saw Christie and Redgrave on television, the more she realized that, despite glowing reviews and audience acceptance, *Prescription Murder* was a small-time effort. And as much as she loved Monte Rubin and admired his work, she had to admit that the other nominated directors were real heavyweights. The days crept by slowly as Oscar night approached. Since she was not working, it became more and more difficult to expunge the competition from her consciousness.

"Hell, it's only a little golden statuette!" she kept telling herself. "What in the hell am I getting so excited about? It's not going to change my life any. I'll always find work, Oscar or no Oscar."

Such talk was all sophistry and she knew it. No American actor or actress who works in Hollywood can avoid the realization that careers are made and broken on Academy Award night. And with the whole civilized world watching to boot! It was almost too much to contemplate. She grew more and more nervous, started drinking just a little too heavily, found herself snapping at Belinda, and often became offended by the slightest oversight. She realized that she was thinking a lot about her father, who had been dead now for more than fifteen years. It was strange that whenever she was in a stressful situation her mind turned back to the man who had so profoundly influenced her in what she considered to be a negative way. Yet, she remembered many good things he had told her, particularly the advice that he had given so freely yet never seemed able to follow himself.

One night in a troubled dream she found herself back in Hubbardsville, pouring coffee for a bunch of noisy, drunken miners, who were playing poker in the Kolinski parlor. Her dad was the biggest loser and she was terrified that he would drop his entire salary for the week, preventing her from buying food for the rest of the kids. She pleaded with him to quit, but he kept borrowing money from his pals, who seemed only too eager to finance him again and again in what was obviously a losing venture. But Cass just kept betting heavily, shouting to his cronies to stop telling jokes and continue dealing. At last a mammoth pot accumulated in the center of the table as raise after raise upped the ante.

Trudy's dad refused to fold, borrowing more and more money as each raise increased the tension. At last the betting was completed. Cass had miraculously filled an inside straight and won the pot and the evening.

One of his disgusted friends asked, "Cass, how the hell did you stay in with such lousy cards, a four, five, seven, and eight?"

"I learned a long time ago from my pappy. You play 'em like you got 'em!"

Trudy awoke with a start. Instead of being upset, her face even in the dark was wreathed with smiles. "Play 'em like you got 'em." By God, that's how she'd play those fucking Academy Awards. She'd play as if she was going to win. That day she went out and spent, for her, the unheard-of sum of $5,000 for a designer dress with gold lamé tassels. Sure, she knew it was the kind of gown that all the cognoscenti would sneer at and call lowbrow. But she didn't care. Trudy Coles would set the standards, for Trudy Coles was an Academy Award nominee!

At last it was April 10, 1972. Monte and Betty had insisted on accompanying her to the Dorothy Chandler Pavilion in the new Los Angeles Music Center. She had invited Richie Stevens but, graciously, he had refused to be her escort.

"This is your night, Trudy. I'm rooting for you to win. If we're together, there will be all the gossip dredged up from the past. Besides, I'll be so nervous, I'll sweat all over your gown. I'm going to stay home this trip and cheer you on by television."

"Can I come, Mom?" Belinda piped up.

"Why not?" Trudy answered with a broad smile. "When I was six the biggest thing in my life was to watch a square dance in our church on Halloween. Why shouldn't my daughter be queen of the Academy Awards?"

Belinda hugged her mother in silent gratitude. She was dressed like a delicate angel under Richie's direction.

Outside the pavilion the usual crowds had gathered hours before the doors opened to struggle for a glimpse of the arriving stars. A television reporter thrust a microphone in Trudy's face and, turning her toward the camera, asked, "You're a top favorite, Miss Coles. How does it feel?"

"Well," she answered slowly, giving all of America a chance to drink in her magnificent beauty, "it feels like champagne and caviar, it feels like winning the Rose Bowl, it feels like Frank Sinatra is singing me a love song, that's how it feels. Wonderful!"

"Thank you, Miss Coles. We wish you bluebirds!"

It was an evening filled with tension. From the moment she entered the packed auditorium, with flashbulbs popping like firecrackers on the Fourth of July, the nerve endings throughout her body tingled. She strove to appear calm and collected, smiling graciously to her many friends in the industry and waving just a little bit too enthusiastically to her competition in the best actress category. There sat her competitors, just a few rows away, all looking determined yet striving to be casual. There were Guzman, Christie, Redgrave, and Jackson, regal and incredibly lovely, and looking as if they had just been released after a week's stay at the beauty salon, every hair in place. Trudy felt just a blush of shame, realizing that she was making a statement in her golden, shimmering gown. But then she thought of Cass Kolinski. "Play 'em like you got 'em!" She smiled and took her seat, proudly leading Belinda beside her.

At long last, the ceremony started. It moved at a snail's pace. Hour after hour the painful ceremonies went on. Patience, Trudy cautioned herself. You might not give a damn about the best cinematography, outstanding special visual effects, or the best story and screenplay based on material never previously published—or was she just jumbling up the categories in her nervousness?—but someone's dream was coming true on that stage and for them it was very important. She'd have to try not to sweat so profusely when—or rather, if—she won. She'd look her worst in front of all these people and all of those millions watching at home. But who had the control, the strength not to feel the tension? My God, it was your very life being played out on that stage right before your eyes.

Then, finally, the moment arrived. They actually were announcing the nominations for best actress. She could feel the throbbing in her temples, the coursing of blood speeding through her arteries, her temperature rising uncomfortably, her pulse jumping madly out of control.

Would he never open that damned envelope? Never?

"And the winner is . . . Trudy Coles!"

She sat there dumbstruck, too stunned to move or react. All around her people were clapping and cheering, but Trudy Coles was immobilized.

"Mommy, you won!"

Belinda's words brought her back to reality. She rose to her feet, smiled; and slowly, regally, she walked to the stage. She climbed the stairs as she had seen so many others do for so many years, moved to the microphone, accepted a kiss from each of the presenters, and bravely signaled for quiet. Her speech was the shortest of the evening.

"I came here from West Virginia twenty-six years ago. Now, I've won this," she said holding the golden statuette aloft. "Believe me, I'm not going back! Thank you for making this all happen."

The auditorium was swept by thunderous applause. Trudy smiled monarchically, raised her hand, and signaled again for silence.

"I promised myself I'd mention one more thing if I was lucky enough to win this," she added, holding the golden statuette for everyone to admire. "I was here at this same podium two years ago, when I didn't deserve it, and I got hauled away. Just goes to prove you can bounce back fast if you care enough. I hope everyone here and at home cares as much as I do. Believe me, it works miracles."

Now, there was no holding back the tumultuous reception for the lady who had won it all but wasn't afraid to admit that she had suffered in the valleys as well as been victorious on the peaks.

Her joy at winning was somewhat lessened when *Prescription Murder* did not win for best picture. Nor was Monte Rubin victorious for best direction. Those honors went to *The French Connection* and William Friedkin, respectively. Monte did not seem too badly let down, for after all, he had been predicting his own fate. The picture would go on to make millions for all involved despite the fact that it did not win the top award. But Trudy had won an Oscar. It had taken long years of work, disappointment, sorrow, exaltation, strain, pressure, all of the mixed emotions that together make up a life. But she had won. As her dad had advised: She played 'em like she had 'em, and she really did.

At long last, Trudy Coles was a star of international significance. She was offered only the best roles and accepted the few parts that gave her a chance to prove all that she had learned and all that she had suffered in a quarter of a century lived to the hilt in the Hollywood caldron. Monte and Betty Rubin became her best friends, and together they basked in their triumphs. Monte delivered yet another winner with Trudy as star, and even though it was not a *Prescription Murder,* it was a big hit artistically and financially, too. Trudy grew rich and famous; her life was ordered and at times even dull. But she never thought of it that way. She saw Belinda regularly, renewed her friendship with Richie, and even forgave Manny Silverstein when word reached her that he was very ill. She visited him in the hospital on one of the last days he was permitted visitors.

"So, Polock, you're a big star now!"

"Surprised?"

"Hell, no. With tits like yours, how long could they hold you back? I knew it the first time I saw you balls-naked in that back room."

"You want to go back there tonight? I'll break my date."

"Shit, I couldn't get it up tonight even for you! You know Tillie always suspected that I was humping you but never could catch me at it. Believe me, she would have broken my ass if she had. Anyhow, she's gone now, and the way I feel, I'm gonna meet her again real soon."

"You shouldn't talk that way. Think positive, like you used to tell me. Old bastards like you don't die that easy."

"Maybe you're right. Maybe I gotta suffer a little more."

He slipped into a coma the next day and was dead by the end of the week. There was an enormous funeral, attended by everyone who was anyone in the film capital. Trudy cried throughout the ceremony and wondered in retrospect if she was crying for Manny, his family, or for herself. She knew she was furious when she heard some tasteless gagster remark as they left the funeral parlor, "The old bastard! God better check his bank account!" She wished Manny could have been alive to defend himself.

She felt a tap on her shoulder as she walked to her car. She turned suddenly and gasped for breath as she saw Leonard Rush standing behind her. It was the first time they had met since she had left the sanatorium, though she had read several column items alluding to his recovery from "tuberculosis." Now, standing there and watching him smile that crooked, knowing smile of his, she realized in a flash how much she had missed him.

The loneliness she had suffered now found its cure in the renewal of an intense relationship with Leonard Rush. Like two adolescents madly in love, they sought each other's company wherever and whenever it was possible. Trudy could not believe how this homely, aging professor could arouse her. All of the tenderness she had felt for Richie Stevens, all of the animal magnetism she had felt for Jocko Rachubinski, all of the innocent discovery she had enjoyed with Rob Wenger, all of the wickedness she had enjoyed with Manny Silverstein, all were rolled into one incredible, emotional bombshell that exploded within her at every meeting. She could not get enough of him, nor he of her. Even her newly won status as a superstar had little meaning when matched against the intoxicating reality of her love for Leonard Rush. She longed for that time when they could spend their lives together.

Although he never broached the subject, Trudy could not but be curious about Rush's relationship with his wife, Shirley, now that he was apparently cured of his alcoholism. She hesitated bringing up the subject but she was, after all, the woman in his life and believed she had a right to ask.

"Len, how are things with you and Shirley?" she questioned directly one morning as they enjoyed a drive to Zuma Beach.

"It's such a beautiful morning. Why intrude with talk that can only be painful?"

"At Reynolds you often spoke of her and we managed to resist the pain. Why not now?"

"Reynolds seems like a million years ago. Here is here and now is now."

"I'll respect your privacy if that's what you want."

"It's not a question of privacy. It's a question of survival. Shirley is Shirley. Times may change and I may change but Shirley will flow on forever."

Trudy was not satisfied with his answer but decided not to press the issue. Besides, she had news to break and wondered if this were the moment for it. She decided to take the chance.

"I've been asked to leave the country for four months. Monte wants me to do his next picture. We're shooting in Yugoslavia. Want to come?"

"I'm afraid a capitalistic economist would hardly find himself welcome in Yugoslavia."

"Even a Nobel Prize winner?"

"Especially a Nobel Prize winner. Unless I applied for a job as a lifeguard in Dubrovnik. And I can't swim."

"Four months seems like forever to me, being separated from you."

"So why not refuse and stay home? You spend most of your energy turning down pictures anyhow. Accept one that will be filmed here in L.A."

"Getting work is not the problem. Getting the right picture and the right director is what it's all about. Monte Rubin made me a star. I can't refuse him. He made me a star after twenty-five years of struggling. I won't run away when he needs me."

"That, my dear Trudy, is pure nonsense. He didn't make you a star. He steered you into the right channel and you emerged. He couldn't make me a star, could he?"

"In my book, you are a star. But I think you're jealous. And that makes me happy."

"I sure am. I wish I had a silver beard like that and a physique that belongs to a young kid. I feel like a mildewed prune when I see him."

"Prunes are good for me."

They had borrowed the use of a friend's apartment and spent the day alternately walking on the beach and making love. It was an idyll that only mature lovers could appreciate.

The following morning Trudy was rudely awakened by the ringing of the telephone. She peered at the clock through sleepy eyes and observed that it was not yet eight o'clock. For reasons she could not explain, early morning phone calls always frightened her. Good news never arrived that early in the day.

"Miss Coles?" an unfamiliar male voice queried.

"Yes?"

"This is the Los Angeles sheriff's office."

"What's wrong?" Trudy asked in alarm. So few people were familiar with her private telephone number that a call such as this must concern someone very close to her.

"We've taken a woman into custody who is a friend of yours. A Miss O'Neill. Miss Penny O'Neill?"

"Yes. She is a friend. What did she do?"

"Narcotics. She's been dealing. We caught her red-handed. Trying to sell a load of coke to one of our undercover agents."

"Did she tell you to call me?"

"No. She won't talk. We traced her back to Milton Sanatorium. The director there told me that she was a friend of yours and that you helped her a number of years ago."

"And who are you?"

"McGuigan. Sergeant David McGuigan. I'm the duty officer.

We're here at the courthouse. Can you come right down? Maybe we can help."

"Thank you very much. I'll be there in less than an hour."

Trudy was ushered into a private office, where Penny was being held. She couldn't believe her eyes. Dirty, emaciated, her teeth yellowed with age, her thinning gray hair unkempt and matted, Penny O'Neill was a derelict. At fifty-six years of age, she looked more like her own grandmother than the sexy, rose-skinned beauty with whom Trudy had shared so many confidences. Her wan smile of greeting was one of shame, nothing more.

"I didn't tell them to call you, Trudy," she said by way of apology. "I'd die before I'd do that, believe me."

"I'm happy they did. Maybe I can help. Have you had any food?"

"Yeah. The sergeant's been real good to me. Just had two hamburgers, fries, and a Coke."

"I don't think she'd eaten in two days," Sergeant McGuigan interjected.

"Sergeant, can we talk alone?"

"Sure. Come on into the inner office. You stay here, Miss O'Neill. Right?"

"There's no place for me to run to, Sergeant."

Sergeant McGuigan indicated a chair for Trudy to sit in and offered a cigarette.

"Thank you, no. Tell me what happened."

"The usual. She's a user. Heavy user. She ran out of dough, needed a snort, and fell for the real dealer's line. They're always looking for new pushers. Sort of makes them a wholesaler and cuts down their own risk of exposure."

"Sergeant, I love that woman. She's the best. Life has crapped on her so often it's no surprise she can't tell right from wrong. I'll do anything to help if we can save her from jail. I guess I'm asking a nice young man like you to compromise yourself. But sending Miss O'Neill to prison won't accomplish anything. I'll send her to a sanatorium and support her so she won't be here again, I promise."

"Miss Coles, once they start dealing, if they're too old to walk the streets, if you know what I mean, they always come back. Well, almost always. But my boss the D.A. wants us to try to help first offenders like Miss O'Neill, especially if they have a responsible sponsor. So I'm not compromising myself. The D.A. knows that I called you."

"I'm happy to hear that."

"Thought you would be. Now there is one thing that's absolutely necessary if we're to sort of bend the rules. She's gotta talk. In private and in confidence, of course. We have to learn where and when and how she's been getting supplied. Then, we can go out and crush those bastards—excuse the word—like the roaches they really are. If she helps us, I'll see that the case isn't even booked, so she'll have no record. If not . . . well you can finish the sentence yourself."

With a little persuasion, Trudy convinced Penny that it was in her best interest to cooperate. Her dealer never could trace it to her, since the case wasn't booked, and Trudy supplied money to hand over to the dealer, which allegedly had come from Penny's sales. Several days later, as prearranged, Penny slipped from sight and was taken to a private hospital more than one hundred miles south of Los Angeles. It took more than eight months to dry her out and break her habit, but in the end she did it. Trudy supplied the money for Penny's convalescence and supported her upon her release until she found work again. Though hardly the ravishing beauty of old, Penny regained her health, her self respect, and was blessed, it seemed, with a new lease on life.

Trudy left for Europe the following week. She and Leonard had one last evening together, shortened unfortunately by his need to attend a late-night seminar at the university. Trudy suspected that the real seminar was the need to get home and abate Shirley's temper tantrum over his constant absence, but she decided against expressing the view on this, their last night together for many weeks. She had noticed, or perhaps she had imagined, that he was drawing back just a hair in the ardor of his attentions. It wasn't anything specific; it was just that there seemed to be more seminars, more conferences, more family crises as the weeks rolled by. Well, a very wise man had cautioned her many years ago to avoid entanglements with married men. Words that enter the ear do not necessarily penetrate the heart. Trudy felt that as long as she lived she would remain a slave to Leonard Rush.

Things did not move favorably in Yugoslavia. Although the Communist technicians seemed eager to please, they simply lacked the know-how of American filmmakers. Their facilities were generally modern but here again they would not be in a position to compete seriously with Hollywood for many years. Trudy developed a bad cold and found it difficult to concentrate on learning her lines. Her leading man was an aging bore who tried almost immediately to enter her bedroom and her life.

"Larry, I want you to realize that there *is* a man in my life. Just because we work together does not mean that we must screw together. You get my point?"

"My dearest Trudy," he replied, "acting is always more effective when it is backed by an element of truth. Here we must perform some of the most ardent love scenes ever filmed. Wouldn't it be so much more meaningful if we really felt true love for each other?"

"Maybe. But the fact is that we don't. So we'll just have to be actors—which is, after all, what we're getting paid for. If you need to, why not approach that pretty little ingénue who's been making goo-goo eyes at you from the first moment we got together in New York? I really think that's the kind of true love you're looking for."

"Trudy, you're a cold, cruel woman!"

"I'm really not, Larry, but you'll never know it."

Every evening she scribbled a few lines to Leonard, which were flown out in the morning packet. His letters, in return, were not as frequent, but he did call occasionally and profess his love. Once during an overseas call, when he told her how much he missed her, she suggested that he fly over for a week's visit.

"I'll pay for the flight. I'm making a barrel now and I might as well enjoy it," she argued.

"I've got the money. That's not the problem. It's the time. I'm in the midst of preparing a paper for an international conference of economists in Toronto. It's got to be ready in ten days and I'm up to my eyeballs in work."

"I still have eight weeks of shooting. I hope I can survive."

The eight weeks dragged on to twelve and finally the picture, a disappointing melange of maudlin sentimentality, was finished.

"The lions have labored and brought forth a mouse," Monte Rubin said cryptically as they left for home.

"Mice pay," Trudy retorted. "Just ask Walt Disney."

"This is a shitty mouse. Not Mickey. If I knew a way to scrap it I would. But then there's ten million dollars tied up and I've got to give the studio a chance to win it back. Otherwise they'll think I keep all the good stuff for my own productions."

Actually, the film, though not up to Rubin standards, did moderately well at the box office. The Trudy Coles name and image were enough to bring folks out of their homes and into the theater despite that little black box that was now spewing color all over America. Whether it would gross two and a half times its negative costs, thus guaranteeing a profit, was questionable. But at least it was not a bomb.

Trudy tried to phone Leonard during a brief layover in New York, but he was not in his office. She left word with his secretary as to the exact time of her arrival at Los Angeles International Airport, but apparently the message went astray: he was not there to meet her when the plane touched down. It was a bad omen.

"What's the matter, kid?" Monte questioned. "You look like you just swallowed a kosher pickle."

"The truth is I'd like to swallow a kosher pickle. But he's not here."

"That sounds awfully Freudian to me. Hey, there's Betty. See, she's waving to us from that window."

She was so exhausted from the change in time zones that she fell asleep the moment she reached her home. All was just as she left it. Aside from missing Leonard and not seeing Belinda, it was almost as if she had never been away. She rose twelve hours later, took a steaming hot bath, and went immediately to the phone. It was seven o'clock but there was no way to resist calling him. She tried to reach him at work but there was the expected recorded message that the offices were closed until the following morning. Hesitating, she decided to risk phoning him at home. If Shirley answered, well, she'd figure out what to say. Slowly, deliberately, she dialed the number, her heart fluttering nervously as the circuits engaged and the ringing began. Finally, after four or five rings, there was a click and a foreign voice answered the phone.

"Rushes' residence. May I help you?"

"Yes. Is Dr. Rush in?"

"Who is calling, please?"

"Tell him it is Mrs. Hubbard."

It was a code they had developed. After an interminable pause, during which she could hear her heart pounding, he was on the phone.

"Yes, Mrs. Hubbard?" he asked coldly.

"Dr. Rush, I was wondering if you knew where I could get my dog a bone. You see I've just returned from overseas and—"

He cut her off abruptly. "I think this is a matter that can wait until morning. Please arrange to call my office."

And he rang off. Trudy cried herself to sleep after tossing and turning for at least five hours. This was his idea of love? For five months they had been separated with only an international phone hook-up as a bridge between them. Could he really have missed her if he couldn't even send a hint of his affection? The fact that he was not at the airport to meet her was bad enough. But no note, no flowers, no telegram, and now this sharp, unfeeling dismissal. She decided that she would not contact him until he called her, regardless of the emotional price she might have to pay.

He called the next morning. It was immediately obvious that something was seriously wrong in their relationship. He offered a half-hearted apology for his brusqueness the previous night when she had phoned him at home.

"Sorry about last night, darling, but the ever-conspicuous Shirley was hovering like the Angel of Death over my right shoulder. I hope you understand."

"No. I don't. I thought that after so many months apart you might have sent some signal that you missed me."

"People who are maturely in love don't need signals."

"This mature person does."

"Well, here's my flasher going off full blast. How about dinner tomorrow evening?"

"Not today or tonight?"

"Darling, it's just impossible. You know I had no advance notice as to when you'd be arriving. I'm up to my you-know-what in appointments. We'll make up for it tomorrow night."

They met the following evening but it was a great disappointment. Trudy couldn't put her finger on exactly what was missing. Leonard was attentive, considerate, interested in her report on her experiences in Yugoslavia, but it was more a conversation between two involved colleagues than a long-awaited meeting between two lovers. What was most shocking, however, was that Trudy was certain he smelled of liquor when he pecked her on the cheek at the restaurant. Her suspicions were confirmed when he ordered a martini before dinner.

"The doctor approve?" she asked in surprise.

"Well actually he prefers Beefeater."

"It's not meant as a joke, Len. I thought you were instructed to stay away entirely."

"Oh, that's been changed for months. I can manage it."

He had another drink before dinner and insisted that they order a bottle of white wine with their entree. He seemed to be able to handle it but there was just a hint of unsteadiness in his gait as they left the restaurant. They headed for Trudy's home as they had on so many nights in the past. Leonard followed his usual route and from all appearances was driving soberly.

Once inside the house, he requested a brandy—"a lover's nightcap" as he called it.

"We must toast our reunion."

"I really think there has been enough toasting tonight, Len. Let's sit and talk like sane adults."

"I talk better with a drink in my hands. Unties my tongue."

"Leonard, what's wrong? Are you trying to get up enough nerve to tell me something? If so, go ahead. I'm a big girl and I can take it."

"It's hard to articulate, Trudy. We've been separated from each other for five months. It's given us both a lot of time to think. I've never been very good at deception and it strikes me that I've been unfair to you and to Shirley. I'm just using you both for what I want at the moment. To translate an old Yiddish saying, 'A man can't keep his ass under two canopies at the same time.'"

"Are you concerned about me or about Shirley?"

"About both. And about me."

"I think that's the gist of it. I've known you were married from the beginning. From what you tell me, Shirley is a bitch on wheels and doesn't deserve consideration. It's you, Len, that's the problem."

"Perhaps."

"Okay. So here's the solution. Tell Shirley you want a divorce and marry me. Money is no problem. There are no little children to worry about. If it's religion that's got you troubled, forget it. I'll convert. Some of my best friends are . . . you know the joke. Maybe you are right. Maybe you had better decide which canopy you want to cover that ass of yours."

"I need a little time to think."

"How little is little?"

"A few days. Maybe a week."

"Take them. But please don't call me until you have made up your mind."

He tried to take her in his arms for a passionate good-night embrace, but she gently, firmly pushed him away.

"Not tonight. I'm really not up to it. If and when, we'll have our lovemaking. And Leonard, while we're talking straight to each other, I'm worried about your drinking. I saw you down that quickie at the bar when you told me you had to use the men's room back at the restaurant."

"Not to worry. Everything is under control."

He stopped at a bar on the way home for more liquid reinforcement. They turned him out at three-thirty, a half hour after their normal closing hour. At four in the morning, her telephone rang, jangling her back to consciousness. She grabbed for the phone, fearing the worst. It was a female voice that accosted her.

"Miss Coles, is my husband still with you?"

"Who is this?"

"Who do you think it is? It's Shirley Rush. He told me he was going to see you tonight—'for the last time'—and that he'd be home early. He's been drinking again, heavily, and I'm worried sick."

"We did have dinner together in Westwood."

"I know. At Marino's. Leonard tells me everything, Miss Coles. You haven't been fooling me, believe me."

"Leonard left here hours ago. He did have a few drinks but he seemed to be under control. What should we do?"

"I don't know what you should do. I know what I'm going to do. I'm familiar with his favorite watering holes. I'll call them, then I'll call the police."

Trudy slept no more that night. Unbelievable! Shirley had known of their affair all along. And he had pretended that their romance must be cloaked in the greatest secrecy. Could it really be possible? Could she have been such an incredible fool?

She rose at six, showered to sharpen her senses, made herself a pot of strong, black coffee, and, cigarette in hand, tried to clear her brain. Was it possible that she could not ever win a man and keep him? Why was it that the men she loved always seemed to waver when she was most intense? Here was Leonard Rush, truly an unattractive human being, at least fifteen years her senior, and yet she could not satisfy him. She had made every effort to avoid the very practices that he had described as being so hateful in Shirley. And to think that all the time she had been playing the game, his wife had known of the affair and apparently had been willing to go along with it while she herself was being so noble about protecting his reputation as a respected, world-famous social scientist who could not stand the glare of notoriety. It had been a long time, and she couldn't understand why she was thinking of her father these days. She remembered him saying, "There's no fool like an old fool." But was she old at forty-two? Or was she just a fool at any age?

He called at nine in the morning, obviously hungover and somewhat abashed. He knew about Shirley's call but didn't know exactly what she had revealed. A friendly bartender with a bachelor pad near the bar had insisted on taking him home, leaving his car in the tavern's parking lot. He had been in no condition to drive. After four hours' sleep, he had arisen, showered, and returned to his home.

That was the last call she ever received from Leonard Rush. She did get a letter several days later, obviously scribbled at a moment when he was terribly distraught. She could practically read its contents without unsealing the envelope. He was unworthy of her and had taken cruel advantage of their love affair. Shirley was a bitch but she was, after all, his bitch, and she had stood by him through all the alcoholic excesses and all of the pain. Months later, and quite by chance, she was to bump into one of the supervisors she had befriended at Reynolds, and learned that Leonard Rush had again been admitted as a patient. By then her pain would have subsided. But now, tearful and smarting, she had to compose a fitting answer.

She wrote and rewrote her reply, each time deciding that what she had written was too ugly or too mean or too forgiving or too maudlin. Finally, she settled on a brief note. It read:

Len,
  You are right. You are unworthy of me and my love. I'm a star. You're a phony.
  Trudy Coles

CHAPTER 22

1973

After the Leonard Rush debacle, Trudy returned to the one thing she did best, making motion pictures. Occasionally, she was invited to participate in a television drama, but the truth was she didn't really enjoy the kind of quickie production that the small screen required. Besides, she was a giant star now and few television shows could afford her. In addition, and only to herself, she admitted that at age forty-three, her appearance was beginning to be more and more of a problem and television didn't have time to play the kind of illusionary games she demanded with regard to makeup and camera angles. Her latest features had been disappointing, though the Trudy Coles name usually was a guarantee of capital recoupment if not big profits.

She was seated one day with her agent, Sid Keyes, in El Padrino at the Beverly Wilton for a luncheon conference. She had avoided the Wilton for a long time after her unpleasant residency, but now that she was a major star they treated her with great deference. With the Jason Arnold office just down the street, it was the customary setting for meetings of this kind.

"Well, this room sure is early California," she said for openers. "I wonder if there are any gold nuggets under the tiles."

"I doubt it," Keyes answered, peering through his horn-rimmed glasses at the group coming through the entranceway. "Maybe there are. I just see Don Clancy from ICM. They wouldn't be here in our territory unless there was some precious metal to be mined. So how the hell are you, Trudy?"

"Fine. Just fine. But I could be better if you guys in the blue pinstripes would get me another hit. I'm tired of the dreck you've been feeding me."

It was an old Hollywood technique. Never let your agent rest. Make him think he's been letting you down.

"Well, we're working at it. That's why I wanted to talk to you. We've got a great offer from Fox. One million guarantee and ten percent of the net. Can't beat that."

"They'll see to it that there never is a net, won't they?"

"No. Not in your case. They really want you badly."

"Tell me about the script."

"It's a dandy. Written by a bright, young genius named Steven Kantakis, a Greek kid from Rhode Island, of all places. He's had two best-selling novels, a string of television hits, and this is to be his first feature. It's based on a series of short stories he did for *The New Yorker*. It's about a teenage boy who falls in love with his best friend's mother. Great drama."

"And I'm to be the mother, right?"

"I hope so . . . but there is a problem."

"Like?"

"Like a lot of blatant sex. Very explicit. Might just have a little trouble with the rating boards. Not frontal, of course, but a lot of nudity. A lot of 'let's get a good long look at this Trudy Coles.'"

"And as my agent you think this is good for my image?"

"Yes, I do Trudy. You may hate me at the end of this luncheon and want to hit me with one of those leather thongs hanging from the wall, but I have to tell it like it is. The market is tired of middle-of-the-road romances involving aging beauties. You blame me for not getting you better material but don't for a moment think I'm not working my ass off to do just that all of the time. The problem is one of changing tastes in America . . . for the entire world for that matter. I'm fifty-two and you're pushing forty."

"Don't be kind. I was forty-three last Thursday."

"The point is that the average moviegoer is nineteen to twenty-two. They can see all of the old movies they want on television. They want something more stimulating when they pay to see the big screen. Sex and violence are in and they're getting bigger every day. My crystal ball tells me that by the time 1980 rolls around they'll be showing grandparents screwing. It'll be like ladies' night at the Turkish bath. So, here are the alternatives. Wait for a fair flick every eighteen months or so and gradually fall out of favor, or join the flow and show your butt. I really can't imagine anyone with better equipment, even at forty-three, which incidentally you should not admit to."

"The equipment is fine, thank you, and still working now and again. It's the layers of fat covering it that may be a problem. Not to mention its owner's reluctance to wade in the gutter."

"You're going to have to lose the weight no matter what we accept. You're going to have to wrestle with the moral issues yourself. Personally, I can't see what's wrong with showing the human form. The great artists and sculptors of antiquity did so. Why are we suddenly so Victorian?"

"We're not. It's just that I didn't pose for Michaelangelo and I'm going to have to get used to standing nude before a pack of leering cameramen and grips. Let me think about it. By the way, who's directing?"

"They'll give us our choice of about ten. All good."

After several days, Trudy decided to do it. She started dieting immediately, realizing that at least twenty pounds had to be lost. Drinking was out completely. She enrolled at a local health spa. She re-enrolled in dance class, and even took to swimming twenty laps a morning in her own modest pool. It was dreary, painful work most of the time, but Trudy was determined to look her best once she showed it all. She looked at herself critically in full-length mirrors each morning and she had to admit that she liked what she was seeing. In all, she took four months to prepare for her role in *Cradle Snatcher,* a mediocre film that got more than its share of publicity even before production began. Here was Trudy Coles, one of Hollywood's own, not some skinny model from New York who emerged through the cover-girl, high-fashion route, who, though a fabulous star of international repute, was going to do a nude scene. Trudy Coles, showing it all for the first time and admitting that she was "an older woman" having an affair with a youngster. It made "great ink," as the press agents termed it. Trudy always had been a publicist's dream. Now, she played the game to the hilt, permitting herself to be photographed in a host of suggestive poses as she was preparing her body for the great revelation.

"How're tricks?" Sid Keyes asked in one of his biweekly, stay-in-touch phone calls.

"Fine. Just fine. A few old friends think I'm nuts. Monte and

Betty have practically disowned me. I've been getting obscene phone calls. Third time I've changed my number. I can't believe there is all this excitement about an old woman's ass. I think the world is sex crazy."

"Well, until something better comes along. Keep at it. I thought you looked sensational, as they say in show biz, when I saw you at Ina's bash. You look any better, I might just give up my priestly vows and take a shot myself."

"You? Never! I know the Jason Arnold credo. 'Never fish off the company dock!' "

The film was to be shot in New York. Trudy was fortunate enough to locate a lovely apartment in the East Seventies, overlooking the river. New York was always a city that made Trudy feel young and vibrant. She hadn't made a feature there in years; it was exciting to be coming back as a giant star.

The city, eager to develop its film-making potential, had been most cooperative. There was a huge press party culminating with a ceremony on the steps of City Hall as the mayor proffered the keys to the city. She thought about Leonard Rush now and again, but in the excitement surrounding the new project, she found ways to subjugate her feelings. It was one of her saving graces: the ability to bury bad experiences of the past and look ahead with courage. In a moment of confidence a friend once asked her if she didn't bear scars from the bitter valleys in her life.

"Hell, no," she responded. "I don't remember much my Polock father taught me. But I do know he told me to be like a ball and bounce higher after each defeat. I never had much time as a kid to learn how to cry."

Vinnie Stagg, the young actor who was to play opposite her, proved to be a sheer delight. He was twenty-one, but looked more like seventeen. His hair was ash blond; deeply set blue eyes gave his face an inquiring, quizzical look. Tall and thin, he walked with a rather hesitant gait that made him look vulnerable. He had been well trained, having spent the better part of three years in the Off-Broadway arena before trying his luck in Hollywood. Even though he had been an overnight sensation, he respected Trudy's long years of experience and was delighted to have the opportunity to play opposite her.

From the first moment she met him, Trudy knew that this would be a good experience. She was right. Vinnie Stagg was a joy to work with. She soon "adopted" him as her surrogate son as well as her on-screen lover. The director had wisely postponed the filming of the nude scenes until everyone on the set had gotten to know each other well and was working as a cohesive team. Also, blessed by good weather and few technical hangups in the outdoor shooting, he had time to give his stars plenty of rest and urged them to relax between takes.

"That was great, today, Miss Coles"—he never called her "Trudy" on the set—"and we won't need you again until Thursday," he announced at the end of a day's filming.

"Thank you, Hal. Sure you don't need any clean-ups? I'll be happy to be on set tomorrow if you want me."

"Not really. We're fine. The rushes looked great last night and we're ahead of schedule."

Faced with the delightful prospect of a day of leisure, Trudy headed back to the hotel. She thought she would luxuriate in a hot bath, have luncheon in her suite, nap, then head out for a day of shopping. She really hadn't had a moment to herself since coming to New York.

As she crossed the lobby, she was accosted by a smiling young woman who appeared to be in her late twenties or early thirties at the oldest. She was tastefully, though not expensively, dressed. She smiled broadly and since she had stationed herself between Trudy and the bank of elevators there was really no way to avoid an encounter.

"Excuse me, Miss Coles, but I'm the niece of an old friend of yours and I told her I'd say hello."

"Oh? Who is that?"

"Minnie Carson."

"I'm afraid I don't recognize the name. Where did I know her from?"

"My aunt worked at Continental Studios for years. She was in the costume department. She helped design clothes for you many times."

Vaguely, Trudy recalled a seamstress named Minnie whom she had nodded to a few times in her early days at Continental. Minnie Carson had never designed costumes for anybody, but Trudy saw no point in raising this as an issue.

"Oh, yes, of course," she lied. "I remember your aunt very well. How is she?"

"Fine. She's retired now. Every time she calls she tells me how very beautiful you are and how she told everybody you were going to be a big star the first time she dressed you."

Another exaggeration, of course, but here, too, Trudy decided it was best to play along. No need to dampen the young lady's enthusiasm. Since the woman just stood there and smiled, Trudy smiled back, not quite knowing how to break off the impromptu meeting though she had the strong suspicion that the rendezvous was not an accident but rather a planned event. Finally, not knowing what else to say, she asked, "And your name is?"

"Lillian Roman. I'm an actress, too. I was wondering if I could impose on you for some advice. I promise I won't take ten minutes of your time. Aunt Minnie says you were always the kind who tried to help other people, or I wouldn't have had the nerve to ask."

So this was it. Trudy wondered if there really was an Aunt Minnie or if it was all a fabrication, a ploy to get her attention. Well, she'd have a cup of coffee with the girl and get it over with.

"All right, I'll try. I'll buy you a cup of coffee here in the Maple Court. It's a lovely spot, no?"

"It's beautiful. You're very kind."

The ten minutes dragged into an hour and a quarter. Lillian seemed delighted that she was getting so much attention since everybody recognized Trudy and, no doubt, wondered who the attractive young woman with her was. Lillian's story was not unusual. At college she had acted and played the lead in all the school plays. Her boyfriend had whisked her away, married her, and presented her with two small children by the end of their fourth year together. Lillian had tried to continue studying and even had auditioned unsuccessfully for a few Broadway shows. Her plight was more difficult because her husband worked at night and she was more or less mired at home.

"Having two great kids isn't bad, Mrs. Roman. Sometimes I wish that I had more time to be a good mother."

"Please call me Lillian. Well, sure I want to be a good mother and I love my kids. But I have a talent and I keep telling Marty that I have just as much a right to express myself as he does."

"What's his job?"

"He's a singer. He works with a lot of bands around town and once in a while does some recording work. I'm not sure he's got what it takes to make it real big. But it's a living."

"I see. Now, how do I fit into the picture? What can I tell you that you don't already know? I'm hardly what you'd call the model career mother."

"I thought maybe he'd listen to you. I keep asking him to let me have my chance and he keeps telling me there's only room for one show business star in a family . . . not that he's a star or I'd ever be one. But I'd like to try. I thought maybe if he heard from you that it's wrong to keep me pinned down, he'd change his mind."

"Are you sure that's all you wanted from me?" Trudy asked with a smile.

"Well—I guess I have to admit that I thought because of Aunt Minnie and all, maybe you could get me a small part in a picture. At least with a film you don't have to be at the theater every night of the week."

Trudy smiled. Well, you had to give this aggressive little lady credit. She regretted ever having gotten started with her. But now that she was in it, she saw no way to break off the relationship abruptly.

"Lillian, I'm not a casting director. And I rarely make films in New York. I'm sure you wouldn't want to leave your kids and take a job on location somewhere. Would you?"

"Not now. Not yet, anyhow."

"If you really think it will help, I'll talk to your husband. Then, if I hear of anything, I'll keep you in mind. Maybe you ought to count your blessings, though. Two kids and a good husband are harder to find than jobs in Hollywood."

Even as she spoke the words, Trudy knew they were falling on deaf ears. Well, she mused, we all have dreams.

The next day Trudy received a call from Marty Roman. He asked if he could buy her a drink at her hotel so she wouldn't be inconvenienced. Reluctantly, Trudy agreed, feeling that this was the quickest way to rid herself of an association that she had neither requested nor desired.

She met him in the lobby at six o'clock, after she had had time to clean up following the day's shooting. He was a charming fellow whose initial, major claim to fame seemed to be a mop of curly brown hair that virtually covered his forehead, as well as a pair of deep, brown eyes that were furry and soft like the orbs on a cocker spaniel puppy. His voice was velvety smooth and he handled himself with great aplomb. He had a way of saying things that were just noticeably flirtatious and yet, if repeated, would not indict him as a philandering husband. Trudy found him an interesting challenge and she wasn't really certain why. The fact was that after a half hour and two drinks each, the talk shifted away from Lillian and on to his own career.

"Are you good?" Trudy asked curiously.

"I think I'm damn good. But why shouldn't I? Hey, I've got an idea. I'm working a small club tonight down in the Village. Let me take you down there and you judge for yourself. . . . How about it?"

The conversation was developing dangerously and yet predictably. Trudy didn't have to show up on the set until the following afternoon and she really hadn't had any social pleasures since arriving in the East. She did feel a tinge of sympathy for Lillian at home with two small kids. But . . .

Marty Roman was really quite entertaining. His singing voice was pleasant, if not outstanding, and he handled a tune intelligently. His way with a jazz band combo was most convincing. He had a knack of imitating the various instruments in the band and alternating with them in riffs that sounded more like melodic accompaniment than the tones of a vocalist striving for individual dominance. The band egging him on, now he was a saxaphone, now a trumpet, now a slide trombone, and now a base fiddle. The audience loved it. Trudy had to admit that she, too, was impressed. She hadn't expected him to be quite that good. She also was flattered when he stepped to the microphone and, looking directly at her, said, "I'd like to dedicate the next song to the most beautiful woman in the world. This is for Trudy Coles."

Most of the crowd had not seen her in the darkened, smoke-filled room, but the light man picked her out with a small travel spot and there was sustained, thunderous applause throughout the room. Star though she was, Trudy felt her ego scandalously stimulated. She started feeling warmer emotions for Marty when he sang "If I Loved You" from *Carousel* and followed it up with "I've Got a Crush on You," both of which he handled deftly.

It turned out to be a long, hand-holding evening. Eventually, inevitably, the talk got around to "Nagging Lillian," as he always referred to her. According to Marty's version, she had trapped him in college, had gotten pregnant so that marriage was the only honorable alternative. She had kept him on a short leash, thereby limiting his career chances, and generally making his life miserable with all the accusations about his being an anchor on her career aspirations. Frankly, he confided to Trudy, Lillian was a lousy actress even in college.

He escorted her back to the hotel and tried to come up to her suite, but she resisted. There was a boyish charm about him and he was show-biz "hip," but on this first night alone with him she really couldn't picture herself entering a serious relationship with someone so young. As for Lillian, strangely, Trudy felt not the slightest bit of guilt. "You live by the sword, you die by the sword," Trudy thought. Marty settled for a stolen kiss in a deserted corner of the lobby, especially when she agreed to see him again the following night.

From that day on, Trudy Coles and Marty Roman became, in the language of the columnist, "an item." Whenever she could risk a late night she traveled to where he was appearing. He visited her on the set, took her to lunch, sent her roses, charmed her with considerate but inexpensive gifts, and generally courted her with the fervor of a young man in a first romance. They made love on the third date and Trudy found him a very exciting, uninhibited partner.

"What does your psychiatrist say about your need for a mother image?" she asked humorously.

"He wants to know when I can introduce you to him. You're the youngest mother I ever met . . . and the greatest!" And he was on top of her again, striving to enter her for the fourth time in an hour.

Aside from the Leonard Rush disaster and the intermittent couplings with Manny Silverstein, Trudy had never really had a sustained relationship with a married man. Besides, Marty was a young father and it pained her to think that maybe she was taking him from his family when they needed him. As far as "Nagging Lillian" was concerned, she felt no guilt. Straying husbands were the rule rather than the exception in Hollywood. Trudy reasoned that this aggressive lady could take care of herself.

What began to trouble her was the realization that she was becoming dependent on him, a man who really was not in a position to enter into a permanent relationship. It wasn't that she thought of marrying now as a necessity, but the sad experience of the Rush affair did weigh on her mind. She had decided that the next man who professed to love her had to be hers and hers alone. The Marty Roman affair had all the earmarks of just that, an affair.

"Marty," she asked him one night in her suite as they were preparing to go to bed, "how do you see us next year?"

"What do you mean?" he asked innocently.

"Just that. Hal tells me we'll be through filming in about two weeks. My work is essentially in California. You could be a big hit out there, especially with a few of the right introductions, but are you planning to be with me or not? I guess that's going to sound to you like 'Nagging Lillian,' but a woman likes to know that she's more than a bedmate."

"You know how I feel about you. I'm nuts for you."

"That I know. But are you nuts enough to leave Lillian and the kids for me? That's what I don't know."

"Well, hell knows it's been on my mind a lot lately. But I was never sure how serious you were about me. I've got no illusions, Trudy. Sinatra, I'm not. Tony Bennett I'm not. And you can have all the Hollywood leading men you want."

"That's true. I probably can. But right now I've chosen Marty Roman. I think we could be happy together. That is, if you don't have some silly sort of pride that will get in the way. I've got all the money we'll both ever need. I can help you in your career. I don't want any more children. I wasn't much good at being a mother, Belinda can tell you that. So you had better think about it. I'm not going to keep being your after-work lay forever. I want your decision. And soon, sweetie."

Early the next week, Trudy received a surprise phone call from Lillian Roman. Amazingly, she was controlled and not in the least hysterical.

"Marty tells me that he is thinking of leaving me for you, Miss Coles. I thought he still loved me but I guess in today's world you have to be ready for shocks."

"I have had my share of shocks, too, Lillian."

"Yes, I know. I've read enough screen magazines and gossip columns to feel that I really almost know you. I didn't think you'd be quite cruel enough to turn on an innocent mother who had come to you for help and advice."

"Stop it, Lillian. You're breaking my heart. Marty says you were a lousy actress in college and, frankly, you haven't improved any. I knew you were out to use me the day we met. So forget the 'innocent' act."

"Actress or not, I do have two kids to worry about. Who's going to support them if he leaves me?"

"I haven't discussed Marty's finances with him. They're really not my business."

"Yes, they are, if you're trying to steal my husband. He never made a lot of money. With the traveling, the new orchestrations and arrangements, the tuxes and the rest, we didn't save a hell of a lot. Now, if he goes, money is a big problem."

"I think Marty is a responsible man. He knows he can't just walk out on his wife and kids and not provide for them."

"That sounds great in a movie, Miss Coles, but I live in the real world. Here's what I told Marty and I wanted to repeat it for you so there is no big mistake. If Marty wants his freedom from me and the kids, it's going to cost him plenty. That's the only way I won't contest a divorce and claim desertion."

"And what is 'plenty' in your mind?" Trudy queried.

"Plenty is two hundred and fifty thousand on separation and guaranteed support, until I remarry. Then, you can have him with my compliments."

"At that price I don't need any compliments, Lillian. But thank you for calling. I had visions of a crying wife on her knees begging me to release her erring husband. At least it's good to know you're a cool businessman."

"I'm a cool business person, Miss Coles. Good-bye."

Well, at least there was little equivocation. "Nagging Lillian" got straight to the point. It was obvious that Marty Roman didn't have that kind of money. Trudy would have to pay heavily for the joy he might bring her. It was a strange thought and a novel experience for her. Bill Peters had been constantly "on the take," of course. But he was a gigolo, nothing more, and there was never even a thought of permanency with him. Here, Marty was essentially a decent man. He needed parole money, and if Trudy wanted to own the key to his cell she would have to provide the wherewithal. It would take some deep thinking on her part.

The picture was all but finished. Only the compulsory nude love scenes had to be shot. Trudy looked forward to them with a bit of trepidation. Yet, when the days came, they really posed no problem. Hal Hopkins, the director, saw to it that only the barest skeleton crew worked those days and Vinnie Stagg remained on the set only as long as the cameras rolled. There was an introductory scene shot in half-light in which Trudy, having emerged from a steaming bath, is turned on by viewing a pair of lovers in action across the street. Although the camera shots were not terribly graphic, it is obvious that she is excited and begins to fondle herself just when her son's friend, played by Vinnie, happens to ring the bell. She answers in a flimsy negligee, and from there on nature takes its course. Hal saw to it that Trudy was protected with a tiny G-string so that at no time was she witnessed totally nude. She admitted to him afterward that she was "into" the plot so intensely that it would not have troubled her if she had been naked. Vinnie, who had filmed nude scenes before, found the work natural. As he explained with a very obvious pun, "I've been in 'Stagg' films before." But never, he had to admit privately, with a beauty of Trudy Coles' stature. Everyone gasped when they viewed the final rushes. Even Trudy liked the way she looked. Delighted with the results, she called Sid Keyes in California that night.

"Get me more work in the altogether. I just discovered I've got a great ass!"

Not an hour later she received a call from Richie Stevens. Belinda had been taken very ill and the doctors were concerned about her slow progress in fighting off the infection.

"What is it?" Trudy asked in alarm.

"A staph infection. It seems to involve her entire upper respiratory system as well as her heart. She's been sick for two weeks, but since you didn't call, I didn't trouble you."

"What is she like tonight? Any better?"

"Not really. High fever. Won't eat. Listless. The doctors think she really isn't determined to get well. When you finish the picture, I think you should come home. She might like to see you."

"I'm finished. Just last night. They're planning a bash to celebrate but I won't stay for it. They'll understand. Pick me up tomorrow around noon at the airport. I'll catch the early United flight. There shouldn't be any problem about reservations. I know that Fox has connections, if there is."

She called Marty at home. "Nagging Lillian" answered the phone and informed her that he was asleep. Trudy insisted that she had to talk to him and, sarcastically, Lillian answered with words to the effect that she would add it to the bill. There was a long, uncomfortable wait. Finally, Marty picked up the phone.

"Trudy, I hope Lillian wasn't insulting on the phone."

"Don't worry about that," Trudy interrupted. "I called to let you know that I have to leave town suddenly. My daughter is very sick and they need me in Los Angeles. Call me in a couple of days. I gave you my private number."

"Sure. I'm sorry as hell. Can I help? Need someone to take you to the airport? I'll be glad to drive you to Kennedy."

"Thanks, no. The studio will supply a limo and I really need time alone. Call me in a couple of days. Good night."

The flight home was agony, the longest six hours she'd ever experienced. Richie's houseman picked her up at the airport. Belinda had taken another turn for the worse and Richie didn't feel that he should leave her alone. Happily, the new domestic, someone she had never met before, was discreet and said very little during the long drive to Beverly Hills.

Belinda smiled wanly when she kissed her. She seemed so thin, so helpless, that it almost broke Trudy's heart. The child was nearly eight now and she always impressed her mother as mature beyond her years, a probable result of having been raised in a one-parent household. Now the guilt of so many years of absence poured down on the famous mother.

That night, home in her bedroom, she prayed for the first time in years. The child whom she had more or less deserted was very ill. Her father, the one who really had raised her, had been present to be by her side. Her mother was off in New York having an affair with a young, married man and posing nude for all of America to gape at. The child seemed to lack the will to live. Ergo, it had to follow logically, that the absentee mother was to blame. She cried for hours on end and, her system disturbed by the change in time zones, found it impossible to get any sleep.

The next morning found her at Belinda's side, where she was to remain for many hours. Richie kindly suggested that she move back into the house until the child recovered, but somehow it just didn't feel right. She drove back and forth twice a day and was there to monitor the slightest change in Belinda's condition. It took more than three weeks, but finally there was slight improvement. Belinda started to smile a bit, seemed to want more food, and regained some of her strength as her temperature began slowly to level off. By the end of a month her return to health was assured. Although she seemed grateful that Trudy was with her, it was to her father that she turned for love as she grew stronger. Trudy realized that now was the time for her to beat a strategic retreat. She came less frequently, stayed for shorter periods, and gradually withdrew from the scene.

During the entire period of Belinda's illness, Marty called regularly and offered to fly out to California if Trudy wished it.

She explained that, as much as she missed his company, her time belonged to her daughter. She really had no room in her heart or brain for romance. But now that the child was almost her old self, Trudy knew that hard decisions had to be made. She asked Marty, as a personal favor, to let her have a month without calling to decide if marriage was the proper course. He acceded to this wish, as he always did, to please her.

Alone now, Trudy found herself growing sadder and sadder. Somehow, when Belinda was ill and she spent her days by her side, there was a direction to her life. Now that the child was fully in the care of her father, it was as if the very *raison d'être* of her life, the cause and direction for living, were gone. She began spending long days and nights alone, asking her secretary to refuse all business contacts on her behalf. Even Sid Keyes' insistence that he must see her on urgent business was rebuffed. Trudy wrote him a brief note:

> *Sid,*
> *I know that the actor who refuses to see his agent is doomed. But you must trust me. I need time alone for me.*
>
> *Love,*
> *Trudy*

Even the presence of her housekeeper began to weigh heavily upon her. She insisted that she go home every night right after dinner. She started drinking again. Slowly, imperceptibly, the old depression crept up on her. She started reaching for the pills, the liquor, both. This time, fortunately, she knew when it was time to blow her own whistle. She phoned Dr. Gordon, with whom she hadn't spoken since that happy day when he discharged her from Reynolds Sanatorium. He was out of town but phoned from San Francisco as soon as he got word that she had called.

"Nice of you to call long distance, Dr. Gordon."

"I always call immediately when I hear that an old patient needs me, Miss Coles. I'll be back at my Los Angeles office on Friday. Can it wait or do you want to talk on the phone?"

"I'll make it work, Dr. Gordon. I'll see you in your office Friday morning. Ten o'clock okay?"

"Perfect. That gives me time to make morning rounds at the

hospital. I don't go out to Reynolds until Saturday afternoon, so we can have a long chat."

That gave her forty-eight hours to pull on her inner strength and avoid the temptation for self-destruction. She had only one drink with dinner, took a single sleeping pill, and, supported by the knowledge that help was on its way, got six hours of blessed rest. Thursday was more of the same, and though she still felt shaky, she survived until Friday morning's appointment.

"So, Miss Coles, you look marvelous. How has it gone? Do you hear from our friend, Dr. Rush?"

"That's all history now, Dr. Gordon. I was doing fine—for a while—now I'm in trouble. My child was very sick and for weeks I sat by her side, helping to nurse her back to health. You may remember that her father has almost complete custody. I only have visitation rights. But this was a crisis and he invited me to help. It made me feel really useful. Now that she's better, I somehow find myself wondering if there really is anyone who needs me . . . on a personal basis of course."

"Career going well?"

"Fine. I'm a bigger star today than when you saved my life last time at Reynolds. I just finished a pretty good picture. Maybe you'll see it. The working title was *Cradle Snatcher*, but that will be changed fifty times before it's released. They're thinking of calling it *His Friend's Mother*. Anyhow, it's my first experience with screen nudity."

"Well, I don't think there's anything terribly serious here. You look well. Your career is going well. Your daughter is better. I think we all get depressed once in a while when our current crises are solved. And yet, maybe you have a special problem, a problem that you haven't seen fit to tell me about."

"You are terribly bright, Dr. Gordon. There's a man in my life. And I really don't know if I can handle it."

"I'd like to hear about him."

In a few hundred words, Trudy told her story involving Marty Roman. Even to the point of admitting that she had to buy him away from his current wife.

"Well, I wish someone loved me enough to put out that kind of money, or to even consider it. Trudy, I don't think I've ever taken the risk of saying this to any other patient. You know my technique. I ask question after question until the answer is apparent to the patient and I don't have to play God and give advice.

In your case, I'm going to risk it. I think you need someone to share your life with. Sure, you've always got that big, booming success story in the films. But you seem to need more than that. That's why you gravitated so quickly to Leonard Rush, who was much older and from an entirely different world. This man—obviously it is difficult for me to make judgments about someone I have never even met—seems to need you. And I think that's what you need. Someone to take care of. I can't pass judgments about the money and the support and so on. That's for you and your business manager. But if that can be handled, I think Marty Roman may be just what the doctor ordered."

"I feel better already. Thank you for seeing me."

She rose and, as she headed for the door, turned, smiling, and said, "Incidentally, Dr. Gordon, since you've been so complimentary to me, let me return the favor. You look great, too!"

"Thank you. That's because like the old psychiatrist in the tired joke, I never listen to my patients' troubles. I only pretend."

"I know the joke—and it doesn't apply to you. You listen damn well!"

She called Marty that night. He packed, left home, and was in California by Sunday evening. He moved in with Trudy immediately. With Lillian's cooperation, and Trudy's purchase money, he won an uncontested divorce in six months. Trudy and Marty were married the next day.

CHAPTER 23

1974

Trudy wanted Belinda and Marty Roman to be warm friends. She invited the child to dine with them whenever possible, shared recreational jaunts with her, and urged Marty to try and treat the child as if she were his own.

"I love kids," Marty assured her. "Hell, if it weren't that you knocked me out, I would never have left my own kids to start with."

Marty did try his best to win the child over. He brought her gifts, complimented her, joined her in small confidences about her mother, even took her with him at times when Trudy was involved elsewhere. He made it a point never to say anything that in any way was critical of Richie Stevens.

Despite all of his efforts, it was obvious even to the casual observer that Belinda disliked him. Trudy decided that the best way to handle the issue was head on. One day when she and Belinda were alone she broached the subject.

"Sometimes I think you don't love your new Uncle Marty very much."

"He's not my uncle. You just call him that."

"That's true. I thought you would like having an uncle you knew since all of my family is so many thousands of miles away and your dad has no sisters or brothers. An uncle can be nice to have."

"I don't want one. Not 'specially Marty."

"What's wrong with Marty?"

"If you want the truth, he's gross."

"What's that supposed to mean?"

"You know. All the kids say 'gross.' It means 'icky,' like that."

"And why do you think he's so icky?"

"Lots of reasons. Daddy says so, too. Daddy says he's so greasy if you don't watch out he'll slide off the chair."

"That wasn't very nice of your daddy. Marty likes him."

"Well, Mom, the truth is I don't like Marty. And I don't like him patting me on the tush all the time."

"Now what are you talking about?"

"I didn't tell Daddy 'cause he'd get real mad. But every time I'm alone with Marty he's always kissing me and hugging me and then he usually ends by patting me on my behind. He calls it my baby love seat."

"I'm sure he was just joking."

She faced Marty on the subject that night when they had finished dinner and were alone.

"Marty, please keep your hands off Belinda, understand?"

"I don't know what you're talking about."

"It's very clear and very simple. Don't touch her. She says you've been patting her behind and she doesn't like it."

"Now that's ridiculous! I give the kid a little pat once in a while to be friendly and she makes a big thing of it!"

"No. I'm making a big thing of it. I'm not interested in discussing any gory details but I had a father who liked to pat me. That's where it starts and here's where it ends. Don't you ever touch that kid again!"

From then on, Trudy made certain that Marty and Belinda were never alone together. She was so troubled by the incident that she discussed it with Milton Gordon. She had taken to seeing him about once a week as psychiatric "insurance."

"I suddenly had visions of my father pawing me. I could have killed him when Belinda told me."

"Don't overreact. He may really have been just trying to make friends with the child. You can't carry that club against your father for the rest of your life and swing it against every living male."

"Come on, Dr. Gordon. When was the last time you patted some eight-year-old girl on the butt? Is that the way to get friendly with a child?"

"You're forgetting the ground rules. I ask the questions."

"Well, ask yourself if Marty Roman doesn't have the makings of a child molester."

The bigger problem, perhaps, was helping Marty find work. In New York there were hundreds of small clubs with combos who welcomed singers. In Los Angeles, it seemed that all of the singers wrote their own material. They all played guitar, or an occasional piano, and came on as singles. When they were with a band, it was usually heavy rock, and they were geared for a much younger audience. A few of the larger hotels had orchestras and there were the usual number of "in" society bands, but all of these seemed married to vocalists who had been with them for years and had absorbed their style. They had no interest in making a change.

She contacted a number of her friends in the casting departments of the big studios. Here, too, with the breakdown of the studio system, no one really kept a basic staff of musicians—or actors for that matter—on payroll. Once in a while, a film would call, for example, for a shipboard scene where the major characters danced the night away, and she was successful in getting Marty a spot job. It was hardly enough to sustain him. He didn't seem to mind very much. She thought he might object to her supporting him, especially on their shopping trips when it became obvious that she controlled the purse strings. Marty opted for the most exclusive shops on Rodeo Drive and when he selected clothing it was always the best.

"Don't you think two hundred for a casual sweater is a bit much?" she asked, just barely holding back her temper as they drove home.

"I don't set the prices. I thought the wife of—I mean the husband of a giant star like Trudy Coles should look his best."

"And that's what Dr. Gordon would call 'a Freudian slip.' I'm the wife, *your* wife, remember. You're the husband."

"I'll take it back if you want me to."

"No. Keep it. But until you're really earning money I think you should take it easy."

"Just say the word. I'll take it back."

"Forget it."

He finally found more or less steady work through a connection Trudy enjoyed, heading a band that had a long-term job in a new private club called "Limbo," a reconstructed factory loft with a decor that was patterned after an early American saloon. The work seemed to perk up Marty's spirits and had an equally restorative effect on their marriage. Trudy wasn't working, but she loved to use the evenings for her favorite pastime, reading. Marty was out until about four in the morning, slept well past noon, and seemed to have little inclination to leave the house during the day, so they had lots of hours together.

One night when she knew that he had planned to try out some new arrangements, she decided to surprise him and stop by for a drink. He usually went on about eleven o'clock for his second of three sets and she arrived just as he reached the bandstand. The room was crowded so she just waved her greetings to the maître d' and took a seat at the back of the room, where she was also out of the bandstand's view. No need to make Marty nervous or to rain on his parade. A big star like Trudy always caused a commotion and she was reluctant to do anything that would detract from his performance. He obviously did not see her come in. Otherwise he would have refrained from his rather obvious flirtation with a curvaceous young blonde, seated at a ringside table, who seemed eager to encourage his attentions. As the set ended amidst loud applause, Marty headed for the nymph's table and invited himself to join her. He probably would have spent the entire night at the blonde's table but one of the waiters who had witnessed Trudy's entrance subtly gave him the word. Startled, he flushed, rose quickly, and, surveying the crowd, waved feebly and self-consciously to Trudy, moving rapidly in her direction.

"Honey, what are you doing here?" he asked in what he hoped passed for joyous surprise.

"I thought you might need support for those new arrangements, but it seems that you can get all the help you need."

"Come on now, Trudy. She's a kid. She was asking me for advice for her boyfriend. He wants to be a singer, too."

"My advice for her boyfriend is to buy a guard dog. Especially when you're around. Well, I have to be up in the morning. I have a cab standing by. See you tomorrow."

The incident at Limbo was just one of a series of flirtations that Trudy learned about. There were definitely spider-web cracks appearing in their marriage. Marty's obvious and juvenile antics did little to stimulate Trudy's affection for him, but strangely aroused little anger. She looked upon him as a pathetic, insecure man who needed constant reassurance to disguise his own shortcomings. That he was so obvious in his efforts to win feminine approval amused her.

"What did you say to Greta that made her so angry?" she asked him with a smile as they returned one evening from a cocktail party at a friend's home.

"Angry? I didn't make her angry. I don't know what you're talking about."

"Yes you do. I saw her glower at you. And Charlie made it a point to remark that he was wondering when you'd get around to his wife, since you'd made so many obvious passes at all the other women."

"Charlie just doesn't like me. That's his way of starting trouble."

"Marty, you're full of it. If I don't satisfy you, why don't you just move out? There's no reason why you can't move back East. I'll bet Lillian will be happy to win you back."

"That's all over and you know it."

She turned to Dr. Gordon for solace.

"Well, Dr. Gordon, it seems as if your advice has backfired. I can't stand him."

"The advice I gave you was based on information you gave me. Do you want me to meet with him and see if I can't get at the basic trouble?"

"It really won't help much, but I owe it to both of us to try. I'll ask him to call you."

Marty agreed to seeing Milton Gordon, though he freely admitted in advance that he put little stock in psychiatrists. Although he had never really been to see one, a number of his friends had done so in an effort to ward off marital problems. Since they had all ended in divorce, Marty had little faith. But since the prospect of being forced out of his comfortable home by Trudy frightened him, he agreed and called Gordon for an appointment.

"Trudy tells me that things are not going well in the marriage. How do you see them?"

"I don't think there is any serious problem. Women are always looking for paradise. When two people see each other seven days a week there's bound to be some friction."

"Are things getting better or worse in the relationship?"

"I think they're about the same. Maybe a little better."

"Why do you think Trudy wanted you to see me?"

"Beats me. You know she's had a lot of problems with men over the years. Being such a giant star and so beautiful and all, she tends to get very jealous when there's no reason to. Like last week we went to a party and I teased the hostess about her low-cut dress. Trudy got all uptight about it and told me I was a male chauvinist pig and that there was more to women than the size of their boobs."

"Don't you think there is?"

"Sure. But everyone likes big tits, don't they? And if Greta didn't want me to notice them, how come she wore such a low-cut dress and a revealing bra that barely covered the action? You can't have it both ways, you know. Dress like a nun, get treated like a nun. Dress like a hooker, get treated like a hooker."

Milton Gordon took such an immediate dislike to Marty Roman that he phoned Trudy after the session and told her he thought it might be better for Marty to see a doctor who wasn't so closely attached to her. He explained that it was difficult to be objective under the circumstances.

When Marty was home at night, he spent most of his time watching ball games on television and occasionally listening to tapes of his own performances. To the best of Trudy's observations, he never read a book or glanced at anything but the sports pages of the Los Angeles newspapers. The relationship was unsatisfactory from so many viewpoints that she saw no reason to try and preserve it. Slowly but inexorably, they started going their own ways, treating each other civilly but with little warmth. At least the fighting had edged off. For that Trudy was grateful. One Sunday morning Trudy decided to attempt a civilized separation.

"Marty, why don't we just end this thing peacefully and get a friendly divorce? We'll both be happier and you can be free to find someone you really love. This makes no sense, just tolerating each other."

"That's okay for you to say now. You made me divorce my wife, give up my kids, move out here where I have no real connections and can't find decent work. And wherever I go I'm nothing but Trudy Coles' husband. Now you want to toss me out like a used toothbrush."

"I didn't 'make' you do anything. You jumped at the chance, after telling me that there would never be a woman in the world who could turn you on like me. Six weeks later you were eyeing the field like a buyer of horseflesh at a country auction. I really can't go on this way. You must get out sooner or later."

"Later," he answered nastily. "I'm staying."

She called Sid Keyes and set up a luncheon. They met once again in the Beverly Wilton, this time in the more exclusive Il Lino d'Oro, where they were less likely to be interrupted. The same maître d', Jacques, was working the room and Trudy blushed remembering the many times she and Bill Peters had drunk themselves into oblivion here. But life was different at the top. Trudy was a real star now and even Jacques treated her with humility and deference.

"Miss Coles, what a treat to see you looking so well! Mr. Keyes is waiting for you at a very special table."

That, thought Trudy, will cost the Arnold office another ten bucks. God knows they can afford it. No actor worth his salt ever forgave his agent for nipping off that ten percent. He or she might be grateful for a good assignment, he might trust his agent in the selection of properties or in the negotiation of fees, but when push came to shove, it was agent against performer and the latter always begrudged the former for riding on his back. As one wag put it: "There are more agent jokes in Hollywood than agents. And most actors don't really think they're so funny!" Trudy tried her best to bury all such hidden animosities when Sid Keyes rose to kiss her.

"Hey, Sid, you're looking great."

"And you, too, Trudy. Sit down and enjoy. I ordered you some white wine."

After the usual exchange of amenities, Trudy got down to business in a hurry.

"Sid, you've got to find me a new picture. And I want to go on location. The farther from California, the better."

"That bad, huh?"

"That bad," she answered. "I need out of here for a change. Besides, California is beginning to get to me. I'd like a change of seasons as well as a change of location."

"How would you feel about working with Monte again?"

"How would he feel about it? The last time I saw him and Betty they practically ignored me. They still won't forgive me for doing that semi-nudie. They think I prostituted myself. You should hear my ex, Richie Stevens, on the subject. He says the curse of Manny

Silverstein is still on me. He threatened to keep me from seeing Belinda if I ever did another. Personally, I think they're all full of it. God gave me my face and God gave me my ass and if I want to show either one of them, that's my prerogative. Right?"

"Right. But we were doing the nudie to prove a point. And, incidentally, to gross fifty million, which it has by the latest reports I received from the New York office this morning. But there's no need for that now. What Monte has in mind is something entirely different. He's talked to me about it several times but I was reluctant to approach you, especially since I knew the two of you were more or less on the outs."

"Hell, I like Monte. Betty, too. I'd work with him again in a minute if the property was right."

"It's not working with him that's the issue. It's the person he wants as co-star."

"Co-star? I remember a hundred years ago when Marjorie Hansell screamed when a reporter referred to me as her co-star. Now it's my turn. Trudy Coles needs no co-star, Sidney. I make the pictures that people pay good money to see. I don't need any help. I don't need reinforcements. Either Monte Rubin sees me as his star or he can go and pound sand."

"Hold on, Trudy. This isn't a female co-star. It's a male. Hell, even Hepburn needed Tracy. Teamwork can be great when it's right."

"And who does he have in mind?"

Sid Keyes paused for dramatic effect. He'd worked with actors too long and too continuously to be guilty of throwing a line away.

"Benitez. Manuel Benitez."

"Benitez? Do I read you right?"

"You read fine. It'll be an international pairing that's got to knock the world on its ass."

In a sense, the film that Monte Rubin chose to make, pairing Trudy and Manuel Benitez, was an old-fashioned romance set in the Swiss Alps. He wasn't sure why this particular story intrigued him except that it offered two major roles and was warm and moving in the early Hollywood tradition. The major characters meet at a ski resort, fall madly in love, and then are forced to figure out a way to disentangle their lives with spouses whom they thought they loved. In the finale, they part, deciding that it is better to suffer personal dissatisfaction than to destroy so many innocent lives around them.

Benitez had read the screenplay and agreed to work in the picture subject to finding the right leading lady. Trudy, knowing of his reputation as a brilliant but erratic superstar, agreed to accept the challenge. Even Sid Keyes was amazed at how easily he arranged the marriage. He had expected more resistance.

Location shooting in Switzerland was not scheduled for at least three months. The earlier portions of the movie were to be filmed in a studio in suburban London. The cameras were to roll in approximately four weeks. Trudy met with Monte and Betty, and a warm reunion resulted. As usual, she was diligent in her preparations and conferred with Monte on many occasions before they left Los Angeles. She broke the news to Marty just a few days before she flew East. She did not want to give him the opportunity to make plans to join her; the less notice she gave him, the better. Actually, he had teamed up with a small combo that was preparing to cut some audition tapes for presentation to one of the larger recording companies. He really had no interest in a trip to London at this time. Besides, even though the two of them had not been working at their marriage, he would enjoy much more freedom for philandering with Trudy out of the country.

Shooting on opening day was scheduled to start at seven in the morning. Since her hotel was located about twenty miles from the suburban studios, Trudy left a call for four A.M. In that way she would have plenty of time for her morning ablutions, a small breakfast, and a leisurely limousine ride away from London. Unfortunately, it was as if she were hexed. First, the hotel clerk slept through her call, and only her own instincts caused her to rise at four-thirty, a half hour late. Because the hotel staff was not accustomed to providing room service at that early hour, the breakfast arrived twenty minutes later than ordered and was so cold and tasteless that she settled for a glass of juice and black coffee. There was also a problem with the hot water, slowing down her morning bath. Finally, the limousine driver hired by the producers got his signals switched and showed up at the wrong hotel. A number of hectic calls resulted in his being properly instructed, but also caused a further forty-minute delay.

Trudy arrived on the set more than an hour late. A restless crew and cast were upset by what, to them, was apparently a cheap shot by a star who wanted to establish her credentials. British workers are taught promptness from their earliest years and look with disfavor upon tardy behavior. American actors will forgive many oversights but they don't like to have their noses rubbed into a turgid ego puddle. As for Manuel Benitez, he had stomped off the premises after waiting just ten minutes for her to arrive.

"Tell fat ass," he hissed to Monte, "that real stars show up on time. The next time she is late for the cameras I might just take a week off."

Trudy made her apologies to all assembled, trying to describe the series of misadventures that had caused the delay. Some seemed sympathetic, others were noncommittal, and the balance, still slightly hostile, adopted a wait-and-see attitude. Trudy cooled her heels for more than a half hour after Benitez had received word that she had finally arrived. He entered with a flourish, took a seat in an area that had been reserved for him, and didn't even turn his head in her direction. Sensing a conflict brewing, which he wanted to nip in the bud, Monte Rubin walked over and quietly invited him to join Trudy and her entourage at the far side of the set.

"Bring her to me!" Manuel ordered imperiously.

Well, Monte thought reluctantly, if the fur is going to fly, it might as well fly quickly. He returned to Trudy's seat and invited her to meet her co-star. Trudy sneaked a look in Benitez's direction, but he was looking away and there was no possibility of their eyes meeting. Since she had been late, she decided to forget the usual demands of chivalry and walked over to him. He still refused to turn in her direction, and Monte Rubin had to tap him on the shoulder after he and Trudy had stood uncomfortably in front of Benitez's chair. It was all the more embarrassing since the entire company, privy to what was transpiring, was watching every move, anticipating with glee the fireworks that surely would ensue.

"Manuel Benitez, this is Trudy Coles."

Slowly, Benitez turned, neither rising nor smiling in response. There was a long, electric pause as the two handsome stars sized each other up for the first time.

"I'm sorry I was late, Mr. Benitez. If you take the trouble to investigate you'll learn that it was not my fault."

And still they stared at each other, part in amazement, part in childish combat. Finally, Benitez rose and smiled slightly, taking her hand in greeting.

"Well, at least the mountain came to Mohammed."

"That's the first time anyone has ever referred to me as a mountain, though I've had my weight problems from time to time." Trudy wondered whether the reference to her weight was intentional.

"So I have heard," Manuel replied with a twinkle, "but soft women have always been my weakness. Do not worry about a few extra pounds. We'll teach the camera to lie."

Since he spoke the words with a smile, Trudy didn't really know if he was trying to put her on the defensive or if this was really his attempt to be humorous. As for "teaching the camera to lie," she didn't think his help would be needed.

"Thank you for the offer. And I'll see that it focuses on me when you're a bit hungover."

Now they were even and the battle was joined. In all the years Monte Rubin had been making pictures, he was not prepared for what transpired when Manuel Benitez and Trudy Coles joined talents for the first time. Though they clashed constantly and publicly whenever the opportunity arose, it was the fighting of lovers and not the hostility of enemies. Within a week of that first meeting, they were sharing a bedroom. Both swore that in all of their years of romantic encounters they had never tasted of love so violently wonderful as that which they experienced together. Even on the set they exchanged terms of endearment. It was immediately apparent to all but the blind that this was one of the great love matches of all time.

They continued to skirmish on the set, but instead of hampering the project, their squabbling merely served as an incentive for each to act at his highest level. Monte felt that he really didn't have to direct. He was merely in a position to steer a mighty torrent of talent as it cascaded from scene to scene, reaching ever-higher plateaux of artistic accomplishment. Now and forever, the team of Benitez and Coles would be internationally acclaimed both off and on the screen. The word was spread in columns throughout the Western world before the company traveled to Switzerland. Even in far-off California, Marty Roman got wind of what was happening in London and how his financial security might well be under attack. He decided to fly to England and restake his claim.

He arrived unannounced and swaggered onto the set in the midst of a torrid love scene. For Trudy and Manuel there was little acting involved. They simply continued, with obvious acknowledgement of the rules of the Hollywood rating system, what they had been doing all night for several weeks running. Monte Rubin's sole contribution was a reminder to both of them that the film was inflammable. Hotter than the love scene being filmed was the reaction of pathetic Marty Roman, who had to sit by and watch his wife practically ravished by the man who threatened his future. He waited a few minutes before joining Trudy in her dressing room after the filming was completed.

"Hell, Marty," Trudy said with practiced nonchalance, which was more irritating than a show of temper. "It's a long way from Beverly Hills. What brings you to merry old England?"

"You. And the kind of carrying on I just witnessed out there on the set. I guess you didn't know I saw the whole display. And you tell me I'm vulgar."

"Of course I knew you were out there. Do you think our security is so weak that you could just burst on the scene and nobody would tell me we had visitors? As for that 'vulgar display,' do you mean that Monte Rubin needs you to help direct? What the hell do you know about making pictures anyway?"

"Pictures I may not know much about. But sex and infidelity I know about."

"Right. On infidelity, you've got your Ph.D."

"Very funny. Look, Trudy, you may not be crazy about me but there are laws and they say you're married to me and have certain obligations. You can't go carrying on with this greasy spic while the whole world watches and expect me to take it lying down."

"You can take it up the kazoo as far as I'm concerned. I told you to move out months ago."

"Yeh. You still talk like West Virginia, don't you? If you won't listen, I'm going to tell him."

"Great idea. Manuel is in his dressing room right now. I'm sure he'd love to hear from you."

It was not the first time that Manuel had played such a scene in real life; irate husbands had accosted him numerous times in the past. But he had never played one with so much relish. From the little Trudy had told him about Marty Roman, he had developed an intense dislike for him, and he resented the effrontery of Roman's invasion of the set during the filming of an important scene. When his dresser told him that a Mr. Roman was tapping at the door, Benitez asked that he be shown in. He pivoted around in his swivel chair in front of his makeup mirror and purposely neglected to ask Roman to have a seat.

"Yes? What do you want?"

"I don't like the way you've been carrying on with my wife—on and off the screen. There are lawyers to handle marriage busters like you."

"I don't mind being referred to in such uncomplimentary terms if the insult comes from a real man. But when a parasite, fortune hunter like you has the gall to invade my privacy, that's where I draw the line."

He jumped up and grabbed Roman by the shirtfront. Even though he was considerably older, it was a terrible mismatch. He towered over the startled singer by at least five inches.

"I'm going to marry your wife one way or the other as soon as we're both free. If I were you, I'd back off as soon as possible. Maybe you'll get more money that way. And if you ever dare to threaten either of us again, and have the temerity to come on set while I'm making a picture, I'll beat you to within an inch of your life. You understand me?"

So saying, he pushed Marty against the wall; then, seeing the fear in his eyes, released him with a less-than-playful shove.

"Now get out of here before I really lose my temper!"

Marty Roman didn't wait for a second invitation. He scooted to safety as soon as he realized he was free to leave. That night he called Trudy once again. He suggested that they have a mutual cooling-off period to see if they couldn't recapture the affection that they had felt for each other when they had first met in New York.

"It won't work, Marty. I could never love a man I didn't respect. You've disappointed me in so many ways that I could never love you again. Why not get out now before we cause ourselves and everyone around us a lot of unnecessary pain?"

"Okay. I'll think about it. I'm flying back to California tonight."

"Have your lawyer speak to Allen Rosenthal. He handles all of my personal legal matters."

Marty Roman was keen enough to hire one of California's agile divorce lawyers, Barney Simkins. Simkins, who usually represented the wife in domestic squabbles, found the Coles-Roman battle unusually challenging. In the end, despite Rosenthal's stonewalling tactics, it cost Trudy a half million dollars, paid up front, to win her freedom. From that day on she referred to

Marty Roman as her "three-quarters-of-a-million-dollar mistake." Manuel Benitez was not as fortunate. There were international complications galore since he was Spanish, his wife Italian, their marriage license was issued in Dubrovnik, and they claimed their main residence in Ireland. In addition, both were Catholics, though neither practiced their religion with any degree of seriousness. The results, however, were similar. Manuel paid $1 million and agreed to $2,000 a week in alimony until his wife, Lisa, remarried. As he put it rather crudely to Trudy: "Marriage. The fucking you get isn't worth the fucking you get."

"You haven't asked and I haven't agreed," Trudy answered. "I'm not going to be ready for marriage vows for a long time."

CHAPTER 24

1975

For the Good of All, as the initial Coles-Benitez collaboration was entitled, developed into the smash hit that everyone expected it to be. Its gross receipts, $60 million, were five times its production costs. Future rentals from television, cable, overseas theatrical presentation, and the like, were bound to add another $10 to $15 million. Benitez had been clever enough to insist on a percentage of the gross, taking a moderate fee in front in exchange. Trudy could hardly complain, since she was paid nearly $800,000 as soon as the cameras stopped rolling. Most important from the industry's standpoint, however, was the fact that a new romantic duo had been forged that was destined to make motion picture history.

Following completion of the picture in Switzerland, Manuel and Trudy went off together for a three month pre-honeymoon. Wherever they landed, traveling without schedule throughout the Continent, they were lionized like visiting royalty. Trudy was decked in garlands of flowers at every airport. Screaming females rushed to Manuel's side, demanding a kiss, a lock of hair, an autograph, any memento that might remind them that they had touched him. An international star of long standing, Manuel was accustomed to the adoration but somehow bored by it. Trudy, on the other hand, loved every minute of it.

"God, I wish they would leave us alone," he sighed after one particularly hairy escape from a flock of boisterous cameramen at International Airport at Elinkon, just south of Athens. "I thought those Italian paparazzi were bad. Hell, these guys make them seem tame by comparison!"

"Don't complain. I've had years when I couldn't get anyone to take my picture for love or money. Believe me, lover, this is better."

"Don't I satisfy you?" Manuel asked in amazement one night after four straight hours of lovemaking.

"It's like eating soup with a fork," Trudy answered. "You know that old saying. I never get enough of you. Any complaints?"

"Not from me. My pecker may need a holiday when this is all over."

"I hope it's never over," Trudy responded, throwing herself on top of him, determined to arouse him once again.

Trouble dribbled through the cracks appearing in their idyll for the first time in Rome, where their holiday was scheduled for completion. They were strolling arm in arm down the Via Veneto when Manuel was accosted by a lovely young thing dressed stylishly in a fashion to advertise her multitudinous, curvaceous charms.

"Manuel Benitez! I can't believe it! Here I was just telling Jimbo the other day that I hadn't heard from you in months, when here you are practically in my back yard!" With that, she threw her arms around his neck, planting a fervent kiss on his lips that left no meaning unstated. In so doing, she completely ignored Trudy, who stood by uncomfortably, watching the two friends renew what must have been an old and ardent relationship. If Manuel was embarrassed by the embrace, nothing in his demeanor indicated it. He just kissed back, hugging the delectable female with a passion equal to her own. Finally, after what seemed to Trudy to be an excessively intimate greeting, Manuel stepped back and, as if by afterthought, introduced the two ladies.

"Trudy, this is a friend of mine, Natasha Orsatti. Half-Italian, half-Russian, she combines the worst characteristics of both. Nat, this is Trudy Coles."

"Not *the* Trudy Coles," Natasha cooed. "I've been an admirer of your films for centuries!"

"Well, we remember the first light bulb, but not much before that," Trudy answered caustically.

In an effort to avert what could well have shaped up as a nasty cat fight, Manuel broke in.

"Trudy, this girl has one of the great senses of humor in the business. We met during my last film. Nat played the second lead."

"Not for long, I'm sure."

"How kind of you to say so," Natasha responded, pretending that she had not understood the obvious barb tossed in her direction. "Say, we met just in time. I'm throwing a party tonight and you two simply must come. Carlo is letting me use his estate. You'll see thousands of people you both know."

"We'd love to come," Manuel replied, not giving Trudy a chance to refuse. He could tell that she had taken an immediate dislike to Natasha, and he did not want to risk a refusal.

Back at their hotel, dressing for what promised to be a memorable evening, Trudy seemed out of sorts.

"What's the trouble, my pet? Swallow a hot pepper?"

"Better than a hot Orsatti," Trudy answered churlishly.

"You really make up your mind quickly, don't you?"

"It doesn't take much instinct to know that girl is out for no good. How long should it take to know one?"

"Not long, my pet, if you've been one yourself."

"And just what in the hell is that supposed to mean?"

"Obviously, it means that there's no need to be a bitch about an old friend I knew before we even met. Am I supposed to ignore her when we meet on the street just because your eyes are green?"

"The color of my eyes and your obvious insult have nothing to do with it. That scene you two threw on the Via Veneto was right out of an X-rated film."

"Thanks. At my age that's a hell of a compliment."

The argument stalled there, but it was obvious that Trudy meant to put a crimp in their evening. Manuel was just as determined to have a good time. Wearing a sable cape over an off-the-shoulder black crepe gown, Trudy made a smashing picture as she sashayed under the canvas canopy that had been erected to shield guests from the slight rain falling as they arrived at Carlo's villa on the outskirts of Rome. Even the hired help, trained in impersonality in their dealings with the beautiful people, had to turn and stare. Manuel turned a few eyes himself in the white silk outfit he wore. His dark complexion and coal black eyes seemed to come alive above the contrasting whiteness, which set off his Spanish grace and elegance. Together, they were a couple destined for attention in any assemblage.

"Let's dance," Manuel demanded as soon as they had reached the main ballroom. Not waiting for an answer, he swept her into the center of the swaying crowd. Among his many other talents, Manuel was as graceful as the matadors in the bullrings of his native land. Trudy, no slouch herself, loved to dance with him whenever the opportunity presented itself.

"Now I know why they call you the Fred Astaire of Castile," she said jokingly as the tempo mounted and the dancers sped their steps.

"Fred who?" Manuel replied humorously.

There was a brief intermission while they refreshed themselves with champagne cocktails being circulated among the guests by waiters garbed in white tie and tails and carrying the chilled ambrosia aloft on sterling silver trays. A series of tables circling the floor offered gourmet hors d'oeuvres to satisfy even the most discriminating taste. Stacks of delectable caviar, presented in delicate crystal swans, stood guard over finely sliced quail presented in birds' nests constructed of toasted Oriental noodles. Pâtés of goose liver shared billing with tiny Mediterranean shrimp overflowing platters of the finest china. And pastries of every description were abundantly present to tempt the palate of those who refused to count calories on such a night.

The music started up again and Manuel whirled Trudy back onto the dance floor for a fast-moving rumba. Then the music shifted to a rock beat and the more sedate dancers made room as boogie-woogie ruled the floor. Trudy could have used some rest but Manuel loved the beat. As the seemingly endless medley from *Hair* blared on, he whirled and shook and vibrated with the best of them, Trudy matching him step for step.

The set ended and Trudy felt as if she had just emerged from a blazing hot steam bath.

"Whew! You'll have to excuse me for a few minutes, honey. I'm off to the ladies' room for a fix."

"You still look as lovely as ever," Manuel replied. "But go dry out. I'll be here when you return."

But when she emerged five minutes later, he was nowhere to be seen.

The task of locating Manuel in the crowd that was jamming the villa's ballroom proved more difficult than Trudy had imagined. It seemed as if a new couple arrived each time the band leader waved his baton. Trudy was convinced that all of Rome's beautiful people were zeroing in on what must have been heralded throughout the city as the party of the season. At one point, Trudy thought she caught a glimpse of her man whirling about the dance floor with Natasha Orsatti on his arm, but investigation proved otherwise. To make matters worse, she was being pawed at constantly by ambitious young men who insisted that she favor them with a dance. The hour was growing late; she was irked, weary, and almost tempted to leave alone when she heard a tremendous scream of delight as the dancing stopped suddenly and the leader announced, "To the gardens for the new fountains of Tivoli."

She was half carried, half propelled toward the glass doors opening onto the terrace. Once outside in the cool, night air, the jolting crowd swallowed her up, preventing her from seeing what was causing them all to shriek in laughter. Looking around, she spotted a low granite wall that separated the terrace from the lower walk level and led to the gardens themselves. Eagerly she stepped up on the wall and, by standing on her tiptoes, could finally see the object of everyone's hilarity. A large fountain, bathed in changing pastel lights, formed a centerpiece for the formal gardens stretching about it in a manicured tapestry of medieval orderliness. There in the center of the fountain, stark naked and engaged in joyful sodomy, stood Manuel Benitez and the lovely, young Natasha Orsatti. It was a memorable tableau. The crowd cheered them on but they seemed unconcerned.

Trudy felt the hot flush of anger in her cheeks, followed by bitter tears. She jumped down, nearly falling over a pair of drunken guests who had decided to try and emulate the fountain dwellers, stumbled, recovered her balance, and rushed inside to where her wrap had been checked. Recovering it quickly, she pushed toward the main entrance, asked the doorman to summon her a cab, and tearfully directed the driver to her hotel.

She flew to Paris the next day to meet with Sid Keyes, who, fortunately, was on vacation in France. They met for dinner in a quiet restaurant near Notre Dame.

"Trudy, you look simply ravishing."
"You lie like all agents. But I love it. Try it again."
"How is Manuel?"
"Dead, I hope."
"That bad?"
"Worse. He left me two nights ago at a great party in Rome.

I found him, and so did everyone else present, with his tool in the mouth of a young hooker who threw the party. They were naked, standing like statues in the large, colored fountain in the garden."

"Pretty original, right?"

"I guess so. I've never been left like that before. Tell me, Sid, and try speaking the truth this time even if it hurts, are all men such bastards?"

"Let's not stop at men. Everybody can be a bastard once in a while, you know that."

"But look at my history. I'm supposed to be one of the world's great beauties, right? Besides, I'm a movie star and that's glamorous, right? So how come men always screw me and run away? Why do I chase them? Tell me."

"I'd say that 'always' is a rather broad statement."

"Maybe. But I chased Rob Wenger to his grave. I lost Jocko Rachubinski to some rich bitch. Richie Stevens picked a young boy rather than sleep with me. Leonard Rush rushed back to his wife. Even Bill Peters finally left me. True, I threw Marty Roman out on his ass, but even he was fooling around every time he thought I had my back turned. And now, Manuel Benitez, the love of my life, the man who tells me he never knew what real love is until we made it, can't stay the course with me without drinking himself into oblivion and screwing some worthless tramp in a fountain. What do I do to them? There's got to be an answer."

"Trudy, if I knew the answer to why men cheat on women and why women cheat on men, I'd be the richest philosopher in California, not an agent at Jason Arnold."

"I'm going back there and talk to Milton Gordon. I used to laugh at psychiatrists when I was younger but I believe in that man now. He helps me see all the answers."

"This is no time to go back. There's nothing there for you to work on, believe me. Every studio and every independent is breaking its neck to do some kind of catastrophe film. They don't need stars. They need bigger fires, larger floods, more powerful earthquakes. And what with the new vogue of science fiction films, they'll turn you into an ape and shoot you to the moon in a rocket. They're making better features here in Europe. I think what you need is some more work here. Then, when they come to their senses in Hollywood, you'll return. By that time, you'll have your head in order and you won't need Dr. Gordon."

"Simple as all that, huh?"

"Absolutely. Trudy, I could make you weep for a week of Sundays if I told you about my problems. I used to feel better when I did that, but about fifteen years ago I took a vow to suffer alone. It works better that way for me."

"Sorry if I seem a cry baby. But you're about the only one left I can find to cry to."

"Grab a shoulder and cry. I'm not objecting. What I'm saying is, don't take every rebuff as a permanent snub. Making it in a fountain sounds like fun. Especially when you're drunk. You and Manuel Benitez are a brilliant team. I've seen the rushes. Go back to Rome and make up. Grit your teeth and say hello. Then start making pictures together. It's what you do best. And in the end, what you do best makes you the happiest."

Trudy Coles stayed in Paris three weeks. Then, on an impulse, she returned to Rome and checked into the Excelsior. She found Manuel at the bar that night, drinking with a male friend. There was an empty seat beside him. She quickly walked over and sat down.

"Where's my drink?" she asked.

"I sent for it. I want the best Scotch in the vault." He didn't bat an eye, pretending that she had been upstairs dressing and that he had merely preceded her to the bar for a quickie before she arrived. With proper apologies, he shed his friend and they dined alone. They moved back together that night, a night that was spent entirely in lovemaking. At four in the morning, Trudy said, "Let's go in the shower. We'll make believe it's the new fountain of Tivoli."

CHAPTER 25

1978

Three years raced by. Trudy and Manuel made a series of souflé-like comedies, all of which were resoundingly panned. Because of the huge salaries they had demanded, none was a money maker. It was getting more and more difficult to find producers for their films, despite their own personal magnetism.

Their own relationship had grown more and more strained as their professional failures added tension to an already stormy romance. The gossip columns of the world were always full of reports of Benitez-Coles squabbles. After one particularly bitter fight, Trudy returned to Los Angeles alone. Benitez remained in Italy to star in a third-rate potboiler. Neither of them made any reference to marriage plans or even to the probability of resuming their relationship as they said their cold, bloodless good-byes.

Back in California now, and after two days of excitement over being home, she began to feel depressed. Belinda, almost twelve, had been sent to a summer camp and would not be back for eight weeks. Richie Stevens greeted her coolly and requested that she not visit the child.

"I had enough trouble convincing her that she would have a grand time riding horses in the fresh mountain air. She was terribly homesick for days. Now that she seems to have settled in, let's not disturb her. Send her a letter. You haven't written in twelve months," he said sarcastically, "so there should be plenty for you to say."

Never one for correspondence, Trudy tried phoning instead. She was informed rather curtly that the camp discouraged calls from parents. Besides, Belinda was off in the mountains backpacking on a three-day trip. A letter was far more appropriate.

There is no life more lonely than that of a person without friends in Beverly Hills. It struck Trudy that though she had called Los Angeles home for more than thirty years, she really didn't have a friend she could call her own. For her, work in films was a kind of sexual necessity. Without it, she felt starved, deprived, unfulfilled. Yet, despite word in the trade press that she was back in Hollywood, no producers were beating a path to her door. She set up a luncheon with Sidney Keyes. Even he was too busy to see her right away. She had to wait ten days before he found an opening in his schedule.

"Trudy, you're as beautiful as ever."

"Sid, you're as full of it as ever. I look horrible."

"The world thinks otherwise."

"The world has passed me by. I need a picture so bad I can taste it. I've been back in town a full month now and not an offer."

"Things have changed here. It's not the same old Hollywood, you know. Stars are still in vogue, but it's the picture that counts now. And between the natural catastrophes, the science fictions, the nudies, and the sheer, brutal violence films, they just aren't making the kind of pictures we like to see you in."

"Bullshit, Sid. You're an agent and I'm a star. When stars don't work, agents don't eat. I'll bet you're finding roles for those young cuties you represent."

"You got it all figured out, Trudy, don't you?"

"Pretty much."

"Why don't you think about all of those losers you and Manuel made in England. Money's tight these days, Trudy. It's hard to come up with the bread to finance a film. And when the stars are half-drunk all of the time and the shit they turn out looks like class C potboilers, that doesn't help much. I never hear you saying thanks to me for the big pictures I put you in. All I ever get is grief when you're between roles. Has it ever occurred to you that maybe you're not the easiest sale anymore? Think about it."

She had never seen Sid Keyes so angry before. It was obvious to her now that he had little interest in her career. Hell, he hadn't even called her when she got back to town. Then, when she finally swallowed her pride and called him, it had taken ten days before he could find time to spend an hour with her. That was the dead giveaway that he had given up on her chances for continued success.

"I'm thinking about it and maybe you just don't know how to handle an international star. Maybe you're better with those twenty-year-old blondes with the big boobs. Think about that!"

Sid Keyes was ashen. He rose suddenly, placed a fifty-dollar bill on the table, and looked squarely in Trudy's eyes.

"Eat hearty, my dear. You keep up the boozing and the lousy flicks and you won't be able to eat here at Ma Terrasse much longer."

With that he turned on his heels and walked out. Trudy was certain that everyone within screaming distance had witnessed the fight. She was probably right. The next day Bob Wendt's "On the Town" column in the Hollywood *Reporter* had these words for an opening:

> The only thing shorter than an agent's loyalty is a star's short-sightedness after the fall. Ask the maître d' at Ma Terrasse, who yesterday witnessed the greatest fight since "The Thriller in Manila."

Alone now, she settled in for what threatened to be a long, long period of watchful waiting. She shopped on Rodeo Drive, pouring out dollars on expensive items for which she had no real use. She read all of the latest best-sellers. She called a few old friends and found, not to her surprise, that most of them had been divorced since last they met. In search of new mates, they didn't want Trudy for company or competition. She went to what passed for good theater in Los Angeles and was generally disappointed in what she saw. She forced herself to volunteer for charity work and found herself bored beyond description. She even fended off a few feeble passes from the current crop of Hollywood's cadre of kept men. Professionally and socially, her life was in a dead calm and she wondered from where, and when, the breeze would originate to fill her sails again.

Manuel called occasionally but offered little hope for a hasty reunion. The film he was making was not going well. A local directors' strike was having its effect on all film making on the Continent. They hadn't shot a scene in three weeks. The producer, Malatesta, was having a terrible struggle just keeping the company together.

"Then why not pack it in?" Trudy asked brightly. "Come on back to the States. Momma misses you fierce."

"Darling, you know I can't desert an old friend just because the path is rugged. I'm a professional and I'm under contract. If I leave, Malatesta is absolutely washed up."

"Do you hear me clearly? Is this a good connection?"

"Yes, of course, my dear."

"Then I say to hell with Malatesta! We can make films together in the States and have fun doing them."

"Much as I would like to say yes, I cannot. Please be patient."

"I'll be patient for a short while. But we must spend Christmas together. How about a holiday in New York? I'll meet you there."

"Sounds lovely. And we shall try our best."

His best wasn't good enough. Two weeks before Christmas he phoned to inform her that the strike was settled, filming was underway, and he knew he would be tied up for at least another two months. He never even suggested that she fly to the Alps and join him for the holidays. She was tempted to suggest it herself, but when there wasn't the slightest encouragement from Manuel, she thought better of it and held her tongue. Instead, she called Richie and asked for permission to take Belinda away to Palm Springs for a week's vacation. Reluctantly he permitted a three-day weekend. Belinda, no stranger to the resort, tried to be an enthusiastic guest. But the truth was that there was little to interest a prepubescent girl in Palm Springs that was not part of her daily life in Los Angeles. The weekend was uneventful and dull. Both mother and daughter were secretly relieved when they kissed good-bye. Trudy had hoped that there would be those little intimacies that would surely bring them closer together. They never developed. They parted still virtual strangers.

At a time in her life when she could least afford it, she received another emotional setback. She had kept a tenuous line of communication open with Penny O'Neill, but what with her own problems and frequent overseas travel, she really had had fewer and fewer personal contacts with her troubled friend. She strove to comfort herself with the thought that should Penny need her, she would be contacted. That really was not Penny's style, but in the past someone always found her when her friend needed help. This time, they found her again, but there was little she could do but bring down the curtain on a Hollywood-nurtured human tragedy. Penny was dead. She had taken her own life with an overdose of sleeping tablets. They found her body in a tenderloin-district roominghouse where beds were rented for a dollar a night. She left a simple, hand-scribbled note for Trudy, which was carted along with her body to the county morgue. Trudy hardly recognized her when she, being the only known contact, identified the body.

> *Trudy dear:*
> *I won't be bothering you anymore. I never deserved such a good friend and you didn't deserve a pain in the ass like me.*
>
> *Love,*
> *Penny*

Trudy insisted on making all of the arrangements herself. There was a simple church ceremony attended by the few friends from the past Trudy could contact. Lee Landis, in his seventies and infirm with age, cried silently throughout the service. Trudy bought an elegant, satin-lined bronze coffin and banked the church with flowers, transforming it into a virtual fairy land. She paid for perpetual care at a quiet, wooded burial site and refused all efforts of financial help from Lee Landis, who sincerely wanted to pay his share.

"No, Lee, thanks just the same," Trudy said. "Penny was my responsibility from start to finish. I loved her. I can't share that love with anyone now that she's gone. I just hope somehow she knows you're here and still care."

Though stoic and completely under control throughout the entire service, Trudy broke down utterly once she returned to her home. Her spirits already weakened by her prolonged separation from Benitez and strained by the unexpected fight with her agent, she was easy prey for the emotionally draining experience of Penny's sad death and burial. As usual, feelings of guilt took over and she blamed herself for not keeping closer watch over the vulnerable friend who had been so kind to her in her own hour of need. That in turn brought thoughts of her father, his deep suffering while she was away from home, and the ever-indelible thoughts buried in her deepest subconscious that their frustrated love for each other had driven her from the family home.

She cried openly, the tears gushing from the same gorgeous emerald orbs that had hypnotized generations of moviegoers. She wept without shame, without control, without restraint. As an actress she had been trained to keep her feelings always within control, programmed to express them only upon summons. Now, she wept openly, as if the oceans of tears would cleanse her and serve as catharsis for her deep, deep sorrow. She cried for Penny. She cried for Trudy. She cried for the years of suffering her friend had known and her own inability to bring her solace.

Finally, the tears would come no more. Exhausted, she went to the bathroom and washed her face with icy water. Somehow, the boil of sorrow had been lanced and peace was returning to her soul. She went to bed hoping that her mourning for Penny would have a positive effect on her own life.

Just when her spirits were at a low ebb, about two weeks into the new year, she received a surprise phone call from Sid Keyes.

"Peace?" he queried. "Or are we still in a state of war?"

"I'm too old for vendettas, Sid. What did you have in mind?"

"Work. We represent the producers and a number of the creative people planning a new feature. There's a part in it that's just perfect for you."

"The lead?"

There was a long pause. Then a frank statement.

"No, Trudy. I won't kid you. It's not the lead. But it's a juicy part that will let you grab all the focus if you do it right. And it could lead to one hell of a TV series later on."

"Tell me more."

"We can meet for drinks this evening."

"No drinks. No lunch. Just facts. I don't want the Arnold office to waste money on someone who is difficult to cast and harder to handle. Just give me the facts, Sid."

"Okay. It's the story of three generations of Boston Brahmins. You would be cast as the matriarch who has little time for convention even in that rigid society. You hold the family together and make it function according to your principles. In the end, everyone credits you with the family's survival at the top."

"How the hell old am I supposed to be? Methusalah's mistress?"

"Not at all. You're forty-eight when the story opens. Your husband has just been killed in a plane crash. His secretary, who is also his lover, has died with him. You are having an affair with the minister. Very today story."

"Can I read the script first? I'm entitled."

What Sid Keyes had not told Trudy was that the script was written by Stan Marcus. Somewhere in his subconscious he had memories of there having been trouble when Trudy and Stan had last worked together on *Mrs. Donovan's Defeat.* He couldn't put a number on it but he did recall that there had been some sort of estrangement. He was certain that he was correct in his recollection when Trudy's name came up as a suggestion at a casting conference attended by Marcus. He just clammed up, saying not a word for, or against, her being offered the role.

Trudy spoke up again.

"Well, do I read it or not?"

"Sure. Sure. We'll messenger a copy over to you first thing this afternoon. I did want to mention one thing. . . ."

"Yes."

"The film script was written and conceived by Stan Marcus. . . . Is that a problem?"

"Why should it be? Stan and I have known each other for a thousand years."

"Candidly, there were rumors of some sort of trouble between you at the end of *Donovan.*"

"No trouble at all. I admire him and respect his talent."

"Good. You'll have the script within the hour."

Stan Marcus. So their lives would probably cross again. More than four years had passed since she had seen him, and then only casually. Even in her own mind she never could understand why they had drifted apart. He blamed himself for the Sophie Thurston debacle, but logic would explain that he really played no causal role in the break-up. She thought back to their first meeting, when, as a fifteen-year-old girl, she had first seen him in the courtyard of that broken-down apartment complex. Even then she had been drawn to him, more out of deep respect and affection than passion. But Stan had played the perfect gentleman, something that punk Skipper Dawson could not believe. She had never forgotten being treated like a lady. And it was to Stan

Marcus that she always attributed her cultural awakening. Before him, books to her were something you read in school, then tossed aside.

She liked the script immensely. Work was scheduled to begin within two weeks and that, too, pleased her. She took the initiative and called Stan, unaware that he was now living alone. He had recently gone through a painful divorce, his second failure. He suggested that they have dinner together that night and happily she agreed. He had a great need to talk about his divorce.

"I know how it feels. I've been there several times."

"The next time, if there is a next time, I swear I'll make it work."

"I'm hardly the one to talk. My record is not what you'd call exemplary."

He left her at her door. They dined again three days later, then lunched the following day, and enjoyed dinner the day after that. Her feelings for him had intensified to the point where even she couldn't differentiate between respect and deep affection. It was certainly a confusing situation since she still burned a brilliant torch for Manuel Benitez. Could I be moved simply because I'm on an emotional rebound, she wondered? And once again, why is Stan so reluctant to take me into his arms?

Filming of *The Boston Calhouns* went smoothly and was completed in six weeks. She saw Stan regularly but never on an intimate basis. He used his own ingenuity to avoid ever finding himself alone with her in a compromising position. Their friendship deepened, their feelings for one another were positive, but they seemed destined never to become lovers.

There was a small cast party the night filming was completed. Stan accompanied Trudy that night and, for the first time in a long, long time, kissed her warmly when they said good night.

"I'll miss you, Trudy."

"Me, too. It won't be the same having dinner and not looking into a pair of horn-rimmed glasses."

Meanwhile, news of Manuel Benitez's frolicking took some time to drift to California, but, in the end, the inevitable occurred. Column items started appearing, linking his name with Carla Langordio, the tempestuous Italian beauty who was costarring with him. At first Trudy chose to believe that it was merely a publicity stream put out by the film's press agent. It was not unusual to link stars romantically when they really hated each other in order to drum up interest in a feature being filmed. But when the second item, and the third, and the fourth made the columns, and when she saw pictures of Manuel and Carla frolicking in the Alpine snow stripped to their waists, she decided that her territory might just be undergoing attack by an invasionary force.

A shock awaited her on her arrival in Zurich. Manuel's film had been completed weeks earlier and he and the cast had dispersed. A modicum of checking through the hotel where he had been housed revealed that he and that lovely young lady he had been living with had returned to Italy, leaving no specific forwarding address. As a matter of fact, they had been returning all of his mail to its senders for the past ten days.

Never one to run from a challenge, Trudy took the next flight to Rome. She was familiar with all of his favorite watering holes and finding him dining with Carla Langordio was no prodigious feat. Winning him back was a much greater challenge, for Carla was not one to release her hooks from a man she loved without a spirited, valiant struggle.

CHAPTER 26

1979

A rude awakening awaited Manuel Benitez the day following a stormy reunion with Trudy. Police deputies seized him and locked him behind bars on charges of failure to make timely alimony payments, as required by his divorce from his former wife, Lisa. Of proud Sicilian descent, she, too, had read of his scandalous carryings-on with Carla Langordio. Though now officially separated from him by binding legal decree, she felt her honor was nonetheless besmirched by his alley-cat activities, all of which were vividly reported in great detail by the Italian press. With somewhat mixed emotions, Trudy visited him in jail after twenty-four hours of string-pulling enabled her to gain entrance.

"So, Manuel, a woman scorned can be a terrible enemy. You agree?"

"Bitch! Cunt! Whore! How dare she do this to me?"

"Oh, you don't like her."

"Very humorous. Very funny. You're probably delighted that they've done this to me."

"Not at all. Do you think I enjoy being in love with a jailbird?"

"Love. Hmph! Love. All women are jailers at heart. I can just hear you and Lisa and Carla laughing at my predicament."

"Carla has threatened me with bodily harm if I so much as come near you. Lisa never spoke to me after you divorced her."

"All right. So tell me how I get out of this situation."

"I've been working on it all day. I've hired the best lawyer in Rome. He thinks he can get you released later today if you pledge enough assets to cover the back alimony payments, plus a large bond in case you skip the country to avoid future obligations."

"What does he think I am, the Bank of Rome?"

"Why, I can't explain, but I told him I'd be equally responsible for your debts if you failed to make any payments. Italian courts are very funny, he says. They don't like to see their decrees ignored. Especially not in divorce proceedings, which are looked upon as 'something dangerously anticlerical and somewhat heretical.' The language, incidentally, is his. So, as they say in the business, it's pay or play."

"I told my attorneys in London to see to it that the payments were made on time. I can't help it if they weren't efficient."

"Whatever the reason, the court wants you to put up a two-year bond now so it won't happen again."

"Get me out of this infested rat hole and I'll get the money up in twenty-four hours."

Actually, he had been treated like visiting royalty. Not many Italian families enjoyed the luxuries in their own home that his confinement quarters boasted. He was being held in a luxurious suite reserved for the highest political prisoners. To the liberty-loving Benitez, however, a loss of freedom was the greatest effrontery.

The Italian attorney was true to his word. Manuel was freed several hours later and, with a joint guarantee from Trudy Coles, was permitted to post bond. The lawyer was careful to obtain guarantees that Benitez would always be free to leave the country if his payment schedule was not in default. The matter became academic several months later when Lisa, still beautiful, met and fell madly in love with an Italian tycoon of noble blood. They were married almost immediately when she discovered that she was pregnant. This lifted Manuel's obligation and his bond was released.

"Well, old man," Trudy joked, "now you have enough money to marry Carla Langordio, she of the big tits and curvaceous ass."

"You will never need a computer, my love. No elephant has a memory to compare with yours."

"There's only one way to prove that to me. Marry me and make an honest woman out of me. We've been seeing each other intimately for three years."

"Is that what you desire?"

"I think so. You're not getting any younger. I don't want you to die and leave your fortune to some young chick."

"A mind like a safety deposit vault. That's why I love you," he said, pulling her to him in a rapturous embrace. "And I don't even have to search for a wedding gift."

He went to his dresser, opened the top drawer, and took out a small velvet box. Proudly, he brought it to her as she smiled up at him from the foot of her bed. She opened it slowly, like a child trying to prolong a pleasant surprise. It was a gift so magnificent, so brilliant, so original in its artistic perfection that when her eyes gazed on it she gasped for breath.

"Oh, Manuel! It's not to be believed!"

Lying in its velvet resting place was a brooch formed of diamonds, rubies, and emeralds, surrounding a huge sapphire. The precious gems were intertwined in golden filigree. It was the work of some Renaissance master. Tears of joy gushed from her eyes as she stared in awe at the unexpected but all-the-more-treasured gift. Slowly she rose, carefully placing the brooch on a nearby night table, wrapped her arms around him, and held him in an endless embrace.

"Manuel, do I really deserve this?"

"This and more," he answered proudly.

They were married in a quiet ceremony two days later in a small chapel on the outskirts of the city by a renegade priest who didn't care to seek unnecessary information about religion and former divorce actions. They had a legal marriage license, paid handsomely for the ceremony, and got God's blessings and a free sip of sacramental wine from a special bottle he kept for just such purposes. They leased a palatial estate on the Costa del Sol for their month-long honeymoon. Each day they motored into the countryside so that Manuel could show his bride the beauties of the land of his fathers. It was the greatest bliss Trudy had ever known.

Lying in bed at night, awaiting Manuel's emergence from his shower and anticipating another passionate session of lovemaking, she could not help but think back to the many incredible twists and turns in the pathway of her life. Yes, she had traveled an unbelievable road from that impoverished coal town of West Virginia. Now she had more joy than she had ever considered possible. She prayed in her own way that it would last forever.

Even Trudy realized that that was impossible. Toward the middle of the fourth week she could feel Manuel growing restless, itching for the activity for which he had become famous. She, too, admitted to herself that she had been away from the cameras an inordinate amount of time. Waiting for what she considered just the proper moment, she made a suggestion.

"Manuel, let's go to California. I'm getting homesick."

"And what will we do there, my love?"

"Make a picture together. We haven't worked together for more than eighteen months."

"I've resisted Hollywood all of my professional career. I really don't think I'd be very happy there."

"Certainly you would. Hollywood is no different from any other city. There are good people and bad people, fine places and bad places, good friends and bad friends, and they make good pictures and bad pictures. But we will make a good picture together, that I promise you."

"Promise me one more thing."

"Yes, my love?"

"Promise me that if we try, really try, to be happy there and it doesn't work, you will not resist our leaving. I in turn promise you that I will try my best even though I vowed never to live there."

"That's a fair deal. You'll try. I'll try. If it doesn't work, we'll move on. Nothing can mean more to me than our being happy together. After all," she added with a smile, "you're my old man."

"I'm not sure I enjoy being called old. But so long as it cements our love, I'll be Methusalah."

Trudy returned to Beverly Hills with more enthusiasm than ever. Sid Keyes immediately signed Manuel to an agent's contract, thereby gaining new prestige at the Arnold office. There were plenty of bright agents; there were not many "signers." To sign a client of Benitez's international repute was a real coup. It was an accomplishment reported in headlines in the film trades as soon as it became known. Manuel was amused.

"In America it is not necessary to make great pictures to become famous. All one does is sign a contract for representation and right away one is a national hero."

"Not quite," Trudy responded. "You are a big, famous, international film star. When an agent signs you, that is big news and, obviously, a promise of big earnings for his agency. You should have seen the fuss they made out here when the Morris office signed Secretariat, the horse that won the famous Triple Crown."

"I see agencies feel the same way about horse's asses."

"If the shoe fits . . ."

"Horseshoe," Manuel corrected.

Although Trudy found contentment upon her return to Hollywood with the man she loved, she realized that one tile was still missing in the mosaic of her life.

She wanted the best possible relations with her daughter, now a beautiful young lady of fourteen, with her own aspirations to be an actress. She also wanted Manuel to meet Richie Stevens, the man she had loved so many years and still respected professionally more than anyone else she had met in Hollywood. Her attempts at bringing Belinda and her former husband, Marty Roman, closer together had been such a fiasco that she was almost fearful of trying to form a bridge this time. Yet she knew that Manuel Benitez was a man of such stature that her fears were really unfounded. Belinda would certainly be thrilled to meet an actor of Manuel's international fame. Fearfully, she broached the subject to Richie on the phone.

"How about bringing Belinda over for dinner? Just the four of us. I do want you both to meet Manuel."

"I'm not sure Belinda will approve. You know she's still a little girl at heart. I think she feels that you deserted us. I've told her the truth, Trudy. Nothing shocks kids these days. I hope you won't be hurt if I say she still feels that I stood by her while you ran away."

"There's nothing I can do about that, Richie. She's right, you know. I did run away. I did it because I knew I could never adjust to your way of life, and I did love you very much."

"Thank you, Trudy."

"The only way I can ever prove to her that I didn't desert her entirely is by trying my best to keep in touch. Ask her to come to dinner. Tell her I miss her very much. I'll call her directly if you prefer."

"No, let me handle it. I hope it will work."

Quiet and introspective, Belinda was a young woman with very definite ideas about right and wrong. She thought for a moment when Richie relayed the invitation.

"Just because I don't approve of everything she's done doesn't change the fact that she is my mother. Will you feel uncomfortable if we go?"

"Not in the least."

"Well, good. I'll call Mom right away and tell her to expect us both."

It was obvious from the moment the two men met that they would have little trouble communicating. Indeed, their knowledge of each other's accomplishments fostered respect and admiration. Belinda was also immediately attracted by Manuel and easily won over. Perhaps it was because of his worldly manner. Perhaps it was because of his handsome face and physique. But most likely it was because Manuel did not strive to impress her. He was completely relaxed, preferring that she come to him when she was ready to accept his friendship. It was not a stratagem conceived by the older man to win the girl over, but rather his natural manner that she found so attractive. Trudy was delighted that everyone seemed so comfortable.

After dinner they gathered for brandy in the living room while Belinda, permitted a glass of white wine, sat at their feet and dreamed of her own future career. It was Richie who set the conversation on a practical course.

"Well, Manuel, now that you have finally reached Hollywood and found that we don't have horns, what are your plans?"

"Nothing definite at the moment, but I am beginning to get a bit itchy, as you Americans so aptly describe it. I miss the cameras. And what is your current project?"

"Like you, I'm between jobs. The studio has a few potboilers they're urging me to direct but I'm resisting. I still look for that super feature that will let me utilize all of the skills I've developed after a whole life in this crazy business."

"I guess we all have the same dream," Manuel added with a smile.

"I used to chastise Trudy for not sharing the dream. She has so much to offer, and I used to be very bitter because she let herself be used for third-rate material."

"Sometimes I think you never saw me for what I was, Richie,"

Trudy interjected. "What little I accomplished was because you pushed me. But I never had the talent you thought I had or my pictures would have been more consistent. Don't you agree, darling?" she asked, turning to Manuel for support.

"No. And the worst thing for an artist to be is humble. Acting is a make-believe game. If you can make believe you are Marie Antoinette or Dolley Madison or Madame Curie and do it convincingly, you ought to be able to make believe that you are Sarah Bernhardt as well. Your audience wants you to be great. But if you doubt yourself, you're lost."

"Bravo! Bravo!" Richie said enthusiastically. "Spoken perfectly and exactly my own views. Remember those words, Belinda. You can't be great in this business without thinking you can be."

"I'll try, Dad. And if I don't, you'll think so anyway," Belinda added with a laugh.

There was a lull in the conversation, which afforded Richie Stevens the opportunity he had been seeking all evening.

"I have a confession to make," he said abruptly.

"I'm not a very convincing priest," Manuel said, "but I can try."

"It's not that kind of confession. It's professional, not moral. I was happy to come to meet you this evening and delighted to be reassured that we can all be good friends. But I did want to find time to tell you about a project I have in mind that can bring us all together on a working level. May I?"

"Speak."

"By all means, go ahead."

"Okay. I've never even told Belinda about this. For years now I've been dreaming of making one picture, a picture so moving and so significant that all of the crap I've turned out for Silverstein and Continental will have been somehow justified. And I know just the story I want to make."

He paused for dramatic effect. Richie Stevens was not above being a salesman, especially when the idea was so important to him.

"I want to make a film that tells the story of Abélard and Héloïse. Are you familiar with their lives?"

"Only in the broadest outline," Manuel admitted.

"Frankly, I never even heard of them. Tell us about them," Trudy urged.

"I planned to," Richie confessed pleasantly. "Pierre Abélard was a French philosopher and theologian of the late eleventh to mid-twelfth centuries. He fell madly in love with a beautiful young student named Héloïse. They were married secretly against the rules of the church. Unfortunately, Héloïse was the niece of the canon, or leader, of the cathedral at Notre Dame. She denied the marriage because she didn't want her husband's career in the church ruined. But Canon Fulbert eventually learned the truth. In penance, Abélard became a monk and Héloïse a nun. But he was condemned as a heretic nonetheless and had to flee to a district far removed from Paris. Many of his loyal students followed him there, and later Abélard installed his former wife as Mother Superior in a convent. Their love then took the form of letters written in flowery prose that are beautiful to read. He died first but she continued to love him for many, many years. It is one of the most beautiful, most moving romances in the history of mankind. I've been working on the project for years and the script is near completion."

"Who wrote it?" Trudy asked.

"I did. With help from a professor of French history from UCLA. And now, my secret, which is not too difficult to guess. I want you, Manuel Benitez, to play Pierre Abélard. You, Trudy, must be Héloïse. Together, we can make motion picture history."

There was silence in the room. It was difficult to speak; Richie was obviously so taken with his project that perspiration had gathered on his forehead as he told the story. Finally, Manuel spoke.

"The best way to kill a friendship is to pour ice water on an artistic project that somebody else believes in. So, frankly, I must pick my words like someone tip-toeing through a mine field."

"You can speak your mind. You won't hurt my feelings."

"We've just met and I admire your intentions. But it's difficult to talk politics, religion, or art even with the most broad-minded fellow."

"Please, speak out. It's okay."

"Richie, why do you want to do this difficult picture?"

"I thought I explained. I believe in it."

"But why do you believe in it?"

"Because it's about the most attractive subject I know, love."

"True. But love in the twentieth century means a lot of things different from love in the twelfth. Abstinence, virginity, celibacy, these values are sneered at by today's young people. And need I remind you that youngsters make up eighty percent of today's movie-going audience? You know that."

Richie paused. There was truth to what Manuel said, and he did not say it unkindly. The pause gave Manuel confidence to continue.

"I've longed to do many pictures in my life. But often I pulled back and realized that maybe I was being led by my heart, not my brain. Costume dramas are expensive and terribly irrelevant in today's world. Don't you agree?"

"My heart won't let me agree. And I'm sure my heart won't separate itself from my brain in this instance. You see, Manuel, I learned a valuable lesson many years ago. I was at Continental when Kazan wanted to make *Gentleman's Agreement* at Fox. Everybody told him he was crazy, crazy to waste time on a meaningful film that was bound to alienate half the country and dealt with a touchy subject like anti-Semitism. Kazan said—I overheard a conversation one day when I wasn't supposed to be listening—'This is a movie I have to make. I have to do it now. I have to do it well. The public is ready for this subject, and I owe it to them and myself to treat it at its highest level.' Result? It won the Oscar for best picture and so did Kazan in the directorial category. He believed. And a lot of money flowed toward Twentieth Century as a result. That was back in 1947 and I have never forgotten it."

The more he spoke, the more intense Richie Stevens became. He was like an evangelist spreading the word of Christ. Manuel felt himself being swayed even against his will. Trudy decided that perhaps she should ask the embarrassing question.

"Richie, I hate to mention it, but didn't you feel the same way about *Helen of Troy?*"

"I did. I was wrong then. I'm right now."

"Are the costs manageable?" Manuel asked.

"Yes. It's an expensive project. I've worked out a tentative budget in the range of thirty million. But it could easily balloon to fifty million. That doesn't frighten me."

Manuel whistled. "You are a courageous man. Has anyone agreed to finance the film?"

"Believe it or not you are the first to learn of it. If you join my team, I'll start looking for financing first thing tomorrow."

"That's really very flattering. I'm beginning to be affected by your enthusiasm. I have to think about it. And so will Trudy. We'll want to do some reading first. I'm sure the library here has information about this great romance."

"The story of Héloïse and Abélard has been told and retold. The Beverly Hills Library has at least five books on the subject. Her collected letters are thrilling to read."

"Trudy and I will read them. Give us a week, no more, and you'll have our answer."

But the answer was to take far more than a week. Early the next morning, heading for the pool for a pre-breakfast swim, Trudy slipped on the pavement in the garden, which was still wet with dew. Struggling to maintain her equilibrium, she caught her heel in a deep rut and went sprawling down a sharp embankment that separated the pool from the balance of the lawn. She heard the crack as she hit the cement. Writhing in pain and unable to stand, she realized that she had suffered some serious injury. Her back had never been too strong after her severe injuries from the motorcycle accident in Mexico many years before. Whimpering in agony, she crawled to the pool and managed somehow to dislodge the phone from the small cocktail table. She called a private line in the bedroom and cried for help. The entire household staff, led by Manuel, came running to her rescue. She was rushed to the hospital by ambulance with Manuel riding by her side.

Within an hour, X rays told the sad story. She had dislocated her hip, fractured a small bone in her left ankle, and, most serious of all, had crushed three vertebrae in her lower spine. Surgery was absolutely necessary. Recovery, if indeed the operation was successful, would take at least four to six months. *Héloïse and Abélard* had suffered its first setback.

She was operated on the next day in a complicated procedure that took the better part of six hours. Her dislocated hip already had been reset and a small, flexible cast placed on her left ankle. It took nearly two hours before she regained consciousness and she was barely able to communicate with Manuel by nightfall.

"Everything went fine," he informed her. "The doctors expect no complications."

Looking down at the lower-body cast that she would have to wear for at least six weeks she mumbled weakly, "Peeing is going to be a complication."

Then she fell back into a troubled sleep. Since her pain was intense, she was given a number of powerful sedatives and was really not speaking clearly until the next morning. By that time postoperative depression had set in and she was in no mood to speak to anyone. Manuel tried his best, engulfing her room in flowers and waiting loyally close by so that he would be there if she needed him. Professional nurses were on duty around the clock, but the support of a loved one is indispensable when one is suffering real pain and discomfort. He asked if she wanted to see Belinda, but her reply was negative.

"No visitors, please. And you mustn't feel like a prisoner here. You haven't had a good meal in days. No need for you to suffer because I'm a clumsy klutz."

"A beautiful, clumsy klutz," Manuel corrected.

"I don't feel very beautiful in this plaster chastity belt."

"Now that you're thinking about sex I know you're well on the road to recovery."

It was a long road, a slow road to travel. At forty-nine years of age, bones aren't eager to mend quickly, especially if they've been seriously damaged before. Her pain was so intense during her convalescence that the doctors were compelled to prescribe narcotics, and she worried about her propensity for addiction. The memory of her days at Reynolds Sanatorium was still vivid, so she strove to deny herself pain killers for as long as it was physically possible. Sometimes, she just could not get by without them.

There were emotional problems troubling her as well. First, the realization that she could not go before the cameras for many months was terribly disheartening. Indeed, she wondered if she would ever be able to act again. Her hopes of working with Manuel had been raised, since he seemed so excited about Richie's proposal. She was also worried about Manuel and his frame of mind. He had come to Hollywood to please her, against his own better judgments. He was fretting for work, and though he had been a perfect saint in attending her during her three weeks of hospitalization and during this long recovery at home, she knew men and she knew him well enough to understand that she could not count on immobilizing him forever. Richie Stevens had come to see her the first day she was home to reassure her that even though he had not received her approval, or Manuel's either, he would not go ahead with his grand scheme until such time as she had fully recovered and made her decision.

"You are Héloïse," he assured her. "Without you, the picture won't be the same."

"You're sweet, Richie. I don't look or feel very romantic these days. Maybe that trip in the garden was not a mistake. I sometimes think that I am so accident prone, God must be trying to tell me something." Then she laughed and added, "I don't know why I said that. I've never been religious. And if there is a God I don't know why he would take time out to try and teach me a lesson."

"I hear God is into beautiful women," Richie answered.

After six weeks at home, Trudy faced her first, real crisis. Sid Keyes relayed an offer to Manuel that was hard to refuse. It was a quickie, made-for-television film that was to be shot entirely in New York, which was becoming more and more important as a film production center. The property was an interesting one, written by one of the rising young New York playwrights. Shooting was to be confined to four or five weeks. Manuel's fee was to be $500,000. Of course, he would get sole billing above the title. Manuel turned it down, explaining that he could not leave his wife alone while she was still laid up.

"But she's not alone," Sid argued. "You've got more excellent medical and nursing care for her than most private hospitals have for their entire list of patients. I'm sure Trudy would not want you to miss this opportunity."

"That may be true. But I won't ask her."

Sid Keyes, right or wrong, thought he read a message. He would ask her when Manuel was not around. He knew that Manuel enjoyed playing golf and learned that he usually visited a local country club on Wednesday afternoons. Sid popped in unannounced the next Wednesday and found Trudy alone with her day nurse. She insisted that he stay for a late lunch. He smoothly directed the conversation in the desired direction.

"How's Manuel holding up with all of the inactivity?"

"He's doing his best to fool me but I know he must be suffering. Actors like to act and he's been on the beach now for nearly a full year."

"Maybe he could get some short-term assignments that wouldn't keep him away too long."

Trudy looked at Sid steadily without speaking. She surmised that he had something in mind.

"You can tell me, Sid. Where, when, and for how long?"

"New York. A month at most. It's a great made-for-TV film just right for him. And the money is great. A half million with an option to do a second for three quarters of a million."

"You like it for him? Not just the commission? You know it's his first American feature and I want it to be great."

"Trudy, it's perfect. He likes it too, but he doesn't want to leave you if you need him."

"I'm his wife, not his jailer. He'll accept."

It took a bit of convincing, but not too much. Manuel was bored to death with the idleness that had characterized his life for the past several months. Like a pit bull straining at the leash, he longed for action. Now that Trudy was winning the slow battle of recovery, he wanted to—he had to—act again. That was his destiny and that was what he did best. Trudy assured him that she could carry on without him. He needed no further persuasion.

They dined alone the night before his departure. After dessert and cognac they engaged in a bit of straight talk.

"I'll miss you terribly, Manuel, but I'll be happy knowing that one of us is back doing the job we love most. And, speaking of love, I don't expect you to be faithful to me. It's not in your nature."

"Dearest, I'll be faithful. I'm not an animal."

"I'm not sure I want you to be otherwise. What I do insist is that you do not fall in love with somebody else. I don't think I could stand that."

"Really, Trudy, this talk is preposterous."

"On the contrary, it's real and quite mature. Fling your fling if you have to, but don't get involved in anything that even looks like it could be permanent. If you do, I'll know it. I'll look at your marvelous brooch and all the stones will turn to paste. When you come back in a month, I want you still to be my man."

"I'm condemned to love you forever. It's a life sentence."

"You bet your ass it is!"

They made love that night for the first time since the accident. The act was performed gingerly but it was all the more meaningful. Trudy thought of it as a reaffirmation of their deep feeling for one another. Manuel considered it a rededication to the principles of marriage. He hoped he would have the strength to remain true to his pledge.

He slept fitfully that night. Why, he thought as the hours ticked by, did life have to be so terribly complicated? Or had civilized man—and woman—taken a simple thing and drowned it in convolution?

He rose early, showered, kissed his still-sleeping wife on the cheek, and left for the airport. He wondered what adventures lay ahead.

CHAPTER 27

February 1981

Though he hated to admit it even to himself, Manuel Benitez was delighted to be in New York, having escaped the purgatorial torture of Hollywood and environs. New York throbbed with life. It was a young, vibrant, creative city, which brought out the best of his creative genes and charged his blood through his veins at a dashing pace. Hollywood was turgid, placid, phony, and plastic, or at least that was its impression on him. There was no dictate commanding him to prefer California over New York. But the fact that Trudy was bedridden, or nearly so, made him feel slight pangs of guilt. He managed, however, to subjugate those feelings as he buried himself in his work. Quite predictably, the four-week "quickie" took seven to film and was immediately followed by a sequel and yet another sequel.

"Can I help it if he's such a damn good actor he makes a picture happen?" Sid Keyes asked Trudy with seeming innocence. "Did I know he was going to be there this long? They told me four weeks, outside six."

"They lied and you knew they were lying," Trudy said with a smile. "But I'm not angry. It's Manuel's work. You can't blame him for loving it."

"Hey, I just thought of something," Sid said.

"So?"

"You never call him anything but 'Manuel.' Doesn't anyone ever call him 'Manny,' like Silverstein?"

"Never. Silverstein's real name was something entirely different. He liked the sound of 'Manny.' He once told me it sounded kind of macho to him as a boy and it was Jewish without sounding too Jewish. Manuel Benitez inherited his name from six generations of Spanish noblemen all similarly named. I would no sooner call Manuel 'Manny' than call the Pope 'Stosh,' and I'm Polish, too. But whatever I call him, damn it, I miss him."

In nearly six months of work in New York, Manuel Benitez returned but once and then only for a weekend visit. Trudy was mending now and was tempted to ask him if she could join him. But she knew that he objected to any interference when he was working on a film. Besides, she felt that the idea of her visiting New York should spring from him and not vice versa. She had no doubt he was seeing other women. The telltale column items had already begun sprouting. Whenever they did, he called her immediately and cursed out their source as being completely inaccurate.

"I really don't care," Trudy responded. "I gave you free rein. Just don't fall in love."

"Darling, you know that after you all other women are like nothing."

"Nothing or something, just remember the ground rules. Flirtations, yes. Love affairs, no. Your brooch will tell me everything, darling."

"Fortunately, there is nothing to tell." And he rang off feeling just a twang of guilt.

Alone at home, deprived of the opportunity to act, Trudy began feeling restless. She saw Belinda now and again but the child was fast becoming a young lady and had friends and interests of her own. Trudy was determined to avoid any "command performances," which her daughter might find unpleasant. They met only when Belinda sincerely wanted to be with her. Obviously there were no suitors in her life. She was a married lady now, generally disabled. Even had she sought excitement, there would be few takers of any worth. So she spent her time reading, watching television, and exercising under the careful scrutiny of physiotherapists. Life, to put it bluntly, was a bore.

She found herself drinking again. First just a cocktail or two, then a bit more, as if in response to some inner demon. Aside from her domestic help, there was no staunch friend to counsel her. The hired help did not dare. She started to gain a lot of weight. Her face became unnecessarily flaccid, her attention span greatly reduced. Help came from an unexpected source. Belinda became worried by her mother's obvious deterioration.

"Dad, I know it's not your problem, but I'm worried sick about Mom. She looks awful and every time I'm with her she stinks of liquor. I think she needs some help."

"Did you ever discuss it with her?" Richie asked.

"I can't do that. She's my mother. I'm still a kid."

"You sure it's that bad?"

"It's worse. She is sick."

Richie Stevens was a man of compassion. Besides, Trudy was his daughter's mother and, as such, deserved attention. He called Milton Gordon in the morning.

"Dr. Gordon, I'm Richie Stevens. I was once married to Trudy Coles."

"Of course I remember you, Mr. Stevens. You may recall the long discussion we had at the time that Trudy was at Reynolds. Is there a problem?"

"Apparently. My daughter, Belinda, tells me that Trudy is alone and drinking heavily. She'll resent it bitterly if she knows that I know, and her daughter is concerned that she might be considered a spy or the like. I was wondering if you could sort of initiate your own investigation, if you don't consider it some sort of professional indiscretion."

"We psychiatrists are usually more effective when the patient seeks us out rather than the other way around. But Miss Coles and I have a strong relationship and I think I can handle the approach sensibly. Thank you for the call."

"No. Thank you for caring."

Like a child waiting to be disciplined, Trudy was secretly delighted to receive a friendly summons from Dr. Gordon. He was shocked at how bad she looked, a fact made even more telling because of the physical injuries that made it impossible for her to move with her accustomed grace.

"Well, Dr. Gordon, here I am, back again. Still a dirty old drunk."

"Hardly. But you don't look well. I'm not a very good liar, you know. If this were our first meeting I'd insist that you commit yourself to Reynolds for at least a short stay."

"That won't be necessary. I'll see you as often as you'll permit and I'm positive I can get hold of myself."

"We'll try, under the condition that if you don't make good progress you'll let me care for you at Reynolds. Is it a deal?"

"I really don't have many options."

Almost on a daily basis, Milton Gordon and Trudy Coles met and explored her inner depths, which boiled with pain and sorrow. Using his questioning technique, he probed and probed, striving to exorcise the devils that inhabited her psyche.

"Now, let me ask the question, Dr. Gordon. Why is it that every man I fall in love with eventually turns his back on me? Here I am this raving beauty—I'm not modest about my looks—here I am this great big movie star—and one by one they say 'So long, Charlie,' and leave me. Why?"

"The last time I broke my pledge and gave advice, you married Marty Roman. I couldn't have been more wrong. Why trust me now?"

"Because you're about the only one in this world whom I really do trust. What do I do that makes them drop me like a hot potato? Even Manuel Benitez, who told me I was the love of his life, has had his fill of me. He's in New York chasing chorus girls while I'm slowly drinking myself to death. Why, Dr. Gordon? Why?"

"To find that answer won't be easy. We have to go back a long, long way. And the pain you'll suffer remembering might be worse than the cure."

"If I don't find the cure, there will be no more pain. I've been on drugs again and several times had a hard time convincing myself that I shouldn't take an overdose. I think maybe the world would be a better place without me."

"That's simply ridiculous and you know it. We've been over this ground many, many times before. Why, you've brought so much pleasure to so many people through your acting that the world might never be able to pay you back."

"I wished I believed that."

"Maybe that's the trouble. Up until now, we've always talked about your life here in California. I know it's a long way off, but I'm convinced we should dig deeper. Where did you say you were born?"

And so the long, painful, exploratory talks began. Little by little, Trudy uncovered the shroud that shielded her subconscious memories of life in West Virginia. Though she resisted it, eventually she made a clean breast of her relationship with her father. She found herself weeping uncontrollably as she recalled the despair she had felt when first he shunned her for Aggie Stephanik.

Bringing herself slowly under control, she said, "Dr. Gordon, I guess I'm something even lower than a common vulgarity, a 'father fucker.'"

"Not really. Maybe you would have been better off if you had been."

"I'm not sure I understand."

"It's not easy.... The fact is that having been rejected by the one man you truly loved, you never escaped from the feeling that you weren't really worth very much. No matter how many accolades the world gave you, you didn't believe them. So you went around not really seeking love, not really looking for sex. What you wanted was to prove to yourself that Cass Kolinski made the wrong decision. Every man you went to bed with was, in a sense, on trial. He had to prove to you that you were the best. No one is up to that task, Trudy. If you don't believe in yourself, how in the hell can I make you be proud? You jumped from romance to romance not because you were such a nymphomaniac who couldn't get enough sex. You needed to be laid—forgive the bluntness—so that you could tell yourself that you really were irresistible. And then when the men got tired of proving themselves again and again, you turned to drink or to drugs or to whatever else you could grasp onto in an effort to assuage your frustration."

"And what do I do now, Dr. Gordon?" The words were spoken sadly and humbly.

"You start by realizing that your father, Cass Kolinski, has been dead for a long time. He turned to you because he was weak and you were strong. He wasn't even strong enough to consummate the love act with you. And he hated himself for wanting to. That's why he turned to Aggie Stephanik. He hoped that she could put out the desire he had to bed down his own daughter, whom he really loved very much. You were rejected not because you weren't desirable but because he knew it was biblically wrong to make love to one's own daughter. You must believe that, Trudy."

"And if I do?"

"Then, from a psychological standpoint, you'll start your whole life over. Maybe for the first time, you'll begin to realize your true worth."

She cried again. He put her into a small waiting room and she lay down for more than two hours. Finally, she rose, washed her face, applied some makeup, and meekly tapped on his office door.

"Dr. Gordon, I have a lot of thinking to do. But I believe I'm going to be all right. I'll call you in a couple of days."

He didn't hear from her for the better part of a week. When he answered the phone, he couldn't believe the change in her voice and composure.

"How goes it, Trudy?"

"It's a piece of cake, Dr. Gordon. You know what I just realized?"

"What's that?"

"I'm a star. From now on, I start acting like one!"

CHAPTER 28

August 1981

In the middle of her fifty-first year, Trudy Coles seized control of her life. She willed herself back to health and in a month had regained all of her strength and most of her vigor. Even her physiotherapists, who had been concerned over her slow recovery, were amazed.

"It's a miracle, Miss Coles, a miracle! In four weeks you've made more progress than in the four months preceding them. I really don't think you'll need our help much longer. Simply follow the exercises after we leave and you'll be just fine."

"Thank you, Abby. And you, too, Gretchen. You've both been a great help to me and I'll never forget you. But I do want you to leave, because from here on in it's me alone. Trudy Coles against the world."

"The world, if you'll excuse the expression, Miss Coles, had better watch its ass," Abby said.

To which statement Gretchen added, "Amen. Amen."

She called her agent, Sid Keyes, and asked for, or rather, demanded, an immediate meeting. Just from the tone of her voice, Keyes knew he dared not refuse.

"Trudy, you look great! I couldn't get better news."

"Thank you, Sid. After nine months as an invalid, it's high time. Now, I want you to find me a picture. I'm not asking for quality or a lot of dough either. I want to work. You can even get me one of those cheapie made-for-television flicks."

"I'm sure we'll find something in the next couple of months."

"You don't read me too well, Sid. I want work and I want it now. I want you to understand that for many years I've ground out a hell of a lot of commissions for your agency. All the time I was being badgered by ICM and APA and MCA and GAC and all the rest of those pirates and I stuck by Jason Arnold. Now I want action fast and if I don't get it, there will be no renewal of my contract. You understand?"

This was a new Trudy Coles, and Sid Keyes was smart enough to grasp that fact. Trudy was working inside of ten days. It was a nothing film but Trudy was delighted to discover that after many months of inactivity she had not lost her touch. The film wasn't a big hit; it wasn't a big loser, either. With a sale to pay cable, syndication in Europe, and theatrical release in Canada as well as the United States, its producers earned a handsome profit. And the filming had only taken six weeks. She was immediately signed to another quickie produced by the same group and it, too, was a mild success. She received, though she had not demanded it, five percent of the net profits immediately.

Now she was ready for Manuel Benitez, who was still gadding about on the East Coast. She sent him a simple letter.

Momma is home and ready. Come home or get lost forever! I'm no nun like Héloïse. Get your spic ass home. Momma misses it.

Manuel got the message and returned to Los Angeles the next week, as soon as he could finish his current project. They had a warm, romantic reunion and within twenty-four hours of his arrival had set up a conclave with Richie Stevens. They signed a three-way agreement, forming the "Helard Company," which was to be jointly owned. Richie had the prime responsibility for raising the funds, but they would all cooperate in every phase of the pre-production work. Years before, when leading film stars had formed United Artists, which they themselves controlled, one wag said it was like giving the inmates the keys to the institution. But times had changed. Many artists now headed their own production companies, as much for financial advantage as for artistic control.

They received their first jolt when they tried to attract large sums of capital. Trudy's persistent health problems were known to all. Manuel's drinking was no secret. Most serious of all, however, was Richie's reputation as an "arty" director. Under Manny Silverstein's control, he had been forced to play the game commercially. On his own, his reputation reeked of expensive, artistic flops. He never had completely escaped from the odors of *Helen of Troy*. For years, Manny Silverstein had brought up the subject every time he wanted to prove to someone that his sense of judgment was infallible. "Arty-farty" movies were what he was against.

Sid Keyes went to several large investment groups on their behalf and had only mild success. One group, which was flushed with cash from oil investments overseas, promised to come up with the last five million, only after the first twenty-five was safely deposited in a company account. That was some help. Jointly, the three partners made a visit to Fox, where Trudy, on loan, had scored some of her earliest successes. Grudgingly, Fox agreed to put up $10 million, provided they kept all distribution rights—which could, in a sense, cover their full investment, assuming that the picture was completed and not a total flop. Now, at least they were halfway home.

Weeks raced by and the funds pledged were still a good $12 million short of their needs. Trudy on several occasions had suggested approaching Continental, but Richie Stevens was against it.

"Continental was and always will be a garbage house. Greenberg wouldn't understand what Abélard and Héloïse is all about. Besides, he's worse than his uncle was."

Following Manny Silverstein's death, a bitter internal struggle had ensued for control of Continental Studios. For a short while, his brother Abe held the reins, only to lead the company to near-disaster. With bankruptcy threatening, the Eastern bankers —who really had the last say—agreed to replace Abe with Jerry Greenberg, a distant cousin of the Silverstein clan. Greenberg was conniving, ruthless, and dishonest to the core. In one of his first executive decisions with the company, he had turned a deaf ear to Trudy's plea for a rest and had consigned her to the windswept cliffs of Colorado, where she had become gravely ill. Trudy had avoided close contact with him ever since as both of their careers had advanced.

"All he can do is say no," Trudy argued with some logic. "I have heard that word a lot lately. If we don't move fast we're liable to lose that oil-group commitment. And how long will Fox stand in line? They could change their minds, you know."

"Look, the truth is that the worst he can do is refuse. But he and I never liked each other and I'm sure I'll give off negative vibes if I attend the meeting."

"I'll see him alone," Trudy said. "He's no favorite of mine either. But we need financial backing and I can stand him for one meeting."

"I'll go along if you wish," Manuel offered.

"No. I think, in this case, alone is better."

Trudy knew she faced a big challenge the moment she entered Greenberg's office. She hadn't seen him in years, and truthfully those years had been good to him. Success was just the aphrodisiac he needed. Characteristically, he raised his right hand to his forehead and brushed his forelock forward, leaning in for a ceremonial kiss. Trudy instinctively turned her head and offered her cheek. After a brief kiss, he took her in his arms unnecessarily and gave her a big hug.

"Trudy, it's been such a long time."

"Yes it has, Jerry. Lots of water under the bridge I'd say. It seems funny to be in this office without your uncle, Manny Silverstein."

Trudy mentioned Silverstein intentionally. It was her not-too-subtle way of telling Greenberg that she knew he sat upon the throne of a better man. There was something about that first kiss and hug that she didn't like. You don't treat stars like chorus girls.

"Manny. Yes, we all miss him, Trudy. I know he'd be glad to know that the ship is in good hands. Here, have a seat. Let's talk about old times."

"What's to say? Let's talk about the future. Have you heard about our new project?"

"Sure. It's a period piece, right?"

"Right. Eleventh and twelfth centuries. It's the great love story of all time."

"I don't think the public wants great love stories. What they want is sex and violence and terror and outer space crap. Show me one love story that made it big in the last five years."

"Generalities are what got this town in trouble. Like that story that no sports picture ever made it big. Then along comes *Rocky* and they can't stop making sequels. Right?"

"True. But *Rocky* is a here-and-now story. Not some costume piece out of twelfth-century France. What's the budget like, incidentally?"

"Thirty million. It's a biggie. A chance for Continental to score real big, Jerry. We've got more than half the money already."

Forty-eight hours had passed since Jerry had received the call from Trudy requesting a meeting. He had been tempted to ask her to come over that afternoon but decided it would be better strategy to seem less eager. He had learned to "play it cool" at Manny's knee. Through the industry grapevine, Jerry had learned about "A and H," as it was referred to in the trade. With names like Benitez, Coles, and Stevens connected with a prestigious property, the chances for success were not bad. This sounded like the very project that might gain him the reputation he so sadly lacked.

There was another plus beckoning him. Trudy. Yes, she was allegedly happily married and getting up in years. But that body and those features were still incredible. More important, the man who conquered Trudy Coles was looked on as a giant among men. They'd forget all about Manny Silverstein once they heard that Jerry Greenberg was Trudy Coles' latest bedfellow.

The trick was to pretend that he wasn't really interested. He'd started on the right note, strongly challenging the commercial value of costume romances. Now came the money talk, the time for practiced reluctance.

"So I heard through the grapevine. But halfway to thirty still leaves a long road to travel." Then, abruptly changing the subject, he said, "By the way, I was going through some of Manny's effects the other day and I came up with some great pictures of you. Have you seen them? You know, the ones taken in this suite, in there," he said, pointing to the inner office.

Jerry Greenberg brushed his forelock consciously this time. There was an evil grin on his face. Trudy wished she had some coffee in her hand. She would have tossed it right in his face. The pictures she was certain he was referring to were some old snaps Manny had made of her in the buff in the early days of their first meetings. He had told her, which probably was true, that he had never seen a body to match hers and he wanted to record it for posterity. Never self-conscious, aware of her own beauty, and eager to please the man who could exert such a positive force on her career, she had acquiesced. Manny had shown her the pictures one time and even offered her copies. She had refused, saying that she knew what she looked like and if she forgot, there were always mirrors around. Later, she was to learn that filming beautiful ladies in the nude was a hobby with Manny. He once boasted that on rare occasions he had met women he couldn't screw. But he insisted that he had never met one he couldn't photograph naked if he spent enough time and energy telling her how great a body she had.

"Would you like to see the pictures?" Jerry asked playfully. "I'll bet you're still in as good shape." He rose and walked to her side, reaching down for her hand.

She pulled it back. Rising with fire in her eyes, she stared at him with disgust.

"You'd lose your bet. That was a hundred years ago. But you know what? You'll never know. You may be king here, Jerry. But to me you'll always be a creep. I wouldn't want your fifteen million if you offered it. You're such a filthy crumb that I wouldn't want your name connected with Abélard and Héloïse. Now I'm sure you want the last word. Say something nasty or I won't remember I was in this office with you."

Shocked by the violence and suddenness of her attack, Greenberg was at a loss for words. He stared back and finally managed, "Why don't you get the hell out of here?"

"That's exactly my plan," she answered with a smile. Turning on her heels, she left. For a long time afterward, Jerry Greenberg stood there brushing his forelock, his face reddened in anger.

Trudy never related the full details of her meeting with Greenberg. Both Richie Stevens and Manuel Benitez knew from the look on her face that the mission had failed. She simply turned to Richie and said, "You were right. I never should have asked him."

Time was running out now and each of the three partners knew that if the other half of the capital was not raised quickly the project would die aborning. At the eleventh hour, Manuel came up with a proposed solution. It might just save the day.

Turning to Richie he asked, "How much time do we really have left? A week, a month, two months, perhaps?"

"I'd say two weeks to a month at best. The oil group's attorney called me yesterday and told me that they must put the money to work before their tax year runs out. I promised him action in the next few weeks. What do you have in mind?"

"I have not been home to my country on an official visit—not counting my brief honeymoon—for years. The reason? Political, I suppose. My family was never in favor of Franco and though there was no open confrontation, I thought it healthier to stay abroad. Now, things are more relaxed but I'm still not sure of my strength. The Spanish government has been eager to increase the number of films produced there in order to stimulate employment. They've reinstituted a policy that was in high gear during the late sixties and early seventies. If we agree to film there and employ a good number—I'm not sure of the exact percentages—of both actors and technical crew who are Spanish citizens, they'll lend or invest a good portion of the money needed. Whether they will agree to fifteen million worth of investment, well that depends on how good a salesman I can be. But this can only be accomplished in face-to-face meetings. If you wish, I'll try. I'm sure we can find scenery similar in Spain to our planned settings in France. What is your opinion?"

"If you don't think it is dangerous, darling, why not?"

"I think it's a marvelous plan," Richie agreed.

"We shall see. But two weeks is not much time to move a bunch of Spanish bureaucrats. Spanish red tape is very sticky. But, we shall try."

He left the following morning, it being agreed by all that it was best if he made the effort alone. Despite his political history, he was somewhat of a Spanish legend and would have to find great popular support. Traveling alone would make it more of a Spanish project, not watered down by the obvious participation of American stars like Trudy. He cabled ahead to several friends who he knew had great power with the current Spanish rulers. They met him at the airport outside of Madrid and immediately put themselves at his disposal. Even though the equivalent of $15 million far exceeded the normal investment limits, the fact that he was Manuel Benitez, the fact that the story concerned such legendary figures, the fact that the royal family was traditionally allied with Benitez noblemen, and the fact that this would be a big picture that might bring the world's attention to Spain as a place to originate feature filming, all helped. Only the time was a hurdle. Two weeks, just two short weeks. Somehow, he accomplished his mission. In just ten days, a smiling minister of culture shook his hands and said, "The money is yours. Now, when do the cameras start rolling? We Spanish are an impatient lot. But you know that."

Filming started outside Tormelinos on the Costa del Sol exactly four weeks after the Spanish government had agreed to the investment. The job of recruiting large hordes of extras was not an easy one, but one that certainly pleased the government.

The simple story of Abélard and Héloïse had been blown up in Stevens' mind to extravaganza proportions. Perhaps that was the basic misconception. Actually, nothing went as planned. Heavy rains during a normally dry period delayed filming day after day. Labor problems arose with the Spanish craft unions, whose leaders claimed that American technicians were being paid far greater salaries than their Spanish counterparts. They made it difficult for Stevens to rent the equipment he needed, so that he was forced to send to the States for much he had planned to lease locally, thus greatly exceeding that portion of the budget. Trudy, not having been exposed to such damp weather for a long time, caught a miserable cold and fever that put her in the hospital for six days. Stevens and Benitez, so compatible in America, did not see eye to eye on many dramatic problems and found themselves at constant odds. Soon, they were practically not speaking on the set and the spirits of the entire company sagged.

As was quite predictable, the projected $30 million budget was soon exceeded. There was a desperate need for an additional $8 million. Since there are no secrets in the motion picture business, word leaked back to Hollywood that *Abélard and Héloïse* was in deep trouble, which made it all the more difficult to obtain additional financing. In one of their rare moments of collaboration, Richie and Manuel, joined by Trudy, just out of the hospital, held a war council. It was decided that only personal appeals might generate the necessary funding. Reluctantly, both men agreed to recontact their sources. Manuel was less successful, receiving a direct turndown from his Spanish government contacts. All he actually accomplished was to blow the whistle on the production and from that day forth civil servants were buzzing around, checking every invoice and every expenditure.

Richie was a bit more successful. He contacted the attorney for the oil investment group and told them there was desperate need for more cash. The attorney called him back several hours later and said that before additional funds were granted, Stevens would have to meet with a representative of the investment group who had the authority to make such a decision. Explaining that it was impossible for him to leave the production at such a critical stage, he countered by inviting the group's representative to visit them in Spain. He, Stevens, would personally be responsible for all expenses involved in the trip. Another delay until morning, then a breath of hope. Mr. Norton William Ardsley would be on a trans-Atlantic flight within forty-eight hours. The lawyer warned that Ardsley was a tough cookie and not one to be easily swayed by show business promises. But at least he was a gentleman and would listen to reason.

There were a few intrepid associates of Norton William Ardsley who had the temerity to call him "Bill"—but not many. He was such an imposing figure that one scarcely had the courage to drop the "Mr." Both Richie and Trudy had heard his name mentioned many times and had read about him in the society columns of Los Angeles newspapers. Yet, apparently he was not the sort of man who frequented charity balls or events of that kind, for neither had ever met him in person. When Trudy got her first glimpse of him she thought he might just be the most handsome man she had ever met. Her heart fluttered like a schoolgirl's. He stood nearly six feet five inches tall, had steel-gray hair, a long, aquiline nose, and the bluest blue eyes she had ever seen. He was broad-shouldered and walked with an athlete's gait, yet there was something soft and sensitive about his face that transcended the obvious physical strength he must have possessed. When their eyes first met, he stared with such unflinching concentration that she was finally forced to turn away in mild embarrassment.

Whether it was his immediate obsession with Trudy's incredible beauty, whether he liked the swashbuckling attitude of Manuel Benitez, or whether it was the sincerity and integrity of Richie Stevens that impressed him the most, was difficult to assess. The fact was that they answered all of his questions honestly, he was favorably moved by the filming they invited him to witness, and even was convinced that the script was an excellent one after several careful readings. But he was a tough businessman and the deal he offered was as follows: If each of the three principals—Richie, Manuel, and Trudy—would put up $1 million personally, he would supply an additional $5 million for an increased profit participation of fifteen percent, which would be taken from the fifty percent they had held for themselves. In addition, he insisted that this new $5 million be adjudged a loan and be the first money returned when and if the profits were earned.

"That's a strong deal for five million," Richie responded firmly but not impolitely.

"Indeed it is," Ardsley said, "but the concept of last money in, first money out is hardly new to motion picture financing. Besides, you people are in trouble, Mr. Stevens, and we already have five million buried in this film that may never see the light of day. Fox can be smug because once afloat, their fees for distribution may well bring them back most of their investment, even if there is no profit to be shared. We are pure investors. If we come up with money in a troubled situation, we must be recompensed accordingly."

It was difficult to argue with his logic. They caucused briefly, each of the principals agreed to a personal investment, and the deal was confirmed with a handshake. There would be papers in due time. But one look at Norton William Ardsley and it was obvious that he was as good as his word. He returned to the States the next day but not before stabbing Trudy with those incredible blue eyes, and not without her second, schoolgirl reaction. More important, however, was her realization that the film would now be completed.

CHAPTER 29

1982

The setting was Sardi's, in New York, where the cognoscenti frequently gather for luncheon while exchanging the latest gossip of the rialto.

"I just heard the most wonderful idea for a show," blurted one of the younger, more naive members of the group. "It's the story of the second coming of the Messiah and it's told with a rock score in the background."

To which one of the more sophisticated, blasé attendees replied, "It is a wonderful idea. And once the magic of the theater takes over, they'll fuck it up!"

Abélard and Héloïse was one of those wonderful ideas for a feature film that sounded better on the drawing board than it really was. And once the imagination of the creative forces took sway, it got worse and worse. In retrospect, it was obvious that here was a simple tale that cried out for simple treatment. Instead, Richie Stevens, despite his many years of experience and his innate good taste, envisioned a huge drama involving thousands of extras and elaborate scenery. In addition, Trudy Coles and Manuel Benitez were hardly professional virgins who would sublimate their carnal desires in the service of the Almighty. It didn't require much perspective to realize that they were badly cast.

Even with the infusion of the additional $8 million, the film ran over budget, leaving Richie with personal debts in excess of $2 million. In a wild gesture of compassion, Trudy and Manuel agreed to absorb an additional $500,000 of obligation each. That still left Richie owing more than a million.

In place of the normal good fellowship that abounds when a team has completed a difficult task, everyone seemed peeved with everyone else. There was no closing-night party when the film was completed. Everyone involved sneaked away. Manuel and Trudy, their normal affections strained by the pains of participating in a losing venture, went off to England for a vacation. But neither one was in any mood for fun. Richie headed back to the States, hoping to touch off a publicity campaign that would hide the blemishes of the picture, which he knew was a dud.

Stevens was not the only one who knew that a turkey had been hatched. The picture was released in several Western test-market cities, then with a fair amount of publicity it opened in New York. Reviews were generally horrible. So much had been written in advance about the film and the great pair of stars in it that the expectations could not have been fulfilled even if the feature had been a strong one. Stevens withdrew the film from circulation as soon as he could, announcing to the world that final editing had never taken place because of certain committed release dates. He then mortgaged his future with another $500,000, re-edited some of the weaker moments, poured more money into a futile advertising campaign, and reopened the film in Los Angeles to even poorer critical reception. *Abélard and Héloïse* became the joke of the industry. Stevens, aside from the problems of paying off his monumental debts, vowed that he would never direct again. He abstained from theatrical films for more than a year; then, finally, in dire need of income, accepted a job directing television features. But his spirit was gone, his best work behind him.

After a month in London, relations between Trudy and Manuel became bitterly strained. Subconsciously, he blamed her for dragging him into such a highly notorious bomb, while she accused him of never having given the film his best efforts. He started drinking again, staying out till all hours, and returning to their hotel suite with obvious footprints of infidelity all over him. At first she tried to be patient with him, realizing that his ego had taken a thrashing in his native country, a terrible blow to his naturally intense pride. But then, as the arguments grew uglier, the insulting and inconsiderate incidents more frequent, she took stock of herself and her marriage and decided that it was a situation she did not wish to tolerate. This was a new Trudy Coles. She was convinced that her destiny lay in her own hands. She would not allow herself to be at someone else's mercy, even a man whom she had loved so intensely. There was every sign that the romance was over. At the very least she was determined to escape with her own dignity and self-respect. The words of that marvelous revelation in the office of Milton Gordon came to mind, not to haunt her, but rather to inspire her with true strength from within: She was a star. She must act like one.

The next night, Manuel left for one of his binges. When he returned he found an empty hotel suite with a curt message from Trudy.

> *I'm going home. Pick a lawyer and have him contact Allen Rosenthal in Beverly Hills. I'll tell him I want a divorce, not a pound of flesh. . . . Thanks for the ride.*

It was what Manuel Benitez knew was inevitable and yet he regretted it. Trudy Coles had been great fun. Now, it was over for both of them and there was no point in brooding. He'd pick up stakes, move back to Rome, and start working again. That was the only way he knew to bury the pain of *Abélard and Héloïse*. Besides, there was that big, big debt to work off.

Trudy returned almost happily to California. As soon as she caught up with the change in time zones, she called Belinda. She was a lovely young lady of seventeen now, not much older than Trudy had been when she first reached the magical shores of Hollywood. As was totally predictable, Belinda was interested in becoming an actress. A freshman at the University of California at Los Angeles, she was playing her first small role at the Pasadena Playhouse and was already madly in love with the leading man.

"Mom," she gushed over the phone, "wait till you see him. He's gorgeous. He tells me he thinks I have great talent, too."

"Have you been to bed with him yet?"

"Mom! Please. We're just friends."

"I never knew anyone who went to bed with an enemy. Watch yourself, young lady. Leading men devour ingénues for breakfast. They're not to be trusted when you're seventeen."

"Mom, I can take care of myself, honest."

"Please do. I'm too young to be a grandmother. Bad for my image, too. . . . How's Richie?"

"Terrible, Mom. He's taking it real, real hard. He says he'll never direct again. George—you remember his friend, don't you?—George says he'll bring him around. I think they're in Acapulco for a couple of weeks. I had a week off from school and offered to fly down with Dad but he said no. He wouldn't be very good company."

"Maybe he needs George now."

"Maybe."

"How about dinner tonight?"

"Can't. Got to study for exams. And there's an early rehearsal at the Playhouse on Saturday. Saturday night I've got a date. But Sunday would be just fine. Okay?"

"Of course. I'll pick you up at seven. Right?"

"Great. Let's try Pinto's. I hear that place is a gas."

"It is . . . if you don't go deaf from the noise. See you Sunday."

The divorce proceedings were relatively painless. Manuel made a halfhearted effort to retrieve the fabulous brooch he had given her, but Trudy resisted.

"Tell him he'll have to kill to get it back," she said laughingly to her attorney. "I'm not interested in alimony or any support. I'm not interested in any share of his assets. But I won't give up that brooch. Tell him it's mine and that's all there is to it."

At home alone one night, Trudy received a telephone call from a man who identified himself as Larry Hocker. Not recognizing the name, she assumed he was another salesman pushing some sort of investment.

"I don't know you, Mr. Hocker, and I'm not interested."

"We've met before, Miss Coles. That day in Jerry Greenberg's office. I was the man, sitting with the receptionist, who chatted with you for a few minutes."

"I really don't remember. And that's a meeting I'd like to forget."

"Me, too. He called me in to fire me."

"Well, I guess that someone Jerry Greenberg fires can't be all bad. What did you want?"

"Fifteen minutes of your time as soon as you can spare them. I've got a project that I want to talk to you about. Just fifteen minutes, please."

"I'm not sure the world is ready for another Trudy Coles film."

"It's not a film. Give me the fifteen minutes and I'll explain."

Hocker was so insistent, she didn't have the heart to refuse him. The truth was that she needed a project now, needed it desperately. Work was the best antidote to help one forget.

They met the next day and Larry Hocker told Trudy about his big dream. *Her Own Woman,* based on a best-selling novel concerned with the women's liberation movement. A Broadway musical with a giant budget.

"It's all very flattering, Mr. Hocker," Trudy said, "but I've never even been in a small Broadway show, let alone a big musical. I'm a screen actress. I haven't sung or danced in years. I admire your courage. But you can find someone better for the part than me."

"I won't, because this is you. There is no one better."

"I think your brief stay out here has twisted your judgment. Me in a Broadway musical. It's a crazy idea."

"Do me one favor. Here's the book. Read it. Then give me your answer."

CHAPTER 30

1983

Trudy went into training for *Her Own Woman* like an Olympian preparing herself to win a gold medal. Although she was naturally graceful, she had not danced in public for many years. Her voice, never strong but always sweet, had been restricted to use in her daily shower. She even sought out Mollie Haines, now in her late seventies, and convinced her to recoach her in drama.

"Hell, I've been retired for years!" Mollie protested. "There's nothing new I can teach you."

"You were there at the start," Trudy argued. "You can help me get rid of all those bad habits I've been developing for years."

Belinda was taking ballet and modern dance lessons and Trudy joined the same classes. She was old enough to be the mother of all of the other students, but none worked harder or showed greater progress.

"You're amazing, Miss Coles," the instructor said in admiration. "You put all of these young girls to shame."

"If I were their age I'd take it easy, too," Trudy responded. "Just to stop my bones from creaking I have to stretch for an hour every morning before coming to class. Next week I start tap lessons. The last time I tap-danced was in studio dance school back in about 1947. Even *then* I wasn't too great at it."

Singing lessons were the most difficult of all. Heading for a Broadway show, Trudy knew that her main problem would be one of projection. It was one thing to sing sweetly and in tune, but what was the point if no one beyond the third row could hear you? True, Larry Hocker had promised her faithfully that even in rehearsal her natural voice would be augmented by a body mike. But even with the wonders of modern electronics to aid her, there were always the uncomfortable moments when perspiration or excessive costumes lead to unpleasant static or interference, and one had to rely on a natural ability to project. As a young actress she had been taught to throw her voice, but that was in a quiet film studio with no other noise to interfere. Now she would be working in a cavernous Broadway theater. That meant that the voice had to be strengthened like a weightlifter's biceps. Her singing coach worked in that direction, more interested in Trudy's ability to sing loudly than to sing sweetly and in tune. The razzmatazz of modern orchestrations covered a lot of flat notes.

"Whom do you have in mind for a leading man?" Trudy asked Larry one afternoon over lunch.

"I've narrowed it down to about five candidates, but I'm really hoping we can get Peter Franklin."

"Who's he?"

"Oh, he's been kicking around the New York scene for years, generally playing second leads. He's got just enough heavy in him to make him entirely believable as Mitchell. He's stodgy-looking, yet handsome in a classy way, and he's got a great lyric baritone that's just right for the part. The composer thinks he would be great."

"Well, since I have to play opposite him, don't you think I ought to meet him?"

"Of course you will. As soon as we're sure he's the one we want. You know I promised you approvals on everyone."

Trudy was to learn rather painfully that what Larry Hocker promised and what he delivered often varied widely. There was the matter of the director, for example. Larry had assured her that she could have her pick of the top five directors on Broadway. He never clearly delineated who the five were, but he always insisted that getting a top director was no big problem. As the months rolled on and no director had been selected, Trudy began growing suspicious.

"Listen Larry, you know this is my first show on Broadway. I want to work with the director long before we go into rehearsal. When are we going to nail one down?"

"There's no really big rush here, Trudy," Larry argued. "I'm still insisting on a lot of script changes. No use sending a bad script out. We'll be ready in less than a month."

But the month grew into two and then three and still no announced director and no selection of a date for starting rehearsals.

Trudy continued working at her dancing, voice, and drama lessons, which were taking all of her concentration; but she started growing uneasy. She decided to consult Richie Stevens who, though still inactive, was beginning to behave more like his old self. She called and arranged to meet him for lunch.

"Do you know Larry Hocker?" she asked after exchanging the usual amenities.

"Slightly. I met him a couple of times in conference in Jerry Greenberg's office. That was while their short honeymoon lasted. Everyone knew they were riding for a fall. Too much like each other, I guess."

"What do you know about him?"

"Not too much. He had a couple of mid-sized hits on Broadway, then a whole slew of flops. He knew Jerry socially, I believe, and Jerry convinced him to come out here. No one seems to like him too much. He's got a reputation for being a hell of a social climber and opportunist."

"Doesn't everybody out here? So what's new?"

"Not much, really. But if you're planning to do a Broadway musical with him I'd ask a lot of questions."

"Like?"

"Like where is the money coming from? Like who is the director? Like does he have a hold on a big Broadway house? It's not that easy to pin down a good musical house in New York and the Shuberts and the Nederlanders own or run most of them. If they don't like the property, you could be in big trouble. I've heard of shows bouncing around in the hinterland for months, like planes circling Kennedy Airport with no runway to land on. One actually had to close because the only house they could reserve on Broadway was too small. Couldn't gross enough to break even."

"I've asked about the director several times."

"And?"

"Larry says he still isn't satisfied with the final script. He says he's waiting before sending it out to potential directors. He says we'll have our pick of the best five in New York."

"I'm no Broadway maven. But even I am expert enough to know that top directors don't just sit around waiting for scripts. Most of the hot guys are booked up for years. I've heard of shows actually postponing their opening for a year so that they could get just the director they want. Believe me, Trudy, the one thing you can be sure about on Broadway is that it is a director's theater. They call the tune. Not the stars. Sure, you generally need a big star to sell tickets. But it's the director who brings a Broadway script—especially a musical—to life. Everyone connected with today's theater understands that."

"Well maybe I'm being too passive. I'd better start asking some direct questions."

"I would. Sounds to me like Mr. Hocker is stalling for time."

Richie's instincts were valid. Larry Hocker *was* stalling, for a very sound reason: lack of capital. With the falling stock market, the soaring interest rates, the general economic stress that had seized the country, raising $3 million was one hell of a challenge. What he really needed in addition to a long list of penny-ante investors were a few heavy hitters. He recently had flown to Chicago, where he had been introduced to Tippy Golden, a fabulously successful attorney and real estate developer. They had taken to each other immediately and Golden had pledged a half million dollars to the project. Larry was experienced enough to know that the half million would probably be sweated down to a few hundred thousand before signing day, but at least he was assured of a heavy investment and Golden's name on the list would have a salutary effect on his meetings with other potential investors.

"How do you feel about Arab money, kid?" Golden had asked him.

"Is it green?" Larry answered.

"It's green and black from the oil fields. I've got a meeting scheduled with a sheik from Saudi Arabia who's crazy about white broads. He'll come up with a hundred grand if we get him a date with a chorus girl."

"For a hundred grand he can take Millie out. That's my wife."

After months of struggling, Larry was still quite a bit short of his goal. He knew that the trick was to interest a movie studio and a record company in the project. Even though the authors held the power to make the sale of the ancillary rights, he could generally wheel and deal since he and the backers were entitled to forty percent of all subsidiary income. Larry was certain that the composer and lyricist would cooperate if it meant raising the capital to make the project fly. Actually, they had been auditioning the material for months all around Los Angeles but to date had stimulated only mild interest. Too many of the movie studios and record companies had been hurt in recent years and had vowed to steer clear of pre-Broadway investments. It was cheaper in the long run, they thought, to wait until they found out that the show was a hit, even if it meant paying through the nose for the rights. All the while the auditioning had been going on and Trudy Coles' name had been used as bait, she had thought that the score was not ready for airing. Larry had played her a tape of only about three numbers, but had insisted that she wait until the whole score was completed. For him, it was a great weapon for delay.

After her lunch with Richie Stevens, Trudy decided she had better pin Larry down. The truth was that by now she was so committed to the project emotionally, she really didn't want it to collapse.

"Larry," she asked him one evening over dinner, "when in the hell is this show going into rehearsal? I can't wait forever. My agent is giving me a bad, bad time. He was against my doing a Broadway show in the first instance. Now, he says if I don't get back to work soon, the public is going to forget me."

"I hardly think that makes any sense. Trudy Coles will be a star forever."

Larry Hocker knew how to massage actors' egos.

"Maybe. But stars who don't work don't make agents any commissions. And this star has her own money problems. I'm still working off that debt from "A and H." I don't enjoy selling off assets to pay bills, you know. I have to know when this show is going to happen . . . if it's going to happen."

The "if" was spoken slowly and with great emphasis.

"Of course it is going to happen. Do you think I'd work for years on something that wouldn't happen?"

"Possibly. I'm sure you're working hard to make it happen. Maybe it's time for us to level with each other. How much of the three million do you have in?"

"Plenty. Well, it's not really in until I call for it. But it's pledged."

"Larry. How much?" Trudy insisted. "You'd better level with me or you'll be looking for a new Linda."

"Okay. It has been tough. I've got a million six definite. I'm about to close a movie deal that could bring me home."

"And if this deal doesn't close?"

"I'll get the money, I tell you."

"When?"

"Soon. Give me another month or so and it will all be in."

Two months later, on serious questioning by Trudy, Hocker admitted that he was up to a million eight. There was still no big record or motion picture deal. The agent for the composer and lyricist warned Larry that his eighteen-month option was winding down. His clients needed the show and they were not going to renew unless he was fully capitalized. The same applied to Rick Crosson, the book writer. His agent was making fearsome noises about pulling back the property unless there was action soon.

In desperation, Larry turned to Trudy.

"I need help. Any ideas?"

"By that do you mean am I going to invest in the show?"

"Well, that would help."

"I'll buy one unit. Thirty thousand dollars. Not a red cent more. And that pledge dies by October first unless we're in rehearsal by then. I'm not going to spend my life waiting for you to raise the rest of the dough."

At the eleventh hour, help came from an unusual source. A group of independent legitimate theaters had banded together in an effort to fight the giants who were getting all of the strong properties in major cities and slowly but surely taking over the industry. They were meeting in Chicago to discuss strategy. Larry offered them a deal. If ten of them would each pledge $100,000, Larry would promise that the attraction would play their theaters following its Broadway run. In addition, instead of owning sixteen and three-quarters percent of the equity to which their $1 million entitled them, he would throw in an additional five percent, which they, in turn, could divide ten ways. It was a hard sell but Larry convinced them. Larry threw in another two percent as commission to the man who had arranged the meeting. Larry Hocker now had his fifty percent producer's share of the earnings reduced to forty-three percent, but he was in no position to fret. He also realized that he'd have to give up more points to a name director. Still, forty percent of a Broadway musical hit was a potential fortune. And in cash-office charges, plus two and a half percent of the gross as a producer's fee, he'd pull down another $8,000 a week. If there were several road companies running at the same time, that figure could be tripled even without a profit distribution. And then, if the motion picture rights sold for millions of dollars, well, the dream was almost too rich to contemplate. In wild euphoria, he called Trudy, striving his best not to sound too excited.

"Hey, Trudy," he said pleasantly, "you'd better start looking for an apartment in New York."

"The meeting went well?" she asked in amazement.

"Better than that. We got all the money. Just like I told you, right?"

"I'm happy for both of us," she answered simply.

One of the investing group of theaters had a connection with an independent group of New York theaters. It wasn't the largest or most desirable theater but at least it was assurance that the show would not be an orphan. Happily, its present tenant's grosses had dropped below what was known as the "stop clause," so that the theater's owner could force it to move out whenever *Her Own Woman* was ready to come in. That eliminated a second big problem.

Finally, there was the matter of the director. Larry flew directly to New York following the Chicago success and distributed his latest draft of the script. There was one taker, a female choreographer named Gerry Serito, who had dreams of becoming a full-scale director. With no alternatives, Larry hired her, then returned to California to obtain Trudy's approval as required by her contract. Reluctantly, he agreed to give Gerry one point of the profits out of his end as well as a $10,000 fee as against two percent of the gross, going to three percent after full payoff. It was an expensive deal with someone who had yet to direct her first Broadway musical, but he needed a director desperately and Gerry Serito was at least professionally acceptable.

Rehearsals started on August first. By the second of August, Trudy had her first disagreement with Gerry Serito. By the third of August, Serito was referring to Trudy—in stage whispers, of course—as "the old bitch." By the fourth of August, Trudy was referring to Gerry as "that dumb dyke," only Trudy made no effort to speak in quiet tones. By Friday, the fifth of August, neither one would speak to the other.

Attempting at first to stay aloof on the theory that rehearsal nerves always caused differences that later were settled, Larry watched in anguish as he saw all of his wonderful dreams about to go up in smoke. He spoke to Gerry that night.

"You have to understand, this is her first Broadway show."

"If she doesn't loosen up, it's going to be her last."

"Christ, Gerry, we've only been in rehearsal for five days. How about giving her a chance?"

"How about giving me a break? You beg me to direct the show and then you saddle me with a clumsy bitch who thinks she can play Miss Hollywood with me instead of taking my direction."

"Trudy Coles is an international star. She's worked with the best directors in the world. Give her a chance and she'll work with you, too. Just remember, she's fifty-three and this is her first Broadway show. She's just nervous."

"I'm nervous, too. But I'll try to be patient with her."

Then he spoke to Trudy.

"You have to remember that this is her first big directorial job. She's nervous."

"So who isn't? The problem as I see it is that she is no director. She may be a great choreographer but we already have one choreographer on this show and he's a dreamboat. She thinks she can push me around that stage like a hockey puck. Doesn't she understand that it's the dramatic parts of this story that make it great, not the motion?"

Larry Hocker knew in his heart and in his brain that it would never work. But where to find another director who would be readily available? And how could he afford to pay off Gerry Serito? What about all of the special orchestrations that Gerry had demanded. What about the sets that she had approved? A new director might well want to change all of these and the show was already about $50,000 over budget. And, the news that he was changing directors so early in the game would be poison on Broadway and have a terrible effect on advance sales. The theater-party ladies always grew overly cautious when there was warfare among the creative staffs of new Broadway shows. All he could do at this time was close his eyes and pray for the best.

But, of course, things got worse. Lines of battle were drawn and people were lining up on both sides. The choreographer, Lonnie Squires, hoping that somehow he might inherit Gerry's directorial robe, sided with Trudy Coles. The author also felt that his script's inner pathos was being ignored and joined the team. The composer and lyricist, on the other hand, felt that the musical had to move and they were beginning to see Trudy as a stiff old lady who could never cut the mustard. By the end of the second week, virtually no one was talking to anyone else and the production stage manager, charged with carrying out the impossible tasks assigned him by the director, was ready to quit.

"I can't take much more of this shit, Mr. Hocker. Not only am I working eighteen hours a day against my doctor's orders, but I can't even communicate with any of them. They won't talk. Shit, it's not my fault!"

Larry called a peace conference involving everyone but Trudy Coles. He tried to be his most charming, most persuasive self. It was an exercise in futility. Everyone was convinced he was right and that the other person was the enemy. Gerry Serito performed the ultimate sin, condemning the star in front of the rest of the staff.

"You can cure all of this in one stroke, Mr. Hocker. Get rid of the old bitch!"

"Maybe you should practice some professional conduct, Miss Serito. We won't have our star spoken of in those terms."

"Sorry. I don't like being called 'a dumb dyke,' either."

Trudy had already called Sid Keyes and he flew in from Los Angeles the same night after setting up a meeting with Larry Hocker. They met in Trudy's suite but Sid insisted that she absent herself from the conference.

"So how's it going?" he asked for openers.

"Fine. Just fine," Larry answered.

"Bullshit. Miss Coles tells me it's a war. She tells me she never saw anything like it in all the years she has been in the business."

"Well, Sid, let's face it. This is Trudy's first Broadway show. It's just the usual rehearsal nerves. It'll settle down."

"Not with my client, it won't. You're into your fourth week and nobody talks to anybody else. That snit of a director has been pushing Trudy around so much she's stiff. Her nerves are shot. She's about to lose her voice. You call that rehearsal nerves? I call it chaos!"

"So?"

Larry's nerves were strained, too, and the only bright spot in the picture was that the box office had opened two days ago to long lines of ticket buyers. That didn't alleviate the cash shortage, which was fast becoming critical. He decided to try and stonewall it with Sid Keyes. That was a mistake. Sid was too experienced an agent not to know his position of power. Without Trudy Coles, Larry Hocker didn't have a chance.

"So, just this. Either you replace that little bitch of a director by the end of the week, or you look for a new star. Trudy Coles has her bags packed and ready and she'll leave for the Coast if she finds that Serito gal in the theater again."

"Now give me a break, Sid. I can't find a new director in two hours. Give us some time."

"You should have started looking the first day of rehearsal. You've got until Friday—that's three days. Either you get rid of that Serito dame or no Trudy Coles. That's it."

Faced with the inevitable, Larry called Serito's agent and tried to soft-talk his way out of her contract.

"It's really not for her, Bobby. You know that. We all made a mistake. She'll come off looking so bad she'll never get another show. Why not walk now while we can blame 'artistic differences' and no one looks bad in the press?"

"We're not afraid of the press. Everyone knows the truth, Larry. Trudy Coles is no Broadway musical star. She's making us all look bad. But my client won't talk. Fire her if you have to. But you'll pay through the nose every goddamned dime she's entitled to. For your sake I hope the show makes it and it runs a thousand years. But you'll pay those percentages for the rest of the show's life. Make no mistakes about it."

Gerry Serito was fired the next day. For an extra $500 a week, Lonnie Squires, the choreographer, agreed to take over temporarily as director until a permanent one could be signed. Finally, there was what appeared to be a stroke of good luck. Moe Drayton, one of Broadway's most successful directors, suddenly became available, having quit the turkey he presently was engaged with in Boston. An old acquaintance of Larry Hocker's, he agreed to fly to New York and observe a few days of rehearsals before accepting the directorial assignment. He finally consented to direct, but his terms were stiff. For one, he insisted on the same economic package enjoyed by his predecessor, and when it came to net profits he demanded an extra two points beyond the one percent promised Gerry Serito. Second, he hated most of the orchestrations he had heard and would accept the job only if most of them were scrapped. What with recopying and additional musicians' rehearsals, that added another $50,000 to the already overstrained budget. The scenery also bothered him. He considered it too heavy, too lugubrious for what was after all a simple story of female emancipation.

"This isn't a funeral procession. This is Broadway. Let's get a little light on stage."

"I don't have the money for a whole new set," Larry argued feebly. "Besides, it would delay the opening by weeks."

"That's another thing," Moe said. "You've got to postpone at least two weeks. This show won't be ready by your scheduled opening night and I'm not putting my name up on the marquee of a sure loser. I'm not sure I can do it with two extra weeks but less than that I won't accept."

"That'll cost us another hundred thousand at the least," Larry moaned. "And all of my theater parties are in the first three weeks. I'm liable to lose them all."

"You won't lose them. Theater parties are used to postponements. Get the ladies on the phone and start pushing them back. Call the league and reserve a couple of new opening dates just in case."

"Moe, you're gonna bankrupt me before I open!"

"You want a winner?"

"Sure, I do. But there's got to be some consideration of cost."

"There is. Give me two extra weeks. No more."

"Okay. It's a deal. But no more."

"There's one more thing," Moe said.

"What's that?" Larry asked with trepidation.

"Peter Franklin has to go. He's no leading man."

"Everyone says he's great."

"Everyone doesn't know what they're talking about. He's a second-rate stock actor. He sings okay. He sings too well, actually. It makes Trudy sound bad in their duets. I checked last night and Paige Robinson is available. Pay that other schmuck off and let's go to work."

"You'll kill me!" Larry moaned.

"No, I'll save your ass."

In the end, everything Moe demanded, he got. A lot of the

heavier sets were abandoned and a few new drops were brought in. The scenery changes added about $75,000 to the budget. Larry Hocker had visions of completely new sets that might run into a quarter of a million, so he was happy. Even though he complained bitterly every time a change was introduced, it was obvious to him and evident to the cast that Moe Drayton might well save the day. All of the bickering, all of the back-biting, all of the internal squabbling ended when he took over.

He started afresh by making the following speech to an assembled cast and creative staff. "I wouldn't be here today if I didn't believe that *Her Own Woman* is going to be the biggest hit Broadway has seen in a decade. Anyone who doesn't agree will do me and himself a favor by walking now." He paused, slowly looking everyone in the eye, then continued. "I like everyone here or you wouldn't still be on the payroll. Tonight, just before you go to bed, strip down, stand in front of a full-length mirror, and take a look at your ass. It's the last you're going to see of it. I have every intention of working it off in the next four to six weeks. And I don't want to hear any more of those bad jokes like, 'Hey, who do you have to fuck to get out of this company?' You're here, I'm here, we're here to work. This turkey is going to shed its pin feathers and fly!"

There was a spontaneous round of applause. Trudy called out, "Here, here!" and the company was off and running. A new spirit took hold of the entire cast.

Larry Hocker faced one additional problem. The advertising agency handling the show was urging him to finance a television commercial that could be aired almost immediately.

"Larry, that's where it is today. Television. You know that." It was Freddy Bornstein, the agency representative speaking.

"Let's wait until we open. What's the rush? We're selling plenty of tickets now."

"You've got to ride the momentum. There's been a lot of bad word about your show on the street. The press has reported all of the fights, the cast changes, the new director. You've got to play it big and confident. Bang away at television like there's no tomorrow. After you open and you're a big hit, maybe then you can pull in your horns for a while."

The argument was convincing.

"And what about the cost?"

"The commercial can be made for about twenty-five grand. Then you'll need at least fifty thousand more for a saturation campaign."

Larry shrieked. "Are you crazy? Where in the hell am I going to come up with seventy-five thousand more? I'm already four hundred big ones over budget."

"All the more reason to play them like you have them. You can't afford to sneak in."

Bornstein was talking sense and Larry knew it. Even though making the commercial lost a valuable day of rehearsal, the TV spot hit the airwaves five days later.

CHAPTER 31

1983

Trudy woke in a cold sweat. It took her a few moments to regain consciousness, and then she realized that her phone was ringing. She looked at the clock and to her amazement it was one-thirty in the morning. She reached for the receiver.

"Hello," she said sleepily.

"Sorry to disturb you, Miss Coles. Are you all right?" It was Higgins, the night clerk again.

"Yes, fine. Why are you calling?"

"I've been ringing for a half hour. There's a Mr. Hocker here. I believe he's connected with your show. He insisted that I keep ringing. Is it all right?"

"Yes. Fine. Send him up."

When she opened the door to admit him, she knew from one glance at his beaming countenance that they had won. His arms were full of newspapers and radio and television reprints.

"You'll never believe it! All raves. Listen to this *Times* headline: '*Her Own Woman* is Season's Biggest Hit!'"

"And the *Post:* 'She Never Stoops to Conquer'"

"And here's the *News*—just listen to this. 'Trudy Coles, who waited more than thirty years to face a Broadway audience, proved last night that talent is talent in any medium. She displayed just the right blend of pathos and determination to make us all love her. *Her Own Woman* is the best thing that has happened to the woman's liberation movement since Adam gave up his rib.'

"We got six raves from television. Only that schmuck in *Female Fashions* didn't like it. And who reads him?"

"Well," Trudy said with a smile, "I guess I'd better sign that year-long apartment lease after all. I've sort of had it with hotel living."

"Trudy, you'd better sign a five-year lease. This show is never going to close if I can help it."

They looked at each other triumphantly. Slowly he dropped the papers and moved toward her. He put his arms around her and pulled her into a passionate hug. His hands dropped and felt for her buttocks. Larry Hocker was unprepared for what happened next. Raising her knee sharply, she kicked him in the groin, at the same time pulling his hands from around her body and pushing him away from her with angry violence.

"Don't you dare, don't you ever dare to touch me like that again! Who the hell do you think I am, some fucking chorus girl?"

Startled, he fought for breath and looked at her in shocked amazement.

"I only thought . . ." he mumbled.

"I know what you thought. Now, go home to Millie and your kids. I'll see you at the production meeting tomorrow at noon."

There were no good nights as he left.

She went to the phone and called the hotel operator. "Get me the Mark Hopkins Hotel in San Francisco." The answer was blissfully prompt. "I want Mr. Stanley Marcus. He's waiting for my call."

"Hey, star, how did it go? How did you do?" Stan asked anxiously.

"I'm afraid I'm still a star. Stan, it went great and the reviews are rave, rave, rave."

"All right!"

"We'll probably run for more than two years, judging from business here."

"Well, you like New York."

"I'll like it better with you here. This is a proposal."

"Trudy, don't let those reviews go to your head. I'm a star, too, you know."

"I've known that all along. You're the one who can't make up his mind."

"Wrong. I made up my mind the first time I saw you. I've just never had the guts."

"Sure you do. Besides, I've got enough guts for both of us. Stan, please come soon. I love you. I miss you."

"Your instructions are a little late, lady. I've already made arrangements to fly to New York first thing in the morning. . . ."

EPILOGUE

The prediction that *Her Own Woman* would run on Broadway for two years was inaccurate: at the end of four years it was still running. There were two road companies touring the States, a company in England, and another being prepared for Australia. Trudy Coles had indeed conquered Broadway as well as Hollywood. Hardly a week passed by that she was not offered a starring role in a feature film, but she would have no part of it.

"Hell, I was born again in this show. I love that feeling of facing a live audience. Sure, I was terrified at first. Never knew if I was a real actress or not. I heard all the cracks about 'made in Hollywood,' where anyone can act. I showed them. More important, I showed myself. I'm going to ride this damn horse until it dies under me."

Her opening night tiff with Larry Hocker was long forgotten. He was rich now, exceedingly rich, and all of his Broadway backers loved him. He told Trudy that he was planning a new show for her but she didn't believe him.

"Larry, you're still full of it," she joked. "You'll keep me in this old turkey until one of us dies of old age. Well listen, kid, *Her Own Woman* is still selling out and I'm hardly ready for the trash heap. Or hadn't you noticed?"

"After a certain well-placed kick to the groin I decided that I'd better look at you from a distance. Frankly, to me you'll always be the sexiest woman in the world."

"I hope you haven't forgotten that this sexy woman has a big date in California right after New Year's. What's the word on a replacement for that month you promised me?"

"Good news for you; bad news for me. Hildy Mitchell, bless her ravenous heart, has agreed to substitute for you. But she'll never hold the gross up Trudy Coles–style."

"You can afford it, buster. There's a man out there who loves me and that's where I'm heading."

"Go. I hate to admit it but I like Stan Marcus, too. I wish I could find reasons to object but I can't. If I can only find the cash to pay for the dress Millie plans to buy for the wedding, I'll have it made."

Trudy and Stan were married on a day that was so beautiful that even the best writers in Hollywood were at a loss to describe it. Even the notorious Los Angeles smog was absent without leave and a cool breeze wafted in from the hills and danced through a cloudless sky. There had been long discussions about when and where the nuptials should occur, but one thing was easily ascertained: this wedding was not to be a replay of World War II. The wedding list was discretely limited to 100 relatives and intimate friends. And double security was employed to keep the press distant.

"I've had the other kind of weddings," Trudy said. "This one is forever and it's not for outsiders."

They held the ceremony in a lovely inn overlooking the sea near Malibu. A mutual friend, a California Supreme Court justice, conducted the brief ceremony. Belinda, looking lovelier than ever, was her mother's maid of honor. Stan Marcus' brother, Charles, a physician from New Jersey, served as best man.

In planning the festivities, Belinda had urged her mother to wear white.

"Mom, you'll be the most beautiful bride that ever was. I can just see you in that flowing white gown with a filmy, tulle veil covering that gorgeous puss of yours. White will be perfect."

"Scarlet would be more appropriate," Trudy joked.

In the end she wore a pale green gown designed not only to show off her magnificent figure but also to highlight the "go-signal" eyes that had helped make her famous.

Richie Stevens, silver-haired and more handsome than ever, at first refused to attend. He called Trudy and told her that he feared he might spoil things for Stan.

"I know I'd be nervous if some former husband were there lurking in the wings," he said.

"You won't be lurking, and it was Stan who suggested that we invite you. Belinda wants you there. And so do I. You played a very important role in my life, Richie. Our bygones have been bygones for a long, long time."

There was one guest whom few of the others could identify. She was a large woman, ill at ease in the tan cocktail dress that she wore with obvious distaste. Her hair, pulled back in a tight chignon, seemed to fit more appropriately with the heavy, horn-rimmed glasses through which she peered at the world.

"I can't figure why you wanted me here with all of these beautiful people," she said after the ceremony as she clasped Trudy's hand. "You must like cops. All I ever did was say no to you."

"Maggie Knudsen!" Trudy exclaimed, beaming, "there will always be room in my heart for you. You gave me courage at a time when I was ready to pack it all in."

"If you had tried, I would have busted your beautiful chops. See you got yourself another cerebral guy. He looks nice. Nicer than that Rush guy I tried to protect you from."

"Leonard had his problems, Maggie, but this is a day for forgetting. My happiness is so complete I don't want any negative thoughts clouding my brain or my heart. Darling, this is Maggie Knudsen, the wonderful nurse who took care of me."

And she was on to the next guest.

"How is it going?" she asked Stan when there was a slight break in the line.

"The only problem here is that the room is too small. The walls just can't hold all the joy. But then again, neither could the Rose Bowl."

The day was filled with marvelous surprises. Belinda, madly in love with a brilliant young director, informed her mother that they were planning to announce their engagement just as soon as his next picture was completed. Larry Hocker relayed the news that the show had just been purchased for a major motion picture contingent upon Trudy's agreement to play the lead. Filming would not begin for at least three years. But the best news of all was reserved for Stan Marcus to inform Trudy.

"The husband can now at last claim steady employment," he said jocularly. "I've been offered a full professorship at Columbia teaching creative writing. That way I can keep my eye on the younger generation as well as on my wife. I'll be damned if I'm going to have one of those long-distance marriages."

Trudy, her happiness complete, turned to another wedding guest, who stood by beaming at all the joyous proceedings. It was Dr. Milton Gordon, the man who had given her real insight into the true Trudy Coles.

"I'm afraid I won't be needing your services anymore, Dr. Gordon," she said. "There's finally 'the man' in my life and I'll never leave his side."